Phantom Orchid

JOSS TALLMAN

JOSS TALLMAN

Phantom Orchid

This book is a work of fiction. Names, characters, places, and other incidents either are the product of the author's imagination or are used fictitiously, and any resemblance to actual persons, living or dead, business establishments, events or locales is entirely coincidental.

The errors: historical, typos, grammar, and all mistakes otherwise are mine alone.

Author's Bridge Publishing
A CyberDiamond, LLC Company
320 Mamie Cook Road
Boone, NC 28607-7844

ISBN-13: 978-0-9882872-1-1
ISBN-10: 0988287218

Cover created by Laurel L. Galvan, Author's Bridge Publishing
Author's website: www.josstallman.com

Phantom Orchid

JOSS TALLMAN

Author's Bridge
PUBLISHERS
A CYBERDIAMOND, LLC COMPANY

DEDICATION

For: Four special people in my life, Big Fred, Sudie Belle, Terry Lee and Susan.

JT

A special thanks to my little dog Toby, whose constant vigilance and unyielding loyalty stayed at my feet during the long hours.

PROLOGUE

Fort Lauderdale Naval Air Station
December 5, 1945, 2:10 P.M.

At 2:10 in the afternoon of December 5, 1945, U.S. Navy Flight 19, consisting of five fully fueled TBM Avenger Torpedo Bombers, lifted off the Naval Air Station at Fort Lauderdale, Florida on an authorized routine training mission. Other than a few garbled radio transmissions, they were never seen or heard from again.

In command of Flight 19 was Navy Lieutenant Commander Jake Galvan. He taxied the Grumman Avenger onto the threshold of Runway 9. He was grim. Although this was a routine training mission, Galvan had an angst feeling in his guts. A qualified senior flight instructor he had flown this mission dozens of times before, but today something was amiss. He could feel it in his bones. Galvan was a Missouri born farm boy and a seasoned combat pilot. He was not a man to be easily reckoned with or quick to be shaken or intimidated. But, he could not explain the phantom feeling stinging his nerves. Somehow, he just knew.

He was pleased with his crew. They were the best of the best. Galvan had handpicked the pilots of the other four Avengers with painstaking care. There was Captain George Edwards, USMC; Lieutenant JG

Joseph Johns, USN; Ensign Jarod Phipps, USNR; and Major Lynn Douglas, a U.S. Army Air Corps pilot assigned to the post-war Navy.

He had combed through their personnel files in great detail and had done extensive background checks on each. Galvan had counseled them for hours and knew each one better than their own families knew them. He had built an inflexible level of camaraderie, trust and loyalty.

"Navy Flight 19 you are cleared for take-off in sequence, runway nine, maintain runway heading straight-out departure approved," crackled a voice in their headsets.

"Roger tower, we're rolling on nine, understand straight-out departure," Galvan said into his microphone.

"Navy 19 do not rendezvous until you are clear of my airspace to the east," said the tower.

"Roger, wilco," replied Galvan.

Once they were all airborne, Lieutenant Commander Galvan dialed his radio from the tower frequency to the standard Navy plane-to-plane channel. "Okay boys," he said, "hold your east heading and we will re-group over the ocean. Keep it in tight let's all stick together." A series of roger-wilcos echoed in his ears.

Galvan looked down at the swirling Atlantic below and at the strange mist rising over the

Gulfstream. He had flown this mission several times before, but today something was different. He glanced at the mission flight plan in his lap; it was same as usual. Steer due east for 64 miles until reaching Bahamian landfall at Hen and Chicken Shoals and execute a practice low-level bomb run. The flight was to continue east for another 77 miles then turn to a northwest course of 346°, which would take them over Grand Bahama Island. Then steer a southwest course of 241° bringing them back over Florida and finally to the Fort Lauderdale Naval Air Station.

Lieutenant Commander Galvan gazed out at the mist below, which was beginning to engulf them. He thought, *Humm, the Devil's Triangle again, well, if you want us, Lucifer—here we are.*

The Devil's Triangle, sometimes called the Bermuda Triangle and has been the subject of endless esoteric intrigue and myths dating back as far as Columbus in 1492. Columbus reported and wrote in his journals that he and his crew observed strange lights low over the ocean at night, and how these lights would dive beneath the sea and travel at great speeds under the water. He also reported his compass spinning and was of no use for navigation. Since that time, hundreds of ships and planes have vanished in the mysterious triangle and thousands of souls lost to the unforgiving sea.

Some say it is paranormal and some say extraterrestrial. Others claim the lost city of Atlantis lies on the ocean floor in the direful expanse of the Devil's Triangle. One constant remains—ships and planes have vanished seemingly into thin air while seeking passage through it. Ships have been found with cigarettes still burning in the ashtrays and food still warm on the mess tables, but no sign of life or the crew. No lost aircraft has ever been found or recovered in the Devil's Triangle.

According to the locals: *It's the Devil's lair, where he lurks and waits—*

"Hey skipper, you'd better listen to this," said the chief petty officer who was minding the radar at the NAS.

"What did he say, Chief?" said the commanding officer.

"Pretty garbled and broken up sir, but it sounded like Commander Galvan."

"Could you make out anything, anything at all?"

"Well, yes sir," replied the radar man, "The commander said both his compasses were spinning and his instruments were making no sense. And sir, he said they were lost."

"Lost?" The C.O. thought for a moment, *lost? No, not Galvan.* "Where are they, Chief?"

"Sir, from what little I could understand, Commander Galvan had a visual on several small islands and thinks they might be over the Florida Keys."

"No, I don't think so," said a Marine sergeant. "They could never have gotten that far southwest without us knowing."

"Unless the commander is looking at a small island chain just northeast of the Bahamas," said the commanding officer. "Radar, what's the last ADF fix you have on their position?"

"Sir," he replied, "his transmission was so weak it was barely readable and impossible to triangulate, but from the best I could tell they would be northeast of the Bahamas, but sir, that's just a calculated guess."

"Then we have got to turn them," said the C.O. "Get a PBY in the air right away to go find 19 and lead them back. Their fuel should be getting close by now."

The radar man looked up from his scope, "Ah, sir, I think I should tell you, the weather is going to hell very fast, sir."

"Deteriorating?"

"Yes sir."

"Thank you, Chief. Make sure that PBY is fully fueled and get her in the air now!"

The British tanker, *Vincent*, was in the area of the lost airmen and was alerted to be on the lookout for Flight 19. The radioman aboard the *Vincent* was able to break into the plane-to-plane frequency and told Galvan to go to another channel. Galvan, barely readable refused saying, "I cannot switch frequencies. I have to keep my airplanes intact."

As the weather continued to get worse, it brought more high seas. Radio contact became very intermittent, and darkness was falling all around them. At 6:04 P.M., Galvan radioed his flight. "Hold a course of due east 090°." By this time, the weather had deteriorated even more, and the sun had since set. Around 6:20 P.M., Galvan's last message was scratchy and barely readable. He was heard saying, "Okay guys, all planes close in tight, we'll have to ditch unless we see landfall. When the first plane drops below 10 gallons of fuel, we will all go down together."

At 7:50 P.M., the tanker, *USS Gaines Mills*, reported seeing a huge explosion in the sky and flames leaping 100 feet high burning on the surface of the sea. The PBY rescue aircraft, with its crew of seven, had mysteriously exploded in the Devil Triangle's boiling sky and was now an oil slick.

Lieutenant Commander Jake Galvan glanced at his Avenger's empty fuel gauge and the churning Atlantic below. Soon he and his flight of five Avengers would plunge into the unforgiving tempestuous maelstrom below and perish in the abyss of a watery eternity.

Or did they?

CHAPTER ONE

Palm Beach, Florida
Offshore
September 8

They say you never see the one that gets you, but this was not true in the case of Bucky Wooster. He saw it, and he heard it, but he never felt a thing.

Buchanan Jay Wooster anchored his 22-foot Seacraft, the *Cloud Nine*, above the coral reef about a half-mile offshore from Palm Beach. He ignored the federal and Florida laws forbidding the dropping of an anchor on any coral reef. In Bucky's way of thinking, these rules applied to everyone else but certainly not to him.

The *Cloud Nine*, all but drained Bucky of the monthly allowance from his trust fund. The upkeep, fuel and dockage fees dug deeply into his pockets, but it was worth it. The *Cloud Nine* was a beauty, and quite a chick magnet. Here he was, heir to the Wooster Chemical & Textile fortune having to exist on a few thousand dollars a month. His grandmother, the old twit, had decided that Bucky was a spendthrift and could not handle his money wisely. So through her lawyers she arranged for him to receive a monthly stipend until sometime in the future when he could show a bit more financial responsibility and maturity.

Leaving the family fortune to her daughter Genevieve, Bucky's mother, was out of the question. Genevieve, an agoraphobic divorcee and hopeless alcoholic, spent her days in the oceanfront mansion drinking and watching soap operas. So even with his extravagant ways, Bucky was an only child and the heir apparent to the family's great fortune.

Bucky had attended several colleges, but he was not really interested in higher education. His longest stint was a couple years at the University of Miami in Coral Gables, where he majored in philosophy. However, Bucky's real major was centered on scuba diving, surfing and the endless stream of bikini-clad coeds packing the beaches of south Florida.

Bucky's world was privileged and a lifestyle that most can only dream of, but it had a dark side. While hanging out at South Beach, instead of attending classes, Bucky had been introduced to the white powder. From the start, he liked it. Soon he discovered the cost of the recreational chemical was digging more deeply into his finances than the *Cloud Nine*. Then the entrepreneur in him stirred.

Why buy it when I could be selling it?

After an exhausting search, Bucky was able to make his way up the organizational labyrinth and finally arranged to receive a telephone call from someone higher up the distribution ladder; however, no phone numbers were exchanged. Bucky had an infallible plan that only he could carry out. In Bucky's mind, *I am a genius.*

The days turned into weeks, and Bucky had all but given up making contact with any of the higher ups in the local cocaine trade. On a sunny Sunday afternoon, he was at the docks polishing and grooming the *Cloud Nine*, when a dock boy stuck his head in the cabin. "Mister Wooster."

"Yes?"

"Telephone," said the acne-faced boy.

"Telephone?"

"Yes sir," said the boy, "The telephone booth down at the end of the dock, sir."

"Okay thanks, Freddie," said Bucky. He liked being called mister and he enjoyed the sirs. He deserved it. After all wasn't he a member of Forbes 500, and heir to the Wooster's net worth somewhere between 400 and 500 million dollars, not particularly impressive by Palm Beach standards where it is joked that millionaires mowed the lawns of the billionaires but a tidy sum nevertheless.

Palm Beach often said to be the richest town in America, the home of the jetsetters and the sophisticates, with its multimillion dollar mansions and lines of chauffeur driven Rolls Royces and Bentleys, where generations of big money has lived for years, most of who never met or ever knew their benefactors.

"Hello?" He said into the telephone.

There was no greeting or salutation. "Is that your red Corvette under the coconut trees?" asked a deep echoing voice.

"Ah, ah, yeah," Bucky stuttered.

"Look under the passenger seat," said the voice and immediately hung up.

Bucky walked at once to his car. Checking around to make sure no one was watching he reached under the passenger seat and pulled out a black canvas bag. In the bag, he found a plain gray cell phone.

Another week passed and Bucky noted the mysterious cell phone remained silent. He began thinking once again that perhaps the contact had forgotten him. On a Tuesday morning, the phone rang.

"Hal-lo," said a groggy Bucky. He usually slept late in the mornings and was not accustomed to doing much of anything before noon.

Again, there was no greeting or salutation. "Be at the Surf & Turf Restaurant on the Boynton Beach Pier at exactly two this afternoon," said the same deep voice.

"Oh man, does it have to be today? I have a two o'clock tee-off time and...." The phone clicked in his ear. The voice had disconnected.

Bucky realized his mistake right away. He could always play golf, but this meeting was urgent. As the days passed, he doubted if he would ever be called again and his white powder habit was becoming more and more demanding. He had to do something. Finally, after ten days had gone by the cell phone rang again.

"Hello?"

It was the same deep voice. "Be at the Surf & Turf Restaurant on the Boynton pier. Sit in the serving area outside on the south side and sit facing north. Be there at exactly two o'clock." The phone went dead.

Bucky would have to hurry to make it by two, but surprisingly he arrived a few minutes early. He walked hastily through the main dining area of the restaurant. He passed the mirrored bar with a large mounted sailfish on the opposite wall and onto the outside dining area of the pier. As instructed, he sat facing north. It was a beautiful Florida day and the blue ocean below him was calm with a few whitecaps.

He was alone on the pier except for a couple enjoying a late lunch under the large umbrella of their table. Bucky could see from where he was sitting the man was having the Captain's Platter, a special of the Surf and Turf.

Typical tourists, he thought. The woman was bleach-blonde and appeared to be in her mid-40s. She was wearing a beach smock over an overstuffed pink bathing suit. The man was clad in long shorts and one of those gaudy Florida shirts with the fish and parrots

11

all over it. Both were wearing flip-flops and both wore dark sunglasses under straw wide-brimmed Panama hats, which they had most likely bought from one of the street vendors.

Bucky checked his $30,000 platinum Rolex, a gift from his grandmother and saw that is was 22 minutes after two and he was beginning to wonder if he had been stood up. He was thinking if worse came to worse he could always sell or pawn the Rolex for more of the white powder. He noticed the dining tourists were leaving their table. The woman still wearing large dark sunglasses quickly disappeared into the restaurant. The man approached his table and sat down opposite him.

"You were early," said the unmistakable voice. Bucky recognized it immediately.

Bucky offered to shake hands the stranger waved him off. "Yeah, a little early I guess. I wanted to make sure I got here on time."

"You were not on time. You were nine minutes early," said the voice. "Do you have a problem following instructions?"

Bucky began to say something and again the stranger waved him off. He was trying to figure out this stranger. His wide-brimmed hat covered his hair, if he had any, and the dark sunglasses hid his eyes. Bucky was no expert, but he was fairly certain the salt and pepper Van Dyke moustache around the stranger's lips and chin was a disguise. The stranger sat on the north side of the table facing Bucky and to the south.

With this arrangement, the stranger had a full view of anyone approaching from any direction.

"Okay," said the stranger. "Tell me about the big deal you want to do with us."

"Once I tell you, when can we get started?"

"I don't make those decisions, what and whom we deal with comes from way up the ladder. I'm just a messenger."

"I sure would like to know who I'm dealing with," said Bucky.

The stranger replied, "That's on a need to know basis and you don't need to know. Now are you going to tell me what's on your mind or shall I leave?"

"No, no," exclaimed Bucky. "Here's my plan. I live on Ocean Boulevard just a bit north of here."

"So?"

"So, what you might know, or maybe do not know, no buildings were ever allowed to be built on the beach. All structures are on the other side of Ocean Boulevard."

"So?" the stranger repeated.

"So," said Bucky, "like many of the ocean front mansions my house has a concrete tunnel, which runs under Ocean Boulevard to our private beach."

The stranger steepled his fingers and appeared to be deep in thought. "Anyone around there, say—late at night?"

"Not a soul," said Bucky. "I could flash a light signal from inside the tunnel and no one could ever see it, except a boat off shore. If you stay past the three-mile limit no cops can touch you."

"And then?" queried the stranger.

"And then we bring the boat in and unload the stuff. We carry it through the tunnel into my front yard, put in a car or whatever and off you go."

"What about being seen in your yard?"

"Impossible. The front yard is behind a six foot sea wall."

"Interesting," said the stranger with the deep voice. "You will be hearing from us if the decision makers are interested. However, only the top honcho makes the decision."

"And who might that be?" asked Bucky.

The stranger looked at him and sighed. "You're a slow learner aren't you?"

Bucky stared at the man.

The stranger said, "Wait ten minutes after I leave. Turn your cell phone on then walk to the end of the pier and throw it over. Don't make a spectacle out of it. If anyone sees you, make it look like you dropped it by accident."

"But, but," Bucky stuttered, "what if?"

"Keep checking under your passenger seat. Goodbye." With that, the stranger disappeared into the restaurant.

Bucky did as instructed and had a feeling that he was being watched. He had felt that same feeling many times over the past few weeks. When he got to his car, on a whim he felt under the passenger seat. There was a black canvas bag and inside a cell phone.

How do they get in my car? I always keep it locked—

Days passed and Bucky was getting antsy. He was thinking that the organization was not interested in his plan when the cell phone buzzed. As usual, Bucky was partying, but he quickly grabbed the phone and made his way to the patio. There was no voice, but a text message appeared on the small screen. It read: Tunnel, 3:20 A.M., Sunday. Do not send any light signal. The message was not signed.

At last! Bucky was ecstatic. At last, he could prove how infallible his plan was. At last, he could make money with the white powder instead of it being such a huge expense to him. He was determined not to screw up this time so he waited on the mansion's front lawn until exactly 3:18 A.M., then he made his way down the steps and into the tunnel. It was pitch black, but Bucky had played in the tunnel since he was a child and knew every inch of it. As he walked toward the ocean beach, he could hear the soft sounds of the surf licking the shore. He sucked the fresh salty ocean air into his lungs and waited.

Suddenly the beam from a high-powered flashlight hit him directly in the face. Bucky was blinded but gasped. "What the hell?"

"No talk," said a man with a heavy accent, who was accompanied by another man. "Where to?" he asked.

"Follow me," said Bucky and began leading the two men back through the tunnel toward the estate. The man who spoke was carrying a neatly wrapped white package. His companion was carrying two.

Soon they were through the tunnel, up the steps and onto the carpeted lawn of the Wooster estate. "Open the gate," said the accent. Bucky obliged and was surprised to see a dark station wagon with its headlights and back-up lights off, backing in the driveway. The men immediately loaded two of the white packages into the station wagon.

"You only brought three? Asked Bucky.

"No talk," said the accent.

"Where was the boat?" Bucky whispered.

"No boat. No talk."

The accent's companion turned to Bucky and said in slightly better English, "For you." He handed Bucky one of the white packages and a manila envelope.

Bucky glanced in the envelope and saw several one hundred dollar bills. "Wow!" he exclaimed. "This looks like a lot."

"It is," said the man. "El Diablo always pays well."

"No talk! Muy Loco!" scolded the accent in the loudest whisper shout he could manage. "You never, ever mention that name!" The accent berated his companion sternly in Spanish. The two men got into the station wagon and quickly disappeared out the gate of the Wooster mansion and into the night.

Bucky felt the blood rushing from his head; the man had let it slip.

El Diablo, the international crime czar—the most feared and ruthless of them all! I've got to get out of this somehow—

The name El Diablo was known worldwide. El Diablo was totally void of any compassion or pity. He was a savage and merciless killer known to run drugs and a long list of other crimes. He was the most wanted by the FBI, the CIA and several other federal agencies. INTERPOL offered a huge reward for the capture of El Diablo or any information about his identity.

Although El Diablo was well-known internationally, no one knew what he looked like, his physical description or where he lived. Even El Diablo's nationally was a mystery, but the one thing that was known for sure; he was very smart and a ruthless, brutal killer. He could put a bullet in the brain of any man, woman or child, then causally go on with his day as if nothing had happened at all.

Bucky felt a burst of terror surge through his body, he never intended to be tangled up with the likes of anyone or anything akin to El Diablo, but this was a worry he would face tomorrow. Right now, he had a whole kilo of some of the finest white powder in the world. He hurried to his bedroom in the northwest side of the mansion. It was nice and it was spacious, being right on the pool helped, as he would often bring his girlfriends in for a late night swim, sometimes with swimsuits, most often without.

Christmas has come early this year, a whole kilo all to myself—I can't believe it!

Bucky carefully cut through the white packaging and there it was an entire kilo of white powder. He laughed aloud. Quickly he placed a healthy amount on the glass top of his coffee table and rolled one of the hundred dollar bills into a makeshift straw. He sucked the powder deep into his nostrils and waited for the rush of ecstasy. Instantly Bucky began to cough and gag. His nose began a series of loud sneezes.

What the hell—

He was puzzled. White powder had never done that to him before. Bucky wet his finger and tasted the white powder.

"Sugar! What? Those dirty double crossing bastards! Sugar! White powdered sugar!" he shouted.

Bucky was stymied. There was no way he could contact anyone. He was beside himself with anger. He had been had. A week passed when the quiet cell phone rang. It was the voice.

Bucky shouted into the phone. "You dirty bastards; just what the hell are you trying to pull?"

"Relax Wooster," said the voice. "That was just a trial run. A test of sorts you might say."

"A trial run? A test for what?" shouted Bucky still perturbed.

"We had to make sure there was no law enforcement around. There's no law against having sugar, and we had to make sure you were legit."

"Well?"

"You will hear from us," said the voice. The phone went dead.

The cell phone buzzed the next day. No voice, it was a text message: "Tunnel, 03:40, Wed. flash light three times, make certain Ocean Blvd & beach clear."

The transition went smoothly without a hitch. Bucky watched, as 22 kilos of white power were unloaded from the boat, carried through the tunnel, and into a waiting van inside the mansion gate. Not a word was spoken. Upon departing, the driver handed Bucky a manila envelope as before except this time there was much more money enclosed. The van drove off into the night and there was no sign of the boat. Both had disappeared. Bucky Wooster was now in the import business.

Bucky's cocaine enterprise continued to prosper and grow. There was a shipment at least once a week. The importers were happy and Bucky was happy. He was especially pleased with the envelopes of one hundred dollar bills he kept receiving. The deliveries were usually 18 to 22 kilos per shipment.

One night in late August, Bucky received a shipment a bit larger than any before, 33 kilos. The cocaine was temporarily placed inside the tunnel entrance in neat stacks. Bucky knew where there was a loose rock on the side of the tunnel and he was sure they would never miss just one kilo. He checked the beach and saw that everyone was still working at the boat. Quickly, he took a kilo and slid it behind the loose rock, and he returned the rock to its place. Bucky knew that stealing from El Diablo could lead to bad trouble, but he also figured there was no way he could ever be caught.

September 8th was a day of which few places on earth could boast. It was an ideal sunny Florida day, not too cold, not too hot—it was perfect. From the deck of the *Cloud Nine*, Bucky could see the water was its usual crystal clear blue purity. Thirty feet below the thousands of colorful little fish were swimming in the turtle grass. The reef of brain coral was a myriad of reds, yellows and a litany of various other colors.

For tank diving, it doesn't get any better than this—

Bucky glanced at his 22-year-old girlfriend, Birdee Birdsall, who was standing topless near the bow of the boat. She had her back to him and her arms outstretched over the water. The water was so clear a dime would have been easily visible on the ocean floor below. Her long raven hair was dancing in the ocean breeze and her eyes, the same aqua blue as the ocean were drinking in the beauty of the reef with its kaleidoscope of colors and thousands of little polychromatic reef fish scurrying about. Birdee was basking in the tingling warmth of the Florida sun and sucking in the salty air. Bucky could not help but admire her perfect figure. She was a bit thin for Bucky's taste, but that detail was certainly compensated for by her sizeable bosom and her enthusiasm in his bed.

Bucky was on his knees hoisting a scuba tank from the well of the *Cloud Nine* when he saw the bullet. It was a .308 caliber missile converging toward him at 2650 feet per second. Everything seemed to go into ultra-slow motion. There was no time to duck not even time to pray. All he could do was watch as the projectile hurtled toward him at four times the speed of sound. He could hear it. The sound reminded him of bacon frying in a hot skillet. Bucky watched. There was no time for fear. He heard the smashing and the crunching of bone as the bullet penetrated his skull just above his right eyebrow.

Sensing something, Birdee turned around in time to see the top of Bucky's skull being blown off and the surprised expression on Bucky's face. The maimed skull fragment, as if fired from a catapult, blew straight up in the air over what was left of Bucky's head and seemed to hover and dance in mid-air as Bucky's brain exploded. His blood and brains splattered against the white bulkhead of the *Cloud Nine* like a coat of scarlet paint fired from a blaster cannon.

Birdee was confused. *What is going on? Something is wrong but what?* Everything is in slow motion—Birdee glanced at her ample breasts and flat belly. Strange—*how did I get covered with all this pink oatmeal?*

It had not yet occurred to her that she was looking at the blood and the brains of the very recently departed Bucky Wooster.

Bucky was right. Stealing from El Diablo could be very bad business indeed. Bucky saw the bullet and he heard the bullet. He even heard the sound of his skull being ripped apart. Bucky saw a flash of light and then nothing as he began his journey into forever.

He never felt a thing.

CHAPTER TWO

Palm Beach, Florida
Offshore
September 8

The Contractor calmly disassembled his *best friend* and meticulously tucked it in the aluminum traveling case. A bronze plate on the side of the aluminum case read: "Computer Consultants, Inc." The Contractor and his best friend had been together a long time. He had made his best friend shortly following his discharge from the Army back in '74, after he got home from the war in Vietnam. He had flown to Germany and personally selected the finest grade stainless steel and had the barrel bored there. From Germany, the Contractor traveled to north central Switzerland, and found exactly what he was looking for in Lucerne, a superior optics manufacturer, who could grind the lens of a scope to absolute perfection.

The Contractor returned home and ordered a block of the finest English walnut for his best friend's stock. He spent months behind a wood lathe forming and shaping the wood until it fit his shoulder and arm perfectly. His best friend was just right, not a single flaw.

The Contractor was a slight man of unassuming build and looks. There was nothing notable or remarkable about him. He could blend into a group of people and go totally unnoticed. His only redeeming quality was that he was the best in the world at what he did.

The Contractor had grown up in the Allegheny Mountains, in eastern West Virginia, in a dirt-poor coal mining existence. Poverty was all anyone knew. His father was unable to work in the mines any longer because of the black lung disease consuming him. Not that it mattered much; the area had been mined out and was all but shut down anyway. To help make ends meet his long-suffering mother took in laundry and ironing from neighbors who could afford a few dollars for such luxury.

The responsibility of putting meat on the table fell upon him early. He was no more than nine or ten years old when he took his father's .22 rifle and went out in the woods to hunt for squirrels and rabbits. Ammunition was expensive in the mountains, so the Contractor learned to make every shot count. He learned well and every time he fired, something fell.

The Contractor loathed the poverty around him and he hated where he lived even more. The muddy streets and rotting buildings made him all the more depressed. He always knew that someday he would leave the mountains and never come back. The opportunity showed itself right after his 17th birthday. On the wall outside the rural Post Office, he noticed a large sign that read: "Be all you can be in the U.S.

Army." He told his mother that he wanted to join the Army. She knew it was best for the young boy and a way to get him out of the mountains. She reluctantly agreed and signed for him. The following week, the Contractor was taking his first trip outside of the Allegheny's to Fort Benning, Georgia, for the Army's basic training.

The Contractor excelled at most everything in the Army's training program at Fort Benning, but most of all his shooting skills far out-distanced the other soldiers in his unit and he soon was outshooting the instructors as well. Noticing this, the rifle range instructors brought it to the attention of a supervising officer who decided the Contractor's skill with a rifle was too valuable to place him in the infantry. He was assigned as a Specialist and dispatched to the Sniper School of the United States Marine Corps in Quantico, Virginia. Although the Contractor remained in the Army, he was under the command of the Marine Corps. He found the sniper training challenging and extremely well-instructed. The Contractor went from being an expert marksman to a superior one. The day after his training was completed he was on a U.S. Air Force transport plane to Southeast Asia.

The contactor blended well in Vietnam, he was a loner, but it didn't take long before he began to be recognized by the higher officers and well respected by his peers as an ace assassin. He amassed an impressive sniper kill list and was soon approaching a record number. Many times, he had been in the hands of the enemy, but he always managed to hide and melt into the jungle foliage undetected; he slipped by them every time. His years of being alone in the Allegheny forests along with his infinite patience had prepared him well.

A few months before the war ended, he was sent back to the United States on a large Air Force transport. He thought it peculiar that he was on such a large airplane and with only four other passengers. The big troop carrier landed at Langley Air Force Base outside Washington.

An unremarkable man in a gray suit approached him as he disembarked the plane. "Come with me," he said. The Contractor nodded. The man in the gray suit led him into the bowels of a huge white building and into a room with a large iron door.

There was no introduction nor were any names exchanged, "I'm from the Agency," the man said. The Contractor was puzzled and looked intently at him. "You know, the Company?" the man said with alacrity. The Contractor just stared.

"Look," said the man, "let's cut through the bullshit. We want you to come to work for us."

"Doing what?" asked the Contractor.

The man in the gray suit sighed. "All that will be explained to you. We are prepared to pay you a starting salary…" The man stopped talking and wrote down a number on the back of a paper napkin.

The Contractor's eyes bulged. He did not know that much money existed in the world. He readily agreed and nodded yes.

"Good," said the gray suit. "We will transfer you to our training facility and you should be there for about six months. Also, we have noted on your Army tests that you scored close to the genius level in almost all subjects. If this proves true, you will be given advanced classes in languages, computer science and other areas germane to your work activities with us."

And so began the Contractor's career with the CIA. He traveled the world many times carrying out company business, and he had amassed a superior knowledge of computer technology. By his 15th year with the Agency, he had earned a sizeable and comfortable nest egg for himself through many wise investments, always off shore and always under a different alias.

One day the event he knew would happen happened. He met a lovely brown-haired music teacher twelve years his junior in Florida. It was love at first sight for them both and after a six-month courtship; they quietly married.

On a windy fall day, the Contractor knew it was time. He quietly and discreetly disappeared off the radar of the Agency, forever leaving no clue of his identity or whereabouts. He knew the Agency would extend an all-out effort to find him but they never would. Thanks to his training at the Company, which had honed his computer skills, he could create identities, credit cards, passports or anything else he so desired. He could be anyone he wanted to be.

He was now, *the Contractor, Computer Consultant.* His real work and identity was completely unknown to anyone. Not even his beautiful wife or the clients who hired him had the slightest idea who the Contractor really was. He was expensive, but he was the best.

The Contractor tucked his best friend's aluminum case in the nook under the bow of the small boat and took one last look in the direction of the *Cloud Nine.* There was no commotion aboard her. He could see Bucky's headless torso lying in a crumpled heap by the tank well, and Birdee standing there in her surreal world with her mouth wide agape. Her flat belly and bare breasts were covered with a sheet of gray-speckled crimson.

He pulled the cord on the small engine and it caught on the first pull. Nonchalantly, he putted south just off shore toward the nearby Boca Raton Inlet.

"Hi Mister Mitchell," said the teenage dock boy, remembering him from the morning, as he seized the bowline of the Contractor's rented boat. "Any luck out there?"

"Hi-ya Randy," said the Contractor reading the boy's nametag. "Yeah, I got a couple King Mackerels. No real size to them but they're legal."

"Here let me give you a hand with that, Mister Mitchell," said Randy as he reached for the Styrofoam cooler in the center of the boat.

"Thanks Randy. Here take that end." He shoved the cooler toward the boy.

"Mind if I have a look?"

"Why sure, go right ahead."

Randy opened the lid of the Styrofoam cooler and admired the two King Mackerels resting on the ice in the Styrofoam chest. "Wow, looks like you did pretty good, Mister Mitchell. Can I help you clean them?"

"No need Randy. I already gutted them but thanks anyway. I tossed everything overboard. The bottom fish have to eat too," he laughed.

"Yeah, we all gotta do that," chuckled Randy. "Which one is your car?" he asked picking up the ice chest and looking toward the parking lot. The Contractor carried the aluminum case.

"Green station wagon," said the Contractor, nodding with his chin as if pointing. "Guess I'd better get these fish home to the wife down in Miami," he lied.

Randy carried the ice chest and the fishing poles to the Contractor's green car happily anticipating a handsome tip. The Contractor had already paid for the boat rental with the Mitchell credit card that he made a few days before. He was always able to hack into the bank websites and make sure there would never be any question about the phony credit cards he issued to himself. He peeled off a ten-dollar bill and handed it to Randy thanking him for his good service.

He was careful not to tip too much or too little. Service people tended to remember you either way. But, if you tipped just right, it was all in a day's work another reason not to be remembered.

At that moment, the highway bordering the boat rental docks was filled with emergency vehicles heading north, their sirens screaming. "Wonder what's going on?" said the Contractor.

"Beats me but must be som-um big. Everybody and their brother are headed up that way," said Randy, jabbing a thumb to the north.

"Well, I hope it's nothing serious," said the Contractor offering a smile. "I've got to get home to Miami. Which is the best way to I-95?"

"Yes sir," said Randy pointing. "Just go up there to the light and hang a left. That's Atlantic Avenue and it'll take you right into 95."

"Got it, thanks Randy." The Contractor was happy with himself. He had planted, "Miami," in the kid's head twice just in case anyone asked about him.

"You're welcome sir; have a good day."

PHANTOM ORCHID

CHAPTER THREE

Boca Raton, Florida
September 8

The Contractor did not go to I-95, he chose instead to drive north on U.S. Highway 1, or as the locals called it, Dixie Highway. He knew exactly where he was. Noticing a vacant lot with two small boys playing stickball he pulled along the curb. One was black; the other appeared to be Hispanic.

"Hey kids," he said, "come over here for a second."

The boys looked apprehensive and made no move toward this stranger. "Come on, I'm not going to hurt you," he said, reaching into the Styrofoam cooler. "Here, take these to your mothers." He handed each of the boys a King Mackerel. The fish were fresh. He had bought them at a local supermarket that morning along with the ice and cooler making sure to pay in cash.

"Gee, thanks Mister," both boys exclaimed as they raced off with the evening's supper toward their squalid apartments.

The Contractor drove another mile. He spotted a large dumpster behind a Chinese restaurant. No one seemed to be around so he pulled the station wagon close. Meticulously he wiped down the fishing rods, the reels and the cooler and quietly slid them into the dumpster. He then went into the only stall in the restroom of the restaurant and stripped off his clothes including his underwear, hat and sunglasses. Quickly he donned a necktie and the business suit he had brought. As a boy growing up in the poverty-stricken Appalachians, the Contractor only owned one pair of ragged dungarees and a tee shirt or two. His bare toes would often peek through his only pair of canvas shoes.

He promised himself that someday he would be an immaculate dresser. A promise he kept. With his first paycheck from the Agency, he spent on a nice wardrobe. Unless working conditions prohibited, the Contractor always prided himself in wearing a neat and clean business suit and always looking sharp.

The Contractor tore off the sticky mustache on his lip, and stuffed everything in the bottom of the trashcan and covered them with paper towels and a newspaper.

Traveling north on the Dixie Highway, he soon came to Palmetto Road where he turned west several miles taking him to a small airport amid many expensive houses, a fairly common real estate investment in south Florida. You could have your home and your own private airport right out the front door. He drove by the perimeter of the little airport choosing not to stop. He would come back later.

A few miles away, the Contractor parked in a remote parking area of a Wal-Mart to wait for dusk. Under the cloak of night, he would draw the least attention. As the evening began its blanket of darkness, he drove back to the small airstrip and again he parked and waited. Once satisfied that all was quiet and with no lights on in the station wagon, he drove to a hangar on the west end of the field. He pushed the button on the automatic door remote. Once the door was open wide enough, he drove the station wagon into the hangar and quickly closed the huge door behind him. He parked the station wagon next to his airplane, a red over white A-36 Beechcraft Bonanza.

The Contractor had learned to fly during his tenure with the Agency, a skill that had served him well over the years. The Bonanza was a bit extravagant, he readily admitted, but it saved him the stress of airport lines, the idiotic groping of the TSA and eliminated the worry of checking his best friend. Besides, with his own personal airplane, he was on his schedule not that of the airlines. The Contractor went to work.

He had no fear of the owners of the house and hangar discovering him. The Contractor always did his homework. He scouted an area long before the day of the contract. He took hundreds of digital pictures. He knew the areas and the people, their habits and their schedules.

On his computer, he had learned the McGriff's', his unassuming hosts, which owned the beautiful place were still in their summer home in Maggie Valley, North Carolina, and not expected back in Florida until mid-October. It was ideal for him especially since the McGriff's' had left their station wagon in the hangar, keys and all.

He checked the aluminum foil that he had placed over the only window in the door of the hangar. Satisfied that no one could see in he turned on the lights. In the restroom of the hangar, the Contractor took out a small Bic lighter and burned the credit card and ID of Stephen B. Mitchell then flushed the ashes. Stephen B. Mitchell no longer existed.

From a small case in the Bonanza's glove box, he took out two plastic cards. He was now Kevin C. Ward. Patiently he removed several cans of water-based blue paint from the Bonanza and slowly began to spray the airplane's red paint with the water-based blue. It was temporary, he knew that, but just in case anyone happened to see him leave, they'd be reporting a blue airplane, not a red one.

The Contractor took out a roll of white surgical tape and changed the airplanes numbers. From the three he made an eight, and from the one he made a seven. He easily changed the letter 'P' to an 'R'. Now he was ready. All he had to do now was to wait until the early hours of the morning when he was sure everyone would be asleep. He would start and taxi the Bonanza out of the hangar and be in the air before anyone was the wiser.

The Contractor decided to wipe the station wagon and the hangar down. Completely getting rid of fingerprints or any trace of him being there, then he might catch a few hours' sleep, but first there was one more item of business. He picked up his laptop and dialed in a series of codes. His reply came in seconds, a question mark, nothing else. He typed in: **Florida contract completed, 08 September.** Again, he was answered right away, this time with a plus sign. He typed in: **deposit fee to Swiss account number** and he typed in a series of letter and number codes. In seconds, the response came back confirmed.

The Contractor was careful always route his computer messages through Hong Kong, London, Istanbul, and several of the eastern European countries making them impossible to track even for the most skilled. He also changed his ID codes and bank codes daily.

He was just beginning to shut down the laptop when a message clicked again. "**URGENT: stand by for Number One, online.**" The Contractor sat stunned. Number One was online, El Diablo himself! All the years, the Contractor had done business with El Diablo, this was the first time he had ever either communicated with him personally on the scrambler phone or encrypted email.

The Contractor was not particularly fond of El Diablo, he thought the crime lord was far too ruthless and he killed unnecessarily. The Contractor never did that. To him, his job was strictly business, nothing personal. On the other hand, deep down, he really didn't care. El Diablo kept him in work; he paid well and he paid promptly. Ruthless or not he was a good client. The Contractor had no idea of El Diablo's real identity nor did El Diablo know his.

The laptop clicked off a long series of codes and symbols. The Contractor typed in, "received," then he shut down the laptop. He entered the codes and symbols into his small pocket decoder.

It read: McCord Barrett, Palm Beach County, Florida, ASAP.

CHAPTER FOUR

Dallas/Fort Worth Intl Airport, Texas
September 8

"Take off power," barked Captain Luke Sellers to the lanky first officer beside him. The captain manipulated the steering tiller beside his left knee guiding the big Boeing on to runway Three-Five Left.

"Trans Global International 2120, you are cleared for takeoff," the tower controller's voice crackled in their headsets. "Runway Three-Five Left, maintain runway heading, contact departure control at 10,000 on one-three-three point one-five. Good day sir."

"Roger, tower, TGI 2120 is cleared to go, Three-Five Left, going to departure at reaching 10,000. Good day Dallas Fort Worth," replied the captain. "You got her, Spark Plug," he said as he motioned to his copilot indicating that it was his turn to fly.

Alternating flight legs was not only good business but also company policy. Sellers liked the rule. It provided an excellent opportunity for the young flight officers to gain hands-on experience and helped prepare them for the day when they too would sit in that cherished left seat. *It was good for pilot fatigue*, as well, he thought. One pilot flew while the other worked the radios, navigated and tended to other cockpit duties.

I'm gonna work you all the way to Denver, Spark Plug. Someday you'll thank me. It's for your own good.

Captain Lucus Frank Sellers, a veteran aviator was approaching 30,000 hours in the air and his 38th year with the airline. He was a Trans Global icon and the epitome of an airline captain. His brown hair was almost completely gray on the sides and was combed straight back. Two steel blue eyes set in a weathered face didn't miss a thing. Sellers was a pleasant easygoing captain and flying with him was enjoyable, but he expected everyone to do their job. Today he was feeling every bit of his 59 years.

He had seen just about everything in aviation from flying the old DC-3 as a young copilot to senior captain on the mammoth Boeing 777. In many ways he was looking forward to that magic birthday, sixty. The FAA had moved the mandatory retirement age for all airline pilots from sixty to sixty-five, but Luke had already made up his mind. He wasn't staying to sixty-five.

Ah, retirement...no more bouncing from one climate to another, no more packaged soap in hotel rooms, no more rubber chicken meals, and no more overseas trips guessing at clearance instructions and trying to cipher fuel in kilos or pounds. Ricocheting from one time zone to another and taking off tomorrow and getting there yesterday...is it Fahrenheit or

Celsius? And no more fretting over every pilot's nightmare, weather. Been there, done that, and bought the tee-shirt—

Sellers wasn't being hard on the young flight officer. Like most captains, he considered it part of his job to share his experience with these young pilots who would someday be sitting in his seat.

Let's face it... he thought, *some of this stuff just isn't in the books.*

"Ninety-five percent on the epers, Luke," the sound of his copilot's voice snapped his attention back into the cockpit. First Officer Cord Barrett's left hand was firmly gripping the thrust levers easing the power up to 95 percent E.P.R., engine pressure ratio.

Ordinarily Cord would never have addressed his captain, or any captain, by their first name unless specifically invited to do so. It simply wasn't done. However, Luke Sellers liked his crew to be on a first name basis.

Cord's eyes were intently fixed on the airspeed indicator and raced across the endless array of gauges and dials as the huge machine lurched forward with staggering power. Cord could never contain the thrill of 90,000 pounds of thrust from each engine pushing him back in the seat like a huge electromagnet as the gigantic General Electric engines spooled out their enormous power, engines so large that the fuselage of a Boeing 727 could fit inside the cowls.

"Airspeed's alive, eighty knots, we have rudder control," called out Sellers. Cord knew his captain was keeping the airliner straight down the center of the runway with the steering tiller while his eyes welded on the instruments. Both pilots were checking, double-checking and triple checking the myriad of dials and gauges.

"Everything's in the green, Cap."

Sellers nodded as he called out the speeds to Cord. "There's a 100 knots, 110, 120, 130, 140 knots. Rotate."

Cord eased back on the control yoke to a deck-pitch angle of 21° and felt all 580,000 pounds of the huge Boeing shift from its landing gear to the wings. With the grace of a swan on a mountain lake, the 777 left mother earth and climbed into the heavens.

Cord noted a positive rate of climb and adjusted the thrust levers to 250 knots, a speed mandated by the FAA for all aircraft below 10,000 feet. He waved his hand, palm up, indicating to raise the landing gear. At that same instant, Luke was reaching for the big red handle on the right center of the dash, which would retract the ship's 14 wheels, each the size of a small Volkswagen. Cord suppressed a private smirk. Sellers caught it. He loved giving the captain an order.

As if I didn't know," thought Sellers. *"I've been sitting up here longer than you have been living, Spark Plug.*

If the truth be told, Captain Sellers liked it. He didn't want a Yes-Man in his cockpit. He admired a bit of spunk in his first officers, and he wanted them to tell it like it was.

How can you ever expect to command if you don't first believe in yourself?

"That's the new Texas Stadium down there isn't it, Cap?" said Cord, nodding with his chin at the massive football stadium 8000 feet below.

"Yep, home of the World Champion Dallas Cowboys," Sellers emphatically remarked, with Cord mouthing his captain's words in perfect sync.

Thought Cord, *if the captain had his way, the Cowboys would all be presidents and the late Tom Landry would be the Pope.*

"Take off flaps zero detent, Captain," said Cord. Sellers patiently obliged.

Luke Sellers admired the young man on his right. McCord Fredrick Barrett was far too good looking for his own good. He stood an easy six-two and was trim and muscle toned. Sellers guessed him around 33- or 34-years old. His dark blond hair was rich and full. Cord's face was handsomely chiseled punctuated by clear and evenly set almond brown eyes.

Bet he's melted a few hearts with those eyes, Sellers thought. *He's probably broken a few, as well.*

Luke especially liked the young copilot's intelligence and eagerness to learn. Cord was a smooth pilot for being ex-Navy fighter jock, and he keenly adhered to Seller's rules of giving his passengers the safest and smoothest ride possible.

Noting the ship's altimeter, "There's 10,000, Cap, we'd better go to departure," Cord said with a hint of a southern accent.

"Yep," the captain acknowledged reaching for the radio selector dial only to find that Cord had already tuned in the center's frequency, 133.15. Cord smiled to himself remembering the captain's words.

Always stay ahead of your ship. Never take it anywhere you brain hasn't been 15 minutes before. Lesson heard, lesson learned.

Captain Sellers leaned into his microphone, "Fort Worth Center, Trans Global 2120 with you at 10,000 looking for higher."

The center's response was immediate. "Roger TGI 2120," a distinct Texas drawl said, "I have you at ten. Climb and maintain flight level three-five-zero, you are cleared to Denver direct as filed, squawk five-five-seven-four."

"Wilco," replied Sellers, "TGI 2120 is cleared to flight level three five zero, direct Denver as filed. Ah, Center, do you want us to change our squawk code to five-five-seven-four?"

"Affirmative 2120 squawk five-five-seven-four"

"Wilco," said the confused captain, "squawking five-five-seven-four."

Luke reached to his right on the center console to the ship's transponder, a radio device, which allows the center's ground radar to identify them and track their altitude, headings and speed. The transponder is especially effective for separating air traffic in high-density areas. He dialed in the assigned code, five-five-seven-four.

"Hey Cap, why would they want to change our squawk code?"

"Hell if I know, son," said Luke. "That radar man probably hasn't got a damn thing to do except mess with us." He gestured toward the thrust levers. "Climb-power," he ordered.

With his left hand, Cord snapped on the auto-throttles, which set the power of the big machine automatically by one of the onboard computers.

"Oh hell," said Sellers, "We don't want to work today." He engaged the orange button on his steering yoke. "Let George do it." Immediately, the giant Boeing was completely controlled by the autopilot computer, a/k/a George.

Cord could not help but feel a bit disappointed. He enjoyed hand-flying the big machine, but the captain was still, and always, the captain. *If, El Supremo, over there said to let George do it, then George would do it.*

Soon the altitude alarm sounded alerting the crew that they were within 1000 feet of their assigned cruising altitude. The Boeing leveled off at precisely at

35,000 feet. "Okay Spark Plug, what's our en-route time to the mile high city?"

Cord busied himself with the GPS computer.

Wish he'd think of something better to call me than Spark Plug.

"Let's see, Cap, we have 740 nautical miles to go and we're showing an air speed of 459 knots, so looking at Denver in 96."

Captain Sellers was also looking at the computer. "Well," he said, "I've got to tell the nice folks back there something and I'd like to do it in English."

"Yes sir," said Cord, "we're doing a ground speed of 540 mph. En-route time is 1 hour and 36 minutes."

"Thanks, Cord. Call Andi up here, I'd like a good cup of coffee if that's possible on an airliner. I don't think one cup will keep me awake in Denver tonight. Say, Cord, did you get the weather?"

I don't know why he bothers with the weather; we're going anyway.

"Yes sir," replied Cord. "It looks clear in Denver at least for now. We've got some pretty heavy thunder-bumpers brewing over the Oklahoma panhandle and southwestern Kansas, lots of rain and some hail. Radar is painting some heavy turbulence, but we should be able to get around it to the east and probably get over most of the bad stuff. It shouldn't be any problem, but looks like it's going to get pretty wet in Denver later tonight."

"Thanks Cord. Go ahead and call Andi. I want a cup of joe, hot and black; she knows how I like it. How about you?"

"Yeah, I could go for a cup, I like it the same." Cord pushed the flight attendant button.

Both pilots loosened their ties and eased back in the upholstered cockpit chairs. Captain Sellers reached for the airborne radar adjusting its scan to a wider range.

He didn't like what he saw.

CHAPTER FIVE

Florida Everglades, Osceola National
Swamp
Cypress Slough, South Central Florida
September 8

Rita Fleming had never been so happy; she was at the threshold of orgasm. The ginger ale-like tingle was spreading through her lower body. Chills raced up and down her spine as her fiancé, David Winslow, kissed her deeply allowing his fingertips to glide easily along her belly and inner thighs. Her breasts pressed tightly against him in the quiet sanctity of the tent. She was barely aware of the murmur of passion groaning deep in her throat. She was in heaven and just moments away, just microseconds away from immense pleasure, the overpowering exaltation of ecstasy.

Rita and Dave had been planning this camping trip for quite a while. They loved coming here to the Cypress Slough far away from her kids, his kids, exes and the grind of everyday life. Both enjoyed the absence of restrictions and being completely free. Here in the slough they could yell, laugh, make love openly and go skinny-dipping in Moccasin Creek.

Rita was an attractive woman, a brunette with prematuring gray hair and deep blue eyes. She was petite and looked younger than her 41 years. She did carry a few extra pounds, but still not bad for a mother of two, doing her best to make ends meet, and stay afloat financially.

After her husband took off with some floozy named Wanda, she went to work as a second-shift clerk at the Jiffy-Stop, a convenience store on State Road 80 and Farm Road 9 near Clewiston, Florida. Although she was economically challenged, Rita still somehow managed to keep up the payments on her mobile home. Rita kept her kids fed, in school and off drugs. She was thankful. The last thing on her mind was romance.

Dave worked as the manager of the Chobee Boat Rentals across the highway from the Jiffy-Stop, where he rented fishing boats to wealthy northerners or anyone else who wanted to fish the big lake; Lake Okeechobee, a Seminole noun meaning, "Big Water." Dave sold bait and tackle, gas, beer, snacks, repaired outboard motors and a sundry of other duties that went along with being manager. But mostly he sold bait and rented boats to rich Yankees.

His routine rarely changed. Dave would drop by the Jiffy-Stop each evening for his usual Bud Tall Boy to sip on the way home. When he spotted Rita, the normal flirting and teasing ensued, one thing led to another and soon Rita was out on her first date in years. Likewise, so was Dave.

Rita had ignored Dave's advances at first, being a bit gun shy from past experiences, but he persisted and she could not help being somewhat taken with the amiable man. What was left of Dave's dark hair was turning gray and he sported a respectable potbelly, but his smile was genuine and his demeanor was kind. At five-feet nine, Dave was not a tall man, but certainly tall enough for Rita's five-three. He lived with his two teenagers. It had been several years since his wife left. He never said why. Rita never asked. They were an instant item and soon significant others.

Dave was Rita's security blanket and he provided the love and affection she so desperately craved. In return, Rita gave Dave the love and companionship that he had lost so long ago. That coupled with her insatiable libido made Dave a happy camper, literally.

Friday, September 8th had been a perfect day. Dave and Rita had arrived at the slough in mid-afternoon. Both were elated at being alone together. Dave was an experienced outdoorsman and quickly had a campfire going. He pitched the tent, gathered plenty of firewood for the night, and was unloading a second cooler from his pick-up.

"Psssst."

Dave was dumbfounded. There stood Rita stark naked.

Oh! Those breast—her belly—the dark patch.

"Catch me if you can," she laughed as she ran across the levee and dived headlong into Moccasin

Creek. Dave was not far behind tearing at his clothes and kicking off his boots.

For the next hour, they splashed and played in the creek like teenagers. They dunked each other in the cool water, hugged, and made an awkward attempt at making love but soon gave up the idea. It was hardly romantic trying to fight the current of the creek, maintaining their balance and treading water all at the same time. They decided to save it for later.

"Let's dry off," said Dave

"How?"

"Whudda mean how?" chimed Dave. "We jest stand around and let the sun dry us. We still got an hour of daylight left."

"Like this?" asked Rita gesturing with her hands over her naked body.

"Of course like this, baby. Who's gonna see us? We're twenty miles from the nearest town and fifteen miles off the hard road for Pete's sake. Nobody'd ever see us way out here. Who would even know how to get here? Shoot, we wouldn't be here ourselves if my truck didn't have four-wheel drive."

"You're right, Dave. Besides hon, I like being like this with you."

Dave grinned. *If you like it now baby just wait 'til I get my arms around you in that tent tonight.*

The sun was fast going down on Cypress Slough. The lovers cooked steaks over the fire. Dave was an amazingly good camp cook. "Things always taste better in the woods," he bragged. They baked potatoes in the fire and Rita made a salad with the vegetables from the ice cooler. Dave drank a few Tall Boys while Rita sipped on one. Drinking had never been her forte.

Later they sat by the fire looking out over the big Osceola Swamp listening to the little night critters make their medleys of music leaving their vibrato of harmony in the mist. The soft blowing wind swayed the Spanish moss in the cypress trees as it whispered back to them.

"No tellin' what kinds of mysteries lays out there," Dave said quietly, gazing out over the mire.

"Yeah, no tellin'."

"Guess the swamp has thousands of secrets we'll never know 'bout," Dave said thoughtfully.

"Yeah," she sighed.

They sat arm in arm enjoying the beauty and the silence of the dense Everglades. They talked and even sang a few songs together, but the only one they knew all the verses to was, *You Are My Sunshine*, which seems apropos at the moment. Dave thought it sounded pretty good. He usually did after a few Tall Boys.

"Oh look hon," Rita said, pointing to the eastern horizon, "we're gonna have a full moon tonight." Dave turned toward the round golden ball reflecting its yellow ribbons dancing on the surface of the watery marsh like a thousand slivering kite tails.

Both stared at the hypnotic Florida moon rising just above the swamp. "Oh, how beautiful hon, look how big it is," she whispered. The couple basked in the moon's glow watching it shine through the rising fog. It looked like a round pool of churned butter. The lily pads were floating in the mire just a few yards away as the fog began to settle.

Swamp fog is a phenomenon of the Everglades caused by the heat of the day rising and as the air is cooled the fog settles in. It was as thick as chowder, but so beautiful.

The only sound breaking the stillness were the frogs croaking and the cricket's fiddling along with a litany of other critters joining the symphony.

"You know baby, it jest don't get no better than this," Dave sighed.

"You said it, hon."

"Guess we'd better get in the tent before the skeeters carry us off," Dave laughed. Both darted for the shelter with much more on their minds than skeeters.

Dave had made sure the tent was on high ground away from the snakes and a possible curious alligator.

Don't want no visitors, especially not tonight.

He quickly built up the fire and shot into the tent like a ricocheted bullet. He carefully tied the inner-tarp and tightly secured the mosquito netting, wondering why Noah had bothered to take mosquitoes with him on the Ark in the first place. At last, he was in the waiting arms of his beloved.

Their mouths met like two hungry tigers. Tongues touched, kisses were never so deep and passionate. Hands were everywhere. Their bodies pressed together encompassing, touching, feeling, rubbing, caressing, teasing. Their lust for each other was unbridled. Rita had never been so anxious for love and she could feel him against her. She knew he was definitely ready her anticipation was unbearable.

Dave eased on top of her slowly kissing every part of her being. When she could stand it no longer she slide her hand down and guided him into her deliriously anticipating the unparalleled explosion of ecstasy.

Dave was swimming in his own abyss of pleasure as his arms encircled the love of his life. Her eyes were barely open focusing on nothing other than the joy of the moment. Dave felt Rita's body stiffen like a rod of tempered steel. *Man, she's really getting into this,* he thought, quite proud of himself for being such a prolific stud.

Dave's elated self-esteem quickly vanished at the volume of Rita's scream shattering the stillness of the night.

"Whut? Whut the hell?" he exclaimed leaping up in shock from the arms of his beloved, his phallus changing from the Rock of Gibraltar to something resembling a boiled mushroom. "Baby, whut is it? Whut the hell is wrong?" cried Dave in wild confusion.

A dark shadow had fallen over the tent cast from the bright moon. It hesitated then as suddenly as it appeared it vanished into the swamp.

"A shadow hon, a shadow of a man, I saw it, hon!" Rita was trembling with fear. She was about to scream again when Dave gently shook her.

"Stop it!" he could see that she was terrified. "C'mon, calm down, baby. You must have been dreaming."

"No hon, I know what I saw. I ain't crazy and I ain't seeing things. It was the shadow of a man." Rita paused then she hissed. "Something is out there."

"Aw crap, I'll go take a look," Dave muttered, disgusted at having his marathon of carnal bliss demolished.

"No! No hon, please don't go out there, please don't leave me," she begged.

"Baby, I ain't 'bout to leave you, you're jest seeing things that's all. Take a few deep breaths and let Ol' Dave worry about some silly shadow."

Dave fumbled with the inner tarp; all the while listening to Rita's persistent pleading. "Where's my britches?" he mumbled through the darkness of the tent.

"I thought they was right here. Oh hell, what do I need them for anyways? We are a million miles from nowheres."

Dave loosened the tarp and was about to crawl out of the tent. "David," she softly said.

That's funny she has never called me David.

"The man, 'um, the shadow it—it didn't have no head."

"Now baby, I already told you there ain't nothin' out there. You jest imagined som-thin'. Sometimes the Glades can do that to you. Funny things happen out here; make's folks think they are seeing things that jest ain't there."

Maybe Dave is right, a headless man? A headless thing? A shadow? Yeah, guess I was just imagining something...couldn't be anything way out here. Ridiculous. But it seemed so real—Dave must think I am a complete nut. I'm just imagining things.

Dave looked around and found nothing. Soon Rita joined him and they both stood nude in the moonlight by the edge of the swamp looking out over the peaceful quagmire through the thickening fog.

"See baby, I told you that you was jest imaginin' things. A headless shadow? C'mon now."

"Yeah hon, you are right. I'm sorry but it seemed so real. I'm sorry hon."

Dave put his arm around her bare and still trembling shoulders. "It's okay baby, it's okay."

The swamp usually offering a chorus opera from the crickets, frogs and a litany of other creatures was deathly silent. They didn't notice.

The scream came from somewhere nearby in the swamp. It was ear shattering. A screech so loud like nothing they had ever heard before; it was deafening. Both froze unable to move.

Dave was the first to recover his wits and bolted toward the truck as fast as his portly frame would allow tugging Rita behind. Once inside he shouted. "Lock your door!"

"What the fuck was that?" gasped Rita, uncharacteristically cursing.

"Damned if I know," he shouted. "Whatever it is it ain't human. I ain't never heard anything so freaking loud!"

"Start the truck hon," she cried. "Oh hon, we gotta get outta here. I'm so scared! Start the truck!"

Rita did not have to repeat her plea. Dave was grinding the Chevy's starter so hard he was about to break the key off in the ignition. It seemed like an eternity, but the truck mercifully started. Dave slammed the gearshift into reverse and backed up a few yards. He put it in forward and floored the accelerator, and steered on the almost visible road, hurling a volcano of dirt and debris into the sticky night air. The truck was bouncing over the bumps like an out of control juggernaut on a trampoline slinging fishing poles, coolers and camping gear in every direction.

No more than twenty yards ahead, they both saw something in the middle of the road illuminated in the headlights.

Something that turned their blood to ice water—

CHAPTER SIX

1861 Meadow Drive
Winnetka, Illinois
September 8

Today was no exception for Pete Ogilvie. He started today like every day. The alarm clock roused him out of bed at precisely one thirty in the afternoon, after a futile attempt to get a few hours' sleep.

Pete didn't rest well. Besides the insomnia and the frequent calls of some damn body, some damn where, selling cemetery plots in freaking Do Wah Ditty, a free vacation contest or whatever. The noisy kids playing outside along with the sirens going by on the boulevard made daytime sleep impossible. As always, his head was throbbing and his mouth felt like a gravel pit. Even his hair hurt.

He hated this shift.

He poured a generous helping of vodka in some orange juice and nuked a cup of instant coffee in the microwave. Pete took a gulp of the orange juice and finished the potion while he shaved and took a quick shower, forgetting the coffee. He stared at what he saw in the mirror. Two red-rimmed hazel eyes stared back at him.

Holy Moses, I'm 36 years old—I look 66, and I feel 96.

Pete laboriously donned his work clothes, a pair of Levis that were feeling a bit snug these days and a Chicago Bears sweat shirt.

Since we aren't seen by the public no dress code, thankfully.

He tied the laces of his Docksiders and meandered back to the kitchen. The shoes squeaked through the empty house, like an echo in a Teton canyon.

Pete dug out a sandwich baggie from the cabinet and shook out two white pills, swiftly downing them with another liberal helping of vodka. He wasn't sure what they were, but the guy he got them from said they would make him "right." They'd better at 20-bucks a pop. He took a quick inventory of his work needs. Photo ID card, cigarettes, glasses, grease pencil, mouthwash, breath mints and the essential flask topped off with Smirnoff.

He grabbed the car keys from the hook by the door and looked around his suburban house. One couch, one chair, one end table, a bed and a dresser. That's all the bitch had left. Pete Junior's Pacman game was still on the floor where she had left it. "Bitch," Pete muttered aloud. He locked the door and folded his five feet eleven inch frame into his red Mustang.

Peter Michael Ogilvie was a reticent man not at all like some of his more gregarious co-workers. He preferred to stay a bit more aloof, but he was not a wallflower either. Pete was spending more time by the bar lately. He hadn't paid much attention to it. *Nobody would notice….* But Annie noticed and so did others.

He faced his daily dilemma.

Should I take the long way around the lake or should I take the freeway? The lake was always a refreshing drive, but the freeway was faster—but I like the lake drive.

Pete glanced at his watch, a gift from the bitch during happier times.

I outta throw the damn thing in the lake.

"Oh Crap," he said to no one. "I'm going to be late as it is." He dismissed the lake route.

Gotta take the freaking freeway, maybe I should call in sick—nah, no way—I've already used up my sick time, vacation time too. Besides, the president would shit a cow if I called in sick again.

Pete steered the Mustang to the south ramp of the Eden Freeway, traffic wasn't as bad as he had expected. Pete pushed the Mustang up to 70, keeping an eye on the rearview mirror for the ever-lurking blue lights of a police cruiser. He made better time than anticipated and was soon entering the cloverleaf labyrinth intersecting the John F. Kennedy Expressway. He steered on the westbound ramp still pleased with the light traffic.

Pete Ogilvie was not a happy man. "The bitch," had taken everything and split. The pain of losing her was bad enough.

But did she have to take my boy? Petey would be nine in January and he needs me in his life. Who is going to take him to little league? Who will teach him to box? How will he learn to slide into home? What good was visitation every other week and alternate holidays especially since she, the bitch, had taken a state job and moved down to Springfield? That dumb-ass lawyer had let that one get by him. As it is, she gets half of my salary and custody of Petey. I can still hear that senile old fart of a judge barking out orders—I'd like to have given him that gavel for a suppository. Why didn't he just order me castrated and be done with it?

Pete drove through Park Ridge and Schiller Park exiting the JFK Expressway at Mannheim Road. As was his custom, he pulled into a deserted gas station and parked in the rear. He popped another white pill and took a respectable drink from the flask. Pete grimaced as the vodka scorched his throat, but it was working, he was feeling a little better now. He tucked the flask under the seat saving some for his lunch break and he took a swig of mouthwash.

He hated this shift.

Pete covered the half mile to O'Hare Airport quickly. He stopped beside the steel gate and punched his code into the sentry box. The heavy gate swung open allowing the Mustang to its parking space. The large red sign read:

FAA AIR TRAFFIC CONTROL CENTER
AUTHORIZED PERSONNL ONLY

He inserted his ID card into the slot in a secured door and heard the honey-coated voice of Dodie Cunningham. "May I help you please?"

"Ogilvie," Pete spat back knowing that Dodie was watching him through the overhead camera. "Whudda ya know…." Pete sighed, "Hot Hips is actually at her desk today—" referring to the wandering Ms. Cunningham by the pet name given to her by the controllers.

I wonder how short your skirt is today, Dodie. Wish all I had to do were roam around the center chomping on a wad of Juicy Fruit and wriggling my ass at the supervisors.

Immediately the heavy aluminum door buzzed followed by the familiar click and Pete was inside. It took a moment for his eyes to adjust to the darkness of the vast center. The radarscopes blinked at him like the eyes of a thousand Cyclops. The voices of the controllers were buzzing as if he was in the middle of an auction. Pete was feeling good now, damn good. He was home.

"Oh Ogilvie, I'm glad you are here," said the voice of his supervisor, Lincoln Sansbury, as he hurried up to him.

"Lo Mister President, how's it goin'?" Pete retorted. Sansbury cringed at the association of his name with the martyred president.

Mopping his brow where hair used to be the pudgy supervisor said, "I want you to relieve Collegio so you'll be working the southwest quadrant today. Everything okay with you, Pete?"

"Yeah, everything is fine, Mister President."

Why wouldn't everything be okay with me?

"Okay. Then get to it," Lincoln snorted trotting off.

"Roger Mister President."

Pete retrieved a headset from his locker and headed toward the radar stations. He managed a glance at Hot Hips. She smiled flashing a row of pearly white teeth. Teeth were not the only thing she was known for flashing. Hot Hips had hiked her mini-skirt just far enough to get Pete's attention. It did. He had toyed with the idea of asking Hot Hips out, but quickly abandoned the thought.

Shee-it, if it ever got out that we were seeing each other I'd never hear the end of it.

Hot Hips had been bonked by everyone in the FAA who toted a Y chromosome. "Shee-it," he grumbled.

Hot Hips has been hit on more than a piñata— she's probably a bitch too.

Pete eased into his cubicle next to a jovial controller named Collegio. Tony Collegio was a likeable man who was easy to work with and highly capable, a man who remained calm under pressure.

"Okay Wildman, I'm your relief, whatcha got?"

"Hi-ya Pete," Tony said without looking up, he ran his hand through a carpet of thick black hair. "Got them all marked for you," he said motioning to the blips on the radar screen in front of them.

"There's Delta 1720 at the outer marker, I've already kicked him over to the tower, and that's American 3362 behind him and American 626 behind him. Ah, let's see—got two holding over Aurora, one's a United and one's Southwest. Here are the flight numbers, this one is at 17,000 and this one here, the Southwest is at twelve grand. I got about fifteen total. You okay with that, Pete?"

"Sure I'm okay Tony, just a walk in the park," snapped Pete.

Why wouldn't I be okay with that?

The two controllers worked in perfect unison. It was the same procedure every time. Shift change, lunch break, restroom visit, it was always the same.

Tony handed off one airplane at a time until Pete got his rhythm and soon he was smoothly directing the air traffic in the southwest corridor. A layperson would have been amazed how two controllers could maintain a conversation between themselves while juggling fifteen or twenty airliners all at the same time, spitting out directions, frequencies, altitudes and instructions of all sorts. Like sideshow barkers, they directed traffic in a sky dense with airplanes filled with thousands of people.

"Alright Pete, I'm outta here," said Tony. "Oh by the way, you have a Cathay Pacific 747 Captain over North Dakota whining about his fuel burn and he's about to shit a turkey. He's coming in from Hong Kong and threatening to park it in Minneapolis if we don't give him a straight-in approach."

"Okay," said Pete nonchalantly.

I don't give a damn if he goes to Minneapolis or freaking Timbuktu—but the president would shit a duck.

"Oh one more thing, you have a super pissed-off Lear Jet driver just off Midway flight planned to Vegas. That's him right there," said Tony tracing a green blip on the radar screen with his finger. "Niner-Niner-Two-Eight Tango. He's bitching because his fuel load might have burned below regulations. He says he had to wait too long for a flight clearance. The guys over at Flight Standards are cracking down on these hot dogs who don't go by the book. You know the rule, adequate fuel to the destination, plus an alternate airport, plus 45 minutes."

Pete nodded.

"Wait a minute!" exclaimed Collegio. "Wait just a damn minute here. I gave that asshole a transponder code of seven-four-five-five. He's squawking five-five-seven-four!"

"It's okay Tony; I'll take care of it, no sweat. Go on home and open yourself a cool one. You earned it."

"You sure, Pete?"

"Hell yes, I'm sure Wildman, scat."

"You talked me into it, Bro." Tony slapped Pete on the arm and made for the door. He called out over his shoulder, "And don't forget that Lear Jet, Pete." Ogilvie waved his arm in the air without turning around.

Collegio was almost at the center's door. "Hey Tony, the president wants to see you before you go," cooed Hot Hips looking up from her emery board and extending out an arm to admire her newly polished nails.

"Thanks Dodie," nodded Collegio.

Jeez, now what? Tony wondered as he stuck his head into the supervisor's office. "You wanted to see me, Mister President?"

Lincoln Sansbury cringed again, this time noticeably at the use of his cognomen.

Damn that Ogilvie, he's the one who started all this nonsense—now every beating heart from here to Aruba is calling me Mister President.

"Yeah Tony, have a seat," Lincoln said, motioning for him to close the door. "Tony, I have worked the scopes for twenty years," Lincoln began in his most fatherly tone.

Bullshit, thought Tony. *The president worked the scopes for only twelve years.*

"I know how the brother-in-law game is played," Lincoln continued, "Nobody rats out anyone else. It's a brotherhood and you cover each other's butts, C-Y-A, that's the name of the game. Hell Tony, I know that."

Collegio nodded and tried his best to look interested, but what came next floored him.

"Tony, you gotta shoot straight with me has Ogilvie seemed all right to you lately?"

Thoughts were clicking through Tony's mind like a stuck adding machine.

Hell no, he hasn't seemed right—he wasn't right! He has been missing too many radio calls, mixing up altitudes, stumbling through flight clearances and Lord knows what else—With all those damn breath mints and mouthwash it's enough to make a buzzard gag and that after shave he uses smells like a New Orleans bordello—Hell no, he wasn't right!

"Look Mister President," Tony said, leaning forward. "Pete Ogilvie is an ace air traffic controller. I've been working the scopes for 15 years and have never seen anyone any better."

"No argument," said Lincoln, gesturing with his palms up. "But something is wrong. I know it."

"Mister President," Tony began, Lincoln frowned again and wiped his hairless forehead. "Pete's going through some pretty rough times right now. I guess you've heard about Annie leaving and the divorce and all."

"Yeah, yeah sure," the supervisor sounded sympathetic.

"He's still pretty chewed up about losing custody of his son. That's really the guts of the issue."

"I understand…I understand that he is going through hard times," muttered Lincoln. "But damn it, Collegio, we've got 10,000 people coming in or leaving Chicago airspace every freaking hour, 24/7, 365, and they are expecting us, yes us, to provide separation and keep those flying tin cans from running into each other. I can't have any of my people out there asleep at the switch," he blurted, jabbing a finger toward the radar room. "It doesn't matter if he's got personal problems or just won the freaking lottery; in this business error is not an option. If anyone should know it's me."

Tony Collegio sat back in his chair stunned. In the five years he known the, "Great Emancipator," this was the first time that he had hinted about that horrible day in San Diego. Everyone knew but nobody ever mentioned it, at least not aloud.

Lincoln Sansbury was a young radar man just out of the Air Force where he trained and worked as an air traffic controller at Barksdale Air Force Base in Louisiana. Lincoln was working San Diego's north sector that fateful morning. A student pilot flying a single engine Piper somehow become disoriented and steered into the path of a landing Boeing 727 airliner lumbering down the glide path at 180 mph.

Despite his repeated warning to the Piper and a valiant effort to turn the Boeing, the midair disaster was inevitable. People, luggage, fuel, and debris of all sorts rained down on Lindbergh Field that catastrophic California morning.

Lincoln had needlessly blamed himself for the tragedy. The FAA placed him on paid administrative leave and saw to it that he got psychiatric counseling and just about anything else he needed. The one thing he needed, the FAA could not provide was preventing his wife, Sandy, from leaving with his two daughters. The booze and the pills had become too much for her. Too many sleepless nights and when sleep did come it was always accompanied with the nightmares.

Sandy moved back in with her parents in Shreveport. The girls visited him a couple of times and once at Christmas. Last, he heard Sandy had remarried and her new husband had adopted Abby and Ashley.

Just as well—I was a lousy father anyway—they're probably a lot better off this way. Someday, if they want to know who I am, they will find me.

One morning Lincoln was roused from his sleep, or was it afternoon? He was staring at the faces of Charlie Johnson and Frank Holt, two of his ATC coworkers. "What? What the hell? What's going on guys?" he asked through a sleepy fog.

"Hello Lincoln, welcome to your new life," said Charlie.

"C'mon guys, what's going on?" Lincoln muttered.

"Look outside," said Frank, pointing to a screen less window. "You are in Mexico, my friend. A tiny little spot called Ensenada, just north of Tijuana. We got no phones, no television, and no radio. We especially don't have any pills or booze."

Charlie interrupted. "There's all the food you want," he said nodding toward a small kitchen. "There are a couple cases of bottled water, vitamins, plenty of fresh milk, vegetables and lots of soft drinks."

Over Lincoln's protests, Frank said. "You, Mister Sansbury are going back to San Diego sober and straight, like it or not."

It worked. Two weeks later, Lincoln returned to San Diego with Charlie and Frank clean, refreshed and sober. Lincoln never forgot. The memory of his two friends was clear in his mind. Two friends who had taken their vacation time and spent their own money to lend a helping hand to an ailing comrade. Was a word about it ever spoken? Was a favor ever asked in return? Never, you always covered each other's backside and you never, ever ratted anyone out. The whole world hates a snitch. Did he understand camaraderie? Damn right he did—

Later that year he was transferred to Spokane in the scenic Cascade Mountains of Washington state, a quieter place. It was beautiful there and a much slower pace than the bustle of southern California. It was in Spokane where he met Heidi and fell in love all over again. He readily accepted her two children, Chloe and Blake, and a year later, in the spring, Heidi and Lincoln were married. They were a happy family. After a few years passed, the Chicago Air Traffic Control Center had an opening for a supervisor. Lincoln applied and was accepted.

"Alright Collegio, guess that's all, thanks for coming in."

Tony stood. "That's okay, Mister President."

"Oh Tony, one more thing, do you suppose Ogilvie is approaching burn out?"

"Burn out." Two poison words dreaded by every air traffic controller. Candidly put, the job was simply too much anymore. The parasite of stress overcomes the host of skill and coolness. Liquor and drugs no longer made things better and sleep was slow to come. Migraines were frequent visitors. Nerves and marriages fell apart as did mental stability. The FAA had a simple solution. Either you were forced into an early retirement, or you were transferred to some little burg somewhere in the Dakotas or Lord knows where. But some place with very little air traffic.

"No sir, I don't think it's burn out," said Tony. "Pete's just going through a few bad times right now. Give him a few days; he'll come around."

"Yeah I suppose," responded the supervisor. "But let's keep a sharp eye on things. There ain't gonna be no freaking disasters around here. Not on my shift there won't...not on my watch—all right Tony, take care and thanks again."

"It's okay Mister President, glad to help."

"Dammit Collegio, can't you guys help me out here? How about dropping this Mister President crap and just call me Lincoln."

"Yes sir, Mister President sir," said Tony, popping the president a snappy salute. He was out the door just in time to dodge the president's hurtling desk stapler.

Tony walked to his car his mind was racing.

No question about it, Ogilvie is screwing up, screwing up big time. He's not the same and he's getting dangerous—besides, I can smell booze on him every time he comes to work, he smells funny after the lunch breaks too. But you ain't gonna hear it from the lips of Tony Collegio, no sir, not from me, no siree.

CHAPTER SEVEN

Aboard Lear Jet 9926T
Friday September 8

"I told you to get your head out of your ass and get me that clearance!" bellowed Captain Clayton Carson to the young copilot beside him who was still shaking from the captain's badgering.

At twenty-six, Kyle MacFarland was fresh out of flight school, where admittedly he hadn't learned much, mostly because the school didn't teach much. It did, however, comply with the federal regulations. Each student was offered a ground school course and given just enough flight instruction to get through an FAA flight check. If you passed, you were a pilot. The student got a pilot's license and the school got its money.

Kyle was already a private pilot from his junior college days and had earned a commercial pilot license including a multi-engine and instrument rating from the flight school. Like most inspiring young pilots, Kyle was going from one airport to another and sending out resumes by the dozens in the endless and seemingly futile search for employment. Lacking military training and any kind of experience with larger aircraft, Kyle was finding the roads to a flying job were all cul-de-sacs.

Kyle was shocked at the telephone call that Sunday morning. The chief pilot for New England Blue Skies Charters wanted to see him in Boston first thing the next morning. Could he make it?

Hell yes, he could make it—even if he had to swim to Boston.

"Yes sir, I'll be there, you bet!" Kyle almost shouted into the phone giving his best effort to keep his voice calm and under control.

Monday morning at exactly eight o'clock, an immaculate Kyle MacFarland was sitting in Chief Pilot Shane Spencer's outer office when he arrived. Kyle noted that he was clean-shaven, trim and an easy six feet tall, under his arm was a load of papers and a blue necktie was draped over his shoulder. *Probably in his early fifties,* Kyle gathered. Dark blue epaulets adorned his shoulders and the four silver bars clearly indicated that he was a captain. The star adorning his wings specified him as the chief pilot.

Spencer was curt. "You MacFarland?" Kyle nodded yes. "Well then, come on back."

The chief pilot's office was an array of books, charts and maps. Stacks of paper took up one end of a well-used brown sofa. A matching chair sat abeam the sofa facing a wall cluttered with various pictures and plaques of airplanes, mostly Lear Jets. Spencer looking every bit of his Irish heritage was brief and to the point.

He motioned for Kyle to sit. "Look kid," he said in a predictable south Boston brogue, "We don't pay enough to amount to a pile of chicken shit, but we do pay something. The good news is we pay all your expenses. So, on R.O.Ns, that's remaining overnight, we pick up the tab. So, if you want to stay in a fancy hotel and eat at the Governor's Club it's up to you. Or you can curl up in some fleabag and eat at the local choke and puke, and keep the money. It's your call. The expense money is yours; you can do with it whatever you want."

As the chief pilot spoke, the young man listened. Kyle was clean and neatly dressed in a dark blue suit, white shirt and the standard conservative tie. A sprig of red hair peeped over part of his otherwise perfectly combed pate.

Probably from a long line of good New England stock, thought Spencer.

"The hours are long and the work is thankless," the chief pilot continued. "We operate six Lear Dash 60s. They fly like fighters and climb like homesick angels. We go coast to coast and anywhere in Canada and Mexico. We keep three crews per airplane. These babies cruise right at 600 mph, so wherever you're going you'll be there that day. How long? We never know. It could be ten minutes or it could be ten days and nobody's gonna be holding your hand and nobody's gonna be patting you on the ass with attaboys."

The chief pilot sounded as he was speaking from memory. Kyle looked puzzled. "What do we want from you?"

Kyle nodded.

"Not a damn thing. The FAA says we have to have a warm body in the right seat with a license and a medical, and of course, be qualified in the aircraft. Don't do anything unless the captain tells you to." Kyle nodded again.

"What can we offer you?" Spencer went on as if reading Kyle's mind. "Jet time, high altitude turbine engine time with an experienced captain, that's experience you never could buy kid," said Spencer answering his own question.

"All of our captains, except a couple are retired from the military or the airlines and have years of experience flying the heavy metal; you know, 747s, DC-10s, Lockheed Tri-Star 1011s, birds like that. Besides, you'll get paid to see the country." Spencer barely managed a slight smile.

"You want the job, kid?"

Kyle's blue eyes bulged. He couldn't believe what he was hearing. He stared at the chief pilot and finally stuttered, "Yes! Yes sir, of course I want the job

Mister, I mean, Captain Spencer. I don't know how to thank you," he finally choked out.

"Don't sweat it kid, and don't thank me. If it were up to me, I wouldn't hire you." Kyle's heart sank. Spencer was abrupt and a bit gruff, but at least he told it straight.

"Apparently somebody up there in Mahogany Hall likes you," Spencer jabbed a thumb toward the company's executive offices. "Seems like a friend of a friend, or somebody knows somebody, anyhow, they whispered in the old man's ear and he told me to take a close look at you. Translated that means to hire you. It usually works that way."

Kyle could not have cared less. He was in. He had a flying job! And he didn't give a tinker's toot how he came about it. Kyle MacFarland was on his way. On his way to that treasured left seat, but first he had to pay his dues.

Spencer stood an invitation for Kyle to do the same. "I need to make a copy of your license and medical. You'll have to get fitted for uniforms and you start ground school on the Lear Dash 60, next Monday at Logan, eight sharp. Here's the address."

"Yes sir," Kyle nodded to Captain Carson and pressed the microphone button.

"Ah Chicago Center, Lear Jet Niner-Niner-Two-Eight Tango request..."

CHAPTER EIGHT

FAA Air Traffic Control Center
Chicago Illinois
September 8

"Lear Jet Niner-Niner-Two-Eight Tango stand by one," the strained voice of Pete Ogilvie detonated in their headsets, his banter sounding like an auctioneer.

In the mind of Pete Ogilvie, he was in his element. He was on his turf. He felt good, never better. The pills and the vodka had once again done their job. He was at home pushing tin and telling airline captains where to go.

This is my sky! I am an air traffic controller and I'm good at it—damn good—the best! I love this shift.

Pete chattered, "Southwest 722 is cleared to the outer marker, intercept the localizer, track inbound, contact tower on 118.7; American 2812 heavy, you are cleared Star Arrival 12, go to Approach 128.3; Lear Two-Eight Tango with request go."

The controller's reply to the Lear Jet was like a machine gun, no pause, no stop. First Officer MacFarland missed it.

Captain Clayton Carson did not miss it. Disgusted, he keyed his yoke mic and aimed his best contumacious stare at Kyle. "Chicago, Lear Two-Eight Tango leaving 18,000 looking for flight level three, five, zero, ah, are we cleared to Las Vegas yet?"

At that instant, the radio cracked with a clearly identifiable female voice. "Chicago Center, United 1442 heavy, with you at 31,000."

Bitch, Pete thought. *What are you doing up there flying a jumbo jet? What did you do? Cram your husband's nuts down the garbage disposal, so you could tool around up there in the friendly skies and shake your ass at all the pilots? I bet you did—Bet you took his son from him too—Bitch.*

"Roger, United 1442 heavy," Pete said smoothly. "I have you at three-one-zero, you are cleared direct to JFK, New York, as filed, continue your assigned squawk seven-seven-four-three, contact New York Center on 132.2."

"Wilco Chicago thanks," came a very feminine reply.

"Bitch," Pete whispered. *Now where's that freaking Lear Jet?* What the hell does he want? Pete studied the blurry radarscope in front of him. "Lear Niner-Niner-Two-Eight Tango your request approved. Climb and maintain flight level three-five-zero, proceed on course direct Vegas."

Was that Lear going to Vegas? Flight level three, five, zero? Why was he on the wrong squawk code or was he? The hell with it let Denver worry about some damn transponder code.

The gravelly voice of Pete Ogilvie came through their headsets, "Lear Two-Eight Tango, you are about to leave my airspace, I'm going to turn you over to Denver Center here shortly, stand by."

"Roger Chicago, Two-Eight Tango standing by," muttered Carson.

Kyle MacFarland was worried. Clearance Delivery at Midway Airport in Chicago had clearly assigned them flight level three-nine-zero not three-five-zero and Carson had missed it. The high and mighty Captain Clayton Carson had made a mistake.

He was probably so busy chewing on me, he missed the altitude assignment—maybe I should tell him or at least mention it. Yeah, sure, and have him bite another chuck out of my ass again? Not a chance—but what if there is other traffic up here at three-five-zero? It's a big sky but what if? Nah, I'm not saying a word. I'm going to sit right here and not do a thing unless he tells me. Maybe I should do something but what? It would look terrible if I got fired on my first trip—no sir, I'm not saying a word.

Kyle had caught the captain's mistake; unfortunately, he failed to catch his own. The harangue of his captain had unnerved him. He was doing his best to copy the flight clearance as Pete Ogilvie's voice rebounded in his ears like a tape on fast forward. "Lear Jet Niner-Niner-Two-Eight Tango is cleared to the McCarran Airport, Las Vegas as filed, expect radar vectors after departure. Stand by for radar vector sequence, transponder code, and squawk seven-four-five-five." A timorous Kyle reached for the transponder and dialed in five-five-seven-four.

Captain Clayton Carson had been a pilot for Zodiac Air Freight International for as many years as most could remember. There was not a continent and very few countries that Clayton hadn't set foot on at one time or another. Everyone knew him even in the most remote places. He knew the best restaurants, the best places to stay and he knew where the women were too.

Clay was still physically fit and maintained an FAA medical certificate. His deeply set brown eyes were still 20/20 and required only reading glasses. His full head of brown hair was almost gray now and a few extra pounds were appearing around the middle of his five-eight frame. The flight surgeon reminded him on every visit to get rid of the excess corpulence. Clay always assured him and himself that he would. He never did.

Carson was well liked throughout the airlines. He was known to be a professional and ran a tight ship. He was very knowledgeable and the young pilots liked being on his crew because Clay was very tutorial and they learned from him. On the long overseas trips, he enjoyed passing along some of his erudition to the young airmen. To Clay, flying was everything, it was the life in his blood, and he loved being a freight dog. In his words: "There is no greater thrill than strapping a whale to my ass and chase the sun," referring to the giant Boeing 747 that he had flown for so many years.

When Clay retired from the airlines, he was never so depressed. He was empty and lost. Nothing held his interest. The kids were grown and had their own families. He didn't miss them really; he had been gone so much he barely knew them. Clay hardly longed for the company of his grandchildren. They were rowdy and loud. Besides, they made him feel old.

Roma, his wife of 40 years, complained about him being constantly underfoot. She was an attractive woman, brunette and slim and she was accustomed to weeks and months of being alone. Understandably she was annoyed by constantly bumping into Clayton, who was either, "piddling," as she called it or underfoot.

When the offer came from New England Blue Skies Charters to fly Lear Jets Clayton welcomed it like Noah welcomed the olive branch from the dove. He didn't need the money as he had prepared well for retirement, but the chance to fly again, you bet! Clay heartily accepted the offer. "Thank you, God," was Roma's response to the news.

"Get me our estimated time of arrival in Vegas," Clay said to Kyle, this time in a softer tone. He felt a little guilty for riding the young pilot so hard.

I'm sick and tired of them assigning me these snot-nosed kids right out of flight school who do not know their ass from an aileron. They get hired just because their daddy knows somebody. Most of them can't fart and chew gum at the same time—I gotta talk to Spencer when we get back.

"Better check our fuel burn too," he said to Kyle, who was already punching the numbers into the onboard flight computer.

"Yes sir, ah, they routed us a little bit south and we are 478 nautical out, so ETA at McCarran/Vegas is about an hour eighteen and our fuel burn at this altitude level cruise is, ah, 1200 pounds an hour, let's see…it's going to be close, Captain. Looks like we might be burning into our reserve fuel," said Kyle, with a tinge of concern in his voice.

Screw it, thought Clay. *What they gonna do? Frog my arm? Take my birthday away? If Chicago Clearance hadn't kept us waiting so freaking long we'd have plenty of gas—it's their fault,* he reasoned, disregarding the fact that the captain always bears the ultimate responsibility.

I've burned below fuel reserve regulations lots of times and I flight planned this baby right on the money. You don't burn fuel to haul fuel.

"Lear Niner-Niner-Two-Eight Tango contact Denver Center 127.9," came the hurried and confused voice of Pete Ogilvie, *or was it 129.7? Gotta be here somewhere,* he thought, scanning the small desktop for the Lear Jet's flight profile.

"Jeez, that guy sounds like Barney Fife on speed," said Kyle. Clay motioned to his first officer's mic button. *Let the kid do something.* Kyle responded in his best professional voice.

"Roger Chicago Center, Lear Niner-Niner-Two Eight Tango leaving you going to Denver Center on 127.9."

CHAPTER NINE

Florida Everglades, Osceola National
Swamp
Cypress Slough, South Central Florida
September 8

Dave jammed on the brakes of the careening pick-up slinging grass and gravel in every direction. Neither he nor Rita could move. They sat in the stalled truck frozen in terror and stared through the debris kicked up by Dave's panicky braking. The fog had increased, making the visibility all the worse and was slowly seeping across the overgrown road like a thick mist in a steam spa. The wind whispering through the Spanish moss in the cypress trees was the only sound.

In the glare of the headlights, it stood motionless. The light from the bright moon helped illuminate the silhouette of a Seminole warrior. His size was enormous and his two perfectly rounded biceps were bulging emphasized by the rawhide bands tied around them. The abdominal muscles rippled like a washboard. Dave's mouth gaped open in staggering horror and his eyes were like saucers as they welded to the shocking scene before him. The creature stood rigidly still and made no move toward them.

It wore the traditional open buckskin vest of a Seminole warrior. Dave could see red stripes on its chest or was it blood? A string of alligator teeth hung mid-chest and the image of a snarling bull alligator was sewn into the left shoulder of the vest. Through the mist and the haze, Dave could not see the creature's legs. Dave stared at the sight in front of him.

Rita was right—Damn thing must be 10 foot tall and it ain't got no head!

Through the milky fog, Dave could see where the Indian's head had been severed; blood oozed from its neck and had coagulated on its shoulders. He saw the Seminole's fingers were stained dark red where the creature had clawed at the ghastly hole and the dangling tendons and nerves were hanging from the wound like an army of worms.

Dave was flailing in the darkness desperately trying to re-start the truck. He glanced at Rita, who was sitting perfectly still and calm. She was uncharacteristically silent and her eyes were fixed straight ahead not focusing in an unblinking stare. She was petrified with fear.

Dave ground the starter of the mistreated Chevy until he thought his thumb would snap off. He constantly stomped the accelerator. *Oh no! I've flooded it.* The sound of the truck's engine grinding down was unmistakable. The pick-up's battery was almost spent.

A dead battery? "Oh sweet Jesus," he prayed. "Not now! Oh dear God, please no, not now—"

CHAPTER TEN

FAA Air Traffic Control Center
Denver Colorado
September 8

Gilbert Brokowski stared at the radarscope in front of him trying to make some sense out of what he was seeing. His forehead furrowed.

Man, something here just isn't right.

Gilbert had been working the radarscopes a little over a year. He had graduated from the FAA Academy in Oklahoma City and by a stroke of good fortune; he was assigned to his first choice domicile Denver, Colorado. At the Denver Air Traffic Control Center, he was apprenticed to seasoned controllers. Subsequently he was signed off by an ATC supervisor and then finally he was on his own. Gilbert knew that he was scheduled on a work shift with lighter air traffic and was assigned to a radar sector that wasn't quite so busy, a normal procedure for rookies.

Fine by me—leave the rush hour and the bottlenecks to the veterans.

Gilbert Brokowski was young and at 28, he was settling into one of the highest stress jobs in the world. He loved it. His closely cropped blond hair was always neat and he stared at the scope through a pair of narrowly set blue eyes. He was not a tall man, barely five feet five and he carried around a few extra pounds. But what Gilbert lacked in looks he made up for with a witty and amiable personality.

Gilbert focused on the radarscope.

I don't like this...somebody has screwed up somewhere—I don't like this at all—

He reached up to the right of his small desk and pushed a white button, which illuminated a light above his console.

I'd better get a supervisor over here—I'm still the new kid on the block and I'd rather ask a few dumb questions than to make some big mistake.

Almost immediately, shift supervisor Betsy Gomez appeared. "What ja got, Ski?" she asked, using the nickname for which he was best known.

Earning the position of Center Supervisor had not come easy for Betsy Gomez, but it was well earned and well deserved. After a stint in the Navy, as a tower controller at various Marine and Naval Air Stations, Lieutenant Beth Sue Finnegan moved to Washington

DC, where she worked in the Capital's assiduous Air Traffic Control Center.

In Washington, the former Beth Sue Finnegan met Raul Gomez an accountant from Denver. They married, each for the second time, and did their best to keep their marriage together with 1,700 miles between them. As soon as she could, Betsy transferred to the FAA Academy in Oklahoma City taking a position as an instructor. Oklahoma City was a lot closer to Denver and Raul than Washington. The following year, Denver Center had a position open for a supervisor. Betsy was a shoe-in.

She was a pretty woman and hardly looked her 44 years. At five feet-six she kept her figure thin due to the jogging and exercise regimen she maintained and she usually wore her shoulder length dark brown hair in a ponytail. Betsy was well known throughout the FAA as a highly skilled professional and widely respected as a no-nonsense but fair supervisor. But, most of all she was known for her abundant bosom.

"Hey Skipper, take a look here," said Gilbert, dragging a yellow pencil along an imaginary line on the southeast area of his radarscope.

Betsy leaned over his chair her green eyes surveying the radar blips in front of her. Gilbert still sitting spun around in his chair in order to make eye contact with the supervisor. He didn't make eye contact, but what his eyes did contact were two enormous breasts straining at the white cloth of Betsy's blouse aimed directly at his cheek. A collision was inevitable.

Who wants to be tall? Gilbert thought to himself *if I'm ever reincarnated, I want to come back as Raul's fingertips.*

"See Skipper, this is a Lear Jet out of Midway Chicago and somehow he's managed to get on the wrong transponder code. He's on a Dallas/Ft. Worth squawk."

"That's fucking impossible!" exclaimed Betsy, never one to mince words. "Why didn't those lazy bastards in Chicago catch that? Find out who the hell is supposed to be working the southwest corridor out of Chicago, and Ski, pull up that Lear Jet's flight profile on your data base."

"Already did, boss; here it is." Gilbert handed her the computer printout. "And see, that's not all, here's another thing. Clearance Delivery in Chicago assigned him flight level three-niner-zero. Now look here at his transponder read out. The sonofabitch is level at three-five-zero, and nobody caught that either!"

"Okay Ski, just relax," said Betsy, resting her hand on Gilbert's shoulder. "We still have a few minutes. Try to raise him on, umm, let's see, what frequency did Chicago assign? Never mind, here it is, try raising him on one-two-niner point seven."

"I've been calling him on one-two-niner-point seven, Skipper, but he's not responding."

"All right," she ordered. "Go to the international emergency channel on one-two-one point five, maybe he's monitoring that, most crews do."

Gilbert dialed in 121.5. "Lear Jet Niner, Niner, Two Eight Tango this is Denver Center, do you copy?" "Lear Jet Niner, Niner, Two, Eight Tango, Denver Center, listening on one-two-one point five, do you read?" The radio was silent.

"All right Ski, keep calling and try all the Chicago channels and keep an eye on that Lear. I've got another light, be right back."

Betsy strode off to answer a light at another workstation leaving no doubt in anyone's mind why she had acquired the nickname, "Bouncing Betsy." She appeared behind the shoulders of Phil Kennebrew, a seasoned controller. "What's up, Phil?"

"Hey boss," said Phil. "This may be nothing, but I heard you and Ski talking. Put an eyeball on this," he waved both hands at the radar screen in front of them. "That's the Lear Jet up here, see? He's en-route to Vegas. Now look down here to the southeast." He traced a line across the screen with his thumbnail. "That's a Trans Global triple seven out of Dallas/Ft. Worth going to Denver International. Now I've got a..."

Phil didn't finish the sentence. Betsy saw the situation instantly. "Have you got a coordinance on them, Phil?"

"Being printed out now, boss. Yep, look here," he said tearing a printout from the radar computer. "See? I was right. That Lear Jet is on a course of 241°, and the TGI heavy is heading 330°. Hey, sum-thin' else too, what about this?" Phil's voice was getting louder. "The radar is panning some real heavy crap over southwestern Kansas and the Oklahoma panhandle, high altitude cumulus, heavy rain with lightning and hail. Boss, we've got to raise them before they get in that shit! Another few minutes they won't have the visibility of a blind man."

Betsy was studying the computer data intently. Her eyes froze on the radarscope. "Holy Mother," she whispered, the two airplanes were at the same altitude and on the same transponder code, and both were headed into severe weather. A chill swept up Betsy's spine.

The Lear Jet and the Boeing were on a direct collision course.

CHAPTER ELEVEN

Aboard TGI Flight 2120
September 8

The sound of the crew key rattling in the cockpit door was quickly followed by the voice of Andi Marokris. "What wonderful and magnificent things have I done on planet earth to deserve flying around the sky with the two most handsome pilots in the whole TGI system?" she crooned in her syrupy Alabama drawl.

Lead Flight Attendant Andrea Marokris, looked ten years younger than her actual age of 39 and she was far more cute than she was pretty, and pretty she was. Andi probably had more time aloft than did many of the younger flight officers. Her tenure with the company marked 18 years of unblemished service. Tonight she was wearing her shoulder length jet-black hair in a bun and her dark brown eyes were accented by a conservative application of mascara. Andi's light blue over dark blue TGI uniform fit perfectly on her petite figure.

"Whatta you mean just TGI? How about the two most handsome and most daredevil pilots in the whole airline industry?" teased Luke. "Besides, I bet your boyfriend would have something to say about that," he said, referring to Andi's significant other, a pilot with another carrier.

"Shoot, that little dickens, he's supposed to be in Berlin tonight. He's probably hitting on all those pretty frauleins and soaking up that good German beer," Andi teased back, wrinkling her nose as she laughed.

It was obvious to Cord that the captain and Ms. Andi Marokris were close friends and had flown together for years. She said, "Now Lukie-boy, you'd better stop flirtin' with all us gorgeous flight attendants or the next time I see Carolyn I'm gonna tell on you."

"Oh, she won't mind if I flirt with the girls, Andi. It's those ball-bearing flight attendants that upset her."

"Lukie-boy, you are so bad," she exclaimed, feigning a slap at the captain. "Hey Cord, how come all those red lights are on?"

Cord had busied himself with the in-flight test of the engine fire bottles required by FAA regulations on each leg of the flight. If an engine temperature got out of control, or in the event of an engine fire, a horn would sound in the cockpit alerting the crew to the emergency. On the captain's command, an overhead lever would be engaged shutting off the fuel to the affected engine and discharging a copious volume of CO_2 hopefully extinguishing the problem. On each engine are two CO_2 bottles and when discharged a red light for each one lights up on the overhead of the cockpit indicating that the bottle had been spent.

The test was simple. Cord had engaged a circuit breaker override, which fools the computer into a fire mode. The computer, thinking there is an urgent temperature change, responds accordingly without discharging the CO_2 bottles. So at the time of Andi's inquiry all four of the red lights were illuminated.

"Well Andi," Cord replied thoughtfully through a row of perfect white teeth. "Whenever anyone who is a virgin steps up here on the flight deck those red lights always go on."

Through the laughter, Andi retorted. "Well Cordie-boy, when we get on the ground in Denver, you'd better get that dern thing fixed!" more laughter.

"Andi, did you build a pot of that good TGI coffee back there?" Sellers asked.

"Yes sir, I sure-nuff did, El Capateen," she replied, mussing his hair. "I was just fixin' to get you some. How about you, Cord?"

"Love some, Andi."

"All right, I'll be right back."

"Oh Andi," said Luke, "would you look at the passenger manifest and see if we have any doctors on board?"

"Sure, I've been meaning to do that anyway. Let me fetch yawl some coffee, I'll be back in a jiff," she drawled locking the cockpit door.

Another thing not in the book, thought Cord. "Say Cap, I see you always check the passenger manifest for doctors; I guess the reason is obvious."

I usually do, Spark Plug. A few years back, I was flying a South America turnaround from New Orleans. We were about five hours out of Caracas when this guy in the back started having bad chest pains. In fact, Andi was the lead on that trip too. Anyway, the timing was really lousy. We were a thousand miles from nowhere and not a damn thing below us, but air and ocean. We were too far out to go back, we couldn't go to Cuba and Miami was too far, so I diverted to Cancun.

The good news is we had a doctor on board who had some nitro pills. He popped a couple under the guy's tongue and got a few aspirins in him and that kept him going until we got on the ground at Cancun. The emergency unit was there waiting on us and as far as I know everyone lived happily ever after. So, I like to know who is back there.

He jabbed his thumb over his shoulder toward the rear of the plane. "Just a precaution, that's all."

Cord nodded his acquiescence. At that moment, Andi reappeared carrying two steaming plastic cups of coffee and placed them in the beverage holder in the center console between the two crewmen.

"Hot coffee for my two most handsome pilots."

"Thanks sugar plum," said Luke. "Did you get a chance you look at the manifest?"

"Sure-nuff did. We don't have any physicians on board, but we do have a veterinarian with us, so if anyone has a sick parakeet we'll be in good shape."

"Where's he sitting?" asked Luke.

"Well Captain Chauvinist, he happens to be a she and she's in 33A by the window; has the whole row to herself," said Andi. "By the way Cord, she's quite a looker. You might want to check her out."

Cord didn't respond. He was intently studying the ship's weather radar.

She was about to exit the cockpit when Luke spoke, this time his voice carried a much more staid tone. "Andi, better have the folks back there buckle up and button-up the cabin. The radar's painting lines of cells and echoes just ahead looks like we're in for a few bounces."

A few bounces he calls it, thought Cord. *A few bounces my ass—it looks more like we're in for a freaking rodeo—*

CHAPTER TWELVE

Florida Everglades
September 8

    Dan Hatcher, the highly acclaimed network news anchorman, grimaced through his pearly-capped teeth. "Well gang," he muttered to the crew crammed in the rented van. "That sure was a waste of time and money." Dan and his news crew had been in southwest Florida filming a TV special entitled, "*Hurricane Charley, Nine Years Later.*" Charley, the second most damaging hurricane at that time in U.S. history, had slammed into Florida's west coast in August 2005, bringing with it nine tornados, and sustained winds of over 130 mph. The storm killed 15 Floridians and left over 14 billion dollars of damage in its wake. It raged across the state like a runaway locomotive and into the Atlantic. Then the storm turned north, making landfall again at Cape Romain, South Carolina. Dan and his crew were surprised to see that most all of Florida had been rebuilt or restored and little of anything was left to remind anyone of the deadly storm.

    "There's no story here, nothing," he said. "Whatta you say, guys? The company jet is at Palm

Beach and if we head out now we could probably get back to New York late tonight." Everyone agreed.

"Hey, Carlos." Dan said to the van driver. "How long will it take us to get back to Palm Beach?"

"If we stay on this road, probably a couple hours, maybe a little longer." Dan sighed but said nothing.

"Mister Hatcher," said Carlos, "I know a back way. County Road 9 runs east and west and cuts through the Everglades. It could save us a half hour or so and it comes out at Southern Boulevard and from there it's a direct shot to the airport."

"Do it," said the anchorman.

It was no mystery why County Road 9 was called the back way; it was miles of a flat two-lane road running through the heart of Florida's massive Everglades. It was dark and there were no lights and no traffic. Only the light from the full moon lit up the shorelines of the canals running on both sides of the road. Dan relaxed, put his feet up and stared out the window. He could see the log figures of alligators floating in the water and on the banks along the road.

I wonder what is out there that I can't see. This place is downright scary—I sure would hate to be out here alone.

Dan was just about to doze off when the van rounded a slight curve in the road flooding the inside of the van with flashing red and blue lights. "Hey Carlos, what's going on? Can you tell?"

"No sir Mister Hatcher, but it must be something big. I see two State Trooper cars and two Sheriff Deputies. And there's a fire engine and a tow truck too."

Always on the alert for news Dan said, "Stop Carlos, let's take a look. Maybe there is a story here."

Dan approached one of the state troopers who was writing furiously on a report sheet clipboard and listening to a pot-bellied man ranting about something he had seen in the Everglades. The man was clad in a greasy pair of ragged boxer shorts that had undoubtedly been used for a grease rag, which he had found behind the seat of his truck. The man apparently thought this was proper attire for the moment and it probably was since that's all he had. Dan noticed the reason for all the commotion. A pick-up truck was resting nose down in the side ditch adjoining County Road 9. Dan whispered over his shoulder, "Get Kylee out here with her camera, quick! Hurry, get a camera out here."

We might have a day's work after all—

The bright lights of a video news camera flashed on and Dan said to the trooper. "May I?" nodding toward the man.

"Be my guest he's all yours," replied the trooper.

"Put that away," Dan said to the man pointing to the hole in front of the boxer shorts where his uncircumcised phallus was jutting out like a forlorn turtle withdrawing in its shell. The man adjusted himself.

Dan quickly checked his hair and his capped pearly whites with his pocket mirror and said into the camera, "This is Dan Hatcher coming to you live from deep in the heart of the Florida Everglades. With me is," he shoved the hand microphone under the man's chin.

"Dave Winslow," he meekly said.

"Thank you, Dave. I hear that you have had a rather exciting evening."

"Yep, dang sure did."

"Can you tell us about it?"

"Yes sir, dang sure can. I've lived around these here Glades muh whole life, you know?" Dan nodded. "And I'd heard 'bout this here headless Indian since I was a kid, but never believed it, you know?"

"Yes, it is a little hard to get a grip on," Dan agreed.

"Well sir, it's true. Damn sure is cause I seen it with my own two eyes, ya know? I seen it! He was a-standing right in our camp and I seen it."

"Well then," said Dan, "can you tell us a bit more about it?"

"Hell yeah, I dang sure can. Sum-bitch was ten foot tall, he was and he didn't have no head neither. Blood and stuff all over him. It was Osceola, plain and simple, that's who it was, ya know? I seen him!"

"I can see how that would be very frightening."

"Nah, it didn't fret me none," Dave boldly lied. "I wuz gonna go after him. I wuz gonna get me a piece of him, ya know? But the little woman was a-scared to death, and all, you know?"

"The little woman?" questioned Dan.

"Yeah, the little woman, she's over yonder in the truck." He pointed.

Dan walked over to the truck, Kylee and camera followed. Leaning in the cab, he said, "Miss would you like to talk to us?"

Rita sat covering her nakedness in a bright yellow raincoat graciously loaned to her by a sheriff's deputy. She didn't respond. Rita looked out the opposite window.

"How humilatin'—" she muttered.

CHAPTER THIRTEEN

Aboard TGI Flight 2120
September 8

Both pilots tightened their shoulder harnesses and prepared to face the gathering tempest outside the windscreen. Luke flicked off the auto-pilot. You always hand flew an airplane in rough weather never leaving it up to George. "Just stay your course, Spark Plug," he calmly said. "Hold her steady as she goes."

"I've got it, Captain, looks like we may stay out of most of it if we steer a little more to the west." Cord shouted, trying to make himself heard over the shattering noise of the hail and rain striking the airplane at 540 mph. Through the streaks of lightning, illuminating the sky like a battery of flashbulbs, Cord could see the tumbling mass of boiling purple clouds bringing its wrath upon them.

"I think you are right, Spark Plug; go ahead and steer a little more west," said Luke staring at the radar.

"But Cap…"

"No buts Cord, and never mind the course, just try to hold the damn thing right-side-up," the captain said smoothly. Both pilots were gripping the control yoke like a vise. Cord noted that his captain never changed expression or showed any concern other than the business of flying the aircraft.

At that moment, a bolt of lightning exploded in front of them. The radio panel directly behind the copilot's seat burst into flames showering them with sparks and melting plastic. Cord did not wait for the captain's order. He immediately jumped up, doused the panel with the cockpit fire extinguisher, and tried to maintain his balance in the tumultuous airplane.

"So much for our radios!" he shouted.

Luke motioned for Cord to sit back down. He still had not changed his expression.

No matter what happens—I don't care if we're on fire—always fly the airplane first.

"Steer between those two yellow cells," he ordered, pointing to the radarscope, "I think we may be coming out of this crap."

As the Boeing passed between the two storm cells, a huge bolt of lightning crashed across the boiling tar-like sky illuminating the heavens accompanied with deafening thunder.

Both pilots saw it at the same time. A Lear Jet filled their vision and was on a direct collision course, no more than an eye-blink away converging at 1200 mph. Luke and Cord let out a gasp and threw their hands in front of their faces in a futile attempt to protect themselves from the inevitable impact.

CHAPTER FOURTEEN

Aboard TGI Flight 2120
September 8

At the first sign of bad weather and lightning, the veterinarian in seat 33A found an airline blanket and snuggled under it shivering with fear. She was back to that horrible day in a small town in east Georgia.

She was only four years old when her father roused her before daylight early one stormy morning in the squalid corner of the warehouse in which they were living. He dressed her in the only dress she owned, a second-hand white pleat trimmed in pink, and he tied a little pink cap in her golden hair. She was dirty and she was hungry; shoes were a luxury she did not have. Her father pinned a note to her small chest and led her to a battered old car that sometimes started but most often didn't. This morning it started.

He drove her to a tin shed where the school bus stopped for kids each morning. With tears in his eyes, he told her, "You wait right here and when the school bus comes get on it. When you get to the school show this note to a grown-up," he had said, tapping the note on her tiny chest.

The last time she ever saw her father was when he drove from the bus shelter in the smoky old battered car and disappeared in the rain of the oncoming storm. She had never known what happened to her mother. Now the little girl was alone in the world.

The roaring of the thunder and the rain pelting the tin bus shed was deafening leaving the little girl terrified. To escape the streaking lightening and the clamorous scream of the storm she bolted out into the rain searching everywhere for the battered old car. It was nowhere to be found and she ran, and ran, and ran. Around noon, a policeman noticed her cuddled up on the steps in front of the old abandoned warehouse sobbing. He gently lifted her and took her to the police station.

At that time, the small town had no provisions for homeless children or orphans, but the police did call the local Methodist Minister. The Reverend Joshua Pepper and his wife, Stephanie, a couple with no natural children of their own, but they were the parents of one adopted child approaching her teens. Although the Peppers were middle aged, they were most happy to make temporary accommodations for the little girl. Upon seeing her, Stephanie exclaimed, "Oh, what a beautiful child!"

Turning to her husband, "Joshua, look at her; it's the face of an angel!"

Reverend Pepper looked at the rain-streaked note pinned to the little girl's chest. "I can't make any of this out."

"We couldn't either, Reverend, other than 'Have somebody take care of her'," said the policeman. "We got people out looking for her parents. But as you can see, she's scared to death. Som-thin' about the storm really got to her."

"And?" Asked the preacher.

"Nothin' yet, Reverend, only thing that's happened around here last couple days is a suicide this morning over in Baxter, next county over."

"Suicide?"

"Yes sir, suicide," answered the policeman. "Looks like somebody just passin' through must a gassed hisself."

"Carbon monoxide?"

"Sure looks like it, Reverend, some old rattletrap of a car, no ID on him, no license plates."

The preacher shook his head slowly then holding out his hand toward the little girl, he said, "Come little angel, let's go and get you a bath and some hot food." The little girl took his hand.

And so, a new life for the little girl began. After almost a year had passed, the reverend and his wife petitioned the court and were granted full adoption of the little girl, when the judge ruled in favor of an adoption everyone was jubilant and hugging one another.

"Let's go home," the reverend had said, "You have a mom and dad and a big sister now."

The reverend made a mental note. *We have got to get this child some counseling for her horrible fear of thunderstorms.*

Outside TGI flight 2120, the storm raged.

CHAPTER FIFTEEN

FAA Air Traffic Radar Center
Denver, Colorado
September 8

"What happened, Phil?" exclaimed Betsy Gomez coming up and peering over the shoulder of Controller Phil Kennebrew. A small crowd had gathered and all eyes were glued on the radar screen. They held their breaths as they watched the two blimps careening toward each other.

"Can't tell, Skipper."

Betsy exhaled a lung full of air making a titanic effort to keep her voice under control. "Whatta mean you can't tell, Phil?"

"I can't tell yet because of all the weather and both planes are right in the middle of it. The radar is overstressed as it is. You can see for yourself, its one hellava storm up there."

Everyone stood hypnotized on Phil's radar screen as they watched the two jets converging at 1,200 mph. The two dots on the radarscope slowly merged into one.

They waited.

CHAPTER SIXTEEN

Aboard TGI 2120
September 8

"Did he miss us?" Luke shouted. "Did the sonofabitch actually miss us? How the hell did he miss us? In 38 years, I've never had anything so friggin' close!"

"Can't tell, Captain," Cord shouted back. "We don't have any emergency lights; no horns are going off. Maybe he just clipped us. But at least we have some clear weather ahead in case something is wrong," he exclaimed tapping his finger on the ship's weather radar screen.

"Yeah, you're right. It looks like we are coming out of this crap. I don't know, Cord, the controls seem to be okay. He must have passed us just as that lightning and thunderclap hit. Go to emergency electric power," the captain, ordered.

Cord flipped the emergency electric power switch. "Nothing Cap," he said looking at the dial, "all our generators are out. We still have the emergency batteries though."

"No, hold off on that, Cord. We might need them to land this damn thing. I can't take the chance of using up our batteries this far out." Cord shook his head that he understood.

"Okay Cord, our radios are shot, better go to code 7600 on the transponder and let the center know we don't have any radios."

Cord dialed in 7-6-0-0, a universal code on the ship's transponder, which signals the ground radar stations that an aircraft's radios were not functioning. Both crewmen knew the radio-out procedure. Once the center received a 7600 squawk code they were alerted that the aircraft's radios were not working properly and the aircraft was to proceed to its destination airport. The ATC Radar Center would clear all air traffic from their course and they were cleared to land at their destination as filed in their flight plan.

At that moment, Andi burst into the cockpit. "What the hell was that?"

"We don't know yet, Andi," said Luke. "We took a lightning hit from the storm and a near miss from some crazy bastard in a Lear Jet."

"More like an onion skin miss," added Cord.

"It must have got our internal power too," she said. "I don't have any electric in the back at all."

"That's the least of my worries right now, Andi," said Luke, staring at the myriad of instruments in front of him, which were not working. "I hope it didn't damage our landing gear system. I still have to get this big sonofabitch on the ground somehow."

"Better tell everyone back there we took a lightning strike and that everything is okay," said Cord.

"Roger that," said Andi. "But the intercom is out; I'll have to use a bull-horn."

"Yeah, do that Andi," said the captain. "I'll send Cord back for a look as soon as we get through the emergency checklist. And Andi…"

"Sir?"

"Don't mention the near miss." Andi nodded and left the flight deck.

The pilots quickly went through the emergency procedures observing every switch and dial in the massive cockpit. They found nothing critical or out of order except for the radio and electrical power outage. "Take a walk back there, Cord, and see if we missed anything."

"Okay Captain, I'll be back in a minute or so," said Cord unbuckling his shoulder harness and donning his hat and uniform jacket.

"Oh Cord, you're gonna need this." He handed him a cockpit flashlight. "Make sure and take the panel off in the rear galley and look at the control surfaces and cables. I don't want to rely on these gauges. Let's make sure everything is okay."

Cord nodded and gave a thumb up. He left the flight deck once again admiring his captain's thoroughness and concern for safety. He passed seat 33A.

Whispering to Andi, he asked. "What's with this?" gesturing to the rumpled blanket with a shivering form underneath.

"I don't know, Cord, that's the veterinarian I told you about. She's been buried under there ever since the storm started."

He shrugged and began slowly to the rear of the airplane smiling and assuring the alarmed passengers along the way. He reached the far aft galley and quickly opened the rear panel.

Cord beamed the flashlight inside.

CHAPTER SEVENTEEN

ATC Air Traffic Control Center
Denver, Colorado
September 8

No one spoke. A deathly silence fell over the radar room as everyone stared at the screen. No one breathed. After what seemed like an eternity, the dot slowly began to split and emerged as two distinct dots on the radarscope. Everyone gasped a sigh of relief followed by a few who were clapping their hands, everyone except Betsy Gomez.

"Thank you sweet Jesus in Heaven," she whispered.

Betsy stomped off toward her office shouting in a voice loud enough to be heard in the next county. "Get me Las Vegas Approach at McCarran and use the red phone. There's not going to be any freaking mid-airs out of Denver, or near-misses either, not out of my center, not with my people and damn sure not on my watch!"

Shouting at Gilbert, Betsy ordered, "Ski, find out who the mother-fu—," she checked herself. "Find out who the crazy sonofabitch is flying that Lear," still clenching her fists at her sides Betsy half-shouted, "Do it now!"

"Yesss ma'am."

"And Ski."

"Yes ma'am?"

"I want the tail number of that Lear Jet, the captain's name and his flight profile." Oh and Ski..."

"Yes ma'am?"

"Find out who the hell is working the southwest quadrant out of Chicago and I want it yesterday!"

Betsy stretched out on her office couch and put her hands on her forehead. She rubbed her temples.

Not going to be any mid-airs out of my center, not on my watch there damned sure won't—not on my watch.

CHAPTER EIGHTEEN

Aboard TGI Flight 2120
September 8

"How far out from Denver are we, Spark Plug?"

"I can't really tell, Cap. That lightning took out our GPS computers and the power generators." Cord busied himself with a slide rule. "Best I can figure is about 120 nautical miles."

"Okay Cord, ease back on the power a tad. We'd better start getting this big mother down lower. We want to arrive at DIA at traffic pattern altitude."

Cord disengaged the auto-throttles and retarded the power setting. With no electric power, he manually adjusted the elevator trim tabs allowing the Boeing to begin a gradual and comfortable decent.

"You didn't notice anything unusual back there in the rear panel, Cord?"

"No, nothing sir. Nothing I could see anyway, but I could feel it. Kinda like the tail was doing a hula dance."

"Yeah, I felt it too," said the captain. "Maybe he got the yaw-damper," a device that helps to provide a better ride for passengers the combination of tail wagging and rocking from side to side.

"Maybe?"

"Yeah, maybe, no way to tell. Get out the landing checklist Cord. We'll be at Denver shortly."

"You want me to try the landing gear, Captain?" Cord pointed to the long red handle.

"No. Not now, Cord. We may have only one shot at it and I don't want take the risk of using up our emergency batteries. Make sure the anti-skid is on." Cord nodded his agreement and checked the overhead panel.

Soon the rotating green and white beacon of DIA appeared through the night sky aiding the crewmen to spot the Denver airport.

"Take Runway Three-Four Left," said Luke, "it's the longest. Gear down," he commanded, giving Cord a palms down signal. Cord engaged the landing gear handle and both pilots held their breath. Almost immediately, they heard the whining sound of the landing gear being deployed. The emergency battery power had activated an electric motor, which ran the hydraulic pumps lowering the landing gear.

"Captain, I think the gear went down, but with no cockpit power we can't tell if it's locked. No lights," said Cord, dragging his index finger along a row of 14 dull green lights, which when illuminated indicates the landing gear is down and locked.

"No shit," said Luke. "Tell me something I don't know. If it's not locked, the wheels could collapse under us at touchdown. We'll know soon enough. Tell Andi to prepare everyone back there just in case."

"Roger that," said Cord.

"You want me to squawk 7700 on the transponder and let them know we have an emergency?"

"No need, Spark Plug," said Luke calmly flexing his jaw muscle. "They'll have all the emergency equipment and everything but a Dixieland band waiting to greet us."

Doesn't anything rattle this phlegmatic old man? Thought Cord.

"All right," said Luke. "There's the runway straight ahead, let's reduce the airspeed to 160 knots."

"Yes sir. But Captain, don't you think this should be your landing?"

"It's your leg to fly, Spark Plug. Now do your job," said Luke sternly.

Cord peered through the sea of rotating blue and red lights ricocheting through the darkness from the emergency vehicles aligning both sides of the runway as he steered the Boeing in a direct path to Runway Three-Four Left. As they crossed the runway threshold, he pulled off the power and pitched the nose up to a deck angle of 15 degrees. He waited for the airplane to settle on the long expanse of concrete.

The pilots waited for the impact through gritted teeth. Both held their breath.

CHAPTER NINETEEN

Aboard Lear Jet N9928T
September 8

Kyle MacFarland's eyes nearly exploded from their sockets at the sight of the giant airliner filling the Lear's windscreen. There was no time to blink much less brace for the inevitable smashing of metal coming together at almost twice the speed of sound. There was nothing he could do; it was over in a micro-second. Captain Clayton Carson never saw it.

Did we miss it? Did it miss us? How did we miss? We were right on top of each other! Carson, you petulant horse's ass, you almost got us killed—This is it—Flying job or no, nothing is worth getting killed for.... And worse yet killing hundreds of others—I'm going to Spencer when we get back, if we get back.

At the same time, in a trespassed hangar in western Palm Beach County, the Contractor stretched out best he could in the back seat of the Bonanza and tried to get a few hours' sleep. He set his wristwatch alarm for four A.M.

The Chicago Air Traffic Control Center at that moment was overwhelmingly busy, as usual, with air traffic stacked up for miles. Pete Ogilvie was at his station jabbering incoherently to a litany of airplanes sending them in all directions with ridiculous and confusing instructions. Two FAA Security Agents appeared at each side of Pete accompanied by Lincoln Sansbury.

"Mister Ogilvie, you have to come with us," said the taller of the agents.

"No can do, amigo," exclaimed a giggling Ogilvie, waving both arms above his shoulders. "I got too much traffic up there."

"Let's go now, Pete," said Lincoln firmly. "This is not a game and we're not playing."

The two agents hoisted Pete up by his arms and immediately another controller sat down in his seat. The agents escorted Pete out a side door. A blue FAA van was waiting.

Meanwhile in the Denver FAA Air Traffic Control Center, the usually equanimous, Bouncing Betsy Gomez was still stretched out in her office couch exhausted. She leaned back and interlocked her fingers. With her thumbs, she pinched her eye sockets inside the bridge of her nose.

No near misses or mid-airs on my watch—not out of my center. Thank you dear God in Heaven.

CHAPTER TWENTY

DIA, Denver Intl Airport
September 8

Cord wiped the sweat from his brow on his sleeve. With knuckles turning white, he clasped the steering yoke in a vise-grip.

"Relax son," said Luke, placing a hand on Cord's shoulder. "Just a normal landing, that's all it is. Put her down gently, just like always."

The big airliner crossed the airport perimeter fence at 145 mph. The tires screeched as the massive airplane settled on 16,000 feet of concrete.

"Touchdown, reverse thrust," Cord blurted. Luke was already reaching for the throttles to throw the engines into reverse thrust to aid braking the hurtling airplane. Using the toe brakes, helped by the reverse thrusters, Cord brought the speeding juggernaut to a stop at the very end of the runway. He expelled a lung full of held breath. "Whew," he breathed, "another day at the office." Both crewmen heard applause from the passengers.

"That's it Spark Plug, just another day at the office. We're cleared to taxi."

"Taxi?"

"Yeah, sure, see that green light from the tower? I think we're at gate 22," said Luke, gripping the throttles and the steering tiller. "I got her, Spark Plug."

The old man has got to be the center block of cool and calm—never once did he show any emotion nor did he ever change his expression. The original iceman— Lesson learned. Thanks Captain.

Once the Boeing was chocked and the engines shut down both pilots donned their uniform coats and grabbed their overnight bags. Cord headed for the cockpit door. "Hey Cap, maybe we should take our flight bags, I don't think we should leave them in here overnight."

The captain nodded his agreement. "Not the jet way Cord, use the stairs."

Cord gave him a quizzical look. "Stairs?"

"Yeah, the stairs Spark Plug. The lobby will be full of reporters and photographers hoarded around like a herd of buffalo. We'll go down to operations and out though the crew room."

"Good idea, Cap."

"I have a haystack of paperwork ahead of me as it is," said Luke. "When everything goes right nobody ever says a damn thing, but let something like this happen and they're around like flies on a pile of cow dung."

"Good point," replied Cord.

"You go ahead. I gotta call the main office. Take the FAs with you and I'll meet you all at the Marriott."

"Roger that, Cap. We'll be in the bar."

"No doubt," replied Luke. "Order me a thick steak and a tea glass full of scotch," he laughed.

Cord laughed, "Yeah, think I'll have a double too." He signaled Andi for the other flight attendants to follow him to the crew bus.

CHAPTER TWENTY-ONE

Marriott Hotel, Denver, Colorado
September 8

After checking in with the hotel desk, Cord made his way to room 522 and placed his overnight and flight bags on the suitcase butler. Pursuant to TGI policy of no drinking or being seen in a bar wearing a company uniform, he quickly got out of his clothes and donned a pair of tan slacks and a blue pullover. He ran a comb through his hair, brushed his teeth and headed for the Marriott's restaurant lounge.

Since the captain and the lead flight attendant were required to notify the company headquarters in Miami after any unusual incident happened aboard a flight they didn't arrive until an hour later. Spotting Cord, they joined him at the table.

"Say now, that was quite a ride this eve'nin'," Andi drawled. "Good job, Lukie-boy."

"All in a day's work," smiled Luke modestly. "The Lord makes the weather, I just fly the plane. But it wasn't me. Cord here did all the heavy lifting. Besides, it was good experience."

Cord laughed, "I know I need to build experience, but tonight was an experience I could have done without!"

They were all laughing when Cord started to say something. Interrupting himself and looking toward the entrance to the bar he said, "Holy jumping Jupiter—what is that?"

They all looked toward the wide arch leading to the lobby. "Cordie my boy, that's the veterinarian I was telling you about," whispered Andi.

"Gad Andi, you didn't tell me she was Miss America!"

"I told you she was a real looker."

"A looker?" exclaimed Cord. "That's like comparing Air Force One to a skate board. She's gorgeous!"

"That she is," added Luke, looking over a shoulder toward a petite figure with dark blond hair. She was modestly dressed in a pair of faded jeans and a light green blouse, which seemed to broadcast that she was not a person of means. Her deep blue eyes were searching the area. A sweater was tied about her waist.

Cord thought. *She's probably living on the edge of poverty after four-years of college and four or five years of vet school. Those clothes are right out of Goodwill.*

"That's a nice package," said Luke admiring the girl's figure.

132

"She's coming this way, she's coming this way," Cord loudly whispered at the same time nervously knocking over his water glass.

Andi mopped the spill with a cloth napkin and said. "Jeez Cord, relax; it's not like she's from the IRS."

Recognizing Andi, she approached their table. In a voice sweet as honey, she nervously said, "Pardon me, aren't you the pilots on 2120?" Both men stood.

"Fraid we'll have to plead guilty to that as charged," said Luke. "Have a seat, please." He motioned toward the last empty chair at the table.

"Thank you."

"What may we get you to drink?" Luke asked.

"A chardonnay would be nice, thank you."

"Done," said Luke, signaling the waitress. Pausing a moment he added. "We were about to order dinner, care to join us?"

"Oh, I don't think…"

Thinking of her economic situation, the captain interrupted. "We insist. What'll you have?"

They all placed their order with a tired looking waitress. Luke and Cord decided on the grilled sirloins while both ladies ordered a chicken salad.

Luke said, "Well, first things first. I'm Luke Sellers, this is Cord Barrett, and the pretty lady over there is Andi Marokris."

"Pleased to meet you," she nodded shyly.

"Do you have a name?" asked Andi.

She smiled and said, "Yes, I'm sorry, my name is Peri."

"You got a last name attached to that?" asked Luke.

"Yes sir," Peri said looking down and a bit embarrassed. She hesitated. "It's—it's Pepper. My name is Peri Pepper."

Cord had said nothing. He just sat and stared at the pretty doctor.

"Humm," said Luke. "I'm told that you are a veterinarian."

"Yes sir, I am. I just graduated last month."

Luke thought for a moment. "Wouldn't that make you a DVM, a doctor of veterinary medicine?"

Peri nodded. *Oh, here it comes—*

"Well now, wouldn't that make you, Doctor Pepper and you're drinking chardonnay?"

"Yes sir, it would." She replied sighing. "I hear that all the time, but that was the first time today." They all laughed.

Peri looked at Cord, "Captain, I wanted to ask…"

Cord interrupted. "Sorry ma'am. I appreciate the promotion, but that's the captain over there," he said, jabbing an index finger in Luke's direction.

"What can we do for you, Doctor Pepper?" said Luke.

"It's Peri, please. I'm trying to get to Miami. I was on a through flight scheduled to stop here in Denver."

"That would have been us on 2120," said Luke. "I don't guess any other carrier is going to Miami tonight?"

"No, I checked. And I don't have enough money to buy another ticket."

"Seems like you are in a bit of a pickle," said Andi.

"We'll figure out something in the morning," said Luke.

Just as they spoke a TGI mechanic in greasy coveralls entered and was looking about the lounge.

"Over here," said Luke, recognizing the gray company coveralls. He motioned the maintenance man to their table. "What's up?"

"Ah, you the Cap-em of 2120?"

Luke nodded.

"Cap-em sir," he said. "Your radios are shot and fried all to hell, sir. And she's dented all to hell too, ah, from the hail, sir."

"Is that supposed to be news?" Spoke up Cord sarcastically.

"Ah, yes sir, the comp-nee is flying in a temporary radio stack tonight and we should have it in about eleven or noon tomorrow."

"And?" said Luke.

"And, uh, yes sir, dispatch says for you guys to fly 2120 to our maintenance base in Miami. The FAA will have you a ferry permit 'bout noon or so. That should put you in Miami a little before dark their time."

"Now ain't that just great?" said the captain disgustedly. "Okay," he sighed. "Guess we don't have much choice. Thanks a lot. Oh, by the way, Tom," he added, reading the mechanic's airport ID tag. "Make sure they button down my airplane tonight. We just came through a helluva storm and it looks like it will be in here around midnight or so."

Cord noticed Peri's face had begun to ashen at the mention of the storm but said nothing.

Tom said, "Yes sir, Cap-em, radars been painting that stuff all night. I'll make sure your bird is safe and sound. Looks like she took a helluva beating. Good night, sir."

"Good night, and thanks, Tom."

"Say Cap," said Cord pleadingly. "You suppose Doctor Pepper here could hitch a ride with us tomorrow?"

"You know the FAA prohibits carrying passengers on a ferry flight, Spark Plug."

"There's no rule about flight attendants going," interjected Andi. "It's required."

"Humm," said Luke. "I think I'm understanding your drift, sugar plum. Do you happen to have an extra uniform with you?"

"Of course I do. We always carry an extra. You know that."

"Aren't you two about the same size," he asked.

"Yeah, like five foot nothing and a hundred and nothing," spoke up Cord. Andi wrinkled her nose and made a funny face at him.

Andi gestured with her hands by her shoulders palms down. "Yes, we are about the same size and I'll never tell if you don't. We could all swear pinkies," she laughed.

"How about you, Cord?"

"I'm like Sergeant Shultz," said Cord. "I know noth-thin—but we all know, just like everything else, it's always the captain's call."

Luke pondered for a moment. "Okay then Doctor Pepper, we'll meet you for breakfast at the restaurant in the morning. You can get with Andi for a uniform and we'll get you home."

"Miami is not home, I'm from Georgia."

"Why are you going to Miami?"

"I have a sister nearby in Palm Beach and I'm hoping she can help me get a job."

"You spent all that time in vet school just to trim poodles in ritzy Palm Beach?" said Cord.

"No," she replied, "I specialized in large animals, horses, cattle and livestock like that."

"Large animals? A little thing like you? Well, that area is a good choice. There's quite an equine community west of Palm Beach; it's called Wellington."

"Yes, I've heard of it."

Cord continued. "A lot of wealthy folks show their prized horses there in the winter. You know, race horses, polo ponies, hunter-jumpers and the like." Peri nodded.

"Doctor Pepper, do you have a place to stay tonight?" asked Cord. "I'm in 522 and you can have my room and I could double up with the captain here," he said jerking his thumb toward Luke. "Our rooms have two queens in them so no problem."

"I'm good, thanks and it's Peri, please."

Their dinner arrived and everyone began to dig in. Cord noticed Peri's hands were folded and her head was bowed. They all embarrassingly waited while Peri gave her thanks, as she was raised to do by the Reverend Pepper.

While Peri and the crew ate, a dark figure exited the fifth floor elevator. Slowly it crept through the shadows of the hallway and stopped at room 522. In a matter of seconds, the shadow was inside. Quickly it made its way to Cord's flight bag.

Cord took a hot shower and turned on the local news. It had been a couple hours since they had all said their goodnights and retired to their prospective rooms. He stretched out on one of the queen size beds and through the windows; he cringed at the lightning flashing off in the distance.

Good Lord, we flew through that?

From the stress and excitement of the day, Cord felt the lassitude beginning to overtake him. He was completely fatigued and worn out. He turned off the TV, doused the light and was fast asleep almost immediately.

Cord was enjoying a deep, refreshing rest when a light tapping on the door roused him. At first Cord thought, the rapping was a dream. Then it sounded again. Sleepily he stumbled to the door.

"Doctor Pepper, what on earth are you doing out here at two in the morning?"

"Captain…" she started to say more when Cord held up his hand at arm's length.

"Doctor Pepper, as I have told you, I am just the first officer, a copilot. If you are looking for Captain Sellers he is one door down on the other side."

"No, it's you. I wanted to see you. I remembered your room number."

"What can I do for you at this hour of the morning, Doctor Pepper?"

"Uh, is it okay…I mean…is it all right…maybe…if I spent the night with you?" She stuttered shyly looking at the floor.

"What?" exclaimed a shocked Cord Barrett standing inside the doorway in boxer shorts. "Don't…don't you have a room?"

"No, no—I'm sorry, I lied about that. I'm so sorry. I don't like lying about anything. I was trying to sleep on the lounge in the ladies room and…"

Cord interrupted. "Well come inside and bring your bag. You can't be standing out there in the hallway. Why don't you have a room?"

Peri stepped inside. "I am so embarrassed," she said. "I just couldn't spare the money and the storm started and I…."

Cord understood immediately. The little veterinarian was clearly frightened by the storm raging outside the window. "That's quite all right, Doctor Pepper. Go ahead and take yourself a hot shower. I'll call the captain and go to his room. You can stay here."

"No!" she exclaimed empathically. "I want to stay with you—that is—if you don't mind. I don't want sex—No sex. I just don't want to be alone," she said in a voice no stronger than a whisper.

"Sure, sure, Doctor Pepper that's fine by me. Here," he said, fumbling through his overnight bag. He emerged with a tee shirt and said, "Hop in there and take a hot shower. Put this on," Cord tossed her the tee shirt. "It's the best I can do for a nightgown."

Peri half smiled and started toward the bathroom. She stopped and turned. "But what about taking a shower during a storm? The lightning?"

Cord smiled. "Don't worry Doctor Pepper; you never see the one that gets you."

Peri returned a slight smile and entered the bathroom. Cord said, "You will find fresh towels on the rack there, Doctor Pepper. I'll turn down this other bed for you."

Peri took the tee shirt and disappeared into the bathroom leaving the door slightly ajar. From his vantage point on the queen size bed Cord had a perfect view of the doctor reflected through the vanity mirror. Knowing the gentlemanly thing to do would be to close the door or look away he could not resist keeping his eyes from feasting on the image in the mirror.

Cord was mesmerized at the sight before him as the veterinarian undid her blouse. Stretching her arms behind, she slowly loosened the clasp of her bra allowing her pert breasts free. They were flawless. Quickly she peeled off her slacks and slipped out of the pink bikini panties enabling him a full view of her naked body.

The hotel could have been on fire and Cord would not have been able to look away. Peri gazed in the mirror. Their eyes met and they held each other's stare for several seconds. The slightest smile barely parted her lips. Never breaking eye contact Peri slowly closed the door.

Oh, my gosh! Did I really see that? Is there really anything that perfect? He gasped to himself. Did she almost smile at me? I must have died and gone to Heaven!

Emerging from the shower Peri had a towel around her hair and was clad only in the tee shirt. "Why do you have two suitcases?" she asked.

"The black one over there with the big handle and that snaps is my flight bag. It's not an overnight bag."

"Flight bag?"

"Yeah, that's where pilots keep maps and charts. Airport info like approach plates. Things like that."

"Oh. And you always take it with you?"

Cord laughed. "Heck no. We leave it in the crew room at our home base. I'm not about to lug that thing around. I didn't want to leave it on the airplane tonight until I found out what we were going to do."

"Oh, I see."

"I turned down the other bed for you, Doctor Pepper."

"Un-huh. Thank you."

Cord was drifting off to sleep. Outside the storm was not letting up. Rain pelted the windows of the room. Lightning flashed across the Colorado sky followed by the crashing thunder. Through his sleepy fog, Cord felt a warm body climb in the bed with him. At first, he thought he was dreaming until a hand settled in the hair on his chest as she snuggled against him. He felt two warm breasts pressing against his back.

In seconds, Doctor Peri Pepper was fast asleep.

CHAPTER TWENTY-TWO

Boca Raton, Florida
September 9

The Contractor was relieved to feel the smoothness of the morning air under the wings of the Bonanza as it lifted off the grass runway. He had been careful to make certain no lights were on in the adjoining houses. No one would be awake at such an early hour to see him depart the little airport community. He banked the aircraft steeply to the north to get out of sight of anyone who might have seen him leave.

The Contractor was careful to stay low enough to avoid being picked up on the Palm Beach radar. In minutes, he was in the vicinity of the Boca Raton Airport. He climbed to 2,800 feet and turned west.

He smiled to himself. *Palm Beach Radar will never know where I took off from—they will simply think I am a local bumpkin off Boca for a joy ride or an early morning cross-country flight—*

The Contractor began to consult his FAA Navigational Sectional Chart. "Humm, that little field is perfect," he said aloud holding his finger on the chart.

The timing is flawless—I'll be there about daybreak. Perfect.

An hour later as daylight was peeking through the eastern sky; the Contractor lowered his altitude to 1,000 feet and began searching the ground below. He spotted the old abandoned airfield that he had found on the chart and began his decent.

This place is so remote, no houses around for miles. Probably only used by crop dusters if anyone at all.

The Bonanza settled smoothly on the earth, and the Contractor taxied to a turnaround area on the narrow runway. He set the parking brake and hopped out in the cool morning mist without shutting down the engine. Quickly he removed the tape from the airplane's number. The makeshift eight was three again; the seven was back to one, and the 'R' was now the original 'P,' he urinated and was back in the air in a matter of minutes.

Now, if I can only find a little rain cloud.

The Contractor was a patient man. First by nature and second it was often necessary for his line of work to wait for long periods of time. Wait for the right time and the right opportunity to carry out an assignment. He was beginning to get a bit concerned by the time he reached Florida's Gulf Coast. The Contractor swung the Bonanza north up the beach still keeping low and under the radar when he spotted what he wanted. A few miles offshore, he saw a small rain shower, exactly what he needed. It was a few miles out of his way, but the Contractor had plenty of fuel. He banked the Bonanza west and into the rain.

The water-painted blue Bonanza entered the rain shower at 180 mph and emerged moments later in its original red. The Contractor laughed to himself at airplane owners who spent a lot of money to have their airplanes washed and detailed by hand when all they had to do was fly through a light rain. Although this procedure was illegal and highly frowned upon by the FAA, the Contractor was not particularly concerned with the rules and regulations of the FAA. Still keeping the Bonanza low and under the radar, he turned back to the shoreline and continued north until he reached Siesta Key, south of Sarasota.

The Contractor climbed the airplane to an altitude that he knew would be picked up by the Tampa west coast radar center. He turned on the transponder and dialed in 1-2-0-0, the international squawk code for all visual and unfiled air traffic. The 1200 code would blip on a center controller's radarscope identifying him as traffic in the area. He keyed his headset microphone by pressing the black button on the steering yoke.

"Tampa radar, Bonanza Three-Two-One-Five Poppa, off Siesta Key Airport, en-route to Palm Beach," there would never be any record of him being there or not, since Siesta Key was a non-controlled airfield.

"Roger, Bonanza Three-Two-One-Five Poppa, this is Tampa Radar. Squawk zero-four-two-four, and say altitude," said a voice in his headset.

The Contractor dialed in zero-four-two-four on the transponder. "Roger that, Bonanza three-two-one-five poppa, squawking zero-four-two-four and climbing to three thousand, five hundred."

"Roger, Bonanza Three-Two-One-Five Poppa, radar contact. You are cleared direct to Palm Beach."

The Contractor set the course in the auto-pilot and leaned back gazing out the window at the peaceful Florida morning. An hour later, he heard the screech of tires as the Bonanza settled on Runway Nine at the Owen H. Gassaway, Jr. Airfield in Lantana, Florida, six miles south of Palm Beach International. He taxied to the ramp, secured the airplane and headed for the rental car counter, his best friend in hand.

CHAPTER TWENTY-THREE

Cord looked down at the cloud deck below and was thankful for the beautiful clear day. *Quite a contrast from last night.* The foul weather had passed and it was clear blue above and below as the Boeing hurtled through the sky.

"What's our time to Miami, Spark Plug?"

"We're right on the money, Cap, looks like we picked up a little tailwind so we should be in Miami at 1646 local."

"Good," said Luke. "Since we were late getting off the ground in Denver maybe we can make up a little time. What are those women folk up to back there?"

"Dunno," he said and swung the cockpit door open. "Hey you two, what's cooking?"

Andi and Peri were chatting in the forward first class seats on the empty plane. "We're talking about you two bad boys," smirked Andi.

"Ut-Oh," laughed Cord. "That should take up a few hours. Did you gals make yourselves useful and brew up any coffee for us poor hard working pilots?"

"Yep," said Andi. "It should be ready now, I'm fixing to bring you yawl some directly. We'll be right up."

Since 2120 was a ferry flight, the FAA rule of prohibiting the flight deck door from being open during flight or allowing visitors in the cockpit was relaxed. Peri, dressed in Andi's spare uniform, had been escorted through TSA and aboard the airplane without incident or question.

Andi soon appeared in the cockpit with two cups of steaming coffee accompanied by Peri. Turning around in his seat, Luke said, "Take a jump seat there and we'll tell you about our good points."

"That shouldn't take long," grinned Andi taking a jump seat behind the airmen and offering the other to Peri.

"Aw now, go easy on us poor hard working pilots," laughed Luke.

"Hard working, huh, El Capateen?" Andi kidded back. "You just work one flight back there with a full load of passengers as I do, then let me hear about all your hard work up here."

"Just a walk in the park," laughed Luke.

"Hey Cord," said Andi. "Did you catch the news last night?"

"Nope, can't say that I did," he answered, winking at Peri.

"Maybe you should have. There was a story about the Everglades. Aren't you from down there somewhere, Cord?"

"Yeah, I am based out of Miami. In fact, I was born in south Florida, fifth generation."

"Is that a lot?"

"Not really but for Florida it is. My family goes back a 100 years or better. What's this about the Everglades?"

"Oh yeah," Andi continued. "Dan Hatcher ran something last night on the Network News, a story about some headless Indian running around the in swamps down there."

"Oh no," groaned Cord. "Not again."

"Again?" asked Luke. "What's the scoop?"

"Oh Cap, it's a long story about Osceola's ghost and it's all bullshit."

"We got time for a long story and a little bullshit, Spark Plug. We're still a couple hours out."

Cord began to relate to his cockpit audience the story of the legendary Chief of the Seminoles and their famed leader during the three Seminole wars with the United States.

Osceola was born during or about 1804 in northwest Florida, a bit north and west of present day Tallahassee now lower Alabama. He was the only son of a white Englishman, a trader named William Powell and an Indian Princess, by the English name of Polly. He grew up in a multi-culture of Indian, English, Irish, Scottish and some blacks, as well. Osceola himself was all of these. So really, Osceola was not completely a Native American Seminole, Creek, Cherokee, Choctaw, or otherwise, at least not genetically. His birth name was William Powell after his father and he was called Billy. The name Osceola didn't come until much later.

Billy Powell grew up into an era where whites were making their first cultural and genetic impact upon the Indian tribes. Billy rebelled and walked a tenuous line between the two cultures.

In 1818, at the end of Andrew Jackson's military campaign, which was more genocide than military, Billy and his mother, his father had died, moved to an area by the Suwannee River in northern Florida. Later due to white aggression, they were forced to move again, this time southeasterly into the central part of the state. Most likely to what is now Okeechobee City, Florida. As part of the Treaty of Moultrie Creek signed in 1823, the government assigned the Indians a four million acre tract of worthless south central Florida land, the Everglades, which was totally unsuitable for any kind of agriculture or livestock. But, it didn't take long for white encroachment, which was all too frequent, to settle or trade illegally with the Indians. The U.S. Government began to carry out a policy of displacement or extermination of the Indians thus removing them from the path of white settlement. Many Indians rebelled against this treatment by the government and retaliated.

In 1831, Andrew Jackson now president, ordered the execution of the Indian Removal Act of 1830. All Indians east of the Mississippi River were to be removed from their homes, which had been guaranteed to them forever via treaty with the United States. They were uprooted and forced to live in the Oklahoma Territory. This was the infamous *Trail of Tears* where one in every three Native Americans perished from starvation, exposure, disease and the like.

To escape this forced migration to Oklahoma, many Choctaw, Cherokee, Creeks and others from several different tribes fled to the inhospitable swamps of south central Florida carving out a poverty existence best they could by living off the land and surviving through any means possible in the hostile environment of the four million acres of Everglades swampland guaranteed to them.

As one would expect petty battles and skirmishes broke out between the whites and the Seminoles, a word meaning 'runaways,' or 'wild people,' depending on the translation. The whites for their self-adorned right of encroachment on the Indian lands, and the Seminoles for their very survival.

Martin Van Buren, Jackson's close friend, vice-president and protégé, and now president, ordered Colonel Zachary Taylor, later General Taylor, the hero of the Mexican-American War of 1846-48, and future president, into Florida to quell the uprising Seminoles. Among other military leaders were Major Francis Dade and Major William Lauderdale.

The natural leader of the Seminoles was, of course, Osceola. He was half-white, well over six feet tall, a natural athlete and extremely intelligent and cunning. Not only did Osceola speak English perfectly. He understood the culture and the thinking of the white man. He was one of the first to introduce guerilla warfare. To strike with surprise, attack and immediately withdraw, purposely luring the white soldiers into the swampy and hostile Everglades. The white soldiers were poorly equipped to fight with the Seminoles in such a strange environment and could not compete with their cunning leader. After the Dade Massacre, near the Withlacoochee River, where Major Dade and his entire unit of 400 were completely wiped out except for two survivors who reported that the Seminoles, 'just appeared from nowhere and instantly disappeared,' the same for Major Lauderdale. It was reported by the only survivor that the Indians were all of a sudden there, struck and immediately disappeared into the swamp. 'Like magic,' he said. 'It was like fighting ghosts. Suddenly they were there and just as suddenly, they were gone. They caught us by surprise every time. They faded like an invisible mist.'

Melting into the foliage is a trait or secret characteristic of only the Seminoles, which is still to this day unexplained. No Seminole will speak of it.

The government spent 30 to 40 million dollars on the Seminole wars, lost over 1500 soldiers. The Seminole Indians have never made any compromise, treaty or surrender pact with the United States.

Looking over Cord's shoulder Peri said, "But what's this got to do with a headless Indian?"

"Oh yeah, I was getting to that," answered Cord. "Finally the government declared the Seminole War impossible to win, or as they said, incurable. So, the only way they could figure to put an end to it all was to capture Osceola, which was an impossible task. So they trapped him under a flag of truce."

"That's not kosher," said Luke.

"No, it wasn't but that's what happened. Same with Geronimo and Sitting Bull. Osceola was an honorable man, a fierce competitor but still, a gentleman and a man of his word. Unfortunately, he thought the whites would be the same."

"What happened after they captured him?" asked Andi.

"That is the sad part of the story, Andi. They took him to Fort Marion in St. Augustine and from there to Fort Moultrie on Sullivan Island in Charleston Harbor. He was put in a cell and was exposed to a brief celebrity. Since he was so famous, the people of Charleston and others were allowed to come by and gawk at him."

"That would have to be humiliating for such a proud man," said Luke.

"Sure. Of course, it must have been," Cord continued. "But mercifully for Osceola he only lived a month or so. The army doctors said it was from disease, but what I really think is that he died of depression or say a broken heart from being caged there like an animal. He was used to the wide open spaces of the Everglades."

"That's really sad," said Peri.

"Yes, but the real sad part is what happened after he died," said Cord.

They all gave him a quizzical look.

Cord continued. "What happened after he died was worse. Osceola refused to talk to anyone and ignored army personnel and visitors. He did let one person befriend him, a physician, Doctor Frederick Weedon. After Osceola died, Dr. Weedon cut off his head and displayed it in a Charleston pharmacy and later it was given to the New York College of Medicine where it stayed on display until 1866. The scarf he traditionally wore and his other possessions were auctioned off."

"So, that's the headless part of the story?" asked Peri.

"Not quite Doctor Pepper."

"Peri, plezzz."

"Okay Peri plezzz," he teased. "At first nobody knew the Chief's head had been stolen or at least it wasn't publicized outside Charleston. Anyway, years later the Florida Legislature petitioned the South Carolina Legislature to remove Osceola's remains so they could be buried in Florida. So the bones were exhumed and it was then they discovered the missing head."

"Cord, that is a horrible story," exclaimed Andi.

"Horrible but true. Actually, they also discovered the remains of an infant girl, thought to be Osceola's daughter by one of his wives named, 'Che-cho-ter,' 'Morning Dew' in English was also buried in the coffin with him."

"That's terrible," said Andi.

"Sure it is, but anyway, that's how the legend got started. Some say Osceola haunts the Everglades roaming around looking for the person who stole his head."

"Oh, that's just a big myth," said Andi.

"Of course it is," said Luke, sighing. "But you know how it is. When truth and legend conflict, always print the legend."

Cord said, "Don't laugh. You'd be surprised how many really believe it. Especially the Seminoles, they swear it's true. The headless ghost of Osceola petrifies them."

"No doubt," said Luke. "But it seems like your Osceola was quite a remarkable character."

"That he was," said Cord. "A Florida county, some twenty towns, a couple of lakes, mountains and a state park are all named after him."

"A national park and a forest too," said Peri.

"Hey, that's right, Doctor Pepper. Very good! All in all, the bottom line is that he was more accurately an avenger operating out of desperation and a cultural code radically different from that of his white contemporaries and tragically antipathetic to their objectives. Chief Osceola was the George Washington of the Seminoles and to this very moment represents an unconquered people. So I guess poor Ol' Osceola's spirit is out there in the Everglades somewhere restlessly searching for its head."

"No question," said Luke sardonically. "Maybe we'll get a chance to see his ghost in our hotel tonight."

Luke looked at the ship's GPS. "There's Miami 100 knots ahead, Spark Plug."

Cord nodded.

"Pre-Landing Checklist."

CHAPTER TWENTY-FOUR

Pend Oreille Cattle Company
Palm Beach County, Florida
September 9

The Contractor eased into the rental car. He had asked for a small gray or dark green model in case he had to hide it. The darker colors would blend better in the foliage than a louder one. Exiting the airport, he turned west on Lantana Road. Soon he was at State Road 441 and headed south. Several miles passed until his GPS alerted him to turn west again on a narrow but well maintained country road. A few miles later, he saw it, a large arch with a sign.

This must be it.

The Contractor searched the area looking for a place to hide the dark green economy car. After a lengthy search, he was able to park behind some sable palms surrounded by palmettos. He hesitated something was bothering him. He would be forced to walk a half mile or better, but he took some solace in knowing that the area provided adequate places to conceal himself, if need be. The car was well hidden from view of any oncoming traffic, not that he really expected any in such remote place. But his training forced him to always be careful and expect the unexpected. He knew that a contract with El Diablo on someone as well-known as a member of the Barrett family would bring him twice his usual fee.

The Contractor thought of his two young boys, whom he loved more than life itself. His mind drifted to his spacious home on the banks of the Loxahatchee River in west Jupiter, Florida. The five acres surrounding the house provided an ideal playing area for his boys and plenty of room to ride their pony and roughhouse with their friends. Then there was little league, soccer, pee-wee football, Cub Scouts and everything else involved in raising kids. He was determined to give them everything he didn't have as a boy growing up in the poverty drenched Alleghenies.

The Contractor could use the tax-free money. His two sons would soon be in their teens and the expenses of raising them were substantial. The cost of sending them to a private college was worrisome, as well. He didn't want them to attend a state school. But the Contractor was satisfied. He had provided well for his family and invested wisely. His beautiful wife never complained about his absences. She was a jewel among jewels. "How could I have ever been so fortunate?" he often asked himself. They were the typical all American family except, of course, his line of work.

It will be dark before long—I need to find a place soon. Ah-ha, this one is ideal.

The contractor carefully scaled the large oak tree and found the perfect place to sit about ten feet off the ground. The oak provided an excellent view of the long driveway below and any oncoming traffic. He was well camouflaged by the hanging moss. A large limb provided a brace for his best friend. He assembled the rifle and slowly pushed in a .308 magnum cartridge. "One should do it," he said aloud. "He will have to pass right under me—easy target." The Contractor injected the cartridge into the breech of his best friend. He took from his breast pocket a small slip of paper. He re-read: "McCord Barrett, Palm Beach County, Florida. ASAP." The contractor peered through the scope and adjusted the sights. El Diablo wanted Cord Barrett dead—today.

He waited.

CHAPTER TWENTY-FIVE

Miami International Airport
September 9

The crew landed and taxied the battered Boeing to the maintenance hangar where a company van was waiting. A short ride later, they were dropped off at the flight crew room. Once inside Luke said, "I might as well leave my flight bag here on the rack next to yours, Cord."

"Might as well, you'll be deadheading back to DFW. You're not going to need it."

"Yeah, you got a point, Spark Plug. C'mon Andi, we have to catch the hotel shuttle topside."

"Peri, you can send my uniform back anytime, no hurry," said Andi.

Peri started to reply when Cord broke in. He snapped his fingers. Cocking his head to one side he said, "Hey, why don't you all come to my place tonight? We can throw a piece of cow on the grill and have a few beers. We need to kick back a little. Put our feet up, you know?"

"Fine by me," spoke up Andi. "Do you have enough room for us all?"

"Oh, we'll make do somehow," said Cord. "How about you, Doctor Pepper? Captain?"

"Sounds good to me too," said Luke, shaking his head in agreement and hefting his flight bag onto the rack. "I wasn't exactly looking forward to another night in a hotel. Besides, Ol' headless Osceola might be poking around my room."

Peri said, "Ordinarily, I would love to, but I still have to get to West Palm Beach."

"Not to worry, Doctor Pepper," said Cord. "The last shuttle north has already left by now. It's only 50 miles; we'll get you up there tomorrow. Anyway, once you get to West Palm where you gonna stay? And my place will get you at least three quarters of the way there."

Peri gave a pensive look. "Yeah, guess you're right. I haven't been able to get my sister on the phone."

"No?"

"She travels a lot."

"You all come on," said Cord, gesturing. "I'm parked in the employee lot."

They followed Cord to the upper deck of the airport to catch the parking lot shuttle bus. Cord spotted someone.

"Hey, Paco," he called out. "What are you doing here?"

"Oh, Señor Cord, my car, she won't start, we have no way to get home." He said putting his arms around two adolescent children. Luke guessed the girl to be about ten and the boy eight.

"What are you doing at the airport?" asked Cord.

"My wife, Ma-Anne, she go to see her sister in Santa Fe but my car, she is broke. She will not start," he said in a heavy Hispanic accent.

"Okay Paco, come with us," said Cord. "I'll drop you off."

"Hey, Spark Plug, are we going have enough room in your car?" asked Luke.

"We'll make do somehow. C'mon guys, let's go."

They exited the shuttle bus and followed Cord to a maroon Ford pickup. It was the large model, an F450, with a back seat and duel tires on the rear. Luke noted the lengthy horns of a Texas Longhorn Steer painted in gold on the doors of the truck. "Pend Oreille Cattle Company," was painted on the doors under the steer horns.

"Hey, Cord, what's this?" asked Luke, pointing to the horns. "Did you go to Texas University?"

"Nah, Florida State. That's just a logo. Paco, you and the kids hop aboard in the back."

They all piled in the truck and Cord drove north for a while then turned on a rural winding country road. Andi said, "Cord, what is a swinging bachelor like you doing living way out here in the boondocks?"

"I've got a place out here and it's paid for. Besides, I like a little solitude now and then." Cord turned off the winding road onto a wide concrete lane and passed under a wide white arch adorned with a set of enormous steer horns. Bordering each side of the arch were two huge oak trees like a pair of giant bookends. Under the arch in bold print read:

PEND OREILLE CATTLE COMPANY

BDI, Inc.

"BDI?" Luke exclaimed. "Like BDI? Like Barrett Diversified Industries? That Barrett?"

"Guilty, at least that's what they tell me." said Cord.

Luke continued, "Spark Plug, you mean to tell us that you are, "The Barrett," of Barrett Banks, Barrett Shipping, Barrett Petroleum, Barrett Manufacturing, and Barrett—Barrett, God knows what else?"

"Guilty, at least that's what they keep telling me," Cord repeated looking embarrassed.

"You are one of the Barrett's and you're a pilot for us?" exclaimed Andi.

"Well yeah, but the companies pretty much run themselves. We have lawyers and accounts, CEOs,

CFOs and so on. My uncle Ted, who's a lawyer, up in Palm Beach, oversees most of it. Besides, I like to fly airplanes."

"Yeah, it sure beats working for a living," sighed Luke.

Commodore Theodore Barrett, Cord's great grandfather, had relocated to the tiny village of Miami, Dade County, in 1895, from South Carolina just before the turn of the century. The Commodore, a retired sea captain, started a small shipping company and with wise foresight moved his new enterprise to Florida because he saw much potential for growth in the fast developing area.

The fledging Barrett Shipping Company began to prosper almost right away. Instead of splurging from the profits, the parsimonious Commodore in his wisdom reinvested the money in prime Florida real estate. At the time in the early 1900s the Florida lands, if not on the ocean were considered practically worthless and most of it was held in delinquent tax notes. The Commodore bought up literally thousands of acres by paying off the delinquent tax deeds at ten cents on the dollar. Among his other investments, he saw the massive influx of new settlers in the area. Knowing they all had hardy appetites; the Commodore stocked his land with prime beef cattle. Eventually, he teamed up with a New Jersey oil man, Henry Flagler, a partner with John D. Rockefeller in Standard Oil. Together they built the new Florida railroad. The profits were enormous.

A huge addition to his already substantial bank account came during the Depression Era when his son, McCord Barrett, Cord's grandfather, became associated with a politically connected Boston banker by shipping in boats loaded to the gunnels with Scotch Whiskey. No sooner had the ink dried from newly elected President Franklin Roosevelt's signature repealing the 18th Amendment; the Prohibition Act of 1919, the eastern market was flooded with fine scotch whiskey. Again, the profits were enormous.

In the spring of the mid 1930s, McCord was on a hunting expedition in northeastern Washington State, on the Idaho border just below Canada, when his party encountered some of the local Indians. He noticed how the natives wore heavy ornaments dangling from their ear lobes. Inquiring about it, they told him, 'This is the land of *The Pend Oreille*, pronounced Pond-O-Ray.'

Peri chimed in, "That's French."

Cord continued, "Yes, named by the French trappers many years before. The words in French literally mean, 'Hanging Ear.' The senior McCord liked the name and named his Florida ranch the same. 'The Pend Oreille Cattle Company.'"

"Whatta ya know. Four years of French has finally paid off," Peri laughed.

None of them ever suspected Cord to be from such enormous wealth. He was a modest man and never appeared self-assuming. "Cord, I didn't know you were rich," said Andi.

"I'm not. My parents are."

"Both your folks living?" asked Luke.

"No, 'fraid not. Big Fred, my Dad, passed on several years back, but Mom is still with us and is the undisputed matriarch of the family."

"Big Fred? Aren't you what, Cord, about six two?"

"Yeah, six two right on the button. But Dad was six five or six. All American end, Georgia Tech, class of 66."

"Any brothers or sisters?" asked Peri.

"Yep, two sisters, both older. Did you all see that big ranch store we passed a few miles back?"

They all said, "yes."

"My sister, Leigh, owns it with her husband Dean Terry. It's a good couple acres under one roof and a 60 acre feedlot for cattle out behind it."

"And your other sister?" asked Andi.

"The oldest is my sister Elizabeth. She's a physician and on the staff at Miami Jackson Hospital and a professor of radiology at the University of Miami Medical School."

CHAPTER TWENTY-SIX

Pend Oreille Cattle Ranch
Barrett County, Florida
September 9

The Contractor squinted through the scope of his best friend as the maroon pick-up came into view. He flicked off the safety and focused the crosshairs into the cab of the truck. His finger steadied on his best friend's trigger, he softly squeezed the stainless steel. He could feel the wood of the English walnut stock pressing against his cheek. Now in seconds it would be over.

The Contractor drew in a lungful of air and slowly exhaled as he was taught in the Marine Sniper School. His finger tightened on the trigger. Now was the instant to complete the assignment. Cord Barrett was clearly centered in the scope. He saw something else. His head bolted up.

"Dammit, dammit, damn him!" breathed the Contractor.

El Diablo knows better than that. There are kids and women. I don't do kids or women. I have never harmed a woman or kids, El Diablo knows my rules.

The sonofabitch. He knows my rule about kids and women. Damn him!

The Contractor could have easily made a clean shot at Cord through the windshield of the truck. *But what if it hits a bump? What if the bullet ricochets? Surely, the truck would crash after the shot. What about those kids in the back? Damn him, doesn't the bastard have any compassion? Damn El Diablo!*

The Contractor froze and waited for the Ford to pass. He snapped the safety back on and ejected the cartridge in his hand. He made his way down the tree. His mind was racing.

I must plan this mission again. I have to get the right time and the right place.

It was unlike him to not plan the entire operation in detail. Usually he spent several days coordinating an assignment. He always did his research. He took pains to know the area; he took dozens of digital photos. He knew his quarry's schedules and personal habits, as well as they did.

I was careless today. I got in a hurry; I thought this would be an easy assignment. I didn't plan, I didn't think it through. Maybe I'm getting too old for this kind of work. It will never happen again.

CHAPTER TWENTY-SEVEN

Pend Oreille Ranch
Barrett County, Florida
September 9

They all were smiling as dusk began to settle on the Pend Oreille. The drive up the long twisting lane was lined with large oak trees. Colorful flowers were growing against the white wooden fence. The Spanish moss dangled from the branches almost touching the fence on each side of the lane, which enclosed the Black Angus cattle peacefully grazed on the white-topped clover. They passed a large cove on their right, which curved around in front of them.

Noting the questions in their faces Cord said. "That's Matheson Cove named after my mother's side of the family."

"Is it navigable?" asked Luke.

"Oh sure, it winds around into the Inland Water Way and into the Atlantic. The water is a little brackish but mostly fresh."

"Oh, my gosh!" cried Peri.

"What?" they all said in unison.

"Is that an alligator or a big canoe?" asked Luke.

Cord peered through the settling darkness. "Oh, him; that's just Goliath."

"Just Goliath?" exclaimed Luke. "He's as big as a Boeing!"

"Yeah, that's an old gator that hangs around in the cove every once in a while. I had a chain link fence put in down to the water to protect the livestock. He can't get in."

"Goliath can't be too dangerous if he's that old," said Andi.

"Don't fool yourself, Andi. It's the older gators that are the most dangerous. He's too old to chase his dinner so he has to catch what he can, like an unsuspecting dog, a dead animal, things like that. A gator grabs something drags it under the water and drowns it. Then he stuffs it in a gator hole somewhere and eats on the carcass for a while."

"Ugh," both girls muttered. Cord pulled the truck up the wide horseshoe shaped driveway of a huge red brick house. Four white pillars stood erect across the front. There was a cluster of flowers surrounding a water fountain filled with goldfish centered in the half-circle driveway. The tree lined driveway and grounds were beautifully manicured.

"Is this your house or a hotel?" joked Andi.

"This is the Tidewaters, home sweet home," replied Cord.

"The Tidewaters?" queried Luke.

"Yeah, Cap. You're in the south. We name everything."

"Eeek!" Shrieked Andi from the back seat. She was seeing two large eyes, a long hairy face and two stubby horns peering in the truck at her.

"Relax, Ms. Marokris," laughed Cord. "That's only Yardboy."

"Who or what the hell is a Yardboy?"

"Just a pet," said Cord, reaching out his arm through the truck's window scratching the head of the baby Hereford bull. "He lost his mama so the hands brought him up here and we raised him on a bottle. He's harmless but watch out. He likes to lean against you and sometimes he butts a little."

"Butts a little?" said Andi. "Damn thing probably weighs 400 pounds or better."

Peri was already out of the truck petting the affectionate orphan that apparently had free reign of the 20 acres fencing in the mansion from the rest of the property. Yardboy had claimed it as his personal fiefdom.

Cord handed Peri a lump of sugar from a box he kept in the truck. "Here, give him this, Doctor Pepper, and he will love you forever."

175

"Okay Paco, you all hop down."

"Si, Señor Cord. Mucho gracias."

"No problem, Paco. Tell Henry I said for someone to pick up your car tomorrow."

"Si, si, gracias, Señor Cord," Paco said, herding his children toward a narrow path.

"They live around here?" asked Luke.

"Sure, in the employee housing couple hundred yards down around the hangar there on the other side of the airport."

Hangar? Employee housing? A Private airfield? Thought Luke.

"Ut-Oh. My mother is here," Cord said quietly, pointing to a dark blue Mercedes. A uniformed driver was standing nearby smoking a cigarette. "Something must be wrong."

Cord led them up a few red brick steps between the tall white pillars. Just then, unbelievable screeching and chaos broke out. Everyone balked.

"Take it easy, you all. That's Max," Cord said. He extended his forearm to an open perch toward a large colorful parrot. The macaw hopped on. Cord scooped a handful of sunflower seeds from a nearby aluminum container. Extending his palm Max helped himself to the treats.

"He's better than a watchdog," Luke exclaimed.

"He's better than ten watchdogs," laughed Cord. "You might get by a dog, but you ain't never gonna get by a parrot."

"With all that racket he could wake the dead," added Andi laughing.

"Cord," said Peri, extending her hand to scratch the macaw's rainbow belly. "Could Max be a Maxine? Have you had Max surgically sexed? Females are very protective. Is she always this aggressive?"

"No," he answered. "But he, I mean she has a problem with strangers. She always raises all kinds of hell with a stranger. She'll get used to you. Just give her a little time then she'll ignore you. Be careful, Doctor Pepper, Max*ine* can crush a Brazil nut with those jaws."

"Oh, shush. She likes me, see? Does your mother live here?"

"No," Cord said sagaciously. "She has a condo on the ocean in Palm Beach, but ordinarily she wouldn't be way out here at this hour unless something was wrong."

CHAPTER TWENTY-EIGHT

Pend Oreille Ranch
Barrett County, Florida
September 9

Following Cord, they entered the humongous manor. To their right was a large white stone fireplace facing two sides. One side opened into a formal dining room. A long mahogany table that could easily seat 20 sat under a huge crystal chandelier. A wide carpeted spiral staircase wrapped around the fireplace leading both upstairs and down.

The other side of the fireplace faced the largest living room they had ever seen. It was at least 20 feet wide and 40 feet long. To the east side, the entire area was floor to ceiling plate glass windows, exposing a breathtaking view of Matheson Cove as it merged into a lake and then into the Inland Waterway Way. Just outside the tall glass windows a wide veranda wrapped around the eastern exposure looking down on the cove and lake beyond. A small isle was in the center of the lake. A breakfast table and chairs rested on the veranda.

"Can you imagine having breakfast served to you out there with a view like that?" Andi whispered to Peri.

"Not really," Peri shrugged. "My family was poor. Places like this were only in story books."

"Me too," said Andi.

Laying in the middle of a long leather couch, an unimpressed golden retriever was ignoring the new visitors. Cord walked over to the dog. "Bailey, Bailey boy," he said, scratching the animals head. Bailey responded with a small howl and slapped his tail in glee on the expensive couch at the touch of his master's hand. Luke noted a solidly built boathouse on the edge of the cove. Pointing out toward the cove Luke said, "Cord, we are on the second story, didn't we enter at ground level?"

"It can fool you. When my great grandfather and my grandfather first built this place there was a small hill here where they wanted to build the house. In those days, they couldn't get any earth moving machinery out this far. So they built it as you see into the side of the hill. We actually entered from the back of the house, which is at ground level. Out here's the front, second level." He pointed toward the veranda and down to the water beyond. Below Yardboy and two horses were grazing on a two acre lawn of white top clover.

An elderly, rather portly, black lady dressed in a white uniform, adorned with a darker white apron was standing at the edge of the large living room near the kitchen.

"Mista Cordie, yo mama is waitin' in the li-berry."

"Thank you, Miss Julia," said Cord. "We're on the way." He led them to a wide doorway off the dining room and into well-shelved library. The library's walls were lined with tongue-in-groove aspen pine and the room was furnished with a dark brown leather couch and matching recliner chairs. Tan leather armchairs surrounded a conference table. Cord leaned over and kissed his mother.

"Hello, McCord," said an attractive woman sitting in one of the leather chairs. A glass of iced tea was on the coffee table beside her. A note pad rested on her lap. She gazed at Cord and his guests. Raising an eyebrow, she barely nodded toward them asking for an introduction.

"McCord?" Luke laughingly whispered to Andi, who was standing with her mouth agape. "This place is absolutely reeking with money. Mrs. Barrett, she's got to be the poster lady of class and wealth."

"Mother, this is our lead flight attendant, Andrea Marokris," he said, placing his arm around Andi's shoulders, "and my captain, Luke Sellers." Tilting his forehead in Peri's direction, "And last, but certainly not least, this pretty lady is Doctor Peri Pepper. Everyone, this is my mother, Mrs. Sudie Barrett."

Luke had anticipated meeting a slow moving matronly woman with thick glasses in a rocking chair. Instead, he was greeted with a very pretty, nicely figured lady in a tasteful light blue dress. Her hair was mostly silver and perfectly arranged. Her dark eyes reflected a no nonsense tenor and were bright and alert.

Mrs. Barrett's immaculate appearance and formal manner fairly shouted her hierarchy in the Palm Beach aristocracy. Palm Beach, Florida is a town like no other; the winter home of countless millionaires and billionaires. A place where the rich and famous pass for average and not be recognized or just plain ignored. Worth Avenue is Palm Beaches answer to Rodeo Drive in Beverly Hills, it's a place where if you asked the price of something you didn't belong. Thought being, if you had to ask you couldn't afford it.

In an accent, distinctly southern, Mrs. Barrett said in flawless diction, "Captain Sellers, I have heard many nice things about you. Mrs. Marokris, a pleasure. Welcome you all to the Pend Oreille and to the Tidewaters. I hope your stay with us will be enjoyable."

"Thank you, Mrs. Barrett," said Luke. "But the captain, we left back in the airplane. My name is Luke."

"Very well then, Luke. Doctor Pepper, are you a physician?"

The usually quiet and shy Peri took a step toward the dignified lady. "No ma'am, I'm a veterinarian and please call me Peri."

"Fine. Very well Peri, welcome. Welcome all of you."

"Mother is something on your mind?"

"Yes McCord, as a matter of fact, we need to talk. Your guests may join us if they like."

They seated themselves beside the long conference table. Cord gave his mother an inquisitive look.

Looking in Cord's direction, Mrs. Barrett began. "It looks like our headless Indian is back again."

"Yes ma'am, it was on the news in Denver last night," said Cord.

"In Denver? Anyway," she continued, "you know what that means. We'll have everybody and their brother tromping through our land, cutting fences, running the livestock, scattering their trash hither and yon, and Lord knows what else."

"Yes ma'am, especially the news people."

"Somehow this sighting is different McCord. It's not just with the Indians this time. It's been reported by several others. Maybe it's college kids or someone playing what they think is a joke."

"Yes ma'am, I remember a couple years back," said Cord.

"As do I," said Mrs. Barrett sternly. Glancing at the group, she added. "They trashed our land and stole things. Some of our cattle got loose, and they poached the wildlife on the Pend Oreille. It's unbelievable what some people will do!"

Rapping her knuckles on the chair arm, she said, "And another thing, McCord, we don't need any more news people on our property. We don't need the word out any more than it already is."

"Where is most of this going on?" asked Cord.

"On the border of our western pasture—you know where it is, McCord, where our property meets the Everglades." Mrs. Barrett was speaking of the 25,000 acres of pasture land they owned.

"Mother, do you mean Cypress Slough and Moccasin Creek? In that area?"

"Exactly," she snapped. "Old nutty Dave Winslow from over in Clewiston was supposed to have seen it the other night."

"Okay," said Cord, "I'll call Goose tomorrow and we'll go out there and see what we can find."

"I have already called GW. He will be here in first thing in the morning. Be ready, McCord."

"Yes ma'am, okay. We're going to grill a couple steaks and…"

"That's not all, McCord. We have a much bigger problem."

Cord cocked his eyebrow and tilted his head. "We do?"

She glanced toward the three visitors at the table as if reluctant to speak. "I'm afraid so, McCord," she quietly said. "I'm sure your guests will understand and excuse us for a few moments. I will have some drinks sent out to the veranda for them."

Luke picked up the cue and quickly excused himself and led Andi and Peri out to the wide balcony.

Satisfied they were alone Mrs. Barrett continued. "Our Tuscan and Flagstaff banks are showing leaks, huge losses. No telling how many more. I…"

"How bad is it, Mother?"

"We don't know yet. I sent Darcee to Arizona this morning in one of our company jets, but it could be as much as a seven figure deficit."

"Seven figures!" cried Cord. "That's not a leak, that's a damn cascade! How could anyone get our bank codes? No one person knows the both access code numbers and sequence."

Mrs. Barrett raised her eyebrows as if asking a question.

Cord went on. "Those computer codes are supposed to be hack proof. Nobody has access to the computers that allow withdrawal of money, only those that been authorized and use a generated second code. Besides, anyone is going in our offices downstairs they would have to get by the cameras and Max, if it was done from the Tidewaters. You know that's impossible. The bank's system is supposed to be hacker proof. Damn it all, there's something sure as hell wrong here somewhere."

Mrs. Barrett's wrinkled forehead and raised eyebrows told Cord to watch his language.

"I hope Darcee can find the leak. Our main office downtown seems to think it is internal. Someone with inside knowledge is skimming money from us. It's impossible to tell where or how."

"That would take someone with superior computer skills, Mother? I just cannot imagine it being an inside job. We gave our employees a thorough background investigation before hiring them, especially those with powers to make transfers and withdrawals with seven figures."

"Sure, it would. We do have a great secured system. But it is happening."

"Maybe it's just a computer error."

"No, we don't think so, McCord. Too much money is missing."

"Internal, huh? At least you have Darcee working on it. She's a crackerjack accountant and auditor. Darcee will find the problem."

"McCord," she quietly said, "I'm not using Darcee to find the problem."

"You're not?" Cord questioned. "She's the best."

"Maybe she is. But I sent her out there to do an audit so we can find out what and where our losses are.

We will work on finding and fixing the problem here at our corporate headquarters and home offices."

"How?"

"I've hired Michelle Stewart and Associates out of Lakeland."

"And?"

"And they are excellent and a very reputable accounting firm. Furthermore, they have no interest in BDI aside from banking with us in Orlando."

Cord gave an incredulous look. "Why can't our own people handle this? We have expert investigators and security agents already on the payroll especially trained for this kind of thing."

"I know, McCord. But I think it best we have someone from outside BDI; someone who has no affiliation with BDI or any of our corporations or holdings." Cord was silent. Mrs. Barrett looked at him. "It's getting later than I intended to stay, so I'll say good night."

Mrs. Barrett stepped on the balcony. Smiling at the guests, she said, "It's been a pleasure. Please enjoy your stay with us." They all thanked her and smiled back.

"I'll have Mister Ironside see you out," said Cord.

"One more thing, McCord."

"Yes ma'am?"

"Have you been informed that Doctor Lee is retiring at the end of the year?"

"Senior? The Real Doctor Lee?"

Cord was referring to the ranch veterinarian; Doctor Robert Lee had been the chief veterinarian at the Pend Oreille for 34 years. His son, Robert Junior, also a veterinarian, had grown up on the ranch and was retained on a part time basis. Young Robert, an excellent and highly skilled doctor was often subject of the good-natured teasing of the ranch hands as the, "Young Doctor Lee." His experienced father as the, "Real Doctor Lee." The young Lee smiled and took the ribbing in stride. Most of the ranch personnel had known him since he was a boy. The teasing was respectful and in good spirits.

"Of course, the senior Doctor Lee," answered Mrs. Barrett.

"What about our other three vets?"

"As you know, McCord, they are all contracted and on an as needed basis. Dr. Lee senior is the only one on permanent staff."

"Yes ma'am."

"It's up to you and Henry, but I don't think I would offer the position to any of them except Bobby, Doctor Lee Junior."

"I don't think he would be interested in a full time position way out here, Mother. Bobby has a busy practice in West Palm Beach as it is."

"Like I said, it's up to you and Henry. You've got a few months to fill the position. It's getting late. Give Bobby Lee a call, see if he's interested."

Cord stood, as did the others, "I'll get Mister Ironside."

An aging black man in a white vest and a shock of white hair appeared in the doorway. He was stooped in the shoulders and his movements were slow. His deep brown eyes showed ages of wisdom.

"Mister Ironside, would you kindly show Mrs. Barrett to her car please?"

The old man nodded. "Certainly. A pleasure, suh."

Cord departed the library and gathered his guests in the living room. He stepped into a sunken bar and prepared everyone a drink.

"Your mom is quite the lady," said Andi.

"She certainly is," replied Cord, poking at an ice cube in his scotch. "But don't let that Palm Beach demeanor of hers fool you. She's a pretty tough old bird. I've seen her out there on horseback penning cattle, roping calves, mending fences and everything else right beside Big Fred in storms, hurricanes, summer heat, you name it."

"She would have fooled me," commented Luke. Then he whispered to Andi. "Would you have ever thought Cord came from this kind of moolah?"

"Never.   Never in a million years," she whispered.

After a welcome drink, Cord and Peri walked to the rear of the kitchen where Cord opened a walk in cooler.

"This is a first for me," said Peri.

"First what?"

"First time I have ever walked into a refrigerator!"

"Oh, that," he said laughing. "At one time we had to feed a lot of people here on the Pend Oreille before we built the employee housing. So my dad had it built large enough to hang beef. When it gets low, we have a steer sent up, same with pork and poultry. These are for vegetables, dairy, and so on." Cord tapped one of the long shelves lining each side of the fridge.

"Mista Cordie, you come out dat ice box raat now," said Miss Julia's stern voice. "And don you be tracking up my floor neither, else I'll take a hairbrush to yo backside jest like I did yo daddy."

"Yes ma'am, yes ma'am, Miss Julia," said Cord. "She likes to be bossy," he whispered in Peri's ear.

"I done got yo steaks, they's on the counter there. And I lit the grill too. Lordy, Lordy, if yo company had to wait on you they'd starve to deff."

Cord and Peri joined the others on the veranda by the grill. Cord put on the steaks. Luke looked up from his lounge chair out over the peaceful cove and river. "I say, Spark Plug; I find it awfully hard to feel sorry for you."

"It's a tough life, especially when I have to fly with some of you ball-busting captains."

Luke laughed and pointed to the water. "Is that the same Matheson Cove?"

"Actually, it is. But it broadens out here quite a bit, a couple miles wide I guess. So it's really a lake, not a cove. We call it Lake Immokalee."

"Immokalee?"

"It's a Seminole word, means 'my home.'"

"Cord," said Peri, "are Miss Julia and Mister Ironside still working?"

"Lord no, Doctor Pepper. My dad retired them years ago, but they just kept coming to work. Miss Julia still won't allow anyone in her kitchen. Shoot, they've been here at the Pend Oreille long before I was even thought about. Mister Ironside was quite a rugged cowboy back in his day."

"I guess they have been your family's servants for years and years," said Andi.

"We don't have servants on the Pend Oreille, Andi. We have employees," Cord flatly stated.

Peri liked the way Cord affectionately referred to them. She also liked the way he preserved their dignity, always addressing them as Miss and Mister, as did Mrs. Barrett. Peri was quickly becoming more and more enchanted with this handsome pilot, Cord Barrett.

"Spark Plug, I didn't realize that Florida was such a big beef producer."

"Are you kidding, Cap? I know you're a Texan, so don't take offense, but Florida is a huge agricultural state. Most people think of Florida as Disneyworld or beaches, surfing and the like. Truth is Florida was the number one state in beef production for years and years." Luke gave a surprised shrug.

After dinner and a few drinks later, Luke said. "It's been one helluva day. Think I'm about ready to turn in."

"Me too," echoed Andi.

"Of course," said Cord. "Mister Ironside will show you to your rooms. How about you, Doctor Pepper? Would you like to call your sister?"

Peri replied with a soft, "It's late, I'll try later."

"Are you ready to retire for the night, Doctor Pepper?"

"No, if you're going to stay up for a while I'll stay with you. And it's Peri, pleeezz!"

CHAPTER TWENTY-NINE

Flagstaff, Arizona
September 9

It had been a long day for Darcee too. She was tired. Darcee had spent the day pouring through volumes of computer records in the Barrett Bank of Tucson. There was no leak to be found, but the bank was still showing a million dollar shortage. It has to be somewhere. Because Darcee had done such an excellent job by her frugal bookkeeping skills and had introduced many ways to save the company's money, she had been sent to Arizona by Mrs. Barrett. She was trusted and had a reputation of being highly skilled accountant and loyal employee.

Darcee Anne Corbin had been with BDI for only six months. She had been hired by Cord to handle the bookkeeping and household affairs of the Tidewaters. She had strategically engineered her employment by making herself available and being noticed at various functions and events in Palm Beach and barbeques at the ranch, especially when she knew Cord would be attending.

It was difficult for Darcee not to be noticed. She was a tall woman standing five feet ten inches and in low heels an even six feet. Her dark red hair, piercing green eyes along with her perfect figure emphasized by the amplest bosom made Darcee very noticeable indeed.

It had not taken Cord long to eye the stunning redhead. Her carefully calculated plans to wriggle her way into his employ and soon after into his bed fell right into place. They kept the affair quiet, but their secret was hardly a secret around the Pend Oreille and certainly no secret within the walls of the Tidewaters.

Darcee loved everything about Pend Oreille and the picture perfect beauty of the ranch with its sleepy cypress trees, the old oaks and weeping willows with the Spanish moss swaying softly in the gentle Florida breeze. Darcee relished being in such a lovely place and the friendly people. She especially loved the animals.

Her favorite was Max, the parrot that took an instant affection to Darcee. Max would hop on her perch and bob her head with glee at the sight of Darcee. She was often seen around the ranch with the macaw perched happily on her shoulder gobbling the ample inventory of sunflower seeds she always carried. Darcee would ball her fist and place the seeds on top while extending out her arm. Max would attack the sunflower seeds with lightning speed never nipping her or breaking the skin. It was an amazing show enjoyed by the ranch visitors and personnel and quite a love affair between the bird and the beauty.

Earlier that evening the company jet, a Falcon 50, had flown Darcee from Tucson to Flagstaff. She kicked off her pumps and stretched out in her room in the local Hilton. After pouring a drink from the handy bar, she stared at the ceiling deep in thought. She made a decision.

Darcee quickly walked over and opened her laptop. She pulled up, search, and hit the enter key. Soon under a heading, she saw **Cheech & Chong**. She read the blog. "Excellent." She uttered. Darcee dialed the number listed.

Darcee drove her rented Lincoln out of the Hilton on Forest Meadow Road to Route 66. She turned northwest on the Fort Valley Highway toward Grand Canyon National Park and turned left on Bonito Street. She turned left again on Aspen Drive and soon found the address she was looking for. The directions she had been given on the phone were perfect. Darcee rang the doorbell and was greeted by a nice looking gentleman.

"Are you Cheech or Chong?" she asked.

He laughed. "I'm Chong. Cheech will be right out." Just as he spoke, a slender attractive brown-haired woman appeared near the foyer.

She smiled broadly. "Come in, come in, please," she said. "You must be the Red Baroness."

"Yes, both north and south. You must be Cheech."

They all laughed. Cheech said, "I'm Cheech. I'm just putting a few things on the table. Have you had supper yet?" Darcee shook her head no. "Well then come join us, there's plenty."

Darcee, not looking forward to dining alone in the hotel's restaurant and readily accepted the invitation. After an excellent dinner, Darcee joined Cheech and Chong in the den of their stylish home. A warm fire was burning. The conversation was light and friendly.

After several drinks and a few joints, Chong stretched his arms above his head. He said to Darcee, "You've had too much to drink to be driving. Stay with us tonight. We have plenty of room and you will find the guest room very comfortable." He showed her to a large tastefully furnished bedroom.

Alone, Darcee pulled back the queen-size eider down and looked about the room.

Very nice.

Stripping off her clothes, she opened the door of the guest room and walked naked down the hall. Darcee entered the master bedroom through the open door. Cheech and Chong, both nude, eyed her.

Tossing the blanket aside, she said. "Move over. Didn't we agree? I get the middle."

CHAPTER THIRTY

Ensenada, Mexico
September 10

In a luxurious and well-fortified hacienda just outside Tijuana, Mexico, El Diablo's lieutenant was typing. After entering in the computer several secret routing codes through Eastern Europe, South America and Asia to guarantee clandestine communication, he typed in:

"State net from Barrett Banks, Arizona into temporary account."

The answer came back swiftly. *"3 million."*

"Exactly as planned." The lieutenant replied. *"Deposit 1.5 in Georgetown, Cayman's, account and 1.5 in Geneva, Switzerland, account."*

"Understood. Will wire transfer immediately."

He entered a new set of routing codes.

Soon after, The Contractor received a message that read:

"Sources inform Florida project not completed. Explain—"

Again, the response was swift. *"Circumstances not good. Many obstacles. Job completion pending working conditions tomorrow."*

"Okay—But do not test boss' patience. Stand by for new assignment."

The Contractor did not have long to wait.

"New assignment: Nigel Birmingham, account manager, Georgetown. Günter Steinberg, acct mgr. & CEO. Geneva. ASAP."

The lieutenant read the answer. *"Overseas—Fee is twice over."*

"Done," he wrote back and closed the computer.

Darcee sipped vodka and tonic as the Barrett Falcon jetted across the dark Oklahoma sky. The effort to find the leak and complete the audit at two banks had exhausted her not to mention the sleepless night she shared with Cheech and Chong. Still there was no evidence as to where the leak was and how someone had been able to tap into the bank codes. But someone somewhere was siphoning large sums of money from the Barrett's.

She was not looking forward to the work ahead at the four Barrett banks, two in Nashville and two in Atlanta. Darcee reclined the seat back. She stretched out her arms and cracked her knuckles. Sticking a yellow pencil behind her ear, she reached for her laptop.

Let's see—whom do I know in Nashville?

CHAPTER THIRTY-ONE

Pend Oreille Ranch
September 9

"C'mon, Doctor Pepper, let me show you something," said Cord. She followed him out the back door in the rear of the kitchen and down some steep stairs. They emerged into a long recreation room. Peri saw a pool table in the center of the room and a Ping-Pong table was folded against the wall next to a wet bar complete with a beer tap. A fireplace was on the opposite side of the room. The east side of the room was enclosed with jalousie windows. Cord grasped her hand in his and led Peri past a stand-up juke box near the screen door leading out to a wide ten-acre lawn.

The firmness of Cord's hand sent a rushing chill through her body.

No one has ever had this effect on me before—

"Where are we going, Cord?"

"You'll see, Doctor Pepper. Look at that moon," he said pointing to the large golden orb rising above the lake.

"Oooh, just look at that," she whispered.

"We can't waste a pretty night like this can we, Doctor Pepper?" He gave her hand a slight squeeze. Peri moved closer to him and slipped her arm through his. Her breast rested lightly against him. Cord pretended he didn't notice. She knew he did.

The couple walked by the sleepy horses that were ignoring them. Yardboy didn't. He fell in behind Cord wishfully hoping for a treat. He pushed his head against Peri's behind lurching her forward.

"Yardboy, stop that!" said Cord laughing, thumping the little bull on the nose. "Sorry, Doctor Pepper, he doesn't know his strength. He thinks he's a lapdog." Cord reached in his pocket and handed Peri two lumps of sugar. "Here, give these to him."

"Are those working horses?" she asked holding a sugar cube in the flat of her hand for the little Hereford.

"Hardly, we rarely use horses anymore. Those two are just pets. We keep them up here for the kids because they are so gentle."

"Gentle?"

"Yeah, the kids climb all over them. No saddles are allowed on those ponies. If they fall off the worst thing that can happen is a lump on the noggin."

They both laughed and came to a long boardwalk. "Where does this go?" she asked, as they walked out on a wide wooden pier.

"It goes out on the lake a couple hundred yards." Pointing to his right, Cord said. "That's Lake Immokalee and it bends around a little to the west up there," he pointed again.

"And over here?" Peri nodded to her left.

"That—Doctor Pepper is the beginning of the enchanting Florida Everglades."

They stood hand in hand in silence for a while. "Oh Cord, I have never seen anything so beautiful."

Cord bent close to her, so close his lips were only inches from hers. "You're right, Doctor Pepper," he said, staring into her eyes. "I have never seen anything so beautiful either."

Cord softly touched his lips to hers. He held her firmly pulling her body against his own. She felt his muscular body and strong arms around her. Peri felt a rush starting at the bottom of her feet racing through her body and exploding through the top of her head like a hurtling tsunami.

Breaking from the lingering kiss, she was barely able to breathe, "Cord, I, uh…"

"Shhh, no need to talk, Doctor Pepper. I've wanted to do that since I first saw you in Denver."

Peri sheepishly looked at her feet. "Me too," she barely uttered.

Noticing Cord glancing at his watch, Peri said, "It's getting late maybe we should go."

"No hurry, Doctor Pepper. We have the whole night if we want."

"Isn't your friend supposed to be here in the morning? GW is it?"

Cord didn't answer. He leaned against the railing staring into the reeds and cattails. The Spanish moss was slightly blowing in the cypress trees waving over the lily pads. Slivers of moonlight danced on the surface like wriggling yellow ribbons. The vibrato of a thousand crickets and other swamp critters filled the night with their symphony of music each singing and voicing its own aria.

Cord was silent for a long time. Lifting his chin toward the peaceful quagmire, he quietly said. "He's here."

"Here? He's here? Who's here?"

"Shhh, Doctor Pepper, listen."

"I don't hear anything."

Again, Cord didn't answer. Peering through the darkness lit only by the moon, Cord cried out, "Goose." His voice ricocheted into the endless morass followed by a deafening silence. Peri cocked her head sideways wondering what on earth Cord was up to.

Goose? A goose? A goose is here?

A minute passed, Cord called again. "Goose, I know you're out there."

"Cordie, where did you find such a pretty lady?" called a voice from the darkness.

Peri strained her eyes through the dim light then suddenly she saw a movement. A ghost-like phantom was silently moving toward them. It seemed to be floating.

"C'mon Goose get up here. What are you doing out there at this hour?"

"Hello, Cordie. And who might this be?" said the ghost hoisting himself over the railing and onto the wooden walkway.

Smiling, Cord said, "Goose, meet Doctor Peri Pepper. Doctor Pepper, this is Special Agent George Washington Wildgoose of the FBI."

Peri stuck out her hand. Taking it, Wildgoose said, "Doctor Pepper is it? I thought you came in a bottle or a can?"

Peri held her index finger up by her face and raised her eyebrows. "First time today!" she exclaimed, "and please, call me Peri."

Peri stuttered, thrusting a finger toward the swamp. "Why... ah, how is it you didn't make any sound?"

Wildgoose smiled widely and held up his hand like he was taking an oath. "How Kimosabe. Because me Seminole. Me make-um no noise in big swamp. But me speak good white man tongue."

"Knock it off, Goose," said Cord, to his tall friend. George Washington Wildgoose was a fine specimen of a natural athlete. His brown body was finely tuned with muscle and agility. His jet-black hair was combed straight back and tied in a ponytail. His piercing black eyes could stare through marble. A handsome man, he was indeed.

"Do you go by George?" Peri asked.

"Nah, usually GW. Cord and my old schoolmates still call me Goose, but I'll answer to most anything."

"Okay GW," she said.

"Actually, I was named after a president. Bet you can't guess which one."

Peri rolled her eyes. "Why couldn't we hear you walking through the water?"

"Because he didn't want you to," blurted Cord, before Wildgoose could answer. "Besides, Doctor Pepper, he already answered you. He is a Seminole, one-hundred percent."

"But still, I don't understand how anyone could…"

"Don't ask, Doctor Pepper, I've never figured it out either," said Cord. "The Seminoles just do it. They appear out of nothing and disappear into nothing. They are like vapor and damned if any of them will tell you a thing."

"Are we on for tomorrow, Goose?"

"Yes. Your mother called me earlier. I'll meet you here at first light." Cord nodded.

Wildgoose's father, Gary Wildgoose, was a partner of Cord's uncle, Ted Barrett, who was the senior partner of a prestigious law firm with offices in Palm Beach and Washington DC. Cord and Wildgoose had grown up together and been best friends since boyhood.

When Cord left to attend Florida State University, GW had been offered a football scholarship at the Naval Academy. After graduation and a stint in the Marine Corps, he was commissioned by the FBI and was now the federal agent for the Florida Seminole and Missaukee tribes on the Big Cypress Indian Reservation in south central Florida.

For the most part, the Seminole Indians are very xenophobic and kept the whites at a respectable distance; not sharing in the white man's ways or his culture. To this day, the Seminole is extremely recalcitrant and maintains a stubborn resistance to white authority.

Contrarily, the Wildgoose family and other members of the tribe accepted the influx of the modern acculturation and assumed productive and responsible positions in the avant-garde world encompassing them.

Looking out over Lake Immokalee, Wildgoose gestured and said. "Cord, keep an eye on your lady friend. Old Goliath is out and about tonight."

"Thanks, Goose. We saw him coming in. Stay up here on the boardwalk, Doctor Pepper, and you'll be fine."

Smiling at Peri, Wildgoose said, "Yeah, big alligators like Old Goliath love to eat pretty little lady doctors." Peri cringed. "Goliath is no problem, Cord. But we have something else."

"Som-thin' else, Goose?"

"We have a prowler on the Pend Oreille."

"A prowler? Here?"

"I think so. A white man."

"Where?"

"Can't say for sure, where he is now, Cord. But, we definitely have some kind of intruder about. I spotted him earlier and there is a dark green economy car stuffed in behind some cabbage palms near the south entrance."

"Maybe a poacher, Goose?"

"No. Not with that kind of rifle. He's no poacher."

CHAPTER THIRTY-TWO

Miami International Airport
September 9

Late that night a figure walked briskly through the airport pulling a flight case on top of an overnight bag. The figure was immaculately attired in a tailored navy blue uniform clearly showing as a pilot with Trans Global Airlines. Three stripes were displayed boldly on the sleeves and the gold wings on the chest clearly indicated a position as a flight officer.

Unwaveringly, the figure walked past the various ticket counters and rental car booths and made its way directly to the elevators. Exiting the elevator on the ground level and headed to the TGI crew room. At this late hour, there would be only a few crew members napping about waiting on their outgoing flights. On late nights, there would only be a skeleton crew managing the operations and dispatch desks. They wouldn't notice anyone dressed in uniform. In a company the size of TGI, it was not uncommon to see someone they didn't know.

The figure tapped in the entrance code on an unmarked door walked boldly into the crew lounge and went directly to the scheduling itinerary posted on the wall near the operations desk. Running a finger down the list then nodded its head then walked over and studied the weather computer. Apparently satisfied with what was seen, the figure pulled the cart over to the flight bag rack lined with identical black cases. Gripping the flight bag and heaved it up on the rack. The figure spent a few moments fumbling through the bag. Making sure no one was paying any attention the figure quickly opened the flight bag next to the one brought.

The nameplate on the bag read: *McCord Barrett*.

CHAPTER THIRTY-THREE

Pend Oreille Ranch
September 10

Early the next morning, Cord and Wildgoose were loading Cord's truck with camping gear. Peri called out from behind them. "Are you two going camping?"

Startled, Cord said, "Doctor Pepper, what are you doing up so early?"

"I heard you and thought I would see what you guys were up to."

"No good as usual," laughed Wildgoose.

"Are you going camping?" she asked again.

"Not unless we have to," replied Cord. "We're going out to find poor headless Osceola, but we'll probably be back tonight."

Narrowing his eyes Wildgoose said, "Cord, I wouldn't make light of it, especially about things you don't know and that you don't understand."

"Goose, for Pete's sake you are a graduate of the Naval Academy and an FBI Agent," exclaimed Cord, tossing an ice chest on the truck. "Ghosts? You're smarter than that Goose."

Wildgoose's voice took a sober tone. "I'm smart enough to know there are things that we shouldn't be messing with. And I'm smart enough to know there are many surreptitious mysteries with the Seminoles."

"C'mon, Goose, that's a load of horseshit. Get in the truck."

Looking at Peri, and noticing her quizzical look Wildgoose tried to explain. "A lot of eerie and strange things happen in the Everglades." He paused, his voice dropped an octave, "Weird things—weird things that nobody can explain." He climbed into the pick-up.

"Hey, wait a minute. I want to go with you. Can I?" asked Peri pleadingly.

"No, of course not," Cord exclaimed. "Seminole Slough is no place for a woman. Just stay here at the Tidewaters. There's lots of things to do."

"Oh, yeah," she retorted. "I can be just as tough as you are, Mister McCord Smarty-Pants Barrett!"

Laughing, Wildgoose said, "You will have to pee in the woods."

Peri placed her hands on her hips. Tilting her head to one side, she declared, "I'm a country girl, you think it will be the first time I've ever had to pee in the woods? Ha!"

Seeing that an argument would be futile, Cord disgustingly sighed and said, "I see you learn your lessons the hard way, Doctor Pepper. Okay, go get your stuff, but no special concessions just because you are a girl."

"A girl? Ha!" she snorted. "Just give me a minute. Oh, but what about Captain Sellers and Andi?"

"I had Paco drive them to the airport this morning. Paco needs to pick up his car anyway. C'mon, step on it, Doctor Pepper, you're burning daylight."

Cord eased the Ford onto State Highway 441, following it around the south side of Lake Okeechobee until they came to Farm Road 9. Turning south several miles, Cord pointed to an almost invisible trail leading into the dense foliage and said, "Goose isn't this the way to the slough?"

"I'm pretty sure it is, Cord. Better put her into four-wheel."

The ride on the trail was rough and bumpy at best, reminding Peri of what it must be like to be a bronc rider in the rodeo. After driving a few miles into the swampy area, Cord pulled into a large peninsula-like clearing. Once stopped, Peri opened her door to get out.

"Wait, stop!" exclaimed Wildgoose.

"What?"

"Look around you, Doctor Pepper."

"What?" she repeated. "I don't see anything."

"Take a look at those two bumps in the sawgrass beside your door?"

"Yeah, so?"

Wildgoose didn't answer. He exited the truck and walked around to Peri's side. Picking up a good-sized rock, he said. "See anything now, Doctor Pepper?"

"See what?" she said, exhaling and staring out the window at the dense jungle.

Instead of answering the veterinarian, Wildgoose ran toward the two bumps making a kick at them as if he were a football place kicker.

A loud, angry hiss and the distinctive sound of alligator jaws slamming together filled their ears. A large dark tail swung fiercely at Wildgoose, who barely jumped out of its way. Wildgoose let out a shout and waving his arms toward the creature, he bounced the rock off the reptile's snout with a well-placed throw. Knowing that discretion was, for the moment, the better part of valor, the alligator retreated and splashed headlong into the water.

"Holy moly!" cried Peri. "That was a real alligator! A real great big alligator!"

"Aw, not all that big, Doctor Pepper, a seven, maybe an eight footer," said Wildgoose. "Most likely a female and she's probably nesting on some eggs up here close to shore."

"Isn't she dangerous?"

"Hell yes, she's dangerous," spoke up Cord. "But don't worry about Goose; he's been playing with those things his whole life. In fact, he is almost a real Seminole."

"I am real and one hundred percent Seminole," said Wildgoose proudly.

"Nah, you're only part Seminole, Goose. A real Seminole would have jumped on that gator's back and wrestled her into the water."

"Shiiit," sighed Wildgoose, "in your dreams, Barrett." They all laughed. "What say we take a look around? Somebody left a tent and all kinds of stuff over there." He pointed to the tent and gear abandoned by Dave and Rita in their hasty departure.

"Let's go," said Cord getting out of the truck and opening Peri's door. "Doctor Pepper, better stick close to one of us. They don't call that Moccasin Creek for nothing, and there's plenty of gators around." He nodded towards a freshwater creek slowly flowing beside the peninsula.

Stick close to one of them—No worries there—

The Everglades Cottonmouth Water Moccasin can be a dangerous adversary indeed. One of the few reptilian species that will not retreat and has been known to actually pursue opponents. Bites from a moccasin can be extremely venomous.

Cord led Peri over to the point of the peninsula and pointed. "Someone built a fire here no more than a day or two ago."

"Cord is this the Everglades?" she indicated to her left.

"Yep, you're right in the middle of them, Doctor Pepper. That's Moccasin Creek behind you."

Peri looked out over the vast compendious view. The light disappearing into the swampy foliage highlighted the lazy cypress trees with their Spanish moss dangling was breathtaking. Colorful water lilies floated nearby.

"Oh Cord; I never knew the Everglades were so incredibly beautiful."

"They are. But we try to keep it a secret."

"Why?"

"That question should answer itself, Doctor Pepper. We don't want people down here stomping around, throwing their trash out and ruining everything. We want it left just like the Good Lord made it."

"That makes sense, Cord."

She said alarmingly, "Where is GW?"

"Goose? You just now noticed he's gone? He's out there somewhere," said Cord, gesturing toward the swampy jungle.

"I, ahh…I didn't see or hear him leave," she said.

Cord laughed. "You never will."

They drove deeper into the Everglades and stopped as the darkness began to settle on Seminole Slough. Cord said, "Goose we'll better start a campfire and get the tent up while we still have some light. We need to draw our ghost out as soon as we can."

Looking at Peri and gesturing, "Doctor Pepper, there's some insect repellent in the truck. No shortage of mosquitoes out here at night."

"Thanks. Is there enough for you and GW too?"

"No problem. I have on long sleeves and don't fret about Goose. For some reason mosquitoes and gnats, things like that, won't bite an Indian. Before you ask, I don't know why; they just don't."

The three sat around the fire and enjoyed a supper of venison and potatoes they had brought from the ranch. As darkness engulfed their small camp, it was interrupted by slivers of moonlight dancing on the mire.

"It's getting late," said Cord. "I think maybe we should turn in and try to get a little sleep." Everyone agreed. "Doctor Pepper, you sleep in the truck. There is a blanket in the back and the seat folds down. You should be comfortable. Goose and I will stay out here in the tent."

"What's wrong, GW?" said Peri.

Wildgoose didn't change his meditative expression. He shook his head without answering. Something troubling was on his mind. He said, "Let's take a look around before we turn in."

The group walked down to the water's edge and gazed over the stillness of the marshy panorama just as the evening fog was beginning to settle, pointing to a tiny green root structure at the base of a cypress. Peri said, "How beautiful, what is that?"

"That Doctor Pepper is one of the things that makes the Glades famous. What you're looking at is a Phantom Orchid," Cord said with an awed reverence. "The real name for them is Ghost Orchid, but down here we have always called them Phantom Orchids."

"A Phantom what?"

"It's a Phantom Orchid, indigenous only here in the Everglades. It has no leaves, only a thread-thin root, which is invisible unless you really look closely. So, when it blooms you can't see the root. The flowers just seem to float in midair. That's why it is called a Phantom."

"Oh."

"If we weren't so deep in the Glades," said Cord, "there are often security cameras nearby. Those things are fiercely protected both by the state and the feds."

"What about these others?" she asked waving a hand.

"Those are orchids too. There are many kinds. What you are seeing are Ribbon orchids, Jingle Bell orchids, and that one over there is called a Butterfly orchid."

"So beautiful and so mysterious," she murmured.

"There's a lot of mysteries in the Everglades and most of them are hidden in plain sight," said Wildgoose.

They stood in silence for a long time each with their own thoughts. The fog was getting thicker by the minute. Wildgoose waved his hand in front of them. "Hush—Listen."

They listened to the dead stillness of the evening. "I don't hear anything, Goose."

"That's my point. There is no sound. No crickets, no frogs, no gator grunts, no night swamp critters, no nothing. Just silence."

Without looking around or changing his stare, which was fixed on the descending fog, Wildgoose squinted past the trees and flaccid moss. He said, "Cord, take your lady-friend back to the truck and lock it."

"Why? What's going on, Goose?"

"Don't ask, just do it—something is coming...," he murmured. "Something evil."

CHAPTER THIRTY-FOUR

Seminole Slough
September 10

No one questioned Wildgoose. Cord put his arm around Peri's shoulders and made a step toward the pick-up. That's when they heard it. A shriek so loud they cupped their hands over their ears to squelch the deafening scream.

Instantly, Cord spun around. Charging toward the swamp, he yelled, "What the fuck was that?"

Cord was barely ankle deep at the edge of the water when Wildgoose suddenly grabbed his shirt and yanked him backwards. "No! Wait, Cord. Stop!"

"What, Goose?" He yelled. "Let go!"

"No, Cord, look!"

Inches from Cord's boots the dark tea-colored water showed nothing distinguishable. "Oh, my gosh! Quicksand?" Cord exclaimed.

Wildgoose said, "Damn right it is. Get your ass out of there."

"But, Goose..."

"No buts, Barrett." Pointing to the quicksand he said, "You never know where that crap starts or where it ends. Get out of there now!"

Peri stood rigid as if frozen in time.

How does he know? I can't see any difference in the water.

Quicksand is another one of the arcane mysteries secreted in the Florida Everglades. A colloid hydrogel, quicksand's menace is its deceptive resemblance to solid ground giving it a shaky soil-like quivering appearance, often called jelly mud, or quivering earth, by some of the Glades people. Unlike regular mud, which compresses to support weight this quandary collapses easily and is bottomless. Once a doomed animal, and sometimes a person is trapped in quicksand's vise-grip snare escape is impossible and their fate is sealed.

Cord and Peri made their way back to the fire followed by Wildgoose, who remained a few yards behind. Wildgoose was backing away from the swamp, his eyes glued on the now barely visible morass. He saw nothing, but the dense fog closing in on them.

Wildgoose built up the campfire until it was a blaze of licking orange flames lashing into the darkness like whips. A thick fog had settled in all around as they sat talking by the fire.

"Whatever it is out there or whatever made that scream its damn sure, not human or animal," said Cord.

"I've never heard anything so loud," said Peri. "And so frightening," she added gulping in a huge gasp of air and sipping her coffee.

"I have already warned you both," Wildgoose said profoundly. "Things happen out here you just can't explain with logic or science."

"Oh, Goose," Cord groaned. "Don't start that ghost rigmarole again."

Wildgoose whispered. "Cord, I'm telling you, and I'm telling you too, Doctor Pepper; some things just shouldn't be messed with. Something or someone has disturbed Chief Osceola's rest and he's here." Wildgoose paused a long time. "He's here."

The three sat around the fire for the next two hours. Finally, Cord yawned. "It's late. Nothing is going to happen tonight, let's try to get a little sleep. We'll get up in the morning and…"

Cord stopped talking in mid-sentence. Both men looked at Peri, who was sitting facing the swamp. Her mouth was wide agape and her eyes were the size of saucers. Both spun around aghast at the sight before them.

Barely visible through the soupy fog the creature stood motionless. Easily ten feet tall and was stone still. It was attired in Seminole wardress and blood streaked down the torso of its headless body. For a moment, the intruders of Seminole Slough stood frozen trying to grasp and comprehend the stunning sight before them. Gathering his wits, Cord eased toward his truck. Finding a pistol, he turned and charged toward the silhouette.

"No! No Cord. No!" bellowed Wildgoose.

His warning was too slow. Cord was charging at the ghost and was within a few feet when it vanished. The creature evaporated into the thick soupy mist of the swamp as instantly as it had appeared.

The bewildered three searched the area. "It's no use," said Cord. "We'll never find anything. This flashlight is useless and all we got is the moon."

"The headlights from the truck aren't doing us any good either," commented Wildgoose. "Let's wait until morning."

Wildgoose smiled at Peri. "You still don't mind peeing in the woods, Doctor Pepper?"

"No need. I already peed my pants."

CHAPTER THIRTY-FIVE

Florida Everglades near Seminole Slough
September 10

"What the hell was that?" exclaimed Steve Garrett, looking up from the beer he was stocking in the refrigerator.

"Damned if I know," said Bill Fletcher. "I've been around these Glades my whole life and I never heard anything like that."

"You suppose it was a panther?"

"I dunno, Steve. I never heard a panther scream like that. Have you?"

"No, never."

The two crop dusters, close friends of Cord, had earlier flown their small plane to a hunting camp less than a mile from Seminole Slough, landing on the only dry ground available, barely 1,000 feet of dry grass running beside the camp. Close but not really a challenge for a skilled pilot. A hunting camp in the Florida Everglades could be anything from a pitched tent to a lean-to. This camp was different and quite luxurious by camping standards.

It stood tucked away on high ground and back into a hammock of hardwood trees and was surrounded by cypress, sable and cabbage palms. The lodge was barely visible unless one knew where to look and was sheltered by a canopy of tall hardwood trees and the ever-present dangling moss. The building was constructed from lumber brought in by airboat and was fully furnished with tables and chairs. A solid tin roof protected the building from the rain and elements. There were sleeping quarters. Propane gas fueled the stove and a generator, which provided electricity for the fridge and lights.

"We'd better get this place ready," said Steve. "Cord called the other day from Texas or somewhere and we're all supposed to meet out here next week."

"Yeah, okay, but don't you want to know what made that awful scream?"

"Sure, do but not bad enough to go out there in the dark and check."

"Me either."

"Say, Bill didn't you bring a rifle?"

"Yeah, it's in the airplane."

"Oh, that's just great," Steve sighed. "What if we need it?"

As the two friends talked, a sleek figure floated across the murky surface. Sheltered by the dense fog, it glided effortlessly not making a sound.

Standing outside the lodge, it waited.

CHAPTER THIRTY-SIX

Seminole Slough
September 11

After a breakfast of scrambled eggs and bacon cooked by Wildgoose over the campfire, they spent the morning making an exhaustive combing of the area. The searchers found no trace of anything.

"Give it up, Cordie, we're never going to find anything," Wildgoose quietly said.

"There's got to be. Anything like that can't just appear and vanish. There's got to be something somewhere."

"Give it up, Cord. It was Osceola, plain and simple."

"Dammit, Goose, you know better than that. Osceola is dead as a doorknob. There's no such thing as ghosts. Whatever is out here is manmade, and I'm going to find it."

Wildgoose's voice took on a staid tone. "Cord, I wouldn't curse the spirits if I were you. It is not wise to run afoul of those in the afterlife."

"Oh Goose, please!" Looking at Peri, he said, "Doctor Pepper, you're a doctor, a scientist for Pete's sake, tell him. This voodoo ghost hullabaloo is all a stack of horseshit."

Peri furrowed her eyebrows together and brought her hands up to her waist. "I don't know, Cord," she nodded toward Wildgoose. "Like he said, a lot of things happened out here that can't be explained. I just don't know."

"Oh, Doctor Pepper, not you too," groaned Cord.

He shook his head. "Okay, let's go. Goose, as soon as you can get reception on your cell phone, call your dad. Maybe he can shed some light on all this. I need to see my Uncle Ted any way."

Cord looked at Peri. "Get a move on, Doctor Pepper. You're burning daylight."

CHAPTER THIRTY-SEVEN

West Palm Beach, Florida
September 11

Three hours later, they arrived in West Palm Beach. Cord steered the Ford from Okeechobee Road onto Waterway Drive paralleling the Intracoastal Waterway. A few blocks later, he pulled into the parking lot of the BDI corporate office complex. The Barrett Banks home office building rising ten floors stood adjacent on the opposite end of the complex.

Peri followed Cord and Wildgoose through the bank's lobby to the elevators. Exiting on the tenth floor, she asked. "Is all this your uncle's law office?"

"One of them," answered Cord. "They have the whole top floor."

Crossing the spacious reception area, they paused at a large horseshoe reception desk. "Hello Margaret, is my uncle available?" Cord said to a gray-haired woman who was briskly routing calls to the various offices.

"Yes, I believe he's in his office. Go right in."

Cord nodded his thanks and led them down a long hallway adorned on both sides with various degrees and awards. The trio entered a large corner office with a commanding view. Peri's attention was captured by the stunning panoramic scene. She gazed through the wide glass windows overlooking the Intracoastal Waterway and the luxurious mansions of Palm Beach. The blue Atlantic displayed its white-capped waves beyond.

A man looking a great deal like an older Cord sat behind a wide cherry wood desk a pair of reading glasses hung from his neck. Ted stood immediately as the three entered the office. His hair was streaked with silver. Ted's sleeves were rolled up to the elbows and he was dressed in dark brown trousers and light blue shirt. A dark blue tie hung loosely from his collar. Peri noticed Ted was very tall, maybe an inch or two taller than Cord.

He smiled broadly. "Cordie, my boy," he exclaimed as they exchanged a brief embrace. Bobbing his chin toward Wildgoose, he said, "and who is this Chinese bandit with you? Some hitchhiker you picked up no doubt."

Wildgoose grinned. "Hi, Uncle Ted," he said, exercising a lifelong southern courtesy of addressing a person close to the family, never by a first name, but as, uncle or aunt, instead of the traditional, mister or missus.

After a brief embrace of his nephew and Wildgoose, Ted turned his attention to Peri. "And this lovely lady?"

"Uncle Ted, this lovely lady is Doctor Peri Pepper, who will soon be heading up our veterinary staff at the Pend Oreille." Peri was shocked at the bold announcement.

Was this a dream come true? To be head of the veterinary staff of one of the largest ranches on the continent? And to be near this gorgeous man whom she was quickly falling in love—No need to call sis, guess I have a job.

Ted held Peri's hand in both of his for a long time. "Doctor Pepper, it's a pleasure."

"Thank you, Mister Barrett," said Peri. Noticing a name plate on the large desk, she added, "Or should I say, Senator Barrett?" Cord's uncle had served in the Florida State Senate for many years.

Ted laughed heartily. "Nope, no senator, that's just a part time job. Mostly I'm stuck here behind this desk, just a plain country lawyer; anyway, nice to meet you, Doctor Pepper."

"Likewise to you, a pleasure. And, by the way, it's Peri, please," she sighed.

"Peri it is," said Ted. "Have a seat, please," he waved to an office couch and chairs. Choosing not to sit behind his desk Ted eased into one of the chairs. Crossing his legs he steepled his fingers under his chin. "What's on your mind Cordie, but before you start, I'm glad you are here. I have some urgent and rather pressing business to discuss with you anyway."

Margaret appeared at the office door. "Mister Barrett, can I get your guests something to drink?"

"I would like some coffee, please, Margaret. What about you all? We have coffee, tea, and soft drinks, whatever. It's a bit early for booze."

"Do you have any Doctor Pepper?" Wildgoose loudly inquired.

Peri furrowed her eyebrows together. "Ugh, very funny," she muttered sarcastically under her breath. "First time today—"

Ted listened intently without interruption or questions as the three related the story of the headless phantom and what they had seen the night before.

"Yeah, I've heard about it," he said. "That's way out of my league, but we have an expert on these matters at the other end of the hall." Walking over to his desk, he pressed the intercom.

"Margaret would ask Mister Wildgoose to step in here if he's not too busy."

Less than a minute later a man entered the office without knocking. His footsteps made no sound. Peri was amazed at the resemblance of the senior Wildgoose and his son. He was tall for a Seminole. He stood erect and walked with the grace of a panther. Behind his crisp white shirt, she could plainly see that he was athletic and muscular. Like his son, his hair was combed straight back and a short ponytail hung over his collar. His cheekbones were high and firm sloping down to a square Seminole jaw. Separating two piercing black eyes was a sharp nose like a chiseled sculpture.

The senior Wildgoose and Ted had been ironclad friends since childhood and had served in Vietnam together. Ted was already an attorney when he went in the service. Gary Wildgoose had attended law school after the war and joined Theodore Barrett and Associates upon graduation.

After introducing Peri, "Goose," Ted chuckled, using the same nom de plume as Cord did for his lifelong friend. "The boys tell me Chief Osceola is haunting the Glades again." They repeated their adventure to Gary.

Gary listened intently. When they had finished, he didn't say a word. He stood and silently walked over to the windows. Deep in thought he stood and stared at the ocean for several minutes. Turning to Ted, he said, "You and I have hashed this over for years." Making eye contact with them, he continued. "It is something the white man will never comprehend nor ever understand. It's not a ghost. It's a spirit—and it's real."

Cord started to speak. Gary held up his hand and cut him off. He walked back to the window again. A good five minutes elapsed until he turned to them. "It is Chief Osceola's spirit and it's dangerous. You do not know what you are dealing with." His tone was reverent and respectful when he spoke of the famed Seminole War Chief.

"But…" Cord began.

"Hush, Cordie," scolded the Indian slightly raising his voice. Then quietly he added. "He is trying to warn you. Chief Osceola's spirit is out there in the Glades for a reason. But you must treat it with deference and respect. It is not of this world. Some things should not be investigated. Some things are best left alone."

"So, what should the kids do, Goose?" asked Ted.

"Ted, we need to talk privately."

Ted glanced at his visitors, "If you would excuse us for a few minutes."

They did not wait for anything further and hastily left the office.

A half hour passed when the receptionist summoned them back to Ted's office. For the third time, the senior Wildgoose walked to the windows where he stood deep in thought with his back to them. Another five minutes passed. Without turning around, he said, "Boys go home and take the young lady with you. It's against my better judgment, but I will make the right contact. Someone will be in touch." With that, he was out the door.

Cord looked around, "How will we know?" He asked no one in particular extending his palms up in question.

Ted interrupted. "Don't worry, you will know."

"Ah, Cordie, there's something else we need to discuss in private," Ted said his gaze fixed on Peri dismissing her.

"Uncle Ted, if you are talking about the banking situation in Arizona, mother already spoke of it a couple nights ago."

"If it's okay with you, it's okay with me. I guess your mother told you we're missing a helluva lot of money."

"Yes sir. Like to the tune of 3 million."

"I wish it was only 3 million, Cordie. More like 8 or 9 million, maybe more. Not only in Arizona, we are taking it on the chin in Nashville and Atlanta too."

"How? How the hell is that possible? Authorized persons have two codes for only certain computers and one of the codes changes every two minutes. Hacking into our banking codes and programs would be impossible?"

"You tell me? I wish I knew, Cord."

"Maybe we should call in the feds," said Cord.

"No! Not yet," Ted insisted. Tossing a glance toward Wildgoose who he knew was an agent of the FBI. "Accounting, down on the eight floor, seems to think it's an inside job. The last thing we need is national publicity. If it got out that we can't manage our own money, who would trust us to manage theirs?"

"I see your point."

"It's not only the banking, Cordie. As you know, BDI owns securities and stock brokerage houses as well."

"What you're saying, Uncle Ted, if word got out everything could collapse under us."

"Damn right it could. Just like a freaking house of cards in a hurricane. But we have got to find out what's going on and I mean we have to find out now!"

"Darcee is in Arizona as we speak doing the audits, then heading to Nashville and Atlanta. Mother has retained Michelle Stewart. They are bound to turn up something."

"I sure hope so," said Ted. "I know Michelle. She runs a first class operation. What do you know about this Darcee?"

"She hasn't been with us all that long," answered Cord. "But she has always been a loyal employee and her work is excellent. If there is a leak, Darcee will find it. She's a very sharp lady."

"So I hear; but, Cordie, keep a close eye on things. The only possible loose cannon is this Darcee. Everyone else has been with us for years."

"Don't sweat Darcee, Uncle Ted. I know her well. She wouldn't steal a dime if she was starving."

"Okay son, if you say so. But keep an ear to the ground anyway. By the way, I have ordered the installation of biometric scanners for a fingerprint, installed at each location where wiring or transferring of monies is authorized. They are installing one in the Tidewaters computer room as we speak. See Mrs. Richardson on your way out so she can add you into the system."

"Good day, Doctor Pepper."

"Good day, Senator Barrett."

Cord dropped Wildgoose off at his home then he and Peri drove to the Tidewaters. They were served dinner on the balcony overlooking the Cove.

"Cord," she sighed, staring out over the cove and the long pier. "I never dreamed that Florida and the Everglades were so enchanting."

"Doctor Pepper. I've lived here all my life except when I was in college and my time in the Navy. It's something you get used to but never tire of."

The couple talked for a while, but soon the events of the past night and the day began to overtake them. Peri retired to her room as did Cord. Both took a hot shower and went to bed.

Cord was sleeping soundly when he felt the cover sheet being pulled back. He didn't move a muscle. A petite body snuggled against him. A hand rested in the hair on his belly and he felt two warm breasts pressing against him. Doctor Pepper was asleep in seconds.

As the pair slept, a dark figure made its way across the Tidewaters' lawn and silently crept up the back stairs adjoining the kitchen. Without a sound, it made its way through the long living room and softly stroked the head of Bailey, the golden retriever, reclining in his usual habitude on the sofa. Soundlessly, the interloper ascended the circular stairs embracing the fireplace and went directly to Cord's bedroom.

Silently, it stood staring at the sleeping couple.

CHAPTER THIRTY-EIGHT

Nashville International Airport
September 11

At exactly ten P.M. central time, the Barrett Jet touched down on Runway Two Right at BNA, Berry International Airport in Nashville. It taxied to the Signature general aviation terminal and spooled down the engines. Darcee bounded down the air-stair ladder and into the general aviation lounge. Glancing about she spotted whom she was looking for.

"Doctor Feelzgood?" she said to the long-legged cotton-blond dressed in a black pants suit. The woman was as tall as Darcee.

"I am, if you're the Red Baroness."

"The one and the same. The carpet matches the drapes upstairs and downstairs," she laughed.

"Well, we can fix that. I have just what you need at my place."

"Thanks, but no thanks. Think I'll leave things just the way they are. Never know. I might want to get a perm down there someday."

They were both laughing and Darcee added. "Besides, how else could I prove that I'm a natural redhead? Are you a real doctor?"

"Depends on how you look at it. I'm a chiropractor."

"Oh, great. Then you can make me feelz good in more ways than one."

They both guffawed at the thought.

Once out of sight in the parking lot the two women embraced and exchanged a lingering kiss. They both giggled again, "Hey, what about your bags."

"No worries. They'll be delivered to the Music City Hilton."

"Why don't you get them? You can stay with me. I have plenty of room." She gave Darcee a sensuous look.

"We're only going to need one room anyway."

CHAPTER THIRTY-NINE

The Tidewaters, Pend Oreille Ranch
September 12

In his sleep, Cord sensed something. He bolted upright reaching for his pistol.

"Looking for this?" said a familiar voice waving the firearm.

"Goose, you crazy bastard! Don't you know you could get shot pulling a stunt like this?"

"Not as long as I have your gun, Wyatt Earp."

Peri sat up frantically trying to cover her pert and perfectly formed breasts.

"GeeWuuu, please!" she exclaimed.

"Sorry about that, Doctor Pepper. Guess I should have known you'd be in here."

"Duh!" cried Peri.

"How did you get by Max? I would have heard her squawking and raising all shades of hell."

"I didn't go by Max. You think I'm stupid? I came through the swamp and up the back stairs in the kitchen."

"Goose, what the hell are you doing here anyway?" Cord, glanced at the clock on the bed stand. "Don't you know it's five o'clock in the morning?"

"Actually, it's only four-fifty."

"How the hell do you know? You swamp savages never carry a timepiece."

"You white marauders invented timepieces. Us swamp savages don't need a clock to know the time. Get up, Cord, we have a lot to do."

"We got what to do, Goose?"

"Dad called last night we have to meet someone. Let's go."

Cord was out of bed in a flash pulling on a pair of Levis. "Go back to sleep, Doctor Pepper. Miss Julia will have breakfast ready for you whenever you want it."

"No!" She exclaimed sitting up. "If you are going, I'm going too." Peri realized that she was giving Wildgoose another generous view of her still naked bosom.

"GeeWuuu, Pleezzzze!"

"Oops, sorry, Doctor Pepper. Cord, I'll meet you at the pier."

Oops, sorry, Doctor Pepper? Quite frankly, I'm not sorry—I'm not sorry at all!

Cord and Peri soon joined Wildgoose waiting at the pier and climbed into a small flat-bottomed johnboat. They sat in silence as Wildgoose paddled them across the cove and into the murky swamp. The first hint of dawn was breaking through cypress and dangling moss as Wildgoose propelled them down an unctuous waterway barely wide enough for the boat. Peri wondered what lay beneath and what might be lurking in the swampy jungle surrounding them. "Where are we going?"

Wildgoose didn't answer. Instead, he said, "Sha-a-no-kee," pointing a paddle toward a long lumpy form beside the boat.

"What? What did he say?" asked Peri.

Cord chuckled. "Sha-a-no-kee is Seminole."

"Sha-a-no-kee?" she said struggling with the word.

"Yes, Doctor Pepper, Sha-a-no-kee. It means big alligator in the Seminole language."

"Oh, my gosh! A big alligator? Where?"

Cord broke off a small limb and popped the reptile on the snout. "Right there, Doctor Pepper." The animal quickly submerged, its tail lashing out, exploding the surface splashing them with swamp water.

Soon a tasteful house appeared on the high dry ground near the edge of the swamp. Looking at Peri, Wildgoose said, "My place. Maria will have coffee and breakfast ready. We'll eat and then get going."

Peri looked at Cord. "Maria?"

"Yeah, that's Goose's lady friend. She's a pretty little thing, French-Italian, I think."

Maria was a gracious hostess and prepared a hearty breakfast of eggs, bacon, southern buttered grits, toast and plenty of hot coffee.

Wildgoose laughed. "Better go easy on the coffee, Doctor Pepper, not many bathrooms where we're going."

"Oh, you," she replied waving a hand at him.

"All right, let's get going," said Cord. "C'mon, Doctor Pepper, you're burning daylight."

The trio climbed into Wildgoose's modern pick-up. A slightly larger johnboat was securely tied on the bed.

"Are we taking your government vehicle?" asked Cord.

"Its government business isn't it?" chuckled Wildgoose. "Besides, we're going to need four-wheel drive."

They drove for nearly an hour and a half when Wildgoose pulled off the hard road and drove for several miles through swampy water rising up to the bottom of the doors. They came to a wooded knoll surrounded by palmettos and other indigenous growth. The four-wheeler gave a herculean effort and climbed the steep embankment coming to a stop in a dense hammock. Peri alit and stretched while Cord and Wildgoose unloaded the boat.

"Are we where we're supposed to be, Goose?"

"Not yet but you see that big oak tree over there on that island?" He pointed with an oar across the fen to a huge oak a half mile away. Cord shook his head.

"Since us swamp savages can't tell time, we have to be there exactly when the sun is centered in the vee between the lower branch and the trunk of that tree. That should make it about three fifteen."

"Okay, Daniel Boone," said Cord, looking at his watch. "That should be another five or ten minutes."

"Nine," stated the Indian.

Nine minutes passed and the sun settled precisely in the vee of the oak. Wildgoose briskly propelled them across the murky water to the island. Landing, they pulled the johnboat up the steep bank and into some shrubs.

"What now, Goose, we wait?"

"Not for long, I'm sure he's here," Wildgoose said quietly. "In our culture it is considered very bad manners to be tardy."

He turned to Peri and nodded at a clump of palmettos nearby. "Doctor Pepper, if you gotta go, now is the time."

Peri took heed of Wildgoose's advice and started for the palmetto clump.

"Oh Doctor Pepper," he sang out, "If a rattlesnake bites you on your cute little tush, you'll find out who your friends are."

"Oh, haaa, haaa, George Washington Wildgoose." she stuck out her tongue, making a face at him. Doctor Pepper disappeared into the thicket.

Shielded by the coppice, Peri assumed a squatting position as best she could and was tending to the business of relieving herself when she felt she wasn't alone. Looking up, she was staring into the black stiletto eyes of a brown-skinned man dressed in contemporary Seminole attire. Since he was standing behind a thicket of palmettos, she could only see him from the waist up. He had no expression. The Indian was like staring like a granite face on Mount Rushmore.

Peri screamed and fled on a dead run to Cord. She grabbed him in a bear hug. "A man, an Indian—I think!" she shouted, tugging at her Levis and pointing toward the thicket, a tissue still gripped in her hand.

"A what?" exclaimed Cord.

"Relax, you two," said Wildgoose, jerking his head in the direction of the two men emerging from the jungle growth.

The first to approach was a brown-skinned man dressed in blue dungarees and a plain denim shirt. A white, wide-brimmed cowboy hat was squarely planted on his head. His companion, obviously a Seminole was dressed in the traditional clothing of his culture.

"Wildgoose." He stated rather than asked.

"I am Wildgoose."

Looking at Cord, "Barrett?" Cord nodded.

The man speaking glared at Peri for several seconds. He moved his stare to Wildgoose. "Tayki." he said gesturing, again making a statement rather than a question.

"Woman," Cord whispered to Peri.

"No tayki," he said sternly, wagging his finger. The stranger and Wildgoose continued their conversation in Seminole. Cord surmised it was a bit heated with both gesticulating their hands and arms.

Wildgoose came over to Cord and Peri. "Sorry, no matter what I tell him he's obdurate about not allowing a woman to go."

"I see male chauvinism is alive and well in the Everglades," Peri muttered.

"Goose, what am I supposed to do? You know damn well I can't leave her here."

"I tried my best, Barrett. He won't budge. You'll have to take her back."

"What about you, Goose?"

"No sweat. I'll get home." Walking over to the cowboy hat, he turned back to Cord tossing him the keys to his pick-up. "You go ahead and take Doctor Pepper in the truck and I'll…."

"Doctor?" The man exclaimed.

Wildgoose recognizing a window of opportunity spun around. "Yes, white doctor."

Cowboy Hat looked at Peri in disbelief. "The tayki, doctor?"

"Yes, doctor! The tayki is a woman doctor," exclaimed Wildgoose.

Cowboy Hat thought for a moment then walked over to his companion. From where they were standing, Cord could tell that it was an intense exchange by the way the two were wigwagging back and forth. Cowboy Hat stepped back and waved Wildgoose over.

"What are they saying?" Peri asked Cord.

"Damned if I know. They're speaking in Seminole."

Cowboy Hat walked over to Peri. Getting right in her face with piercing ebony eyes, he said, "Doctor?"

"Yes, I'm a doctor, but I am a verter…."

"Shut up, Doctor Pepper!" whispered Cord.

Cowboy Hat walked back to his glaring companion. After another lengthy exchange in Seminole, he turned. "We go," he said waving them toward the brush.

Wildgoose huddled with Peri and Cord. "Listen, you two," he said. "No matter what you must never divulge, or even let slip, what you are going to see and hear. You can't imagine the repercussions if you do."

"Like what?" said Cord.

"I don't know. This is as new to me as it is to you. One thing you can be sure of, they have a way of making certain their secrets are kept secret. Some good, some not so good, if you know what I mean."

Cord shook his head and shrugged.

"The only reason we are here is because of my dad's word." Moving his eyes to Peri he said, "And Doctor Pepper is going because they think she's a real doctor."

"I am a real doctor!" Peri exclaimed emphatically. "But what if someone is sick or someone really needs a physician?"

Wildgoose sighed. "You'll just have to wing it, Doctor Pepper, and try not to get us killed."

Cord, Peri and Wildgoose followed the guides into the foliage never suspecting what lay ahead.

CHAPTER FORTY

Florida Everglades
September 12

The Contractor was careful to keep his distance behind the white government pick-up. His quarry, Cord Barrett, was sitting in the right window seat. He knew that any FBI Agent as sharp as Wildgoose would spot a tail in an instant. He watched the white pick-up leave the paved road and head into the swamp.

The Contractor was being pressed for time. What ordinarily would have been an uncomplicated assignment was becoming more and more arduous. El Diablo considered ordering someone's murder no more than a routine business matter. Cord Barrett was a nuisance, a billionaire nuisance, but a nuisance nevertheless. Now, it was fast becoming a gnawing irritation, and he was getting more impatient by the hour.

The Contractor was in no way aberrantly careless in his work. He was never lackadaisical carrying out an assignment. Every move was meticulously planned and thoroughly thought-out. He resented the pressure El Diablo was putting upon him. The Contractor was a professional, an emissary; his skilled service was a boon to mankind by ridding the planet of undesirables. He would not be hurried or otherwise intimidated by anyone. He was never duplicitous in his work. In his own way of thinking, the Contractor was a gentleman. To him, murder was simply business—nothing personal—just business.

Still, in the back of his mind, he knew better than to get crossways with El Diablo. The man was a psychopathic slaughterer who ordered someone tortured, butchered and killed on a whim. Although neither El Diablo nor the Contractor knew the identity of the other, each harbored a deep degree of respect and fear of their respective collaborator. He knew El Diablo had a network nationally and internationally. No, the Contractor did not want to get on the dark side of El Diablo.

He watched the government truck disappear around a sharp curve behind a tree hammock. The Contractor followed carefully keeping out of sight of the vanishing pick-up.

Although he had been raised and had hunted in the wooded mountains of West Virginia and was an ace sniper-assassin in the jungles of Vietnam, the Contractor was no challenger for the intimidating hostility of the Everglades. He had travelled no more than 50 yards when it became abundantly obvious that the small rental car would never make it through the mushy surface. It gave a gargantuan effort, but the little car coughed and sunk to its frame in the unctuous bog.

The contractor grabbed his best friend and began to dash across the sludge. Bending low and keeping out of sight, he hoped to intercept the trio at a 90-degree angle. It was slow going for the Contractor; he was sinking knee deep in the mud. The gurgling sucking sounds of his feet breaking free of the watery muck sounded like a hungry Great Dane gulping down a bowl of hamburger.

He spotted a tall hardwood tree near a clearing. Reaching the hardwood, he was gasping for breath from the exertion, but managing to steady his best friend against a low limb. Quickly he injected a cartridge into the rifle's ammo magazine. The truck was entering a covered hammock. He only had a second, maybe two. This shot had to count.

The Contractor squinted through the scope and eased his finger into the trigger housing.

Darcee snapped back to the present when she heard the landing gear being deployed as the BDI Jet turned on final approach for Runway One-Zero at the Palm Beach Airport. It was dark, and she was bone tired. It had been another sleepless night in Nashville. She knew now why Doctor Feelzgood was so appropriately named.

In Atlanta, she had combed through tomes of computer programs, codes and various spreadsheets as she had done in Nashville. Still she had not been able to come up with any evidence or a single clue for the Barrett's as to the whereabouts of the missing money or the source of its disappearance.

Deplaning she tossed her bags into the trunk of her company Lincoln and drove the winding road until the headlights shone on the spanning white arch with the Texas Longhorns securely affixed in its center; the entrance to the Pend Oreille. She turned on the white-fenced serpentine lane leading to the Tidewaters. Steering through the ghostly shadows reflected from the large oak trees, Darcee's mind drifted to her handsome, rich pilot. In a short time, she would be nuzzled against his skin in the big king size bed. She was becoming moist with the thought of him kissing her full lips in the candlelight and his fingertips caressing her breasts. A chill ran up her spine at the thought of him entering her.

Darcee was walking down the extended corridor by the ell adjoining the Tidewaters where several of the ranch offices were housed. Fumbling with a large bundle of keys a voice called out to her.

"Hey Max—Pretty Max—Pretty Max—"

Turning to her beautifully feathered friend she said, "Oh Maxie, my colorful darling, I missed you too!"

Extending her arm, "Come on, sweetie," she cooed and kissed the bird on the top of its head. Max overjoyed with the attention of her favorite person eagerly hopped on Darcee's arm and made its way to her shoulder.

Darcee reached down, opened the lid of an aluminum box, and scooped a handful of sunflower seeds. As always, she balled her hand and placed a charitable amount of the seeds on top of the fist by her thumb and index finger. Ecstatically Max eagerly helped herself to the feast.

"Swuaaaak—Pretty Max—Pretty Max—"

"C'mon Maxie, let's go check on a few things." Max enjoying untainted bliss bobbed her head with enthusiasm and rubbed against Darcee's cheek. She entered one of the ell offices and booted up the computer. She thought for a moment, pushing a red curl behind her ear, she began typing a series of data. After entering several letters, numbers and symbols, she was satisfied. She will still have to report that she hasn't found the leak yet. She sat back and scratched Max on the head. Content with her work she hit the enter key. "Com-on Max let's go outside for some exercise."

Sometime later Darcee let herself in the Tidewaters. Due to the late hour, no one was astir. She strolled into the spacious kitchen, made a sandwich, and heated some soup. After wolfing down the food, she made her way up the circular stairway around the fireplace and walked directly to Cord's bedroom. Moonlight was shining through the tall sliding glass doors and bouncing off the water a story below like an unfurled flag on a windy day. Darcee gazed across the balcony at the cove. A light breeze blew across the water, and she felt her nipples becoming erect.

Cord is not home—maybe he's flying? Can't be—he's supposed to start his vacation this week—is something wrong I wonder? No, he would have called—that's so odd—

Strange—she thought. The smell of a woman was apparent in her nostrils. She walked over to Cord's bathroom. The toilet seat was down.

Really strange—or was it—?

Placing Max on the stand near the windows and leaving an adequate supply of sunflower seeds in the food bowl, she took a beer from the small bedroom refrigerator. Darcee stripped off her pants suit and slipped out of her bra and panties. She glanced at herself in the full-length mirror.

Humm—Doctor Feelzgood did a great job on my perm. I hope Cord likes it.

After donning a white silk night gown, Darcee sat cross-legged on the bed. She fluffed up a pillow and popped open her laptop. She typed:

Mrs. Sudie M. Barrett, of Palm Beach is pleased to announce the engagement of her son, McCord Fredrick Barrett, to Miss Darcee Ann Corbin of California. Wedding date and announcements pending.

Darcee tapped send and closed the laptop.

She stretched her arms over her head and yawned. It had been a long day, and Darcee was tired. She opened the top drawer of the bedside table.

Well, Cordie, my boy, I'm here, and you are not—this will have to do.

Darcee turned off the light and turned on the vibrator.

CHAPTER FORTY-ONE

Deep in the Florida Everglades
September 12

They fell in single file behind Cowboy Hat as he led them through the dense growth, his companion following behind. A short distance later, he stopped by a small creek about four feet wide. Companion pulled a canoe from under the bushes and indicated for them to get in the canoe. Cord noticed the canoe was handmade chiseled from the trunk of a cypress tree.

No one spoke as they drifted with the slow current of the creek. Peri sat in awe at the breathtaking scenery. The canoe floated through a labyrinth of winding creeks and tiny streams and through a maze of forks and turns. Beside the small rivulet, she watched a mother raccoon and her three kits peacefully drinking. A doe and her fawn looked up as they passed ignoring them. Two otters made splashing sounds behind the canoe. A dense opaque canopy of oak, cypress limbs and hanging susurrus moss formed a make-shift tunnel. The sun was almost completely blocked out giving a dusky appearance.

This is a vet's paradise—A dream—Peri mused.

The Florida Everglades is host to many secrets and mysteries, which to this day remain in her watery milieu. Sighted things, unsighted things, myths and truths are buried and masked deep in the dark depths of her bosom.

The Everglades, also known as the sea of grass is actually a slow flowing river 60 miles wide and 150 miles long with the current so slow it moves no more than a half mile per day. The origin of the Everglades is not precisely known other than it begins somewhere around Orlando, Florida, near the Kissimmee River, which discharges into the vast Lake Okeechobee. Flowing south, it is fed by underground springs and rivers and empties into Florida Bay at the southern tip of the state. Many high and dry areas known as hammocks punctuate the landscape where thousands of wild animals prosper. Best known is probably the feared Florida Alligator, which thrives in the hostile environment. Many areas of the Everglades are still unexplored and unknown with the possible exception of the Native American Seminole.

"Chen-Te," said Cowboy Hat.

Wildgoose asked, "Chen-Te?"

"Chen-Te," Cowboy Hat repeated waving his paddle in the direction of a large python hanging from a limb spanning the creek. Nonchalantly the serpent swung back and forth then suddenly dropped down dangling inches in front of Peri's eyes. It stared at her unflinching, stabbing its tongue like a whip. She buried her face in her hands letting out a shriek.

Wildgoose rose to his knees and with a spare paddle he held the snake at bay until the canoe passed. "Relax, Doctor Pepper. These fellows don't find pretty little vets very tasty." Smiling, he winked. Looking at Cord, he added. "They'd much rather have a rich airline pilot."

Peri said sarcastically, "let me guess, Chen-Te means Python?"

"Close," said Wildgoose. "Best translation is snake."

It was getting dark when the group rounded another sharp turn and for the first time since they had gotten in the canoe, the tiny channel was straight for approximately 100 yards. The creek was widening and picking up speed pushing them faster. The small boat was reaching a dangerous velocity, which concerned them. The last thing they needed was to be spilled into the coffee-colored water crowded with cotton-mouth moccasins and so thick with alligators, one could almost walk on them.

Cord directed his attention forward and noticed the stream ended and there was a solid clump of fallen tree logs and debris directly ahead. "Hey!" he shouted to Cowboy Hat, who was sitting in the front of the canoe. "Hadn't we better slow this damn thing down?"

Companion in the rear spoke for the first time and mumbled something garbled in Seminole.

"What?"

"He said don't talk," injected Wildgoose.

"How am I supposed to understand that?"

"You aren't."

Both Cowboy Hat and his cohort began paddling frantically with great intensity. The canoe was picking up momentum. Compounding the danger, the creek began to narrow again leaving barely inches on each side, which propelled the small craft even faster. Companion began using his paddle as a makeshift rudder.

"Look out!" Cord shouted. Before them, the barrier was getting closer and closer by the second. The creek obviously ended at the miniature cul-de-sac. It was thick and solid blocking any further progress. At this speed, the canoe was barely maneuverable.

"We're going to hit it you crazy bastards. You'll never stop this thing in time!" Cord exclaimed. He grabbed Peri and crushed her face into his chest in an effort to protect her from the impact. Wildgoose threw up his arms preparing for the crash.

"Down!" shouted Cowboy Hat pumping his hand behind him indicating for them to get as low as they could.

Cord held Peri tightly and closed his eyes as they waited for the inevitable collision, which was sure to obliterate the tiny canoe into splinters.

CHAPTER FORTY-TWO

Deep in the Florida Everglades
September 12

With his eyes clenched tightly shut as they had been fused together with a soldering iron, Cord listened for the crash, but all he heard was a swoosh and the unmistakable slapping sounds of palm fronds. The little vessel narrowly zipped under the logs and parted the obstruction as if were made of papier-mâché. They opened their eyes in amazement trying to comprehend the staggering sight before them.

The palm fronds closed quickly behind them and the small stream was becoming wider. Cowboy Hat navigated the little canoe over a waterfall and through some white water rapids plunging them down several feet below from where they entered. The little creek spread more; 10, 20 now 30 feet across and was flowing at a much faster pace.

Oh, my gosh! Thought Cord. *That barrier was a fake. It was built to hide the entrance to wherever we are.... No one would ever notice it, not in a million years. Where are we?*

Thousands of wildflowers bejeweled the sloping banks on each side offering a kaleidoscope of rainbow colors. Behind it, the banks sloped steeply upward. Wild animals could be easily seen in the thick flora and made no attempt to flee from the intruders.

They all noticed a sudden chill. The temperature had dropped several degrees almost to the point of being uncomfortable.

Peri saw a pair of penetrating yellow eyes frozen on her from the foliage. As the canoe, got closer, she could clearly see the block-shaped head of a jet-black Florida Panther. Its canine fangs were clenched tightly over its lower jaw.

They really do exist. I read about the Black Panther in vet school, but I've never met anybody who has actually seen one—I can't believe it. A real black panther.

Wildgoose also saw the panther. "Coo-Wah-Chobee," he said. "Means big cat." Peri nodded.

"Where are we?" she whispered to Cord.

"Damned it I know. Goose?"

"Don't ask me. I got no idea. But one thing's for sure, we are on the underground river."

"A river? Underground?"

I've heard about it my whole life, but I always thought it was folklore," replied Wildgoose. "I thought it was just more tribal legends the elders handed down over the years from generation to generation."

"Folklore or not, we're here and it looks real enough to me. Goose, there is light. If we're underground, how can this place be lighted?"

Cord referred to the soft light rising from behind the steep banks on each side of the creek giving off a reddish-golden color. Behind them, the lights extinguished as the canoe passed.

Wildgoose shook his head from side to side and shrugged. "I don't know, Cord. I got no freaking idea. I'm having a hard enough time trying to figure out where we are."

They sat in silence for a long time to absorb the scenery around them. Peri tapped Wildgoose on the shoulder.

"GW, I didn't know there were this many alligators in the whole world."

Wildgoose turned to face her. "The Glades has no shortage of gators." Pointing an index finger upward, smiling, he added. "They are protected by law up there in the real world, but us swamp savages hunt them for food and leather."

"Food?"

"Yeah, Gator Tail," Cord said. "Gator Steaks, Gator Stew. You'd like it, Doctor Pepper."

Wildgoose waved his palm toward the bank. The reptiles stared and a few slowly slithered into the water never breaking eye contact on the intruders.

"They probably think we're dinner. See that big one over there? He's the bull, those others sliding into the water are the ladies. His harem."

"How can you tell one from the other?"

"Well, you see, Doctor Pepper, it's easy; that big male over there is complacent, just taking life easy. Now, you see those smaller ones crawling and swimming?"

She nodded that she did.

"Those are the females. You can always tell the women because they are the ones swimming toward the mall."

"Oh, you!" she exclaimed feigning a slap at him.

They were still snickering when the canoe took a sharp turn. Ahead of them lay a Seminole village.

All three sat in awe of the sight. Colorful flamingos and egrets lined the shore. Fires were burning in front of the chickees. Many of the Indian women were preparing the evening meal over open fires. Hundreds of colorful fireflies flickered nearby. The natives were dressed in contemporary Seminole apparel. The men were shirtless and clad in the traditional buckskins and moccasins. The women wore the colorful long dresses indigenous to the Seminole tribe. They seemed to be unaware of the cool atmosphere, which was almost chilly enough to make them shiver.

Cowboy Hat beached the canoe. He did not speak and offered no assistance to help anyone. He bent all four fingers in a follow me gesture. The village fell into a deathly silence. The children had stopped playing and clung to their mothers. Everyone stood and gawked at the strangers as they climbed ashore and followed Cowboy Hat. It was obvious they had never seen a white person before.

"Good Lord," whispered Wildgoose. "We have just stepped 150 years back in time."

Cowboy Hat wagged his finger at Wildgoose. "No talk." He turned to a young man barely 18, wearing buckskin pants, and moccasins and was bare from the waist up. He was the picture of health and rippled with the muscles of a lean athlete. Cowboy Hat said something in Seminole to the boy who took off on a dead run.

"What did he say, Goose?" Cord whispered.

"I didn't catch it, but I did make out Old One, or maybe it was Wise One. I couldn't tell."

In moments, the boy was back and whispered in Cowboy Hat's ear. Using the same all fingers gesture Cowboy Hat said. "You come. The Old One will see you."

He led them through the village of chickee huts and the women stirring large pots over the open fires.

Cowboy Hat paused only once. Pointing to a ladle hanging from a post beside a spring bubbling out of the earth, he said. "Ocala?"

"He wants to know if anyone is thirsty," said Wildgoose. "Ocala is Seminole for spring."

The ocala was belching water from the earth making a small fountain and spilling into a large pool surrounded by lilies and other wild flowers of the Everglades. A duct channeled it down to the creek they had just left. They all took a cool refreshing drink of the crystal clear water. Each noticed the water was freezing cold. They arrived at a well-manicured chickee next to last in a long line of huts. Cowboy Hat held up his hand at arm's length and entered the chickee.

"He wants us to wait out here," said Wildgoose.

"I didn't need a translator for that. Goose, what's going on? Where are we?"

"You'll know soon enough, Captain Marvel. I can tell you one thing for sure. If they don't take a shine to us, we could be in a lot of trouble."

"Yeah, Goose, you're right."

"You bet your ass I'm right and there's no way outta here. I couldn't find the way back if they gave me an airboat and a GPS." Looking at Peri, he said, "You okay, Doctor Pepper?" Peri flashed thumbs up but said nothing still awed by this strange environment.

Two dogs bared teeth at the trio and showed displeasure at the new guests with their snarling. The angry animals were Dobermans and gave every indication they were strictly business and not an opponent to be bargained with.

Cord walked a few paces to the creek. He was intrigued with the anomalous sight before him. Through the dimly lit dusk, the sky had a yellowish color and an oval shape as if they were standing inside a bubble. An odd bluish tint rose above the distant swamp to tree top heights. The strange blue hue was something Cord had never seen before. The leaning cypress trees, the lazy hardwoods, the hammocks, even the gloomy water, and the flaccid moss had all taken on the unambiguous tinge. The swamp was definitely blue.

In the distance, a large structure captured his attention. An Indian burial ground lay in front of the structure. Cord could clearly see that it was the size of a large barn, maybe larger; it was difficult to tell this far away. The construction was also bizarre. It appeared to be built into the side of a mound with a lawn of grass growing on its roof. There was no door or entrance that he could see; at least no obvious door or entrance. In front, a warrior was pacing back and forth. A sentinel...?

I don't know where we are and I don't know what's going on. But everything is really weird—

Cord looked at his watch. *Why is it I can I see? It's got to be pitch dark by now. It's dim, but yet we have light—how could that be?*

A half hour passed, before Cowboy Hat appeared at the door of the chickee. He jerked his head for them to come inside. Sitting cross-legged around a small fire burning in a pit on the floor were two Indian males. They were naked from the waist up and their faces were painted eggshell white. Wide black circles were painted around their eyes and three black streaks adorned their ribs. The Indians heads were shaved leaving only the traditional ponytails of the Seminole men. Cord guessed them early to maybe mid-twenties. A slightly elevated heavily padded mattress was on the opposite side of the fire.

"Holy men," Wildgoose whispered.

Behind the mat on the far wall, Cord noticed an old tanned leather satchel with the initials JRO. It was tattered and appeared worn from years of use.

That's strange, where would something like that come from way out here? That thing's got to be a 100 years old.

"Sit," Cowboy Hat commanded, pointing to three mats between the two holy men. He immediately left. The three sat with Peri between them, her pert nipples were straining against her blouse announcing the cold. The two Indians remained silent and expressionless on each end forming a semi-circle.

Another half-hour passed and Cord was getting impatient when he heard a barely audible rustle from the rear of the chickee. The two holy men rose and disappeared through a flap, which led in the direction of the sound. He could only assume the living accommodations and sleeping quarters were beyond the flap in the rear of the chickee.

The two men parted the flap and an old woman was between them. Hardly able to walk, she slowly and painfully put one foot in front of the other. It was apparent that she never would have made it without the support of the two holy men who were almost carrying her and guiding her to the heavily padded mat opposite them. With great care, they settled the old woman and departed through the frond-woven entry of the chickee.

This has got to be something out of a Stephen King novel, Cord mused.

The old woman sat. No one spoke. She was dressed in what Cord thought was probably a long sack. Her hair was straggly and pallid as snow hanging loosely about her head and rested on her shoulders. Furrowed wrinkles congregated on a pock-marked brown face like a rusted accordion, emphasizing the white hairs budding on the tip of her hawk nose and square chin. Cord thought the old woman's face had the look of tanned leather or maybe like a dried coconut hull.

She did not look up and stared at the fire behind a pair of glasses so dark they would be almost impossible to see through. After a long pause, the old woman waved her hand slowly over the fire. The amber flames instantaneously turned to a dark green.

"You are McCord Barrett," she remarked, in perfect English, still with her head bowed to the green fire.

"I'm Barrett," said Cord.

"Yes, you are McCord Barrett. I knew your father and your grandfather. Your uncle Theodore is my friend."

"You knew my Dad?"

"Yes. A good man, a man of dignity, big strong man. He lives in the land of the blue light." She waved an arm in the direction of the azure swamp.

"My father is dead many years," said Cord quietly.

"Yes. I know. I was there when he passed. But yet he lives. He is now in the land of the blue light," uttered the old woman. "I was there when you were born McCord Barrett."

"You were in the hospital when I was born?" Cord said acerbically.

"I was not seen, but I was there."

The old woman never looked up. "You are George Washington Wildgoose, son of Gary Wildgoose. He is a good man. He is an honorable man and he is my friend. I witnessed your birth. I knew you before you were conceived."

Wildgoose sat silently without expression. The old woman waved her hand again over the fire. They watched it turn blood red.

"There is evil. Something sinister is all around you," she whispered.

Wildgoose spoke up. "Yes, Old One that is why we are here."

"I know," replied the woman.

"You are not Seminole," said Wildgoose.

"No, I am not Seminole. I am half Tequesta and half Calusa. My father was Tequesta, my birth mother a Calusa, the shell people."

The old woman was referring to the ancient civilizations of the Calusa Indians who lived on the southwest coasts of Florida. They existed on a diet of seafood and shellfish. The Calusa built huge mounds of oyster shells and used them in their daily habitude.

She gave a guttural coughing laugh. "Some say we are extinct, the Calusa and the Tequesta."

The old woman was ignoring Peri. Wildgoose said, "Your English is very good, Old One."

"Yes, it is," she replied. "I was educated in the schools on the Big Cypress Reservation and attended the Appalachia College for Indians in Tallahassee. I have taught here since the big war the whites fought in Europe and Asia."

Sardonically Cord said, "All that is well and good Old Person, Wise Person or whatever you are supposed to be. But we are here to…"

For the first time, the old woman looked up her dark lens reflecting them in the crimson light of the fire. Harshly she said, "My eyes do not see well anymore, but I know. I know all. You must learn respect, McCord Barrett." Sternly she said, "Your father always showed respect."

Showing displeasure, she waved her hand over the fire. It turned to a bright cherry red color for a few seconds, and then returned to blood red.

CHAPTER FORTY-THREE

Seminole Village Deep in the Everglades
September 12

The old woman turned her attention back to the fire. Again, she seemed to be entering into a trance. Her head shook slightly and her tongue slipped through her lips when she opened her toothless mouth. The shaggy head shook violently as she opened her mouth further.

Peri, Wildgoose and Cord sat in horrified disbelief. A hairy tarantula crept between the parted lips and paused on the tip of her tongue. Imperturbed, the spider made its way down her mouth and along her throat coming to rest on the old woman's shoulder.

Peri sat astounded and felt chills of electric voltage racing down her spine. Cord also sat stunned at the ghastly sight while Wildgoose, also appalled, but with true Seminole mores, sat without expression.

The Old One coughed and cackled. "This is Shing-Tu, my little darling." Wagging her head and shaking a bony finger sideways, she continued, "Shing-Tu is not an insect; she is an arachnid."

"You have come here to ask about Chief Osceola."

"Yes ma'am, that's right," said Cord, this time in a much more respectful and obsequious tone.

"No. Not now," said the Old woman. "We eat first. We talk later."

She clapped her hands. At once, a slim woman entered the chickee. She was lean and strikingly beautiful with long light brown hair reaching down to her waist. Cord guessed in her late thirties or maybe early forties. She wore buckskin slacks, oddly different from the other women's tribal dress. Cord noticed that right away the woman's skin was substantially lighter than the others. She kneeled and placed a steaming bowl of venison stew in front of him. The woman glanced at him with two deeply set jade-green eyes for a brief moment, and then quickly looked away.

The woman began to stand when a necklace with a gold metal medallion tumbled from her loose Indian blouse. Cord bolted upright when he saw it. He felt the pressure of Wildgoose reaching across Peri squeezing his arm alerting him to keep his mouth shut.

Goose saw it too—

The woman instantly tucked it back inside her chemise. She chanced another brief green-eyed stare at Cord then hastily darted from the chickee.

Two others entered, a boy and a girl, each carrying a bowl of stew for Wildgoose and a wooden plate of baked meat and vegetables for Peri. They were handsome children, also light-skinned like the woman, Cord thought the kids to be about 12 to 15 years old.

Reading their minds, the old woman cackled. "My granddaughter," she said, "and these two are my great grandbabies."

Thought Cord. *These beautiful children don't look Seminole or Miccosukee. Could they have white genes? It looks like I am the only white man around this village—strange.*

He was afraid to think too much. By now, he was starting to believe the old woman could actually read his thoughts.

"We eat now," she said. The old woman waved her hand over the fire. It instantly changed from a deep red back to its normal flame of yellow and orange.

CHAPTER FORTY-FOUR

Western Palm Beach County
September 12

It was late when the Contractor lay exhausted and frustrated in the bed of his suite. Never had he been so embarrassed personally or professionally. The elimination of Cord Barrett was becoming more and more of an escalating problem.

He dreaded emailing El Diablo the news of yet another failure. How was he going to explain a clear shot this afternoon was not possible?

The vehicle in which his quarry was riding was bouncing in every direction on the crude road. Centering the crosshairs on Cord Barrett was like trying to thread a needle in a running sewing machine. What if he had missed? What if he had accidently killed one of the innocent passengers?

I am a professional, I don't kill innocent people.

He knew in his heart that such an excuse to El Diablo was unacceptable. To El Diablo failure was not an option. To El Diablo it would have been a trifle matter of simply killing all three and be done with it.

The Contractor gave a mournful glance at what was left of his suit laying crumpled on the bathroom floor. His humiliation was further heightened by the fact that he was forced to walk through the lobby of the motel in clothes that looked like he had taken a bath in a pig's sty. The sawgrass in the Everglades had made irreparable rips and tears in his expensive Brooks Brothers business suit. His tailor would have to make another.

Moreover, he was shoeless. Somehow, he had become separated from his left shoe in the clutching gravity of the sucking muck. He would have to do something about this too.

The Contractor was exhausted and needed sleep. But first, he must contact El Diablo. He opened the laptop and pensively thought for a moment. The Contractor closed the laptop and leaned back on the pillows. El Diablo would have one of his tizzy rages and he didn't feel like dealing with him tonight.

No, not tonight—Screw him.

He slept.

CHAPTER FORTY-FIVE

Seminole Village Deep in the Florida
Everglades
September 12

The Indians served a delicious meal. Peri, usually a modest eater, gulped down the dinner and remarked how tasty it was.

After the meal, the old woman leaned back. Cord thought she had drifted off to sleep when her head slightly jerked. At last, she looked up, the dark lens blocking any expression she may have had. "Chief Osceola lives," she said, adding a bit of reverence to her otherwise stoic tone. "He is here. He is with us."

The fire was reflecting off the walls of the chickee like yellow licking tentacles.

Cord, in a slight tone of asperity, said. "Are you trying to say that a man who has been dead since 1838 is here in the 21st century haunting us?"

The old woman raised a crooked finger at him. Firmly she said, "I am not trying to say it; I am saying it. I'm telling you, Yaw-Hee lives…and he is among us."

"Yaw-Hee?" Peri whispered to Wildgoose.

"Great Sacred Leader," he whispered back.

Cord flexed his jaw muscle. "Why is he here, Old One?"

"I cannot answer. I am not sure of his raison d'être. But I am sure Yaw-Hee is with us for a crucial reason. Otherwise, his rest would not have been disturbed."

Wildgoose spoke up. "Old One, is Yaw-Hee in search of his head?"

The old woman raised her finger again. "My son, do not listen to the imagined myths of the white man. They only assume they have an understanding of the Seminole and our culture and our ways. They are like blind eagles flitting though the sky going nowhere."

Peri spoke to the old woman for the first time. "Old One, how can this be?"

The old woman scowled. "You ask how this can be. You are no doctor. You are like the others. You have no comprehension in your black heart of the red man or his traditions. Some things are not meant to be understood or explained even with all your science and technology. A doctor would know these things."

The old woman waved a wrinkled hand over the fire turning it back to blood red. She fell back into a trance.

"I see great danger around you, McCord Barrett. You are being hunted as an animal is hunted."

"I am being hunted?" Cord said mordantly. "Who would be hunting me?"

"Someone far away but at the same time someone very near."

In spite of knowing better, Cord felt a chill of uneasiness ripple through his body. "Why would anybody be after me?"

"I cannot answer. I do not know. But I see evil. Wickedness and iniquity surround you. Something ominous awaits you, McCord Barrett you must take great prudence. You father is speaking from the Land of the Blue Light."

"What does he say, Old One?"

"You must implement great care and trust no one."

"George Washington Wildgoose, your grandfather speaks to me from the Great Beyond of our ancestors. Your grandfather instructs you to watch over your brother, McCord Barrett." The old wench was still ignoring Peri.

"Can you do anything about this, Old One?" asked Wildgoose.

"I cannot remove such a curse, George Washington Wildgoose, but I will ask the spirits to guide you."

A dark chill fell inside the chickee engulfing them. Peri shivered and hugged her arms as she watched the vapor from her breath appear in the light of the dimming crimson fire.

The old woman held out her liver colored hands and cupped them together over the fire. Pausing for several seconds, she rocked back and forth. Very slowly, she opened her hands; a tiny wren appeared in her palms.

"This is a good sign," she said. "A small bird is a message from the other world. It brings good tidings." The little bird flew up and hovered above Peri for a brief moment then disappeared into the back of the chickee.

The old woman leaned back and stared at the fire. She tilted her head back and began to make a gurgling sound deep in her throat. With her head back, the old woman extended her tongue with her mouth wide agape.

The three gasped, in shock at the horrifying sight before them.

CHAPTER FORTY-SIX

Seminole Village Deep in the Florida
Everglades
September 12

From the back of the old wench's throat, a pair of pinchers appeared. Behind the claws was a ghastly head with two penetrating black eyes. As it crawled forward, Cord could make out a black scorpion at least four inches long with its stinger held high and ready to strike. The creature turned its horrendous head. Its tiny eyes glared at Cord as it remained motionless on the old woman's tongue.

A full minute passed until the arachnid slowly made its way across the old woman's cheek. It kept its stinger erect as if ready to attack in an instant. It crawled up the bridge of her nose and across the dark glasses. Slowly it crept to her forehead and vanished into the disheveled white hair.

Abruptly the old woman sat up. She held out her arms horizontally and spoke from a trance in words nobody understood. The cold chill immediately was replaced with warmth.

"This is not a good sign the spirits have sent us," said the old woman. "The scorpion represents evil and tribulation. There is great peril and jeopardy embracing you, McCord Barrett. Your father is warning you from the other world—the Land of the Blue Light. You must exercise great discretion."

Cord, Peri and Wildgoose were trying to absorb what they had just seen and heard.

"I am very tired," said the old woman. "You will not see me on this earth again. A guide will return you to the surface and to your world at tomorrow's dawn. You must never speak of what we discussed here or what you have seen in this place. Not even to each other. The penalty could be your life. You have been warned."

The old woman waved her hand returning the fire to normal. "This is the finish of our visit. We sleep now."

She clapped her hands twice and the two bald body painted holy men appeared. One showed them out and quickly closed the entrance to the chickee. The old woman's great granddaughter was standing outside waiting for them. She was a beautiful child with ash-blond pigtails extending to the middle of her back. She stared at the three through the same ocean green eyes of her mother. She looked at Wildgoose then to Peri. "Wha-hi-wa?"

Wildgoose chuckled and replied to the girl in Seminole.

"What, Goose?" inquired Cord.

"She wanted to know if Doctor Pepper is my wife. I told her no, she was yours."

"Mine?"

"Yeah, I thought it best to say that so we'll all be able to stay together. If you were not married, they would have put Doctor Pepper on the other side of the village. That is the custom. We don't need to get separated," said Wildgoose. He laughed, "And, by the way, Barrett, congratulations on your marriage and your wedding day."

"Screw you Goose but roger that. The last thing we need is to get separated."

The young girl led them to a chickee one down from the old woman's and waved them inside. She pointed to slightly smaller chickee close by and indicated that Wildgoose was to stay in there.

Cord was following Peri into the Seminole abode when all of a sudden the entire village went dark. If was as if someone had switched off the light. The only light afforded them was a small fire burning inside the chickee.

The dogs stopped barking.

The village was silent as a tomb.

CHAPTER FORTY-SEVEN

Seminole Village, Deep in the Florida
Everglades
September 12

"Come on in, Goose." Cord threw back the woven palm door of the chickee. "We have a lot to talk about."

"Indeed we do O' Great Vanguard of the Everglades. You sure, I won't be disrupting you newlyweds on your wedding night?"

"Oh, screw you to the tenth power, Goose. Get your ass in here."

The three sat around the fire trying to contemplate the day's events not knowing where to begin.

Finally, Cord said, "Have you ever seen such a load of bullshit in your entire life?"

"Hold on right there, Barrett. I have told you over and over not to make fun of the Native American ways, and things you don't and can't understand."

"Oh Goose, don't start that voodoo crap again."

"Voodoo? Voodoo, Cordie? Then explain how that old shrew kept changing the fire to different colors?"

"That's an easy one, Goose. She probably palmed a handful of powder or some kind of chemical and when she waved it over the fire, it changed color. Where's the mystery?"

"Okay then, Mister Edison, then explain how she chilled the room and where the hell are we? What about that blue swamp and the bird and that frigging scorpion?"

"Don't forget that ugly tarantula, ugh!" said Peri. "I have never seen a yellow sky like that before. Have you?"

"Checkmate. You got me there," sighed Cord. "No, I haven't. But there's got to be some explanation somewhere. Things like this don't just happen."

"Why did she say I was not a doctor and that I have a black heart?" asked Peri despairingly. "Somehow she must have known I'm a veterinarian and not a physician, but a black heart?"

"Checkmate again," said Cord. "We never told anyone any different."

Cord looked at Wildgoose. "By the way, Goose, what is a JRO or who is JRO?"

"If you're asking about the leather satchel that was over in the corner, I got no idea. It's not Seminole through. Looks like it fell off a stagecoach, a century ago."

Wildgoose laced his fingers together cracking his knuckles. "Another thing, did you notice anything peculiar about that woman, the granddaughter?"

"Yeah, besides being a looker and a helluva figure, I caught that medallion hanging around her neck. Didn't you?"

"Of course, I did," said Wildgoose. "I recognized it right away. But even stranger, when is the last time you've seen a Seminole with ocean green eyes?"

"Like never," said Cord, exhaling, "and the great grandkids too."

"Precisely, like never."

"Goose, what's with that big mound over there just past the burial grounds? You saw it didn't you?"

"Certainly, I saw it. You think I'm blind?"

"It's huge; big as a barn. What's it for, Goose?"

"You got me. But I assure you it's something important. Otherwise, they wouldn't be posting around the clock guards."

"I saw only one sentry."

"Don't kid yourself, Cord. If it's important enough to post one there'll definitely be more."

"All right," said Cord. "We'll give it a couple hours and make sure there is no one astir. Then we can sneak over there and take a look."

"Barrett, have you lost your fuckin' mind? Excuse my French, Doctor Pepper."

Peri shrugged her shoulders. "These aren't virgin ears. I've heard it all before."

"Cord, are you completely out of your mind? Have you gone absolutely nuts? That's the most insane thing I've ever heard! If you get caught doing something that stupid, no telling what they would do you and us too."

"Goose," Cord interrupted, "I'm going. So make up your mind. Are you with me or not?"

A dark silence fell on the room. Finally, Wildgoose said begrudgingly, "There is no sense arguing with you when you get that look in your eyes, Barrett. So guess I will have to go because my grandfather ordered me to watch over your slapdash ass. But it's dangerous and it's wrong. And I don't like it."

"What if it is something holy and sacred to these people?" asked Peri.

"Then I'm going to find out," said Cord.

Wildgoose wiped his brow with the back of his hand. "Look Cord, to get there you'll have to slip through the burial grounds. I don't need to remind you how this culture treats its dead. Anyone who passes into the Great Beyond, the land of our ancestors is deeply respected and revered. The burial ground is holy and never to be trespassed upon. Especially," he paused, "especially by a white man. I'm telling you not take these things lightly. The spirits roam the Blue Swamp in the dark of night and they will know."

"Oh, Goose, please—"

"Guess I really shouldn't be concerned," said Wildgoose. "You can't make it past those dogs and you sure as hell could never make it across that swamp."

"Why can't I make it across the swamp? I was raised around these Glades just like you."

"Because you are a white man, Barrett, and a white man would never make it."

"The swamp is only one of your problems, Cord." He continued. "How do you plan to get by the Dobermans?"

"Leave the dogs to me," spoke up Peri.

"Deal," said Cord. "Let's give it a couple hours and try to get some rest. One of us should stay awake. I'll stay up."

"Good idea," said Wildgoose. "At least they fed us good."

"They sure did," remarked Peri. "My dinner was delicious."

Both men laughed. "What's so funny?"

Wildgoose said, "Well Doctor Pepper, you have just had your first dining experience of Seminole cuisine with swamp potatoes, mushrooms and fine gator steak."

"Gator steak? Ugh!"

CHAPTER FORTY-EIGHT

Seminole Village, Deep in the Florida
Everglades
September 13

In the wee hours of the morning, Cord and Wildgoose slipped under the rear of the chickee facing the blue swamp choosing not to use the front in case they were being watched. Peri followed and silently made her way to where they had last seen the guard dogs.

Keeping low, Cord and Wildgoose quickly ran across the open area and were soon forging their way through the jungle marsh. Even in the dark cloak of night, Cord could not help but be in awe of the creepy swamp. Although it had a purplish tint, it was definitely blue.

"It's dark so stay right beside me and watch your step, Davy Crockett," Wildgoose whispered to Cord. "There's quicksand out here and it's fast. You'd sink in seconds and then you'd be the late Davy Crockett."

Cord started to ask him how he knew but decided against it, the less conversation, the better.

Goose was right. I never would make it across here alone—

Wildgoose speaking in a faint whisper said, "We have to get through the burial ground. Stay right behind me and do exactly as I do, understand? I mean exactly."

Cord nodded that he understood.

Crawling flat on their bellies, the pair struggled their way into the holy place. It was slow going, only gaining inches at a time. Seminoles do not bury their dead in the unforgiving mush of the Everglades. Choosing instead to place the body on a bamboo cot structure slightly above ground to keep it from the pottage and protect it from preying animals.

The stench was unbearable and the horrendous odor was stinging Cord's nose. He tried his best not to puke, as the two slowly forged through the sacred ground. Following Wildgoose, Cord reached out his arm to pull himself forward when his hand felt like he had just grabbed a handful of rotting macaroni. A hissing sound broke the stillness as gases escaped from the belly of a rotting cadaver adding to the fetid stench surrounding them.

Abruptly Wildgoose spun around in the darkness like a spinning pop bottle when he heard the repugnant sound behind him as Cord's hand had clawed the rotting corpse.

"Oh God, Oh God, no!" he prayed in a muffled whisper. "You didn't touch it, did you?"

Cord said nothing.

"This time you have really done it, Barrett! You have alerted the spirits. You have disturbed someone's rest. Now they know we are here. I told you to stay right with me and do exactly what I do; I meant exactly!"

Again, Cord did not respond. "C'mon, we gotta get out of here fast," said Wildgoose.

When the two were within fifty yards of the mound, Wildgoose cupped his hand over Cord's ear. "No more talking. We will have to go on all fours and crawl the rest of the way."

"Ut-Oh," still whispering Wildgoose said, "We're going to have to go around to the back of the mound."

Cord mouthed, "Why?"

"Because that sentry over there will hear you or smell you."

Cord started slowly to move away on his hands and knees then froze. A Cotton Mouth Moccasin was crawling directly towards him, its thick body just inches from his hands. The serpent's tongue was licking the night's air like a javelin. Sensing prey through its tongue by vibration and heat the moccasin rose up like a cobra barely an inch from Cord's face, its mouth agape. Cord could see the inside of the reptile's mouth, white as a hospital sheet. The deadly fangs dropped from their normal position high in the snake's gums and protruded menacingly to the strike position.

Cord squeezed his eyes shut and waited for the reptile to lash out. Instead, the snake slithered across his clenched fists, its sensors attention now fixed on a small swamp mouse desperately trying to flee to safety in the palmettos. The vibration of the movement distracted the snake from Cord, who had remained stone still.

The moccasin struck with lightning speed injecting its deadly venom into the ill-fated rodent. Dinner was served. Cord feeling like he was going to explode from holding his breath let out a lungful of air.

A few yards ahead, Wildgoose held up his hand-indicating stop. He pointed in front of his face and whispered, "Trip wire." Following Wildgoose's lead, Cord rolled over on his back and barely made it under the wire. He took his time, his mind still rattled from the close encounter with the venomous moccasin.

I remember Uncle Ted telling me about trip wires he saw in Vietnam—

The two pressed on tediously and eventually came to the rear of the mound.

"We're here," said Wildgoose. "So how do you propose we get in?"

"We dig," said Cord, scooping up a handful of dirt from the mound.

"We dig," sighed Wildgoose. "I should have known you would come up with something original. For this, I went to the Naval Academy?"

As they were digging, Cord's fingers scraped something firm. "Goose, let me have your pen light."

"No asshole, not out here! Are you crazy? Let me see."

After careful inspection Wildgoose said, "It's a tarp, Cord."

"A tarpaulin?"

"Yeah, just like I said a tarp. How do you suppose we dig through that?"

"I didn't crawl through a graveyard and a swamp just to get skunked." He began tugging at the bottom of the tarp. "C'mon, Goose, lend a hand."

"What the hell. Why not tack on burglary and breaking and entering to the list of our other crimes tonight."

They pulled at the tarp seesawing it sideways and outward. Finally, they made enough room for a crawl space. They slipped through.

Inside the mound, Cord detected a musty smell and the faint odor of gasoline

A fuel dump—He thought disappointingly. *Nothing but a damn fuel dump—so, what's the big secret?*

They searched the inside perimeter and proceeded further into the mound, but found nothing in the darkness. The moment Cord turned to leave; he collided with something solid, something very solid and cold to the touch.

"Let me see your pen light, Goose."

"Okay, but be damn careful, Barrett," he said handing Cord the tiny flashlight. "If we get caught in here it will be our asses for sure."

Cord shined the narrow beam on something that appeared to be gray metal. He was feeling his way around it when his head struck something hard. He beamed the light up.

A propeller? A prop—this thing is an airplane! Can't be—

"Goose," he whispered, "It's an airplane! This thing must be close to 100 years old. Just look at this. Exactly like the day it came out of the factory."

"Take a look over there," said Wildgoose.

"It's another airplane," exclaimed Cord. "And there's another, and there's another! Goose, what would the Indians who live like it was 200 years ago be doing with antique airplanes in such pristine condition?"

Wildgoose was shrugging with his palms up when the light hit an officer's insignia below the cockpit.

"Wait just a minute. Wait just a freaking minute Goose! These are TBM Navy Avengers, five of them. See that insignia? This one is a lieutenant commander and that one is an ensign. A lieutenant over there; and this one here is a Marine."

"Keep your voice down, Cord."

"Goose, do you know what we have found? If I'm right, we have just stumbled across exact duplicates of the missing flight. You know, Flight 19 out of Fort Lauderdale that disappeared on a mission a couple months after World War Two ended."

Wildgoose looked bewildered and shrugged his shoulders.

"Goose, why would the Indians have exact models of airplanes that went down in the ocean sixty plus years ago?"

Wildgoose, still shaking his head, threw up his palm. "I got no idea bro. It's as confusing to me as it is to you."

"Try to remember as many names as you can. That one there, the lieutenant commander, says Galvan. He must have been the flight leader. See that painted on the nose, the '*Miss Lisa*,' probably his girl."

"We better get outta here, Cord, it will be almost daybreak by the time we get back. Anyway, I got a feeling this place is very sacred and holy to them."

They felt their way back to where they thought they had entered. Abruptly Wildgoose stopped and held up his hand.

"Shh, be quite," he ordered.

"What, Goose?"

"Something is out there."

CHAPTER FORTY-NINE

Seminole Village Deep in the Florida
Everglades
September 13

Wildgoose grabbed Cord by the arm and hastily led him behind a row of oil drums. They found several pairs of coveralls neatly folded in a pile and a hoard of canvas aircraft covers. Quickly, they slipped under the stack.

From under his hidden lair, Cord heard the rustling of the tarp when it parted and a young Indian warrior entered. At once, dim lights came on in each corner of the mound. From his veiled burrow, Cord could make out a tall, well-muscled shirtless brave who was sniffing the air like a dog curiously seeks the many different aromas in the wind. His cheeks were streaked with white paint identifying him as a sentry.

"He smells you," whispered Wildgoose. Cord nodded and sank back down into the khaki warren.

The sentry cupped his hands to his mouth and made the call of a swamp coot.

In seconds, noises at the other end of the mound caught their attention. Two other guards dressed the same entered. They talked briefly then spread out thoroughly searching every inch of space. They were edging closer and closer to Cord and Wildgoose hiding under the cloth heap. It was only a matter of minutes until they would be discovered.

Cord began to wonder about his fate once they were found. He knew since they had been in the holy burial grounds and had knowledge of the blue swamp; freedom to leave would no longer be an option. Obviously, the mound-like hangar was a hallowed secret, as well.

How will they kill us? What about Doctor Pepper? Would she be killed too? She is completely innocent of this whole mess—

Wildgoose uncharacteristically terrified was also thinking of his demise at the hands of these strange people in this strange world. He would be disgracing not only ancestor's family name, but also the sterling word of his father. He knew the Seminole method of execution. You would wish for death long before you were dead.

Peri Pepper sat a half mile away in the darkness slowly stroking the sleeping Dobermans.

I'm beginning to get worried about the boys. They should have been back by now. Maybe they were attacked by an alligator. A poisonous snake? Maybe some wild animal? No, not Wildgoose. And he would be looking out for Cord. That means only one thing—they got caught—I don't want to think about my life without Cord. I think I'm falling in love with him—No, too late—I am in love with him.

The silence in the mound was suddenly disrupted by a cacophony of rushing and scurrying. A series of squeals erupted shattering the stillness of the mound as scratching feet bustled around the hangar. All three of the sentry braves rushed toward the din.

Cord and Wildgoose hunkered down as far as they could awaiting their inevitable fate. One of the warriors was chasing something and coming at them on a dead run. He stopped abruptly and kicked at the clothes just as a small animal scurried underneath the khaki camouflage concealing the two trespassers. The Indian's moccasins were so close to Cord's face he could have stuck out his tongue and licked them. Cord forced himself to suppress gagging from deep in his guts at the horrible stench filling his nostrils.

To their shock, laughter erupted from the other two sentries and soon was joined by the sentinel who was standing beside Cord's laboring nose. "Sho-kee!" one of them laughingly shouted.

"Kono!" shouted another. The men were doubled over with laughter. They were smiling and slapping each other on the back when the three made their way to the front entrance of the mound. When they exited the dim lights extinguished.

"Goose, what the hell?"

"False alarm. Sho-kee means pig. They think that's what dug up the tarp."

"What's a Kono?" Just as Cord spoke, a small black and white striped animal scampered hastily from under the concealment and disappeared in the darkness.

Wildgoose chuckled. "Does that answer your question? Kono is skunk. Apparently, those guys rousted a litter of pigs that must have snuck in here and made themselves at home. That's what spooked the skunks."

The duo made their way back to the raised tarp; quickly and silently, they slipped outside. Cord sucked in a welcome breath of fresh air. Bending low, they ran to the refuge cover of the palmettos and back into the swamp. The Indian cemetery lay ahead.

"This time follow me exactly," ordered Wildgoose. "And watch out for that trip wire. We've had enough excitement for one night."

Cord indicated he understood.

"And, by the way, Kemosabe, you stink like an Iranian shit house."

"No ain't no morning gardenia yourself, Estee Lauder."

CHAPTER FIFTY

Seminole Village Deep in the Florida
Everglades
September 13

It was breaking the first glimpse of daylight as Cord and Wildgoose eased up to the chickee just time to see a shapely backside scoot through the makeshift hatch from where they had departed.

"Cute, tight little ass wouldn't you say, White Man?"

"Absolutely. Someday I'll tell you all about it, Injun."

"Okay, but I want to hear every single detail."

"Don't hold your breath while you're waiting."

They were both chuckling as they crawled into the chickee.

"Doctor Pepper, I presume," said Cord.

"Phew! You two smell awful! What did you do, take a mud bath in a pig sty?"

"If it makes the hogs happy, it makes us happy," said Cord. "How was your evening? Uneventful, I hope?"

"Nothing to it," she replied, "Just a walk in the park. How about you guys?"

"Later," said Wildgoose. He shuffled over to the entrance of the chickee and peeked through the woven palm fronds. "Just as I thought, we are being watched. How did you subdue the dogs, Doctor Pepper?"

"Like I said, just a walk in the park."

"How so?"

"If you had taken pharmacology, like I did in vet school, then you would have recognized all the philodendron plants around here."

"So?"

"So, the philodendron is a deciduous cataphyll, which contains about seven percent calcium oxalate, or raphides. Epidemiological studies have shown that the juice from the leaves of the philodendron has a mild sedative effect on humans, but it can be toxic to animals like dogs and cats."

"Jeez, Doctor Pepper, speak English."

"In other words, I anesthetized them. They will be fine."

Wildgoose's voice took a staid tone. "Doctor Pepper, did you pick up the leaves after you used them?"

Peri stared at him but didn't answer.

"Oh, shit. We gotta get out of here. Let's go. Let's go now! They are bound to find those leaves and they will know for sure."

"Shouldn't you guys wash up first?"

"No time, we gotta get out of here."

Cord grabbed Peri's hand. "The old woman said our ride will be there at first light. Move it."

The three made their way to the river just as the camp was beginning to stir. The dogs were not barking. As promised, Cowboy Hat was standing by the canoe; his silent companion was holding the boat. They climbed in and Cowboy Hat and Companion began paddling them back to their world.

As the canoe passed the first bend in the river and drifted out of sight, the passengers could not have seen the old woman being carried to the edge of the river in great haste by two bald white-headed aides. She was shouting orders in Seminole to the crowd following her and the young men were scurrying about in compliance getting canoes in the water.

Suddenly, she stopped and held up her arms, as if reaching for a cloud. "Stop," she said in Seminole. Then she mumbled in English, "Providence will take care of those deceitful renegades."

The old woman closed her eyes, "Death is waiting."

CHAPTER FIFTY-ONE

Florida Everglades
September 13

    Everyone sat in silence in the small canoe. The yellow sky was fading out of sight behind them, as they gracefully floated along the underground river. They absorbed the incredible beauty of the foliage and the animals around them. Cowboy Hat and Companion propelled the small boat effortlessly and efficiently making little, if any, sound.

    Sooner than expected, Cowboy Hat made a sharp turn into a small rill plunging them into blackness. The pair began to row with greater intensity picking up speed. All of a sudden, in the darkness Cord heard the familiar swoosh of palmetto and palm fronds and they were thrust into the hindered daylight of a circuitous creek flowing under a dense canopy of moss draped cypress and swamp oaks. Nothing looked familiar. A half-hour later, Cowboy Hat pulled the canoe aside and beached it near a clump of growth.

    The three alit from the boat. Cowboy Hat held out three bandanas and indicated they put them on.

"Blindfolds," said Wildgoose apprehensively. "I don't like this. I don't like it at all."

Companion took a bold step forward silently insisting on the headwear never changing his emotionless expression.

"We don't have a choice," said Wildgoose. "We'd best put them on."

Once blindfolded, Cowboy Hat led them single file, hand in hand, each holding on to the other, through a maze of twists and turns. Even Wildgoose had no idea where they were going or in which direction.

It was windy when Cowboy Hat came to a stop. He said nothing and untied the blindfold from Cord. "Okay guys, blindfolds off," said Cord

Looking about everyone saw they were back in the same place where they had first encountered the two guides. Wildgoose's small john boat was where they had left it tucked under some brush.

Cowboy Hat said something to Wildgoose, in Seminole. For the first time since they had met Cord saw the hint of an attempted smile on the Indian's face. He gestured with his hand toward the horizon as he spoke.

"What did he say, Goose?"

"He wishes us well and to go in peace."

"Thank him and tell him likewise from the three of us."

Wildgoose was just beginning to speak when Cord heard a loud sizzling sound and felt an excruciating pain burning his cheek. The sound of a muffled crack echoed through the peaceful Everglades scattering hundreds of pink flamingos and white egrets into the cerulean sky. The splashing of panicky alligators broke the serenity as the sunning reptiles hurried to the safety of the water. A blue heron crane nesting nearby took flight, its six-foot wing span labored gracefully against the blue firmament.

Cord turned in that instant and heard a whump sound, like a ripe watermelon being dropped on concrete. His hands involuntarily rushed to his stinging cheek.

He watched Cowboy Hat's eyes as they were blown from their sockets. His head exploded splattering his brains and a crimson sheet over Companion and the surrounding foliage. The missile blew the Indian's jaw from his chin. Pieces of Cowboy Hat's tongue and fragments of teeth were splattered in the moss of a nearby cypress like some kind of strange jungle growth.

Cowboy Hat's mangled body crumpled to the ground absent the top of his head and lower jaw. Vacant holes, where his eyes had been, gaped at them like a two-eyed Cyclops. Everyone stood frozen trying to comprehend the sight before them. Wildgoose was the first to gather his senses.

Grabbing Peri, who was standing stunned and dumbfounded, he flung her to the ground like a sack of rocks.

"Get down! Everybody down!"

Cord threw his body over Peri shielding her from any further gunfire. After several minutes, Wildgoose looked up. "I hear a motor. It's far off, but I think whoever fired that shot is gone."

Peri scampered over beside Cowboy Hat on all fours. She took one look and saw what little was left of the Indian's head looked like an opened bowl of crushed tomatoes.

"There is nothing I can do for him," she gently muttered looking up at Companion, who was still standing obviously in shock. He was staring in disbelief at his prostrate comrade. "I'm so sorry."

Cord, gathering his wits said, "Goose, ask Companion, his name. What can we do?"

Goose turned to Companion and uttered something in Seminole. The man stared but didn't respond.

Wildgoose shrugged. "Nothing."

"Ask him again, Goose?"

"Chotkwa No-Co-Se," the Indian answered.

"He says his name is Little Bear."

"Tell him we are very sorry. This is obviously a stray shot from a poacher. We are appalled and apologize for people who do these things."

"I'll tell him, Cord. He might buy it, but I sure as hell don't."

As Wildgoose was speaking, Little Bear sang out in a chant raising his arms to the heavens.

"He says his friend is with Ta-Mal-de-Zue, the Great Spirit."

Everyone stood reverently until Little Bear finished his mantra then helped carry Cowboy Hat's lifeless body back through the twisting maze of growth to the canoe. They covered what was left of the mutilated head with the blood-drenched hat. Showing no emotion, Little Bear slowly turned away.

"Wait," said Peri. She hurried to the edge of the brush and picked up a piece of Cowboy Hat's skull. Leaning over the canoe she gingerly tucked the fragment under the Indian's shirt.

They stood in silence as Little Bear slowly drifted out if sight.

Wildgoose said, "I can't believe all this."

"Ditto," said Cord. "What kind of crazy bastard would take a shot like that without knowing what they're shooting at? Damn poachers!"

"Listen up, Cord. That was no poacher and it was no damn accident. That bullet was meant for you."

"Me? Don't be ridiculous. Why me?"

"Barrett, are you deaf and blind too? Didn't you hear that old woman? Someone is out to get you and if you keep up this cavalier attitude you're going be as dead as Cowboy Hat."

"Oh Cord, you are hurt," said Peri touching his cheek. "That was close as close can get!"

"Let's get back to the Pend Oreille."

CHAPTER FIFTY-TWO

Pend Oreille Ranch
September 13

Cord, Wildgoose and Peri were climbing the backstairs at the Tidewaters when Miss Julia stood at the top, her rotund figure blocking the kitchen door like a Marine Drill Instructor, fists firmly planted on her wide hips.

"Poo-Ooo! Cordie Barrett, you smell like a den of polecats. Don you even think of coming in dis here house like dat. Look at yawl. You been a-wallerin' in a mud pond? And don you go tracking dat mess through my clean kitchen neither. Now you go down to da rec room and take a shower. And you too, GW."

Cord started to say something. "Now git!" barked Miss Julia, "boff of you, else I'll take a hairbrush to yo behinds jest like I did yo daddies."

Cord threw up his hands in surrender and turned around. Wildgoose followed. "I'll send Mista Ironside down wit some clothes or else I'll bring dem. And for you, Little Missy, you march yo-self right to Mista Cordie's bedroom and git in the bathtub. I'll be in to scrub you directly."

Everyone hopped to Miss Julia's commands without hesitation. "And dat goes for you too, Little Missy, don't you go messin' up my clean flo neither."

Peri bobbed her head in humble obedience and made a beeline for Cord's room.

Downstairs, Cord had just stepped out of the shower as Wildgoose was getting in when Miss Julia burst through the door.

"Miss Julia, please!" he exclaimed. "We're naked."

"Oh psst, hesh up you. I been seeing you neeked since the day you wuz born. You too, GW. Here put these on." She laid some clean clothes on the sink. In a milder tone she said, "Come upstairs when you git through. I'll make you sumthin' to eat." Looking at Cord, she grabbed his chin turning his head sideways. "I need to tend to yo face befo yo mama sees you."

Miss Julia marched off still talking in her own soliloquy. "Lordy, Lordy, I been taking care o dem boy's scratches and cuts since they wuz youngens in diapers and their daddies too. Lordy, Lordy, I..."

"Yes ma'am, Miss Julia," they both said. Nobody dared to disobey or get crossways with Miss Julia. They could hear her still talking to herself as she climbed the backstairs to her kitchen.

Peri entered Cord's bedroom looking neither left nor right.

"Well, hello."

314

Peri stopped cold in her tracks and gasped at the attractive redhead sitting cross-legged on Cord's king size bed peering over a laptop.

"Who…who are you?"

"Let's start with who are you?" said Darcee.

"Um, I, ah, I am the new veterinarian," stuttered Peri, her mind racing.

"Well, tell me now, Miss New Veterinarian, are you expecting to find a sick cow in my fiancée's bedroom?" Waving a hand toward Peri's luggage, "Are those yours?"

"Your fiancé?" Peri exclaimed. "Your fiancé? You and Co…, ah, you and Mister Barrett are engaged?"

Not waiting for an answer, Peri burst into tears and raced down the hall desperately seeking the sanctity of the kitchen.

Cord and Wildgoose had settled at the staff dining table gobbling down tuna sandwiches and chips Miss Julia set out for them. A place was waiting for Peri. A large pitcher of iced tea sat sweating on the table. Cord took a bite of a sliced pickle and picked up a legal pad. "Let's go over all this, Goose."

"You sure, there's enough room on that pad?"

"C'mon, Goose get serious. There has been a ton of bullshit raining on us lately and…."

"Cordie Barrett, don you be talkin' no bad language in dis here kitchen. I am still a lady you know, and the Good Lord can hear you too," barked Miss Julia's voice from somewhere in the walk-in pantry.

"Yes ma'am. She has the hearing of a twenty year old," he whispered.

"I always thought she had built in radar," laughed Wildgoose. "Anyway, where were we?"

"Okay Goose, what do we have?" Cord was writing. "To begin with, there's a headless Osceola running around the Glades. We got a 200-year-old Indian Village living out of the past that nobody's ever heard of with a blue swamp and a yellow sky. Then there's that nutty old medicine woman, a hangar full of vintage airplanes, and..."

Wildgoose interrupted, "We shouldn't be talking about this—the old medicine woman said we cannot speak of it, not even among ourselves—remember? And Cord, aren't you a little concerned about the eight or nine million or so dollars missing from your banks?"

"Yes, of course, I am. But we got people working on that, and..."

"Cord, don't you think we'd better turn our attention to Cowboy Hat? That was no fuckin' accident."

"I heard dat!"

"Yes ma'am," they said. "Sorry."

Lowering his voice, Wildgoose said, "Cordie, that bullet was meant for you."

"No way, Goose. Why would anybody want to shoot me?"

"I don't know, Cord, but…"

At that moment, Wildgoose stopped talking when Peri burst into the kitchen. "Cord, why didn't you tell me? Why? I feel like such a fool," she sobbed trying to speak between a flow of tears.

"What?" exclaimed Cord. "Tell you? Tell you what?"

Peri raked her red eyes with the back of her hands. "That you are engaged. That there is someone else," she cried.

"I am…? I am what?"

"You are engaged. You have a fiancée."

"Me? A fiancée?"

"Yes, a fiancée," exclaimed Darcee walking into the kitchen. A marker pen was clenched in her fist. She hurled it across the room at Cord and Wildgoose. Neither flinched.

Cord was becoming agitated. "Where would you get an idea like that?"

"Where? Why? Why would I think that?" demanded Darcee. "You've been sleeping with me since I signed on with BDI. We have attended charities and other events in Palm Beach together and everyone thinks we are an item and now you are denying it?"

"No, I'm not denying anything, but engagement?"

Darcee crossed her arms over her plenteous bosom, and loudly exclaimed, "I have been on the road doing my best to save your financial ass and all the while you have been here at the Tidewaters bonking this little harridan?" She jabbed a finger toward Peri.

Miss Julia, who had remained uncharacteristically silent during the fray, walked across the kitchen and put her arms around Peri. "Come, Little Missy, I'll take you over to the guest house. Mista Ironside will bring yo stuff." Peri still weeping buried her head in surrendered obedience.

Miss Julia ushered Peri from the kitchen giving Darcee an acerbic stare making it abundantly clear her dislike for the redhead. "We'll git all dis settled in the morning after a good night's sleep. C'mon now, Little Missy, let's get you cleaned up." Still crying, Peri followed the matron out of the kitchen never lifting her bowed head.

Darcee started to speak. Cord held up his hand. "Tomorrow."

"But, but…"

"Tomorrow," he sternly repeated.

"Okay fine, tomorrow," said Darcee. "But I am scheduled to go to our banks in Tallahassee and New Orleans."

"Then go," said Cord quietly. "We will talk about this later. I'm not going to say it again."

Darcee stared but said nothing. She turned on her heel and as abruptly as she had appeared stomped out of the kitchen. She went to Cord's room and fetched her computer and Max.

Cord was exhausted. The sleeplessness of the past couple of days was taking its toll on him. When he entered his bedroom, it was empty. He flopped into his bed and fell into a deep sleep.

The next morning, as the first streaks of daylight, pierced the darkness of his bedroom, Cord awoke with a start.

He was not alone.

CHAPTER FIFTY –THREE

Pend Oreille Ranch
September 14

"Goose, what are you doing here?"

"Last night you said to meet you in the morning. It's morning, so here I am."

"Yeah Goose, but I didn't mean to be here before the chickens got up. You're getting nuttier and nuttier in your old age."

"I wouldn't talk about age if I were you, Methuselah. You are, and always will be, two months older than me. Come on get up, you're burning daylight, Barrett."

"Okay, okay."

Wildgoose had a wide grin on his face.

"What's so funny?"

"Nothing, really. I see that you are sleeping alone these days, Mr. Hefner."

"Beat it, Goose. I'm gonna jump in the shower, tell Miss Julia to whip up some ham and eggs for us. I'll be down in a minute."

"Roger that, Mr. Barrett, but I'm not about to tell Miss Julia to do anything."

Wildgoose was on target making this point. Since boyhood, he knew better than to tell Miss Julia. If you were smart, the thing to do was ask. She could be as stern and disciplinary as any parent and still considered them her own little boys.

Cord appeared in the kitchen and gave Miss Julia her good morning kiss. He nodded a greeting to the household staff seated at the long kitchen table having breakfast.

Miss Julia was the first to speak, barking orders like General Patton, "Cordie Barrett, you jest march yo self back in there right now and dry off yo hair. GW is out on the veranda. I'll have yo breakfast sent out."

"Yes ma'am."

"And ask GW if he wants grits wit his ham and eggs."

Cord walked out on the wrap around balcony overlooking Lake Immokalee. Wildgoose sat with his boots propped up on the railing. "She wants to know if you want grits."

"Does a wild bear shit in the woods? Of course, I want grits."

"I'm not about to tell her about the bear but will say 'yes' to the grits," laughed Cord.

The two men were about to dive into a platter of sunny-side up eggs and a thick slab of ham when Peri joined them. Her eyes were red and swollen. She was dressed in white jeans and a maroon pull over top. Her low cut white tennis shoes slightly squeaked when she approached the glass-top table.

Even with puffy eyes and no makeup, Cord thought, *this is the most beautiful woman I have ever seen—*

Both men stood. "Good morning, Doctor Pepper."

"Good morning, I think," she mumbled bobbing her head.

"Sit down please, Doctor Pepper. There's V-8 juice, orange juice and plenty of hot coffee."

Peri sat but said nothing. A staff member in a white vest appeared and placed two brown Rhode Island Red poached eggs in front of her with a mound of hash brown potatoes. A stack of medium brown buttered toast stood near a plate of sliced tomatoes.

Cord and Wildgoose heartily dug into their food while Peri barely dabbed at hers. "There is no way I can eat all this," she said.

"No worries," said Cord. "Miss Julia always thinks her kids are starving."

Peri didn't look up and she didn't smile at Cord's remark. "Doctor Pepper, I know last night was awkward, but please give me a chance to explain. I, in fact, we all want you to stay on with us."

Peri remained silent and stared at her plate. "We are going to need a full time veterinarian on the Pend Oreille. Dr. Lee is retiring and this is a good place to be."

"And the money is good," echoed Wildgoose.

Cord thumped himself of the chest. Smiling he said, "And the people are great."

Peri's eyes focused on her plate, she didn't smile at Cord's attempt at a joke. Without looking up, she quietly said, "What about your fiancée?"

Cord banged his fork on his plate and pointed it at her. "Fiancée? For the umpteenth and final time, I do not have any fiancée! If you are talking about Darcee Corbin, she left this morning on company business."

"She works for you doesn't she?"

"Yes, in a way but not for me personally. She works for BDI—one of our bank auditors."

"And you have been sleeping with her?"

A long pregnant pause fell on the veranda. "Well—yes. But, Doctor Pepper, that was before I met you. She was a friend with benefits—nothing more. Please, I want you to stay. Will you at least wait until I get home this afternoon? We can talk about all this then, and please, let me explain."

"Yeah, I'd like to hear that one myself," said Wildgoose.

"You stay out of this," snapped Cord glaring at Wildgoose.

Gazing at Peri, Cord said, "I want you to stay for personal reasons."

For the first time, Peri looked at him. Very quietly, she said, "All right, we will talk this afternoon."

"Not to change the subject but what did you have in mind for us today, Cord?" asked Wildgoose.

"Good question, Goose. I've been thinking, since you have access to FBI computers, will you find out everything you possibly can about Flight 19? What really happened out there in the triangle that night? And where?"

"Guess I could check it out but…"

"Goose, listen up. Who were those pilots? Find out if the names match. For some crazy reason, those Indians have exact models of the TBM Avengers. Why? Where did they come from?"

"Roger that."

"We know they went down and are no doubt dead. But why?"

"Cord, that sounds like nothing we would have in the FBI files. We would never have stuff like that in our data banks. I will have to go to the District Office in Miami for anything sophisticated as what you are asking. Maybe we should check with the VA or maybe the Office of Naval Records, something like that."

"Well then get on it. I'm going to drive into West Palm and talk to your dad and Uncle Ted. Weren't they involved with something with the CIA during the Vietnam War?"

"Yeah, I'm pretty sure. Some kind of special ops, som-thin' like that. Neither one of them has ever talked about it. All I know is Dad was involved in some special mission and your Uncle Ted was a code breaker, translator or whatever."

"But," said Cord, "even so, you know, as well as I do they both know a lot more than they let on about that Indian village and whatever the hell else is going on out there in the Glades."

"You really think they'll tell you anything, Cord? Especially when we are told not to talk about it."

"Probably not, but I got a strong feeling they still know of a few buttons to push at Langley and in Washington."

"Yeah, but the question is, will they push them? See you later; I have to get down to Miami."

"Roger that, Goose. We'll hook up this evening and compare notes."

"All right, check with you later."

"Oh, Goose, one more thing."

"Yeah?"

"Try and find out what the hell is a JRO."

"I'll give it a try. Check you later White Man."

CHAPTER FIFTY-FOUR

Western Palm Beach County, Florida
September 14

The Contractor was relaxed and stretched out on the bed of his motel suite. He placed his hands behind his head and stared at the fan above. He was pleased with himself. The Contractor smiled.

This has been a difficult job to say the least. I'm glad it's over. The Cord Barrett assignment was a little more than I anticipated. At least Barrett is dead—Now, I can add 50 grand more in my Cayman account, not bad for a couple days work.

The Contractor reached under the bed and retrieved his laptop. He typed in the familiar series of codes and symbols. Then wrote: *"Palm Beach contract completed this date. Please wire fee confirmation."*

He waited for a response. None came.

That's fine. El Diablo is probably busy I'll check later. Think I'll treat myself to a big juicy steak and maybe a bowl of ice cream.

The GPS in the Contractor's rental car led him to an address on Okeechobee Road. The Okeechobee Steak House Restaurant seemed like a good choice. Years of travel had taught him to stay away from the tourist's choices and dine in places the locals patronized. The steak house had been in business since 1947, so they must be doing something right. Since it was the obvious choice of the locals, the food had to be good. Neatly attired in a new suit he was ushered to a corner table where he ordered dinner and a Wild Turkey with water.

Drinking any type of alcoholic beverage was rare for him and strictly against his rules while on an assignment but tonight he could celebrate. Tonight he would splurge a bit. His mission was completed and maybe he would have enough time to fly the Bonanza to his home in Jupiter and see his lovely wife and the boys before leaving for the Caymans and Europe to carry out El Diablo's next transaction avocation.

The medium rare sirloin was excellent as was the baked potato and salad. The Contractor patted his belly as he entered his room.

Life is good—

He opened the laptop and heard, "You have mail." He read: "Florida contract not completed. You failed."

Failed? I never fail— is this some kind of sick joke El Diablo is playing? I have never failed.

"Negative," he wrote. "My work is flawless. I saw the contract carried out myself. Please wire fee."

"Negative," came the response. "What you saw was the wrong subject. Complete project TODAY or I will hire someone who can. Will not tolerate any further breach of assigned contract. No fee at this time."

The wrong subject? That's impossible. You cannot make mistakes in this business. I am perfect—I saw his head explode through the scope. I saw his brains blown out of his head. I saw it myself. It was a little windy, yes, but so what? I am an expert—I am a professional—I never make mistakes—Barrett is a rancher, isn't he? It makes perfect sense that he would be wearing a cowboy hat.

The Contractor was no longer so pleased with himself. His dinner was not so special after all. He had made a mistake and he had killed the wrong man, an innocent man.

The Contractor had always prided himself as a highly skilled specialist. He demanded a premier fee for his services because he was the best and he never made mistakes.

He was embarrassed. Embarrassed personally and embarrassed professionally. The Contractor reached for his best friend. His mission was no longer business.

It was personal.

JOSS TALLMAN

CHAPTER FIFTY-FIVE

Northwest Florida
September 14

Darcee was not on the BDI jet. She had chosen instead to drive her company Lincoln. She needed time to think. She had to find some reason for the leaking codes and the nine million dollar leak in the Barrett bank computers. She was going to have to come up with some answers not only for Cord but for Ted Barrett as well. Cord she could manipulate especially with her sexual charms but Ted Barrett? That was entirely another issue. Ted Barrett was one tough cookie.

Darcee had tried to get Ted's attention. She gave him generous views of her intramammary cleft, but the lawyer had paid no attention to the offered cleavage. On another occasion, she had tried to get his interest in her. She flashed her newly shaved vulva at him by pretending to adjust her skirt just as he entered the office. Still, Ted didn't take the bait. Seems he is obsessed with his wife.

Oh, well—his loss.

Cord Barrett, on the other hand was a different can of worms. She could capture his attention as easily as a rock sinks in an aquarium.

I need a break. Maybe a vacation, some time off. Now, I have to worry about Cord and that—that veterinarian. I have to admit, she is gorgeous. Has she taken my place in his bed?

I am too stressed out. I need some relief, too much pressure.

She slid a disc into the player and heard Willie and Waylon belting out, "She's a good hearted woman in love with a good timing man…"

"How appropriate," she muttered to no one.

Darcee pulled the Lincoln into the parking lot of a truck stop just north of Perry, Florida. "Let's see," she said aloud, "Twenty-nine miles to Tallahassee." Darcee opened her laptop and plugged it into the cigarette lighter.

I hope I can find a hotspot internet connection around here. There never seems to be G4 service in this area. Ah, my lucky day—The Perry Shrine Club has an unlocked wireless connection.

She typed: "Local Swing, Tallahassee, Fl." Scrolling down she stopped at "Threesomes Welcome. Chip and Dale, Discretion and Disease Free Assured," caught her eye. Darcee hit enter and viewed the photo of an attractive nude couple. She typed in, "Red

Baroness is a lonesome traveler would like rendezvous this p.m., is bi ok?"

The reply was instant. "Red Baroness lonesome traveler, please send pic." Darcee raised her photo and entered send.

Again, the reply was right away. "Red Baroness, lonesome traveler, welcome. Prefer shaved. Bi welcomed. Drinks & snacks. 8 P.M."

"Eight 8 P.M. perfect. Please forward address," she wrote.

Back on Highway 29, known to the locals as the Apalachee Parkway, she passed through the tiny burg of Waukeenah and saw the Florida Capitol Building looming ahead atop a steep hill. She turned right on Capital Circle on North Monroe Street and passed Florida State University and the nearby Governor's Mansion.

Darcee had always liked Florida's small capital city with its dogwoods and blooming azaleas along with the towering oaks and a myriad of other colorful flowering plants blooming around the various state office buildings.

It reminded her of how beautiful this little southern town really was. Tallahassee was nothing like south Florida, which has its own beauty but so different. Darcee turned left on the Thomasville Highway noting the short distance to the Georgia state line. Upon reaching the Hampton Inn and Suites, near

Interstate 10, she pulled the Lincoln into the receiving area.

Once in her suite, Darcee yawned and stretched then reached in the mini-bar and took out a chilled white wine. She started a hot bath.

She opened her suitcase and took out a razor.

CHAPTER FIFTY-SIX

Theodore Barrett & Associates, Law
Offices
West Palm Beach, Florida
September 14

Cord and Peri approached the reception desk. He had decided to have Peri accompany him. The drive would give them time to talk and since she had been with them during their adventures in the Seminole village, Peri might be able to help. Besides, he liked the company.

"Your uncle is expecting you, Mr. Barrett. Please go right in," said Margaret.

Cord steered Peri down the long hallway and into the spacious corner office of his uncle. Instead of the usual warm greeting, Ted Barrett stood behind his desk. "Sit down, Cordie." He said sternly. Waving a hand at an adjoining chair, he indicated for Peri to have a seat, "Doctor."

"Just what the hell do you think you are doing?" Ted demanded tossing the society page of the Palm Beach paper on Cord's lap.

Peri's eyes filled with tears as she watched Cord read the announcement of his engagement to Darcee centered on the front page. Under the photos of Cord and Darcee he read:

> "Cattle Rancher and local billionaire, McCord Barrett, finally lassoed! Mrs. Sudie Barrett proudly announces the engagement of her son; McCord Barrett, Florida's most eligible and sought after bachelor, heir to the Barrett fortunes to...."

Cord sat stunned. "Uncle Ted, I—I don't know anything about this. How could something like this get in the paper?"

"You tell me, Cordie."

"I—I don't know."

"Isn't this Darcee the same gal you've been sporting around town and is now working for us?"

"Yes, but—but, this is a lie! It's not true."

"Well, son, true or not, I talked to your mother this morning. She is beside herself and doesn't know a damn thing about your wedding plans, and worse yet, neither do I. If it is true, have you had our security people run a background check on her? If you are even close to thinking of marriage, we have a mountain of legal work to get done; pre-nuptials, trusts, things like that to protect the family's assets."

"But Uncle Ted, this is a lie, a farce. I don't know a thing about it."

"Well okay, it's a farce, Cordie but you ought to know by now if your name is Barrett, you are news. I have told you a thousand times about your philandering and to keep that little thing of yours in your pants. Especially with company personnel; even a pigeon won't shit in its own nest."

Ted glanced at the tearful Peri. "Sorry, Doctor Pepper, I'm sorry to be so blunt." Peri gave a nonchalant shrug.

"We are going to have to do some damage control here," said Ted. "Letting the cat out of the bag is a helluva lot easier than putting it back in. I'm sure you know the party has been urging me to run for governor next year or maybe the U.S. Senate. I haven't made up my mind yet, but I sure don't need this kind of cannon fodder."

"Yeah," said Cord. "What is the old saying? Never pick a fight with anyone who buys their ink by the barrel."

"You got it, son. We need to move on, there's a lot to talk about."

Cord opened his mouth but before he could speak, Ted raised an index finger silencing him. He pressed the office intercom, "Margaret, would you ask Mr. Wildgoose to step in here please?"

"Yes sir."

No sound of footsteps were heard but moments later the senior Wildgoose silently strode into Ted's office giving Cord an icy stare and a quizzical look toward Peri.

"Where is GW?" he demanded.

Cord, sizing up the frigid atmosphere in the room thought discretion might be better than candor for the moment. "He was called to the FBI District Office in Miami, Uncle Gary." Due to the vibes of coolness in the ambiance of Ted's office, Cord knew it best not to say exactly what Wildgoose was really doing with government computers.

After a long silence Ted said, "Cordie, just what the hell were you thinking?"

"Sir?"

"Sir, my ass!" exclaimed Ted slamming his hand on the desk. "You know exactly what I'm talking about. You broke every rule breakable. You snooped in places you had no frigging business or call to pry into and worse yet, you got a friend of mine killed."

"The guy, ah, the guy with the cowboy hat?"

"His name is, or was, Coacoochee."

"It means Great Warrior," said Gary solemnly. "Coacoochee was a cousin of mine. His English name is Ray, Ray Sweetwater."

Cord knew the Seminoles called salt water, bitter water, and fresh water, sweet water.

"I'm sorry. I'm…"

"Being sorry doesn't cut it, Cordie. I gave those people my word, so did your Uncle Gary here. A promise made by you, or by white men, means little or nothing, but to the Seminole a promise is a sacrosanct oath."

Cord started to say something and again his uncle silenced him. "Those people chose to live that way over 150 years ago. They wanted nothing to do with the white man. They still don't. All they want is to be left alone and to live in peace."

Cord sat quietly and stared at his folded hands like a disciplined schoolboy. "But Uncle Ted, there are so many questions."

"Questions?" Ted exclaimed. "No questions. But if you have something to say, say it."

"Hold it," said the senior Wildgoose. Nodding in Peri's direction, he said. "No women."

"Yeah, that's another thing, Cordie. Have you lost your ever loving mind, taking a white woman into that camp?" He waved a hand in Peri's direction. "Doctor Pepper, if you please."

Peri stood and said, "Yes, of course, Senator. Cord, I'll be in the lobby."

Cord shook his head that he understood.

Cord asked his uncle and his partner a litany of questions regarding the trio's recent tour-de-force to which neither responded. When he asked about the satchel, with the JRO lettering, Gary Wildgoose sat with his usual Mount Rushmore stone face, but he could tell that he hit a nerve with his uncle.

"Cordie, I need to speak with your Uncle Gary for a few minutes. Leave us please."

Cord sat with Peri in the reception area for the better part of an hour. Finally, Margaret looked up and said, "Mr. Barrett asked to see you again and to please bring your lady friend."

Cord thanked her and escorted Peri back to Ted's office. "Sit down, you two," said Ted. "Cordie," he began, "the Seminoles out there in the Glades just want to be left alone. You two and GW have been privy to one of the most sacred and closely guarded secrets in the world. To violate that confidence would be a tragedy and bring calamity to their way of life. This cannot ever be dishonored." They both nodded they understood.

Cord said, "But Uncle Ted, there are so many things…"

Ted interrupted, "Let it go, Cordie. I want you both to forget everything you saw and heard out there. You must."

"We will do as you say, Uncle Ted, but I still…"

"Cordie, I'm not asking you, I'm telling you. Can't you read between the lines here? Isn't it clear to you yet without me saying, those Indians would have your head on a platter and your bodies fed to the gators, all three of you, before they would ever let their way of life be exposed or taken from them?"

"You mean…?"

"That's exactly what he means," said Gary. "They would take all three of you out in a heartbeat and never blink an eye. The only reason you are alive right now is because I made more promises to them. And I keep my promises," he added emphatically with an arctic stare.

"Let it go, Cordie. Just let it go. I'm not going to tell you again. Don't you think maybe your attention should be focused on our recent bank losses and missing money instead of the Everglades?"

"Yes sir, there's nine million dollars we have to account for."

"Nine million?" said Ted. "You haven't seen today's audits. Try twelve million."

"Twelve?"

"Yes, twelve, maybe more. We're still stymied and we can't call in the federal people because with that kind of publicity, our stock would collapse like a Niagara cascade."

"I see your point," said Cord. "The stockholders would have a mass withdrawal and dump their stock. Our whole banking system could cave in overnight."

"You got the picture," said Ted. "We do know this much; it is looking more and more like an inside job."

"I just cannot believe any of our people would do such a thing. They all are like family. The most junior person has over 15 years with us."

"It is hard for me to believe this too. However, it is happening and with the security processes we have in place, it appears it must be an inside job. For an outside hacker to make a withdrawal like that would mean, they have access to an authorized computer. I was told by our IT department that every computer that is authorized to be used to make a transfer has something they call a MAC number, it is like the individual computer's fingerprint."

That means someone would have to have access to our computers here in the main bank, at a branch or at the ranch," said Cord.

"True, but not necessarily, Cordie. It could be one of the laptops. I have mine. You know where your's is?"

"Of course, I know where mine is," Cord answered, knowing it is safe in his flight bag.

"Then the hacker must have the monthly security code, plus a code from the code generator, that thing that looks like a small old fashion page that give you a new access code every two minutes."

Cord interjected, "Safe also," knowing one is with his secure flight bag at the airport and the other is in the locked computer room in the Tidewaters.

"Good," stated Ted. "However, we have had another three plus million stolen since the installation of a biometric access point on the authorized computers. I am stumped on how we are still having this theft unless it is an inside job. Michelle Stewart is also at a crawl in the investigation, and the meantime we are losing big money. She can account for every authorized computer and code generator."

"Okay, I'll get in touch with Darcee Corbin," said Cord. "She is in Tallahassee right now and going on to our New Orleans banks. Maybe she can find out what's going on and hopefully find those codes and access issues."

"Sounds like a plan, Cordie."

After leaving Ted's office, Cord and Peri exited the elevator on the first floor of the Barrett bank.

"Hey Captain Sawber," Cord called out to a tall gentleman in a dark blue uniform bearing four gold stripes near his cuffs who was entering the bank.

"Hey there, Mr. Barrett, how are you?"

"Fine, just fine," replied Cord. "I thought you were flying Miss Corbin to Tallahassee this morning."

"That was the plan, Mr. Barrett," replied the BDI chief pilot. "We were waiting at the airport all ready to go and she didn't show."

"Didn't show?"

"No sir. We got a call and were told that she was driving instead."

"Driving? Okay thanks, Captain."

"Yes sir. Good day."

"Good day, Captain."

CHAPTER FIFTY-SEVEN

Pend Oreille Ranch
September 14

The sun was about to set on the cove and a soft breeze was blowing in across the calm water. Cord and Peri were lounging on the veranda discussing the events of the day sipping a gin and tonic. Poking her finger at the slice of lime floating in her drink Peri said, "I guess these limes come from the Pend Oreille too."

"Yep," said Cord. "Most everything we eat here is from the property. Come with me, Doctor Pepper, I want to show you something while we still have some light." Cord led her down the stairs wrapping around the fireplace, past the pool table and out the north door of the recreation room. After passing through a short wooded area, they came to a long line of white painted stables. Yardboy trotted along behind begging for a sugar cube.

"Cord, I didn't know these were here."

"There's a lot here, Doctor Pepper. It'll take a while, but you will learn your way around before long." Cord stopped in front of one of the stalls and opened the door.

"Hello there, old girl. You're soon going to be a mom," he said to a golden Palomino, patting her on the neck.

"Oh, oh, Cord, she is one of the most beautiful horses I have ever seen," exclaimed Peri, running her skilled hands over the mare's belly. "She is about to foal."

"Yes, any time now. Mama here is double registered and a quarter horse with great working lines. She is bred to Regal Webmaster, another working quarter horse with impeccable breeding. That's the proud papa over there," Cord thrust his chin toward a large golden stallion across the breezeway in the end stall. Like the mare, he was light chocolate colored with a silver mane and tail.

"Cord, they are so beautiful. That stud must be a purebred just like mom here."

"You can bet on it, Doctor Pepper. That's Nugget over there; he's my personal horse. Nobody rides him but me. Maybe you would like to take a ride around the property some afternoon?"

"Oh Cord, I would love to! Anytime—around the whole property?"

"Not around the whole property, Doctor Pepper. That would take weeks, maybe months."

"I don't have to ask Henry to teach you to ride, do I?"

"What kind of wacky weed have you been smoking? Of course, I can ride. I'm a country girl, remember?"

They were laughing as they exited the stables. "Here comes Henry now. It's probably feeding time," said Cord.

A tanned robust man approached them. "Lo, Cord."

"How's it going, Henry? We just stopped by to check on the mare."

"She's fine. Any day now, you know," he said eyeing Peri.

"I'm sorry. Henry, this is Doctor Peri Pepper. She will be taking over for Dr. Lee when he retires. Doctor Pepper, Henry is our ranch superintendent."

Henry tipped his hat and said, "Doctor Pepper, ma'am, nice to meet you and welcome to the Pend Oreille family."

"Thank you, Henry, nice to meet you as well, and its Peri, please."

"Peri will do fine. Now, if you all will excuse me, I got some hungry livestock to tend to." He handed the patiently waiting Yardboy a sugar lump and scratched his nose.

Cord and Peri were making their way back to the Tidewaters when Cord said, "Looks like Goose is coming," he indicated down the long driveway.

"Is that his truck?" she asked.

"Yeah, let's go around back, he won't come to the front."

"The back?"

"Yep, we don't allow Injuns or little veterinarians to use the front door," he laughed.

"Oh, Cord, you..." She slipped her arm through his. Peri Pepper was at peace with the world and completely absorbed with Cord Barrett.

"Hey, Goose, what did you find out?"

Wildgoose remained sitting in his truck. "Not a helluva lot, Cord. Hey, Doctor Pepper."

"Hey, GW."

Wildgoose leaned out the window of the truck. "Flight 19 went down in the ocean just like the history books say they did. Not much else about it except they had some bad weather, got lost, and ran out of fuel."

"How would all five of them get lost Goose, especially Naval Aviators?"

"Damned if I know. They never found a trace of them. But I did find out that the Navy Avenger was not all that scarce after World War II. So some collector with a lot of money could have easily bought them from Navy surplus."

"Somebody like my grandfather, maybe?" said Cord.

"Exactly."

"If so, why would he hide them way out there in some Seminole village that no one has ever heard of or even knows about?"

"Beats me."

"Did you check out the names?"

"Sure did. They all match and all dead. But I found out something kind of interesting."

"What, Goose?"

"You remember that one guy you said was probably the flight leader, the, ah, commander?"

"Yeah, Galvan, I think it was; he was a lieutenant commander. What about him?"

"Well, Lieutenant Commander Galvan is long since dead, but his wife or someone is still getting his widow's pension."

"Can't be, Goose. She'd be older than Noah."

"Maybe she is, and like you said, she's got to be older than a redwood, but those checks have been going to someone every month since the end of the war."

"Where are they being mailed to, Goose?"

"I couldn't get it. Blocked. But think about it. If she was married to Galvan, say late in the war, and she was only 18 or 19, at the time that would make her what? About in her late 80's or so."

"Let's see," said Cord. "The war was over in 45 so that would make her...yeah, Goose, that's about right. Maybe she's still living?"

"She would be in her high 80s or low 90s," spoke up Peri, "Math 101."

"Did you look up the others, Goose?"

"I haven't checked on them yet."

"What about JRO?" asked Cord.

"No idea," replied Wildgoose. "Nothing."

Cord frowned and kicked at a dirt clod beside the truck, deep in thought. "Goose, what's that skinny kid's name who works part-time at your office, you know, the tall blond kid?"

"You mean Timmy?"

"Yeah, that's it, Timmy. Doesn't he attend the community college, and isn't he some kind of boy wonder, like a computer wizard of some sort?"

"Yeah, I guess," said Wildgoose. "He's just a part-time file clerk and does entries and filing on our computer and stuff like that, but he doesn't have FBI access."

"Get him over to your office tonight, can you?"

"I guess so. Why?"

"Just do it Goose. I got a hunch. I'll see you about eight."

"Okay, Lindbergh. Eight it is."

"Thanks, J. Edgar."

CHAPTER FIFTY-EIGHT

Federal Office of the Interior
Palm Beach County, Florida
September 14

At eight, that evening, Cord and Peri were sitting in Wildgoose's FBI office located in the Office of the Interior Building. Since Wildgoose was the federal agent for the local Indian Nations, he was housed there rather than in the West Palm Beach or Fort Lauderdale offices.

Soon after eight, a tall extremely thin late teenager ambled into the office. The young man's face was pockmarked with acne and he was so skinny, Cord wondered how he kept his pants up. His long blond hair was messy and hung on his shoulders.

I think it's a boy, thought Cord. *An exact prototype of a computer nerd—*

Timmy peered through thick glasses. "You wanted to see me, Mr. Wildgoose?"

"Yes Timmy, thanks for coming in. We need to get this information," said Wildgoose handing the kid a slip of paper.

Timmy studied it for a moment and said, "Ah, Mr. Wildgoose, this is the VA, Division of Pensions, it is illegal to tap into it."

"It's not illegal if an FBI Agent asks you to, is it?" said Cord. "And Timmy, this is top secret."

"Top secret?" exclaimed the kid, thrilled that he was being included in an FBI top-secret investigation.

"Yes," whispered Wildgoose, "Top secret. You must never tell anyone."

"Ouuu, I won't," promised Timmy. "Top secret, huh?"

"Yeah, man. Top secret," they all nodded.

"You know I'll have to hack in don't you?"

"Yes, we know, Timmy," said Wildgoose. "But this is top secret government business."

"Yeah," whispered Timmy. "FBI, top secret." Timmy sat down at the computer and cracked his knuckles. He began to type faster than any of them had ever heard anyone type before. It sounded to Cord like a handful of gravel being thrown again a tin barn making a constant rat-tat-tat.

An hour and a half had passed before Timmy looked up from the keyboard. "Mr. Wildgoose, I don't think I'm going to be able to crack it and get this lady or her address or anything. Maybe there isn't anything."

Wildgoose sighed. "Okay thanks, Timmy, I appreciate you coming in. I know government codes are impossible to hack."

"Not impossible, sir. But kinda beyond my skill level; something like this would take a real pro or another hacking program."

"You mean it would take a different program to break into their computer?"

"Exactly, sir, actually it's a computer hacking into another computer."

Cord made a mental note. *A computer with a hacking program can break into another computer. Is that what's going on in our banks?*

"Wait," broke in Timmy. "There is one more thing I can try, but I don't think we'd better—I'd have to install...."

"Do it, Tim," ordered Cord.

"Yes sir," he looked at Wildgoose, "If you say so, Mr. Wildgoose."

Wildgoose nodded his approval.

Timmy sat down at the computer; again, his fingers were flying over the keyboard like a jazz pianist. Suddenly the computer began clicking. Cord heard the printer engage.

"What we got, Goose?" he asked as Wildgoose grab the printouts from the printer.

Wildgoose looked unbelievably at Timmy. "You hacked into the CIA database?"

"Yes sir, you said it was top secret FBI business. The CIA was the only ones who might have had it. So, I hacked in and checked."

"Timmy," said Wildgoose, "Can anyone tell if you hacked into their computer?"

"Yes sir, if they check and have the smarts. I better uninstall the program I installed on this machine before I leave."

"Err, okay Timmy, uninstall the program and thanks a lot." Wildgoose said in a calmer voice. "You can go home when you finish, and remember, this is top secret."

"Yes sir, Mr. Wildgoose, top secret." Timmy raised a finger to his lips indicating silence. He unloaded the program and took his leave.

"Barrett, I thought you had lost your mind before, but this is really the top of the volcano. Have you got any idea what they would do to us if we got caught hacking into the CIA?"

"Relax, Goose. What does it say?"

"Relax? Relax, Goose, you say! Barrett, you want me to relax when I could lose my job! When we could all go to freaking prison. Be shot!"

"Take it easy, Goose. You're getting too hyper especially for a cool and calm, great Seminole Warrior. What does it say?"

"Cool and calm in the Everglades maybe, but the CIA! The fucking CIA!"

"What does it say, Goose? For Pete's sake."

"Let's see, Galvan's widow pension is not being paid from the U.S. Treasury, so why would the CIA be paying her? And it's going to a Lisa Finn in Watauga County, North Carolina, county seat there is Boone."

"Where is Boone?" Cord asked.

"May I see that please?" said Peri. She studied the paper for quite a while. "Boone is in the northwestern part of the state, very far north, almost on the Tennessee/Virginia state line."

"I recognize the name," said Wildgoose. "Watauga is an Indian word, means pretty water or close. We have a derivative of the same word in Seminole."

"But Goose, it says there is no listing for a Finn or a Galvan anywhere in Boone. The kid checked the water company, power, property records, everything. All we have is a post office box."

"Looks like that's the best we're going to do, Cord."

"But the lingering question here is why would the CIA be involved in any of this?" said Cord. "All

356

military checks, retirements, disabilities, widow pensions and things like that are dispatched through the Veteran's Administration and paid through the U.S. Treasury. The CIA operates completely separate from any other government agency."

"Yeah, you're right Cord. Nobody knows a thing about the CIA's budget, where the money goes or how it is spent."

Cord was pensive for a lingering moment. "Tell you what, Goose. Meet me at the Tidewaters tomorrow morning at first light."

"Barrett, I don't think I like that look and I know I don't like that tone."

"Be there, Injun. First light."

CHAPTER FIFTY-NINE

Pend Oreille Ranch
September 15

Wildgoose showed up at the Tidewaters early. Cord and Peri were already up and dressed. They were waiting on the veranda. "Morning, Goose," said Cord, "your breakfast is ready." Wildgoose sat down and Cord picked up the phone.

"Good morning, Paco, would you please have the Baron pulled out of the hangar and make sure she's fueled and ready to go."

Wildgoose exclaimed, "Oh, no, Barrett, oh, no. You're not about to get me in that flying tin can again. No sir, absolutely not!"

"Hurry up with your breakfast, Goose, you're burning daylight."

Cord turned to Peri, "Doctor Pepper, are you packed?"

"Cord, if it's all the same to you, I think I'll stay here on the Pend Oreille. If that mare foals, I might be needed."

He thought for a moment. "Good thinking, Doctor Pepper. We'll be back tonight or tomorrow. You look after things here, and while I'm thinking about it, call our accounting office and tell them to add you to the payroll."

"Tell them what?"

"Tell them I said to add you to the payroll. Pick a salary that suits you and call the Barrett Carpool; order whatever car or truck you want." Peri was speechless and sat in stunned bewilderment.

Do dreams really come true? Am I dreaming? No—this is real—Am actually here at the Pend Oreille? Do I really have a job as a vet? And do I have the man of my dreams? Any woman's dream—Do I have McCord Barrett? Just like my daddy, the Reverend Joshua Pepper, promised me long ago — someday, all my dreams would come true.

Looking at the distraught Wildgoose, Cord said, "C'mon, Goose, O great Viceroy of Seminole aviation, we gotta go. Bring your breakfast with you."

"Oh, crap, the things I do for you," muttered Wildgoose, throwing his fork down. "You know I hate to flyin' that little pill box of yours, especially with a wildman like you!"

"Goose, it's a half-million dollar Beechcraft, B-58 Baron. The finest light twin ever built. Move your butt."

"I know, I know, I'm burning daylight," mumbled the reluctant Wildgoose. "We might as well go. You haven't been rowing with both oars in the water since I've known you."

After an end-to-end pre-flight inspection of the maroon and white Beechcraft, the two men strapped in and Cord went over the check-list, mags on, fuel pumps on, boost overrides off.... The engines started smoothly and Cord taxied to the runway. Soon the reliable Baron lifted gracefully off the Pend Oreille airport and banked north.

An hour into the flight Wildgoose peeked from under the blanket he had roofed over his head.

"How fast are we going?"

Cord glanced at the airspeed indicator. "190 knots."

"How fast is that?"

"About, 220 mph."

"Oh, dear Lord," muttered the Indian. "We're over the ocean. You're not taking us over the ocean are you?"

"Damn right, Goose, we're going direct. Don't be such a puss."

"Oh, Lordy, oh, Lordy," prayed Wildgoose. He pulled the blanket back over his head.

Cord teased, "You and Dr. Pepper assume the same flying position."

After three hours passed Wildgoose said, "Where are we?"

"Coming up on the Holston Mountain Vortac. See?" he pointed to one of the myriad of instruments.

"See what?"

"It's a navigational facility, Goose. All we do is fly to the fix then track 125° from it. Let's see, once at the fix, we've only got 26.7 miles and we're there."

"There where?"

"The Boone airport, Goose, straight in front of us."

"How do you propose we get around once we're on the ground, Mr. Hertz?"

"Way ahead of you, Geronimo, I called our bank in Ashville and they will have car waiting for us at the Boone airport."

Cord turned final approach for Runway Three-One. "Might be a little tight, Goose, we only have 2100 feet of runway and at this elevation altitude—"

"Don't tell me stuff like that, Barrett, don't explain!" cried Wildgoose ducking back under his security blanket.

"You're missing a lot of pretty foliage. It's gorgeous around here; especially this time of year."

"I'll take your word for it," came a muffled reply from under the blanket. "Someday you can tell me all about it."

Cord eased the Baron down on the runway and taxied to the tie down area. After ordering the tanks topped off, they climbed into a waiting Cadillac. "Looks like we got the bank president's car," he chuckled.

Three miles later, Cord pulled into the post office parking lot on Blowing Rock Road in Boone. "All right, we're here," said Wildgoose. "What do we do now?"

"We wait."

"We wait? We wait for what?"

"We wait to see who opens that P.O. Box," Cord answered.

"From here?"

"No, not from here, that's why you are going in and pretend as you're addressing something or whatever. Just look busy."

"Yeah, sure, just look busy. And you?"

"I'm going to stay right here and check out every car. We have to make sure we follow the right one."

"For this I went to the FBI Academy," grumbled Wildgoose climbing out of the Caddie.

It was well into the afternoon and the two men were about to give up their stakeout for the day when Cord noticed a white Volvo station wagon parking in front of the post office. A slender chestnut haired woman entered the doors and turned left toward Post Office Box 320.

All right, Goose, be on your toes—

Wildgoose walked quickly back to Cord. "That's her or whoever. Anyway, she opened box 320, so that's got to be our person."

Cord fell in behind the white Volvo as it turned on Blowing Rock Road to Highway 105 towards Banner Elk and Linville, heading south out of Boone. Several miles later, the Volvo turned onto a winding road, next to a tributary of the Watauga River in the tiny parish of Valle Crucis.

They passed the Mast General Store, the sign read, "*Founded in 1883*." Apparently, Mast was about the only store in town. They followed the white station wagon down a long unnamed country lane. The houses were scarce and few. The Volvo stopped in front of a quaint and comfortable looking dwelling commanding a spectacular view of the colorful mountains.

Cord approached the woman as she was getting out of the car. He didn't know to ask for Finn or Galvan. He took a chance. "Hello, Mrs. Galvan?"

"No, my married name is McCutchean. I'm her granddaughter," she said in a heavy mountain accent. "Did you want to see her?"

"Yes, if you don't mind, Mrs. McCutchean." Cord caught himself staring at the lady's beauty. He guessed her in the mid-thirties. She was slim and the chestnut hair bounced around her shoulders.

"That's okay, call me Kaitlyn. Everyone does," she smiled showing perfect white teeth. "And you are?"

Cord thought fast. "My name is McCord Barrett, Lieutenant McCord Barrett, U.S. Navy, and this is Captain G.W. Wildgoose, U.S. Marine Corps."

"Oh, I see." she said. "Are you here to see my grandmother or the commander?"

The commander? He's still alive?

"Yes ma'am, we'd like to see the commander."

"Y'all wait here. Let me check inside. Seems like the commander has been quite popular here lately," she said. Kaitlyn disappeared inside the charming cottage.

"What did she mean by that, Cord?"

"I don't know. I can't believe he's still alive."

Kaitlyn reappeared. "Y'all come on in, but I have to ask you not to be long." They both nodded. She led them into a room in the rear of the house with a splendid view of the mountains. "Granddaddy, these gentlemen are here to see you."

An old man was in the corner of the room sitting in a wheelchair. His hair was snow white and his blue eyes crystal clear. He was sucking on an oxygen mask and extending his hand. The old gentleman was neat and very alert.

"Attention on deck," he shouted as best he could. Cord and Wildgoose snapped to attention and gave the old man a pacifying salute. He saluted back. "Hee, hee," the old man cackled. "Hot damn! I ain't done that in a coon's age. Hee, hee, hee."

"That's my wife Lisa, there," he said. An elderly lady ambling behind a walker entered the room. Even with her advancing age, Mrs. Galvan was still an attractive woman. The visitors surmised that she must have been a pretty hot number in her day. Pointing a wrinkled finger, the old man said, "Been married to my darling there for 68 years, I have."

"Sounds like it might work out," laughed Cord.

"How come you Navy boys are way up here in the mountains?"

"We came to see you, Commander," said Cord.

"Where you from, sonny?"

"Florida, sir."

"Yep, I was afraid of that."

"Afraid of that? Why?"

"I figured you all would find them Avengers sooner or later."

"Commander, you mean they are authentic? The real things?"

"Hot damn! Hee, hee, hee. You bet your sweet ass they are the real things, sonny. Did you see the *Miss Lisa*?"

"Yes sir, we did."

"How'd she look, son? Tell me."

"Perfect, sir, just like the day she came out of the Grumman factory."

"I sure miss that old bird. I flew her all through the fightin' in the south Pacific during the war; I got her shot up all to hell a few times, I did. Hee hee, hee. I won the NFC with her at Midway."

"You were awarded the Navy Flying Cross, sir?"

That explains the necklace on the old woman's granddaughter.

"Damn right I did. I gave it to a medicine woman, with them Indians down there in Florida; good lookin' thing she was too. Hee, hee, hee. Wish I hadn't done that now." The old man went into a series of coughing and sucked deeply on the oxygen. Kaitlyn approached him with a paper towel. The commander spat into the towel and continued.

Cord and Wildgoose did not interrupt as the old man went on obviously enjoying reviving this exciting part of his youth. "Hot damn, we was flying off the Yorktown in them days before the Japs bombed her and shot her all to hell and back. Hot damn what a tussle, hee, hee, hee."

"Admiral Halsey, ya know, Bull Halsey, he was the skipper, the fleet boss. Rough ol' sumbitch, he was. I wuz a young ensign, full of piss and vinegar, you know; all balls, no brains, hee, hee, hee. Hot damn, what a fray! We give them Japs somthin' to think about, we did."

The old commander went into another coughing spree and held the oxygen mask tightly against his face. He spat into the paper towel.

"Commander, can you tell us about the Avengers and how they got in the Everglades?" asked Wildgoose.

"Yeah, I can. But not sure, I will. Hee, hee, hee." He looked at Wildgoose. "You the Marine, sonny?"

"Yes sir."

"Hot damn, what a fightin' bunch of boys them Marines was. They got the shit kicked out of them down in them islands in the Pacific. You know Guadalcanal, Iwo hot spots like -at. Them Marines—what an outfit! Hee, hee, hee." The old man began coughing again.

"Please don't be too long," said Kaitlyn.

They nodded.

"Commander, can you tell about the airplanes?" said Cord.

"Yeah, reckon I will. You boys have a seat. Kaitie, would you get these boys sumthin' to drink. You all hungry?" They both shook their heads no but thanked him.

"You one of them jet jockeys, boy?" He said to Cord.

"Yes sir. Hot damn, if we'd had equipment like - at, we'd kicked them little bastards asses clean back into China! What a ruckus, hee, hee, hee."

Cord and Wildgoose smiled at the old man's enthusiasm. He obviously enjoyed the fight or least telling about it to anyone who would listen.

"You know I could still lick either one of you boys, by damn. Don't care if you are a Marine, sonny," he said setting his jaw in Wildgoose's direction. "I could whup the lot of you."

Both readily agreed with the old commander and almost believed him.

He leaned forward and held up a mason jar. "Hey, I got sum-um' here you boys might wanna taste. Friend of mine makes it over on the other side of Sugar Mountain. Them revenuers don't know a damn thing about it. Hee, hee, hee. It'll put lead in your pencils, boys." Cord and Wildgoose declined the generous offer of the clear liquid.

368

A series of coughing followed. The commander sucked on the mask. "I fooled 'em sonny, hee hee. I fooled em all. I fooled ever' damn one of them Yankee bastards, all these years. You boys sit back and I'll tell you the whole story."

CHAPTER SIXTY

Tallahassee Airport, Northwest Florida
September 15

Before going to her rendezvous with Chip and Dale, Darcee had to make an important stop. She drove the Lincoln around Capital Circle and past the Apalachicola National Forest. Again, she reflected on the beauty of this part of the state. Darcee turned on Lake Bradford Road and into the flower-lined entrance of the Tallahassee Regional Airport.

Instead of turning right to the terminal, she steered left and parked at Sky Ventures Aviation, one of the two Fixed Base Operators on the field. When she walked through the automatic doors, a slightly balding man peered over a pair of granny glasses and gave her an inquiring look. He was showing a slight bulge around his middle and wore a garnet and gold necktie hanging loosely from a ruffled white shirt.

Garnet and gold, he must be a Florida State man—

"Help you, ma'am?"

Reading the man's nametag Darcee said, "Do I call you Mr. MacNeil, or shall I call you Hugh?"

"Hugh fits. But must folks call me Mac."

Darcee, dressed in a low-top blouse, leaned both elbows on the counter and squeezed her shoulders tightly giving the man a charitable view of her abundant creamy-white breasts. In the deepest sensuous voice, she could muster she said, "You charter airplanes don't you, Mac?"

"That's why we're here. We also got maintenance, fuel and a little flight instruction."

"Good. Then I want to charter the fastest plane you have."

"When and to where?"

"Tonight, late; I guess I should say in the morning, early. Like one or two."

"Not all that unusual," said the man, still finding it impossible to keep his eyes from staying glued to Darcee's nipples peeking above the low cut blouse.

"It isn't?"

"No ma'am. Tallahassee is the capital and lot of the legislators' use us and sometimes the hours are a little crazy, you from the senate or the house?"

Darcee didn't answer allowing him form his own opinion. "I want to leave around one or two."

"Yes ma'am, but it's going to cost."

"I didn't ask if it cost, Mac. I said I wanted to leave around one or two."

"Yes ma'am, but if you want to take the Citation Jet, the FAA requires a copilot and I will have to get another crew member out here. There's a charge for her too."

"I didn't ask you that either, Mac. What I asked was how much?"

"Is there going to be a layover? There's an hourly charge and all expenses for layovers."

"No, I have to be back here by morning," said Darcee. "How much?" she asked again.

"Well, ma'am, that depends on where you're going, but at least ten grand and up, and I'm going to need a credit card for a deposit."

Darcee fumbled in her purse emerging with a bundle of Ben Franklins. She counted out fifty 100-dollar bills on the counter. "Mac," she cooed seductively. "Unless you have some another form of payment in mind is money acceptable?"

Mac licked his lips and paused. "Sure, money is always good. You sound like my ex-wife," he smiled.

"There's five grand," said Darcee. "I'll pay you the rest in cash when we land back here." She headed for the door anxiously anticipating her three-way romp with Chip and Dale.

"Oh, ma'am."

"What, Mac?"

"Where is it you want to go?"

"BCT."

"BCT?"

"Yes, BCT, that's Boca Raton Airport, just south of Palm Beach International."

Darcee was half way through the open automatic door when she turned. "Oh, Mac."

"Ma'am?"

"Did I tell you?" she purred.

"Tell me what, ma'am?"

"I shave."

The man's eyes budged as he swallowed hard. The pencil he was holding snapped in pieces.

CHAPTER SIXTY-ONE

Watauga County, North Carolina
September 15

Cord and Wildgoose settled back in their chairs and waited for the old commander to end another wheezing and coughing spell. Kaitlyn brought them some iced tea, which was almost too sweet to drink. In the silence, they waited.

The old man leaned forward waving a liver-spotted arm and said, "You know, the war were over in '45, August of '45. We whipped them Krauts, and we whipped them Nips, on two sides of the world, we did. Hee, hee. We was real fightin' men in them days; not like the bunch of pussies that's in the military today. A woman in a combat? A woman aboard ship? Whoever heard of such a crazy damn thing?"

Both visitors shook their heads in feigned agreement. The old man went on. "We wuz real men; real fightin' men, you know? Anyhow, Ol' Harry, now he were one tough old sumbitch," he jabbed a crooked finger toward an autographed picture of President Truman. "Ol' Harry, now there were a president. He'd tell you where the bear shit, in the buckwheat, in a second. Anyways, Ol' Harry, he didn't take no shit from nobody. He were a Missourah farm boy, he wuz. Jest like me. Tough as an iron skillet, he wuz. Ol' Harry, he weren't no Commander-in-Chief like the panty-waste they elect today." He began coughing. Kaitlyn wiped his mouth and gave them an acrimonious look.

The old nonagenarian held the oxygen mask tightly and sucked in a few deep breaths. "Anyways, like I wuz sayin', Ol' Harry ordered Little Boy dropped on Nagasaki in August of '45. You boys know what Little Boy wuz? Little Boy were the A-Bomb, made out of plutonium, ya know. The Nips didn't surrender right away, so Ol' Harry he ordered another-un dropped. It would have taken them months to build another plutonium bomb, so they dropped Fat Man. That were another A-Bomb, it weren't made outta plutonium, but it did the trick. Them Japs surrendered to Doug MacArthur the next day. I never cared much for him."

Cord and Wildgoose sat intrigued with the old man's rhetoric of his war years, but patiently hoped that he would get to the point soon.

"What about the Avengers, sir?" asked Cord.

"I'm getting to that young man," he coughed. "All you young folks is in such a damn hurry these days."

"Yes sir, take your time, please."

Commander Galvan went on. "Like I said, the war were over in August of '45 and I decided to stay in the Navy. So they made me an IP, that's Instructor Pilot, and I got sent to Fort Lauderdale. Hot damn! What a duty station. Hee, hee, hee, if you know what I mean," he winked.

Cord had been an IP himself. He smiled with admiration for the old warrior and patiently waited for him to continue.

"The war had been over for three or four months when I led Flight 19; but shortly after I got to Fort Lauderdale, a tall skinny fella, named Bobby looked me up, said he'd chosen me special for some secret mission."

"Flight 19, a secret mission, sir?"

"Just keep your pants on there, Lieutenant," the old man cackled. "You young fellers always running around like your asses wuz on fire."

Cord smiled at the old man, "Please go on, Commander," he said. "Who was Bobby?"

"Bobby? His real name was Robert, Robert Oppenheimer."

Cord bolted up in his chair. "Dr. Robert Oppenheimer! The physicist? The father of the atomic bomb, Robert Oppenheimer?"

"Yep, same feller, sonny. Snotty little sumbitch. A Yankee Jew-Boy from up nawth, New Yawk, New Jersey, some place like –at."

376

"Yes sir, I remember reading about him," said Wildgoose. "He was very much against the use of the bomb."

"Yeah, I remember that too," said Cord. "Oppenheimer became very cynical and critical of the Manhattan Project and the use of the bomb. In fact, he quoted from the *Bhagavad Gita: 'Now I am death; destroyer of worlds'*."

"You got that right, boys," he said, wheezing and catching a breath. "That skinny little sumbitch smoked constantly, one Camel right after ta other. You might know it would take the smarts of them Yankees to come up with somethin' as brilliant as the A-Bomb. Fact is, right after the Trinity Project, that's when they first tested the bomb out yonder in New Mexico." He said, "My God, we have created hell."

"Yes sir," said Cord. "Dr. Oppenheimer was brilliant."

"Damn sure was, but that ain't all."

"Sir?"

"That ain't all, son. He come up with something a whole lot worser than any atomic bomb."

"What could be worse than a nuclear bomb," asked Wildgoose.

"Temperature, Captain, Temperature."

"Temperature?" they both said together.

"Temperature, sonny, yep, damn right, temperature. I know it is true cos I seen it. I seen it work with these here two eyes." The old Commander burst into a coughing spasm, which earned them a testy look from Kaitlyn as she wiped his mouth. But they were not about to leave until they heard the rest of the story.

When the old man recovered, Cord gently said, "Commander Sir, can you tell us a bit more about this, ah, temperature? Is it a heat source, like a laser, maybe?"

"Nope, jest the opposite. It don't add heat, it takes it away."

"You mean instead of burning something, it can actually take heat away?" asked Wildgoose.

"That's exactly what I mean, sonny. Damnest thing you ever did see. Some rich rancher down there in Florida allowed the gov'ment to build Bobby a lab on his land way the hell out in a swamp. Built like a brick shit house it were. Damnest place you ever tried to get to in your life. Damn alligators, snakes, and all kinds of friggin' critters all over the place."

Cord felt a bolt of electricity rush up his spine. "Ah, sir, do you know the rancher's name?"

"Yep, and so do you, sonny."

"McCord Barrett?" Cord quietly said. *This sly old fox is sharper and a lot cleverer than I thought.*

The old man smiled. "Two McCord Barretts? Now ain't that one hell of a coincidence. Hee, hee, hee."

CHAPTER SIXTY-TWO

Watauga County, North Carolina
September 15

The Commander's head sagged and he seemed to be dozing. Kaitlyn said, "You can see he's worn out; too much excitement. I'm sorry, but I have to ask you gentlemen to leave."

The old man raised his head and held out his hand like a cop signaling someone to stop. "Hold it, boys. Belay that order."

"But Granddaddy...." Kaitlyn started to say.

"Hang on a minute, Kaitie, darlin'. There's a few more things these fellers ought to know."

He began. "See boys that skinny Yankee, Ol' Bobby Oppenheimer, was one smart little sumbitch. He discovered sum kinda element or mineral, sumthin' like –at out there in them Everglades; actually he didn't discover it really, he got it from the Indians, them Seminoles. He named it Freeonite. Onlyest place in the world they have ever found it is down there in them swamps."

"What's it good for, Commander?" asked Cord. "I mean, what can it do?"

"What can it do, son? I'll tell you what it can do, damnedest thing you ever saw. That Freeonite is the prettiest blue you ever did see and colder than an Eskimos ass. Comes right out of the ground in them Everglades, down there in Florida."

"Yes sir, and?"

"Well, Ol' Bobby, he figured out a way to refine and process it, whatever they do. It can be made into a bomb or fired from a cannon or any way you want to use it. Freezes everything it touches."

Wildgoose said, "You say it just freezes things, that's all?"

"That's all? Hee, hee, hee. That's all, Captain? You don't know what you're talkin' 'bout. This Freeonite, once it's processed, somehow destroys any heat molecules in any substance. Takes it right down to absolute zero instantly, that's what? 'Bout 460° below zero on the Fahrenheit scale? I tell you that skinny little Yankee was one smart sumbitch."

"And did they ever make it into a weapon?" asked Cord.

"You bet they did, sonny. Ol' Bobby named it Phoebe, like the lady's name, Phoebe. I saw it work myself. Damn thing could take out any object. A city block is nothin'. Hell, it could demolish an entire country in one swoop. Everything dies instantly." The old man tried to snap his fingers for emphasis. "Then everything in its path jest disintegrates like a stale cookie. It don't leave nothin'. No buildings, no life, no nothing. Even steel crumbles like baby powder."

"Whatever happened sir? We have never heard anything about Phoebe or this Freeonite."

"Course, you ain't. Cos I fooled them all, made 'um all looked like a bunch of horse's asses. Hee, hee, hee. I tell you, it didn't take long for them OSS boys from Washington to git down there to them Everglades."

"OSS, Commander?"

"Yeah, the Office of Strategic Services, that were before it became the CIA. Anyhow, them OSS boys wuz all over the place like flies around a pile of cow shit." The old man began another series of coughing and gasping into the oxygen mask.

"They give us orders to have some of that Freeonite stuff and Bobby's weapon, Phoebe, flown to some secret place outside Washington, DC, but I fooled um'. I fooled um' all. Hee, hee, hee."

"What happened, Commander?" asked Wildgoose.

"Well, Ol' Bobby, he come to me and said that he was ascared that if Phoebe ever fell into the wrong hands, maybe even ours, and if that damn thing ever got out of control, why hell's bells, son; the whole continent could be wiped out in seconds."

Cord said, "So what did you do, Commander?"

The old man coughed and spit into the napkin again. "We fooled um', son. We fooled ever one of them OSS bastards. We come up with a plan, son. Me and Ol' Bobby.

The old man took a slap at his knee. "Hot damn! Hee, hee. We come up with a plan, we did."

CHAPTER SIXTY-THREE

Watauga County, North Carolina
September 15

"Will you tell us about it, sir?" said Cord.

"I'm going to; the cats already out of the bag now anyways. But you will have to give me a minute I gotta make a head call. Kaitie."

Kaitlyn helped the old veteran into a walker and toward the bathroom. It was a slow process. Wildgoose punched Cord, "Hey Barrett, what did he mean by 'the cats already out of the bag'?" he whispered.

"I got no idea, Goose, but we sure better ask him."

After several minutes, Kaitlyn re-emerged at the old man's side as he slowly struggled to place one foot in front of the other. He fell back on his wheelchair exhausted. He exhaled a raspy breath.

The old commander seemed contemplative and not quite as feisty.

"Boys, I guess you could call me a traitor or maybe even a defector of sorts. Hell, I been AWOL damn near 70 years, hee, hee. What are they gonna do? You think them boys in Washington will put an old bastard like me in the brig way out there in Leavenworth?

"A defector, Commander?" asked Cord.

"Yeah son, a traitor. See, me and Ol' Bobby, we had a plan. We fooled all them sumbitches, we fooled ever one of 'um, hee, hee, hee."

The commander began coughing and pressed the oxygen close against his face. Cord and Wildgoose sat with inquisitive expressions anxiously waiting to hear the old man's story.

"We both figured that if Phoebe ever got out of control, or if she ever got into the wrong hands, even our own peoples, an entire civilization could be wiped out, and we'd end up victims of our own folly. We just couldn't allow it. Fact is, the war were over back there in '45, and we already had atomic power and nuclear bombs. But Phoebe, shee-it, why she'd make the atomic bomb look like a firecracker. So Bobby, he defused Phoebe. There were only five essential parts to it and..."

"How big was it Commander?" asked Wildgoose.

"Weren't nothing to it, sonny. Damn thing weren't no bigger than one of them little Jap cars, mostly made up of casings and lead, stuff like 'at, but it were heavier than a ton of elephant shit. Like I said, weren't but five parts that wuz really essential."

"Like what?"

"Damned if I know sonny. Whenever it wuz compressed or did sumthin' to that there Freeonite and turned it into a murderin' sumbitch." He paused.

"And then?" said Cord quietly.

"Well, Ol' Bobby took that Phoebe thing apart and he give me all five of them really important parts, said for me to git rid of them forever."

"How, sir?"

The old commander gave a despairing look at Wildgoose. "I'm comin' to that, sonny. Did someone stick a branding iron up your butt?"

"No sir. Sorry."

"Them OSS fellers had it all figured out. Each of us had a part to fly. I was to lead a flight and we'd fly them important parts out east of the Gulfstream, just a fifty or so miles off Palm Beach, and land on an aircraft carrier. A sub was s'posed to meet us out there then take us and them five parts underwater to Norfolk, Virginia. Top secret stuff, boys."

"No doubt," said Cord.

"Well—I fooled 'um. Fooled ever one them— hee, hee, hee." The old man stopped talking and looked in the distance.

"Yes sir, Commander go on, please."

"Well sir, I rounded me up four good men. All volunteers; I mean the very best of the best. Boys that I trusted—trusted completely, good boys, all top-shelf, A-One Naval Aviators. And I told them 'bout my plan and the gravity of the situation with Phoebe. I give each one of them boys a part to Phoebe and kept the triggering mechanism myself. I knew that this way no one of us would have all the parts to it."

"So we took off from Fort Lauderdale, but we didn't land on no damn carrier, hee, hee, hee. No sir! Hot damn! What a night!"

"You didn't land, sir?"

"Of course we landed boy! But not on no damn carrier, we didn't. That's when I come up with my plan," the old aviator cackled. "I pretended that we was lost, hee, hee, hee."

"That you were lost, sir?" said Cord.

"Hee, hee, damn right. Hee, hee. That we wuz lost, all five of us lost? There I wuz 59-combat missions in the Pacific under my belt, and an Instructor Pilot, lost. Hardly! But we pulled it off and they bought it. We fooled 'um all. They searched for our asses all over the Atlantic Ocean and the islands too. Hee, hee. They finally give up and wrote us up as dead, cos we run out of fuel. They figured we'd ditched out in that there Triangle, they did."

"How did you manage that, Commander?" asked Wildgoose.

"Actually, it weren't all that hard, sonny. See, down there in Florida they got this big mystery 'bout the Devil's Triangle; some call it the Bermuda Triangle, you know, where a bunch of ships and airplanes have disappeared, so they say."

"Oh yeah, the infamous Triangle," said Cord.

"I think that Triangle stuff is a bunch of horseshit myself, but I made it work for us. We took off from the NAS there at Lauderdale 'bout two, or so, in the afternoon. Plan were to meet the aircraft carrier and the sub out there in the Atlantic. We had concocted a line of hogwash that we knew they would hear on the radios. Stuff like our instruments had gone crazy and wuz givin' us trouble and that we wuz lost. Stuff like 'at, and that we had to ditch, no gas. Hee, hee."

Cord asked, "Commander, you mentioned my grandfather earlier, and I was wondering...."

"Yeah, your granddaddy, helluva a feller, your granddaddy, a real man he were, big feller. I knowed who you wuz the second Kaitie here told me your name. You kinda favor him too."

"But what did he have to do with all this?"

"I was gonna tell you 'bout that, Lieutenant. I went to your granddaddy for help. I needed money and I needed a way for my boys to get away clean. If anybody was gonna take the fall for this, it was gonna be me. I had to look after my boys. You understand?"

"Yes, of course, sir. Any good officer would."

"Damn right." He waved a wrinkled finger in the air. "You think them OSS heavyweights, them bastards, would have let all five of us to git away scott clean and live with a secret like at?"

"Probably not," said Wildgoose.

"Damn right, but no 'probably' 'bout it. Me and my boys would have been shark food for sure once they got their hands on Phoebe and that there Freeonite."

"And my grandfather?" said Cord patiently.

"Your granddaddy, helluva feller—a good man— a tough old sumbitch he were, but a good man. Anyhow, your granddaddy, McCord Barrett, he understood the consequences of Phoebe and he asked me to keep the Freeonite a secret cos he wanted to protect them Indians and I always have 'til now."

"How did he help you, Commander?"

"Simple enough, son, he put me in touch with this Indian woman I was tellin' you 'bout. I don't know her real name, but her English name was Christine; some kind of medicine woman, sumthin' like 'at. Spoke perfect English, good lookin' thing too. She told me what to do. Relied only on your granddaddy's word, he were a helluva man."

"Yes he was," said Cord.

"We wuz to fly due east around Chicken Shoals out there in the Bahamas, then on northeast for a spell and make sure to talk it up on the radio so'd they'd hear us and stay on the radar. Then we shut off the radios and dropped down barely above the waves; ain't no radar gonna pick you up down that low." He paused again.

"Yes sir, go on, please," said Cord.

"Well sir, we headed back west but stayed low and a little to the north. We come up on a little spot in the road called Stuart—Stuart, Florida. We come right over the inlet there, we did. It was gettin' dark and I was startin' to worry about our fuel. Damn worried." The old commander began wheezing and gasped in the oxygen mask.

"Yes sir."

"Like I was sayin', damn fuel was low, damn low and it was dark by then. Boy, you're a pilot. You know how everything can turn to dog shit after it gets dark and besides that we had some pretty bad weather."

"Yes sir, how well I know," said Cord.

"Well by damn, we flew right over the inlet there at Stuart and follered a river to Lake Okeechobee, then we turned due south over the Everglades; oh, I don't know, maybe 50 or 60 miles."

"That would have put you right over the heart of the Glades, sir," said Wildgoose.

"Yep, sure, did sonny. My engine started sputterin' like a sumbitch from fuel starvation, so I hit the fuel boost pumps. That were back in the days when all we had wuz them oscillating fuel pumps in the tanks, you know? Not electric like today's. Anyhow, I were about to kiss my ass goodbye when I spotted a long row of smudge pots a burning out there in the darkness. Imagine that, smudge pots out there right smack dab in the middle of them swamps. Made a perfect landing strip it did, hee, hee, hee. I put her down right there, engine coughin' and sputterin' like a sick crow."

"Tell me about the landing strip, Commander," said Cord.

The old man smiled. "No need to, sonny. If you saw the *Miss Lisa* and them other TBMs, then you already know."

CHAPTER SIXTY-FOUR

Watauga County North Carolina
September 15

The sun was slowly sinking behind the serene Carolina Mountains giving a majestic array of dazzling colors. The old aviator seemed to be nodding off from time to time.

Cord said, "Commander, maybe we should take our leave and come back in the morning."

"I think that would be best," Kaitlyn quickly spoke up. "He hasn't had supper yet and it will soon be his bedtime."

"Supper, ha!" Griped the old man coming alert. "If that's what you want to call it. All they feed me is that baby stuff; they only give me one coffee in the mornings, but sometimes I sneak two. Hee, hee. Hey, boys, you member that good ol' Navy coffee? Shee-it, so strong the spoon would stand straight up in it, hee, hee. Hot damn! That were real coffee for real fightin' men.

Cord and Wildgoose stood and started to bid them goodbye when the old commander beckoned them near.   He whispered, "Hey, how 'bout you boys slipping down to that little place a few miles back towards Boone; it's called the Horn & Hoof.   They make the best double cheeseburger and git me a…"

"Now, Granddaddy, you know better than that," scolded Kaitlyn.

"See? See, how they treat me? Like a damn two-year old," the petulant old man grumbled.

"We'll see you in the morning, sir," said Cord. The Commander had nodded off again.   "If that's all right with you, ma'am," he said to Kaitlyn.

Kaitlyn looked reluctant but nodded her approval.

Kaitlyn was showing them to the door when Cord abruptly stopped and turned. He came to attention and said loudly, "Going ashore, sir, by your leave, Commander, sir." Both men popped a salute.

The old officer, obviously pleased, returned a hardy salute. "Granted, from the Officer of the Deck," he barked.

Cord glanced at Lisa, who had remained quiet throughout their visit. She was gently rocking back and forth, and gave him a smile.   He took her hand. "Ma'am, thank you."

"Certainly, Lieutenant, a pleasure. Anytime." She winked, "Reliving those old Navy days does him a lot of good." Cord and Wildgoose smiled at the pretty lady.

Wildgoose was driving. Cord said, "Not much out here is there?"

"Not much. We have only met one car; that dark Chevy went by us a few miles back."

It was after dark when Wildgoose steered the Cadillac into Boone. "Got any place in mind to stay tonight, Mr. Hilton?"

"Didn't we see a Marriot Courtyard on Highway 105? I can get a room and you can make a chickee out under those fir trees."

"Ha! In your dreams, White Man."

There was only one room available in the Marriot and since it had two queen size beds they decided to take it. "Goose, you got any money?"

Like many men of great mammon, Cord rarely carried any cash. "Oh, don't tell me, not again," groaned Wildgoose, "you mean we are actually at a place you don't own? Just put it on one of your credit cards."

"I can do that, but we still have to eat tonight so we're going to need cash. C'mon, Goose, you know I'll pay you back."

"Ha, Barrett, how many times have I heard that? If you paid me back all the dough, I've shelled out for you the past 20 years, I wouldn't need my FBI pension."

"Aw, Scrooge, quit your bitchin', you're worse than an old granny." The men headed to the elevator.

CHAPTER SIXTY-FIVE

Boca Raton Airport
Palm Beach County, Florida
September 16

In the early morning hours, while Cord and Wildgoose slept in the peaceful mountains, the Citation Jet from Tallahassee lightly touched down on Runway Two-Three at the Boca Raton Airport. Darcee hopped into one of the Barrett fleet cars kept at the airport. She drove not to the Pend Oreille but to a privately owned boat dock.

She climbed into a 14-foot Ski Craft. Powering the boat was a 60-horsepower electric drive system, which quietly hummed rather than making the loud noises of a gas engine. Darcee turned right on the Intracoastal Waterway and made her way into Matheson Cove girdling the Pend Oreille Ranch. She cut the engine and let the boat glide to the long pier.

Staying under the security cameras Darcee silently made her way to the office wing adjoining the Tidewaters. She scooped up a handful of sunflower seeds for the gleeful Max, who bobbed her head in ecstasy at the joyful sight of her favorite person.

Silently, she slipped into the massive computer room.

Somehow—Someway—I have got to find someone to blame for those getting their hands on those computer codes—There's got to be an answer somewhere—If I am on the road at least there is no reflection on me.

At that moment in Cord's bedroom, Peri was huddled over a laptop when the bedside telephone rang.

"Hello."

"Doctor Pepper, this is Henry. I've been trying to call you for some time."

"I'm sorry, Henry, I have been on the phone. What's up?"

"Doctor Pepper, I hate to call you at this hour, but I think you better come down to the stables."

"Henry, what's wrong?"

"Better come quick, Doctor, it's the mare."

CHAPTER SIXTY-SIX

Watauga County, North Carolina
September 16

The next morning Cord and Wildgoose sat comfortably in the snug little mountain home. True to Navy tradition, the coffee Kaitlyn had brought them was strong and hit the spot for both men. The old commander was alert and talkative, but his mood was much more somber.

The old man appeared to be nervous. "I tell you boys, them were the days. Them OSS fellers, you know, them CIA boys, they was 'bout to shit a brick, hee, hee. They had the whole damn Air Force and Navy out there looking for us. I don't think they gave a tinkers damn about us, what they really wanted was Phoebe, and there weren't no way in hell they would ever git their hands on that Freeonite stuff. Your granddaddy and them Indians, shee-it, they weren't 'bout to tell 'um nothin'."

"Commander Galvan, sir, you were going to tell us about the Indians and my grandfather?"

"Yep, it's all out now anyways. We stayed with them Indians, them Seminoles, for 'bout a year.

Damnedest place you ever did see. They wuz livin' like it were a hundert years ago, all underground in some kinda dome or sum'um. I never did figure it out."

"And my grandfather, sir?"

"Yeah, Ol' McCord Barrett, a big tall feller. Ol' McCord, now there were one crusty ol' sumbitch, owned half of Florida he did, had more money than Fort Knox, hee, hee, hee. Anyways, Ol' McCord, he put the whole damn thing together, made a deal with them Seminoles. Did it all on his word and a handshake. That's the way Ol' McCord did bid-ness. He saved our asses. Pulled our bacon out of the fire, he did."

"That sounds like him," said Cord. "My father was the same, did everything on a handshake."

The old man gazed out at the mountains. "Yeah son, you come from good stock. That's the way things wuz done back in them days. A man was only as good as his word. Ain't like it is today."

"And the Seminoles, sir?" queried Wildgoose.

"Them Indians? Well, sir, they took us in and treated us like royalty, shared everything with us. After 'bout a year, after everything cooled down, they snuck us out on that underground river, long winding sumbitch, it was. Came out in some secret place way nawth around Ocklawaha, Florida."

"How did you wind up here, Commander?" asked Cord.

"I'm comin' to that, son.   The Seminoles took four of us up as far nawth as Ocklawaha, where it meets the St. Johns River.   We come up to the surface there.   I tell you, boys, I never was so happy in all my life as to see a blue sky again."

"A blue sky, sir?" said Wildgoose.

"Yeah, them Indians livin' underground had kind of a yellow sky.   You boys ought to know, you was there."

Wildgoose and Cord looked at each other and nodded.

"Anyways, some other Indians, Timucuans, they wuz, paddled us up the St. Johns to Jacksonville and hid us in a safe house."

"What about your crew, Commander?   Whatever happened to them?"

The old man looked despairingly and sighed. "My crew—my crew.   They always put God and country first—all dead now, I reckon.   We never stayed in touch; we wuz ascared to cos…if one of us got found out, they could never be able to find the others.   My crew, all top-shelf boys, ever damn one of 'um—the best."

Cord said, "Ah, Commander, you said the Indians took four.   Weren't there five?"

"Hee, hee, I figured you wuz gonna ask that, hee, hee.   Ol' Lynn that were Major Douglas, the Army boy, a flyin' and scrapping sumbitch, he wuz.   He took a hankerin' to that there good lookin' Indian gal, the medicine woman, hee, hee, hee. She taught school over on the reservation. He married her too, he did. I know cos I wuz there. Ol' Douglas, he stayed there with them Indians, but his daughter got word to me that he died a few years back."

"Commander, do you remember the color of Major Douglas' eyes?"

"That I do, son. Damnedest shade of green you ever did see."

That explains the granddaughter and the great grandkids—

"But it weren't, his eyes." He continued.

"It wasn't?"

"Nope, it were that voice of his—once you ever heard that voice, you'll never forget it. Clear as a bell, it were. Like them fellers on the TV news, sounded sum-thin like -at."

"And the others, sir?" asked Wildgoose.

"We had it all arranged. All of us disappeared to different parts of the country and took us a phony name. Lieutenant Johns, he went somewheres in Texas; one of 'um took out to Colorado and one of the fellers moved to New England. Only one to leave the country was Captain Edwards. He settled in Ireland. Good man, he was a damn good Marine, crackerjack pilot, the best."

"And you, sir, here to North Carolina."

"Yep, and me here. When we got married," he stuck his jaw toward Lisa, "I took her name, hee, hee, Finn. You ever hear of such a crazy damn thing in all your born days? Hee, hee, hee. The gov'ment sends my widder's pension to Lisa Finn. Them fellers always reckoned there were something fishy 'bout our disappearance, hee, hee, but they couldn't prove a damn thing."

"But that pension comes from the CIA's budget doesn't it, sir?"

The commander looked surprised, "Yep, damn sure does, sonny. Since I was the flight leader, and seein' that I was dead and all, they thought my Lisa might know sum'thin'. So, they pay her a tad extra for hush money. Fooled 'um all, I did. Hee, hee. Them fellers always reckoned there were something fishy 'bout our disappearance."

Cord and Wildgoose stood and thanked the old veteran. Cord slipped him a white paper bag, inside was a double cheeseburger. The old man grinned widely and gave Cord a wink. They were almost out the door when Cord noticed Lisa, sitting in a rocking chair was sobbing and dabbing her eyes with a tissue.

"Why, Miss Lisa, what on earth? What's wrong?"

"Hush up, woman!" barked the commander.

"Oh Jake-dear," cried Lisa, "Tell them. Tell them now. Let's get this over with forever!"

The commander sighed and began to speak. "Granddaddy, no!" exclaimed Kaitlyn.

"What is it, Kaitlyn?" Cord said firmly.

"Tell 'um, honey," said the commander. "Mama's right, let's get this damn thing over with."

"But Granddaddy, they said they would come back and kill us!"

"Don't matter none, honey. Tell 'um."

Kaitlyn hesitated, "Last night after you all left, two thugs came into our house, just busted right in! One was waiting in the car. A black car, like a Ford or Chevy, something like that, a rental car, I'm pretty sure. They demanded to know about Phoebe and the Freeonite."

Cord and Wildgoose looked at each other. *A black Chevy?*

"Yeah, damn sure did!" exclaimed the irascible old commander shaking his fist. "I wuz gonna jump and whip both them sorry bastards. The onlyest time my foot would have been off their asses was when I was swingin' it back! 'Cept I was ascared to do anythin' 'cos they was holding a gun on the women folk."

"What did they want to know about Phobe and the Freeonite—how do they know?" asked Cord.

Kaitlyn said, "They grabbed granddaddy by the collar and threw him down on the floor. They wanted to know about Phoebe and where they could get their hands on some Freeonite?"

"How could anybody possibly know about that?" asked Wildgoose.

"Damned if I know sonny. But I didn't tell them a damn thing. I didn't tell them nothin' cos I don't know nothin'. My boys did away with all them parts to Phoebe. Buried 'em I reckon, 'cept for Ol' George, Ol' George Edwards. He deep-sixed his. Dumped it in the ocean, he did."

"What about the triggering mechanism, Commander, what did you do with it?" asked Cord.

"Well sir, when I left that Indian place I give it to that Army boy, Major Douglas and told him to git rid of it. Dump the damn thing in the quicksand out there by them Indian burial grounds or something like at."

"Did he?"

"I don't know. All I know is Douglas said he would take care of it and put it in a safe. A place nobody'd ever find it. A vault, somethin' like at he called it."

"A vault?" That's strange. Where would he find a safe way out there?" said Wildgoose.

"Got no idea sonny, but that's what he said."

"Commander, do you have any clue to who they were? Government men, maybe?" asked Cord.

"Nope, weren't the gov'ment. Too greasy and slimy to be G-men. Onlyest thing I know is one of 'em said that El somebody weren't gonna be too happy 'bout them not finding out anything."

"El Diablo?" Cord almost shouted.

"Yes!" exclaimed Kaitlyn. "That's it, El Diablo."

CHAPTER SIXTY-SEVEN

Pend Oreille Ranch
September 17

A soft breeze blew across the calm cove as Wildgoose and Peri spent the late morning on the upstairs veranda sipping coffee. Cord stayed in his office inside the Tidewaters checking emails and returning telephone messages. Peri listened intriguingly as Wildgoose related their flight back that morning, their trip to North Carolina and the visit with the old commander.

"What about the three thugs, GW? You really think they might be in cahoots with El Diablo?"

"You know about El Diablo, Doctor Pepper?"

"I thought everyone knew about El Diablo, he's been all over the news, many times and supposed to be the most treacherous and ruthless criminal ever."

"Yeah," sighed Wildgoose. "We've been looking for him for years, so has INTERPOL. Problem is, nobody has ever seen him or knows a damn thing about him. He's there and then he isn't." Goose thought, *it's*

strange that Peri brings up El Diablo out of nowhere—
Cord must have opened his mouth.

Peri was yawning and stretching her arms over her head when Cord appeared on the balcony. "You keeping late hours, Doctor Pepper?"

"Oh Cord, I have something to show you; something to show both of you."

"Oh?"

"Yes, come with me." She clutched Cord's hand and the trio walked down to the stables.

Cord peered into the mare's stall and his jaw dropped. There on wobbling legs was the prettiest golden foal he had ever seen. "Doctor Pepper, when…?"

"Last night, when you were in North Carolina, she had a pretty rough time."

"It's a good thing you were here." Cord said, "Is, is—everything okay now?"

"Everything is fine, Cord. Mama and daughter are just fine."

"A little filly," said Wildgoose.

They watched in awe as the baby teetered and swayed on her new legs searching under her mother for breakfast. "Oh Cord, don't you just love her?" exclaimed Peri. "Isn't she the most beautiful thing you have ever seen?"

"Next to you, she is, Doctor Pepper. I'll get the transfer of ownership papers in order this afternoon."

"Oh, no, no, no, Cord! Don't sell her, please, please." cried Peri, her eyes filling with tears.

"I'm not going to sell her, Doctor Pepper, I can't."

"You can't?"

"No. You can't sell something you don't own."

"But, but, Cord, if you don't own her who does?"

"You do, Doctor Pepper. She's yours."

"M,m,m mine—?" Peri looked at him in disbelief. "Oh, Cord, that's the most wonderful thing anyone has ever done for me!" She flung her arms around him, her tears staining his shirt.

"C'mon, Goose, let's leave the doctor and patients alone for a while." The two headed to the Tidewaters.

Walking back Wildgoose said, "You know, Cord, something's really strange here. Doctor Pepper asks me about the three thugs at the commander's house."

"So?"

"Funny thing; I never said there were three thugs. I only said thugs. So how could she know? Plus she mentioned El Diablo."

"Oh Goose, you let your sleuthing get in the way of your common sense. We probably said something about there being three, or maybe you said something this morning."

"No, I don't think so. But this much I know for sure, Barrett. You have the same problem you've had since we were teenagers; you keep thinking with your weenie. Like Uncle Ted said, you need to keep that little thing in your pants and stop using it for recreation."

"Shut up, Goose, your envy is showing. I like Doctor Pepper. I like her a lot."

"So do I, Cord," Wildgoose tapped his temple, "But I think with this head, not the one under my zipper."

They were sitting on the veranda when Peri joined them still ecstatic and jabbering endlessly about the new arrival. The men continued to tell Peri about their visit with the old Commander.

"He certainly sounds like an interesting character," she said.

"Yeah, he was pretty salty too," laughed Wildgoose. "He sure talks like a Navy man."

"Don't let that mountain demeanor fool you, Goose," said Cord. "That old salt could go on Jeopardy tomorrow."

"And win," laughed Wildgoose.

An aging black man appeared, his shock of white hair glistened in the morning sun. "Mista Cordie, suh, telephone for you."

"Thank you, Mister Ironside. Can you have someone take a message?"

"Yes suh, but she say it's urgent, suh."

"Thank you, Mister Ironside. I'll be right back," he said to Peri and Wildgoose.

Cord reappeared on the balcony looking dour. "What's up Barrett? You look like someone just took off with your dog."

Cord gave him a sober look. "That was Kaitlyn on the phone."

"What Cord? What is it?" said Peri.

"Apparently the thugs came back last night and beat the hell out of the old man. He's in the hospital in Boone. They threatened him and held a gun to Lisa and Kaitlyn's head."

"Is he going to make it?" asked Wildgoose.

"It could be either way, Goose. It's touch and go right now."

"Cord, did the old man spill the beans about the triggering mechanism?"

"Fraid so, Goose. But all he could tell them is the same thing he told us. That it's in a safe or a vault somewhere."

410

"Somebody is after it and if they know about the triggering mechanism, then they know about the Freeonite," said Wildgoose. "And that somebody is El Diablo."

"Exactly," replied Cord. "With that thing in his hands he could hold the whole world at bay."

"Then we have to find it before El Diablo does," said an abstemious Wildgoose

"What about your granddad's safe?" asked Wildgoose.

"No, it's in my office. I go in it every day. And it can't be in the safe in the ell offices, anyway nobody could ever get in. The only things we keep in there is an extra code generator for the bank, and it would never be in any of our bank vaults because too many people are in and out of them all the time."

Wildgoose snapped his fingers. "Hold on a second! Wait just a dern minute. Didn't the old man say a safe or a vault, something like that?"

"Yeah."

"And didn't he say Douglas was dead?"

"Yeah."

"And didn't he say the Major had married that old medicine woman?"

"Yes, he did. Where you going with this, Goose?"

Wildgoose thought for a moment. "Look Cord, Lynn Douglas was a white man. That means he could never be buried in a Seminole burial ground. No matter who he was married to or how important he was."

"Why not?"

"A burial ground is very sacred to the Seminoles. Holy, if you will. No white person could ever be entombed in one. So, what they do is coat the body with herbs and spices and wrap it in colocasia leaves. You know what I'm talking about, those big elephant ear plants with wide leaves."

"Yeah, we have a few of them here on the Pend Oreille."

Wildgoose went on, "After the body is prepared they put it in a tumuch, or best word in English is vault. Then it's buried in an adjoining plot of ground but never in a Seminole graveyard."

"Then what you're saying, Goose is that Major Douglas is buried in a vault."

"That's exactly what I'm saying Cord. Seminoles inter their dead above ground. They never bury them. A non-Seminole is buried in a tumuch, a vault, which is underground."

Cord thought for a long time then disappeared inside. He emerged a few minutes later dressed in Levis. "Okay, Goose, let's go."

"Go? Go where?"

"And, Goose, round up a couple shovels. That triggering mechanism for Phoebe has got to be buried in that vault with Douglas."

"Shovels? What are you talking about, Cord?"

"We, my Native American friend are going to exhume a body."

"We what?" exploded Wildgoose.

"C'mon, Goose, you're burning daylight. We are going to dig up the late Major Douglas."

CHAPTER SIXTY-EIGHT

Pend Oreille Ranch
September 17

"That does it, Barrett! This time you have absolutely gone off the deep end. You belong in a nut house. Have you completely lost your fucking mind?"

"Aw, c'mon, Goose—"

"No! Don't aw c'mon Goose me. I'm not budging off this one damn inch, especially with a lunatic like you!" exclaimed Wildgoose stabbing a finger against Cord's chest. "Do you have any idea, any comprehension, of what they would do to us if we get caught?"

"Well then, Goose, let's not get caught."

"No! No sir, this time I'm pulling the plug, Barrett. We should call in the feds or the army, or somebody but sure as hell not us."

"Oh sure, Goose, let's call in the feds. You can explain to them that there is a secret Indian village with a yellow sky, all underground, an underground river and the TBM Avengers from Flight 19 in a hangar in the middle of an underground blue swamp. And while you're at it you can tell them all about a machine with an unheard of element that could macerate the world!"

Wildgoose gave a blank look.

"Yeah Goose good idea. Why don't you tell them that? And, Goose," he added, "Don't forget to mention that we know all this but have no freaking idea where it is!"

"Okay, okay, I get the point," said Wildgoose. "But how do you propose we find it, Mr. Meriwether Lewis?"

"Simple Goose, you are a redskin, you know those swamps. Maybe there is a trail of breadcrumbs?"

"Ha, Paleface, if you remember your Grimm's, you'll know the birds ate Hansel and Gretel's trail of breadcrumbs. They couldn't find their way and got lost."

"C'mon Goose, let's go, you're…"

"I know, I know, I'm burning daylight."

The two men had no trouble finding the clearing where they had first left the johnboat. Carrying the boat, they made their way through the twisting trail through the vines to the small creek.

They drifted with the tranquil current until it took them to the barrier where they thought Cowboy Hat and Little Bear had penetrated, which would take them down the falls and onto the underground river. They tried to ram it with their small boat, but found it solid as granite.

"This can't be the place," said an exasperated Wildgoose.

"It's got to be, Goose."

"Maybe but there has to be another way in. It will be dark in a few minutes, Cord; we better find us a place to spend the night."

"Does that mean I have to sleep with you again, Miss Playboy foldout?"

"Barrett, you might be lovely and all, but don't ogle me with those big brown eyes. You ain't my type."

"Good thing," both men laughed.

Wildgoose cut a few cabbage tree fronds and some palmettos. Soon he had made a small hovel. Both men crawled in for the night.

"Did you bring anything to eat?"

"Nope, but here have an oatmeal bar," said Wildgoose, handing him a package.

"Ugh, rabbit food," said Cord.

"Take it or leave it, Sleeping Beauty."

416

"Goodnight, Sweet Prince." They slept.

Morning broke through the foliage. Wildgoose and Cord searched well past noon for the hidden entrance to the underground river but found nothing. "Hey, Barrett, I've been thinking."

"Didn't hurt yourself did you?"

"Get serious, Cord. Remember, we were supposed to meet Cowboy Hat and Little Bear at a certain time."

"I remember," said Cord. "They were very specific about it."

"Yes, they were. Let's wait a while and see if anything changes."

A couple of hours had passed when Wildgoose exclaimed, "There!"

"There what?"

"See, Barrett, the sun had to be just right. Look to the left of that barrier and follow the shadow of the sun. You see that little dark area?"

"Yes, I see it, Goose; the sun has to be at the exact angle. It's barely a tad darker than the rest of it."

"The sun will only stay at that exact angle for only a few seconds, help me get up as much speed as we can, Cord."

The men paddled furiously and crashed into the blockade. Cord heard the familiar swoosh of the fronds and they emerged at the waterfall and down onto the underground river.

It seemed as if they were drifting through a fairy tale again. The small johnboat glided gracefully between the custard apple trees draped with the moon vines and wild asters. Water lilies were everywhere and of every color: white, yellow and an odd blue orchid, not quite as abundant as the others. The banks of the small river were adorned with an array of wild ferns along with the tall yellow chinquapins and the blue and yellow flag. Purple hyacinths bloomed along the water's edge giving the alligators a natural camouflage.

Eventually, Cord and Wildgoose could see a yellow hue ahead and they knew the village was getting near. Wildgoose skillfully guided the johnboat to the shore. "We better wait," he said. "No sense taking a chance on someone being awake and spotting us."

"And we sure don't want to alert the dogs," said Cord.

They stretched out under a towering cypress. Tree orchids and air plants were blooming above. A bull gator was bellowing a call of romance to the ladies nearby.

Wildgoose shook Cord's shoulder. "Get up, Rip Van Winkle, time to go," he said to the napping Cord.

"What time is it, Goose?"

"About midnight, maybe a little after," Wildgoose's voice took a staid tone. "Cord, if we get caught there's no way out. The absolute worst thing you can do with the Seminoles is disturb a grave. They will kill us for sure."

"I know Goose, but we're in a foot race here. If El Diablo gets his hands on the Freeonite and that triggering mechanism, it's not going to matter anyway."

Wildgoose let out a chest full of air, "I guess you're right. Let's go."

Wildgoose beached the johnboat silently on the shore opposite the sleeping village. Carrying the shovels, they silently crept along the cypress forest to the edge of the blue swamp. Wildgoose cupped his hand to Cord's ear and whispered, "This is it the burial ground for Indians so outsiders would have to be over there." He gestured toward the other side of the cemetery.

"How are we going to get way over there, Goose?"

"Same as last time, we crawl. Now damn it, Barrett, stay with me this time. No mistakes."

"Roger that Goose, no mistakes."

"Here," said Wildgoose, "Take some mud and black your face."

"What about you?"

"No need. I got it naturally. Now follow me exactly."

After a laborious endeavor of crawling in the eerie darkness through the gaping skeletons and rotting corpses, Wildgoose whispered, "That's it over there." He pointed to a small clearing hidden in a clump of mulberries tucked under some mango trees. "That's good," he said, "at least we will have a little cover from the guards at the hangar mound."

"Goose, there is only one grave, and that's his name on it."

"He must have been the only outsider to ever die here."

The men began the arduous labor of digging into the thick muck. The soft earth and rootless area made the digging unproblematic but still a loathsome task. Waist deep and sweating profusely, Cord felt a bump on the end of the shovel. "Psst Goose, I hit something."

Cord lowered himself to his knees and onto the loam followed by a hesitating Wildgoose. Using their hands, they uncovered a casket, which appeared to be constructed from wild Oakwood.

"How are we ever going to raise it? The dern thing weighs a ton."

"We don't have to raise it, Goose. All we do is pop the lid and grab the triggering mechanism. Put your shovel here by mine and pry."

The coffin lid was inexorable and wouldn't budge. Cord blew a drop of sweat from his lip. "It's too dark," he said exasperated. "I can't see a damn thing."

"Cord, we need better leverage."

"Yeah, I know, Goose. Put your blade down there on that end and I will pry it from here. If I put my weight on it, I'll either break the shovel or pop that freaking lid."

Cord leaned his weight on the shovel handle a loud crack pierced the darkness. The handle had snapped. At that same moment, the wooden sarcophagus burst open.

"Damn it, Barrett, are you trying to wake the major or just get the trigger?"

"He's been in here for years; he might be a tad hard to wake. Shine your pen light in there, Goose."

Cord and Wildgoose followed the beam from the pen light and stared into the coffin.

It was empty—

CHAPTER SIXTY-NINE

Seminole Indian Village, deep in the
Everglades
September 19

Cord and Wildgoose busied themselves with the strenuous task of replacing the oak casket and filling the major's tomb with the damp black earth they had dug. Leveling off the surface of the grave Cord whispered, "There Goose. Nobody will ever know."

"Don't bet your weenie on it, Barrett. If we bent one blade of grass, they would know."

"C'mon Goose, help me smooth this thing over."

"Forget it, Cord, we have to get out of here. By the time, we get back to the boat, and down river, it will be light. The whole Seminole Nation will be after us."

The two men crawled back through the burial ground and made it to the edge of the cypress trees and on to the river where they had left the johnboat.

It wasn't there.

"Cord, I know we left it right here."

"Did you pull it far enough up on the bank, Goose?"

"Of course, I did. It wouldn't have mattered anyway. See, the current is going that way," he said pointing. "It could not have drifted off."

"Goose, are you sure we are in the right spot? It's dark as a cave out here."

Before Wildgoose could answer, a voice in perfect English came out of the darkness sending a napalm shock wave of up their spines.

"Did you gentlemen find what you came for?"

The voice was unmistakable. A crystal clear, rich baritone reverberated from somewhere in the darkness very close. Cord and Wildgoose froze in their tracks.

They heard a slight "pfft" sound as if someone had tossed a dime into a bucket of mud. Instantly a purplish deep blue glow dimly illuminated an area ten feet in front of them. A chill filled the air around them making both men shiver from the sudden drop in temperature.

They knew we were here all along, thought Cord.

Through the faint blue haze, Cord could make out the medicine woman called the Old One. She was supported by the two bald attendants and an elderly man stood beside her. There were others, but neither man could see anything but dark shadows.

"Mr. Barrett and Mr. Wildgoose I presume," said the voice. "I asked you a question. Did you gentlemen find what you came for?"

"No, we did not," stated Cord indignantly. "How do you know our names?"

"Cord don't ask dumb questions," murmured Wildgoose.

"You must come with us," said the voice.

"Where?" demanded Cord.

There was no answer. Out of the murk, strong warriors gripped his arms and led them across a rickety bridge, and through the village to the same chickee they were housed in before.

"We will talk when the sun is up," said the voice. Then he spoke something in Seminole to the others. Silently and quickly, as they had appeared their captors melted into the night leaving Wildgoose and Cord alone in the chickee.

"You suppose they posted guards?" Cord said, peeking out of the chickee.

"Now what do you think, Barrett? Of course, they posted guards. Do you suppose they are going to forget the last time we were here?"

"Well, the only things I see outside are those Dobermans,"

"Sure," said Wildgoose. "That's the only things you are supposed to see."

"So, now what Goose?"

"What now, Cord—?"

"They are going to kill us."

CHAPTER SEVENTY

Seminole Village deep in the Everglades
September 19

It was late into the morning when four bald warriors opened the entrance of the chickee. Each stood easily over six feet and said nothing, but indicated for Cord and Wildgoose to go with them. The warriors escorted the two men down the path to the old woman's large chickee.

Sitting in the same place as before was the old medicine woman. An elderly man sat beside her in a comfortable chair. He had a thick mane of silver hair. He was trim and appeared to be in excellent health. His green eyes stabbed at them like stilettos. In the dimly lit chickee, the old woman sat waving her hands over the flickering fire changing it to various colors. Five minutes passed; no one spoke.

At last, the man said with precise enunciation, "Our counsel of senior members met during the night and all this morning. Unfortunately for you both, it was their unanimous decision that you must die by sundown."

Cord said, "Major Douglas? You are Major Lynn Douglas aren't you?"

"The one and the same."

"I thought you were dead."

"Gentlemen, as you can well see I am very much alive. A few years ago we decided it would be best if I were dead."

Cord snapped his fingers. "The triggering mechanism."

"Exactly, Mr. Barrett, if I were dead, there would be no way I could lead anyone to the triggering mechanism of Phoebe."

"Good thinking," muttered Wildgoose.

"It might please you to know that Commander Galvan is improving and convalescing quite well in North Carolina."

"Yes sir, I am happy to hear that, but how could you possibly know?" Cord asked.

"I told you to stop asking dumb questions," whispered Wildgoose.

Cord had often heard of the Seminole's mysterious ability to perceive things through psychic perceptions, but had never witnessed the occurrence. He decided not to pursue it and let the matter rest.

"Now, if you gentlemen will be kind enough to excuse us." The four escorts appeared inside the chickee's entrance.

"Wait!" cried Cord. The major paused. "Since it is not going to matter anyway do you mind if I ask a couple of questions?"

Douglas thought for a moment. "You are correct, Mr. Barrett, it is not going to matter. What's on your mind?"

"Major, sir, we did not come here to infringe upon your secrets or the lifestyle your people have chosen. We came here because we have reason to believe the world could be greatly threatened."

"Yes, I know," said the Major. "You are referring, of course, to the Freeonite and the triggering mechanism for Phoebe."

"Precisely, sir, we have good reason to believe…"

Douglas smiled and interrupted. "You are troubled about the three gentlemen who were sent here by El Diablo to retrieve the element and the trigger."

"Yes sir, that's it exactly," exclaimed Cord. "They were here?"

"Yes they were. Those gentlemen chose to visit us last night an hour or so before you and Mr. Wildgoose arrived. You can relax, Mr. Barrett. They have been dealt with accordingly."

"Accordingly, sir?" said Wildgoose.

"Yes, Mr. Wildgoose. Accordingly," smiled the major. "Those gentlemen departed this life a bit earlier than they had planned or expected to. Our sentries caught two, and one fled. However, he was captured down river and met his maker there."

"Major, can you tell us about the Freeonite?" said Cord.

"Certainly. The Seminoles have known about this mystifying element for centuries. The only place in the world it exists, at least as far as anyone knows, is here deep in the Everglades way below the surface and they developed a way to produce energy from it. The Seminoles knew how to make light 100 years before Edison ever invented a light bulb. Once used, the Freeonite turns into a gas and rises. It mixes with the oxygen in the atmosphere and gives off a yellowish hue."

"How?" asked Wildgoose.

"I can't answer that one, Captain. It's a secret shared only among the Seminoles, a scant few at that. There is no alphabet or writing in Seminole. It is handed down verbally generation-to-generation. The stuff is extremely cold, bitter cold. But the Seminoles learned how to generate both heat and cooling from it. The dangerous part, as you gentlemen know, Freeonite gives off an unconceivable amount of energy, which in the wrong hands could be developed into weapons; weapons capable of destroying entire civilizations."

"What about this village sir?" Cord said.

"The Indians knew about the underground river centuries ago. They drove the white man's army crazy with surprise attacks and their ability to disappear by simply using the river that no one had ever heard of and wouldn't believe anyway."

"So they really don't just fade into the swamps?"

"Oh yes, they certainly do, Mr. Barrett, but don't ask me. I don't know how they do it, but I have seen it many times. Just like a Seminole will never cast a shadow, I can't explain it." Nodding toward Wildgoose, he said, "Why don't you ask your friend there? He is obviously a native."

"He won't talk. Not even to me," said Cord.

"Of course he won't," said the major. "None of them will. Not one."

"This village, sir…" Cord started to say.

The major interrupted. "Oh yes, I was coming to that. Around 1812, or so, there lived a wise Seminole Chief named Sleeping Otter, who apparently saw the invasion of the white settlers as a threat to their way of life and to the land itself. So, he established this underground village here on the river. It is completely self-sustaining and has been for 200 years."

The major stood and started to leave when he turned. "About the triggering mechanism," he said, picking up the brown leather bag with the JRO initials. "It's in here."

430

"That's it?"

"That's it, Mr. Barrett."

"Commander Galvan told us that you had done away with it."

"Yes, that's what he ordered. I just haven't done so yet. There never was any need to until now. But I will dispose of it in a quick way," he smiled.

Noting the initials on the satchel, Cord asked. "What is JRO, Major?"

"Just initials," he replied. "Just initials, that's all. This satchel belonged to Johnny."

"Johnny, sir?"

"Johnny? Why that's Johnny Oppenheimer, the fellow who created the A-bombs and Phoebe. He was the brains behind it all."

"I thought his name was Robert," said Cord.

"You are correct, Mr. Barrett. John Robert Oppenheimer, Robert was his middle name and he was always known as Robert. But we who were close to him called him Johnny."

"Mystery solved," said Wildgoose.

"No mystery, Mr. Wildgoose. Everything happened out of design. Flight 19, everything—we all went different ways. I was supposed to go to Wyoming, but I fell in love with my Christine here, so I stayed with the Seminoles and damn glad I did."

"And the others, sir?"

"Nobody knows, Mr. Barrett. Commander Galvan thought it best for not any one of us to know anything about the others or their whereabouts for security reasons."

"Makes sense," said Cord.

"Now, if you gentlemen will please excuse me you will be shown to your quarters and you are to stay there for the rest of the day. I will have some roast venison sent to you."

Major Douglas exited the chickee as the four warriors entered. Both men looked, but did not see the old woman. Sometime during their conversation with the Major, she had vanished.

Cord and Wildgoose sat in glum silence waiting for the inevitable. Finally, Cord broke the stillness. "Well, Goose, at least we got a few answers."

"A lot of good that's going to do us now, this time Barrett, you really got us in a mess. You never listen to me. I tried to tell you it would be our asses if we got caught. I should have known we would never make in here undetected."

"I'm sorry about all this, Goose, I really am. I know I should have listened. I should have known we could never sneak past a Seminole any more than we could get by Max."

"Sorry doesn't cut it, Cord. Tonight we'll be fucking dead, D-e-a-d, dead!"

"I know Goose, I know. I said I was sorry. But at least we have done a lot of things and we've been a lot of miles together."

"Ha," said Wildgoose, "most of those miles have been in four-wheel drive."

At that moment, the entrance flap was opened by one of the bald warriors.

"Guess it's time, Goose," said Cord. The two men embraced and said goodbye to each other.

The Indians led them out the chickee not toward the river but back to the old woman's chickee. They looked at each other and shrugged.

Once again, they entered the chickee and found Major Douglas alone sitting in an easy chair. He gestured for silence.

After a moment he said, "Gentlemen, there was no execution scheduled for you today, or any other day. I wanted to give you a few hours to think about the gravity of your intrusion and your trespass into our peaceful existence."

Cord and Wildgoose exhaled a massive lungful of air. "Thank you, Major," mumbled Cord. Wildgoose nodded his appreciation.

"You don't need thank me. Frankly, I was powerless to help you. Your reprieve was granted only because of the pleadings of your uncle, and in your case, Mr. Wildgoose, your father. Amnesty was granted only because of their reputations here and the solidarity of their word."

"My...My uncle was here?" stammered Cord.

"Yes indeed, they were both here all morning. They asked that I let you stew on the matter for a while in hopes that you might learn something. Mr. Wildgoose, your father, was aghast when he heard that you were digging up a grave. You probably would prefer to meet the executioner rather than face your father. Best thank your lucky stars it was not a Seminole grave you were violating."

"You know them?" said Cord.

"Yes, for many years. We are close friends. I have visited them many times and they have often been guests in our lodge. I knew both your grandfathers as well."

Cord started to speak; the Major silenced him with a gesture.

"Good day and goodbye gentlemen. I trust that I will not see you again. One more thing," he handed Cord a gold chain with a Navy Flying Cross. "Please see this gets back to the commander."

"But sir..."

"Please, Mr. Barrett. Just do as I ask. My granddaughter and Christine insist it be returned. Anyone with a war record like Commander Galvan should have this and it should stay in his family."

"Yes sir, I give you my word," said Cord.

"I must insist you both keep our existence and our secrets. It pains me to think of the penalty if you don't."

Cord and Wildgoose readily shook their heads in agreement.

"Your john boat and escorts are waiting at the river." With that, the major was gone. The four centurions firmly led them to the river.

The two friends were sitting side by side in the johnboat propelled by the escorts. Both were reflecting on the beauty around them and their sense of being alive when just minutes ago death seemed so eminent. Cord was looking ahead of the boat.

"Hey Goose, what's that in the water?"

"I can't tell from here, Cord, looks like a hat." Squinting his forehead he said, "It is a hat."

"It's a city boy's hat. Nothing like any Seminole or a cowboy around here would wear," said Cord. "Grab it Goose, I bet it's from one of El Diablo's goons."

Wildgoose leaned over the side of the boat and grasped the hat. "Ugh!" he cried, "It's heavy."

"I see why," exclaimed Cord.

"There's a head in it!"

CHAPTER SEVENTY-ONE

Pend Oreille Ranch
September 20

They sat in the soft morning sun. Cord and Peri were holding hands and sipping coffee as they waited for breakfast on the veranda. They shared bits of conversation, but mostly they sat glowingly staring at one another. Bailey lay curled at his master's feet, and below Yardboy was bellowing for a morning treat. Love was in bloom on the Pend Oreille.

A staff member appeared with a heaping plate of scrambled eggs, crispy bacon and sliced tomatoes. At the same moment, Wildgoose could be heard coming up the backstairs giving morning salutations to the staff. He kissed Miss Julia and grabbed a crisp slice of bacon. Behind a harsh succession of unsympathetic scoldings from Miss Julia about messing up her clean kitchen and that she was going to paddle him again, just like she did his daddy, he pulled up a chair.

"Is that plate for me?" he sheepishly asked.

"Goose," said Cord, "how do you always know to show up exactly at meal time?"

"Aw, just a coincidence, Lone Ranger," he said pouring a glass of fresh orange juice and scooping up a generous helping of scrambled eggs.

"It's a good thing I own a ranch," joked Cord. "Keeping you in groceries is harder than trying to feed a wood chipper."

"So what's on your agenda today, Mr. Proprietor of the Whole World?"

"I have to go over to Fort Myers and meet with our lawyers. We're leasing some western pastures over there to a few cattlemen," said Cord. "Doctor Pepper is going with me. You wanna go?"

"You flying or driving?"

"We're flying over, Goose, it's a gorgeous day. You know I don't drive anywhere unless I have to."

"In that case, I'm busy," said a dithering Wildgoose.

"Yeah? Busy doing what, Goose?"

"No, seriously, Cord, I have a few things to do. I'm going to run down to our lab at the FBI District Office in Miami."

"Why?"

"I have an idea I need to check out. We can talk about it later." He stood grabbing a thick slice of bacon.

"Check you later, Neil Armstrong."

"Yeah, check you later, Goose."

Cord and Peri strode down to the hangar where outside sat waiting a pristine Cessna 180E Skywagon. Cord helped Peri into the right seat.

"Cord, I thought your airplane had two engines."

Cord laughed. "That's the Beech Baron you're thinking of. The twin is good for long distance, nighttime and bad weather. The Cessna we use to scoot around the property and short halls, it's very convenient because it has a tail wheel instead of a nose wheel landing gear."

"Why?"

"A tail wheel aircraft allows us to land on off-airport places. In pastures, things like that. It's good for soft short fields and we are able to put floats on it if we want to set down on water."

"And the two engine one?"

"The Baron is built for speed. This airplane will only do about 150 or so, but it's a high wing so you can get a good look at the ground. Here, put this headset on."

Cord scanned over the checklist making sure he didn't overlook anything. The Skywagon lifted gracefully off the Pend Oreille Airport into a crystal clear blue sky. Cord banked the airplane west and stayed low allowing Peri a bravura view of the BDI properties and in a little while, they were over the Everglades. Peri marveled at the vast Everglades with its savannahs and cypress hammocks.

"Cord, I never realized the Everglades were so big and so beautiful."

"Sure is, Doctor Pepper. They go all the way to the southern tip of Florida and empties into Florida Bay, where the Gulf of Mexico meets the Atlantic."

Too soon for Peri, Cord eased the Cessna down, toying with a slight crosswind, on Runway One-Three at Page Field in Fort Myers.

Cord met with his lawyers and the Lee County Cattlemen's Association. With the attorney's approval, he signed papers leasing several thousand acres of BDI land. Once business was attended to Cord said, "Doctor Pepper, it's such a beautiful day, how would you like to have lunch on the outside patio at the airport restaurant?"

Peri readily agreed. The two enjoyed a turkey sandwich, chips and iced tea. Cord said, "That was a good lunch. We should be getting back to the Pend Oreille. Let me take a look at the weather radar and…"

"Cord, why would you look at the radar? It's a perfectly clear day you can see forever."

"I guess you're right, Doctor Pepper, it's only a hop and a skip back to the ranch anyway. Let's go."

At that moment, for the first time in his life, Cord broke a cardinal rule of aviation.

He didn't check the weather.

CHAPTER SEVENTY-TWO

Page Field Airport, Fort Myers, Florida
September 20

Cord lifted the Cessna off the runway. Steering southeast, he set a course heading back to the Pend Oreille. The sun was bright and the sky sparkling clear. He kept the airplane low allowing Peri to have a panoramic view of the endless Everglades and the splendid beauty detailed below. A flock of bright pink curlews hovered below them gracefully flapping their black tipped wings in the warm sunshine. From this low altitude, Peri could easily see a large blue heron crane and snow-white egrets fishing for their lunch in the savannahs beneath the wings of the Skywagon.

"Ut-oh—damn!" she heard Cord cursing to himself in the headset.

"What, Cord? What's wrong?"

"Nothing Doctor Pepper, but you see that dark cloud bank up ahead?" His voice had an apprehensive tone.

Peri looked about 20 miles in front of the Cessna. "Yes, I see them." Her fear of thunderstorms shot the onset of terror up her spine. Then suddenly she felt safe with this man beside her.

"That's the Pend Oreille and there is no way we can fly through that mess."

Cord busied himself on the radios talking with flight service. By now his voice and his expression was showing aberrant compunctions.

"Cord, what's the matter? Is something wrong?"

"Not to worry, Doctor Pepper, no real problem. We just have a little bad weather, that's all," he lied.

The report from the Fort Myers weather station had told Cord that Page Field, behind them was socked in with a bad storm coming in from the gulf and the weather was closing rapidly both north and south of their position. Looking ahead to the east, he could see the dark blue turning black, cumulus clouds subjugating the Florida sky like a boiling ocean of purple tar.

Barrett, you idiot. Cord admonished himself. *How could you be so freaking stupid and make a blunder like this...? Over 12,000 hours of flying time logged, and you don't check the weather? Not even a student pilot would make such a dumb mistake.*

Cord knew only too well how quickly the dark cumulus anvil shaped clouds could build over the Everglades. He was born and raised in south Florida and was well aware of the unpredictable weather patterns and violent thunderstorms, which fed off the rising moisture from the swamps. He cursed himself again.

You have been a pilot since your teens, you know better than to ever go anywhere without first checking the weather.

"Better snug up your seatbelt, Doctor Pepper, and put your shoulder harness on too; looks like we're in for a few bumps." Peri silently obeyed.

Barrett, you dumb bastard! Not only have you put your own butt in a pickle, but you are risking Doctor Pepper's neck as well—!

At that moment, it dawned on Cord that he cared a lot more about Peri than he realized. Cord Barrett had fallen in love with the pretty veterinarian.

The Cessna was bouncing violently as the relentless weather began to deteriorate. Cord wrestled with the steering yoke trying to keep the aircraft level. He dropped down lower fervently searching the endless Everglades for a spot high and dry enough on which to land.

"You're looking for a place to land, aren't you?" she calmly said.

"I'm afraid so, Doctor Pepper, we could never get through that stuff, and it's closing in all around us. I'm going to have to put this thing down soon or we will be alligator supper for sure."

We probably will be anyway.

He maneuvered the Skywagon lower.

Cord and Peri were desperately searching out the windscreen through the pounding rain for a suitable place. Cord said, "Doctor Pepper, you have to look out the side window; you can't see a thing through the front." The search was hopeless and the gathering tempest was getting worse.

Forcing the airplane to an altitude so low, it was barely skimming over the treetops Cord became gravely worried about their safety, but the inclement weather gave him no choice.

Suddenly Cord snapped his fingers. "Wait a minute!" he exclaimed.

Why didn't I think of this before?

Peri gave him an inquisitive look. "We have a hunting camp not far from here," he said, "And it has a landing strip. Maybe we can make it." Cord banked the Cessna sharply and dropped down even lower.

Rain was beginning to pelt the four-seater with greater intensity making visibility impossible. They searched the ground vigorously for the oblique landing strip. Peri could not make out anything. The immense Everglades looked infinite and very much the same except for the cabbage tree hammocks and higher ground punctuating the watery landscape.

The search for the landing strip was exhaustive. Cord was beginning to think they would never find it, especially with the squally weather closing in about them. A bolt of lightning crashed in front of them lighting up the sky.

"There it is!" Cord shouted through the streaks of lightning. He banked the Skywagon so sharply Peri had to reach out and brace herself. Cord immediately dropped all 40 degrees of flaps and pitched the nose steeply toward the earth.

Peering out the windshield through the escalating rain, Peri never did see a landing strip. Soon she heard the soft thud of the landing gear settling on the wet grass.

Taxing back to the strip's threshold a bolt of lightning struck nearby immediately sending a deafening clap of thunder. "Doctor Pepper," Cord shouted over the noise of the driving rain, "When we stop run to the lodge and get inside."

"Why? Where are you going, Cord?"

"I'm not going anywhere, Doctor Pepper, but in a storm like this I've got to tie the airplane down."

"I'm staying with you," she stubbornly said. The two secured the Cessna to the tie-down ropes as quickly as they could. Soaking wet they made a dash to the hunting lodge.

Cord hastily started a fire. "Don't you keep a nice place like this locked?"

"What for, Doctor Pepper? No need. Who could ever find its way out here? The only way in is by boat or airplane."

Peri looked around the roomy lodge. There was a nice fireplace with pine logs, neatly stacked beside it. The walls were paneled with what appeared to be knotty pine; there was running water, obviously from a well. The kitchen was well organized and to the rear of the cozy cabin a couple of separate sleeping quarters. The living area was carpeted and nicely furnished with chairs abutting each end of a long sofa. She especially liked the wide windows.

"This is your idea of roughing it, huh?"

"Well, there's no room service," he laughed. "But we do have flush toilets and color TV."

Cord looked through the cabinets and opened the refrigerator. "Thank goodness the boys have been here and stocked up. We have plenty to eat and the generator is running, so we have power."

"The boys?"

"Yes, a couple of crop dusters, Bill and Steve, they're good friends of mine. Doctor Pepper, you'd best get out of those wet clothes."

"And wear what?"

"There are some towels in there and a few sheets. Or look in that chest of drawers over there, maybe you can find a tee shirt or something." Cord opened the fridge freezer.

By now, it was dark in the Everglades and the rain was coming down harder. Peri disappeared into the bathroom. Cord called out, "Hey, Doctor Pepper, how about some steak and potatoes tonight?"

"That would be great, Cord. I'm getting hungry. And it's Peri, please," she mumbled under her breath closing the door.

Cord had stripped down to his boxers and was thawing the steaks in the microwave oven when he heard the bathroom door open. He turned to see Peri emerge wearing nothing. She seemed oblivious to her nakedness and completely at ease. Casually she strode over to the chest of drawers and selected a man's long sleeve shirt, which hung down to her knees. She tied a knot in the shirt at her waist.

Cord's jaw dropped and he stood in stunned awe at the veterinarian's petite and flawless body. Her melon breasts were pert and advertised a slight chill in the air. "Ah, Lady Modesty," he stammered, "That shirt is way too big maybe you could wear…"

"I don't have to wear anything, Mr. Barrett, but I'll keep this on until after dinner," she teased, giving him a seductive look.

After a scrumptious dinner, Peri chose an E&J Brandy while Cord opted for a Chivas Scotch. They sat by the fire and watched a dazzling display of lightning illuminating the Everglades through the wide sliding glass door of the lodge. They talked for a long while.

Peri tried to squelch a yawn while stretching her arms above her head. Cord took the hint and dimmed the lights. He took Peri's hand and led her to the bedroom.

Outside the tempest raged and beat on the tin roof of the lodge like a snare drum. Lightning crashed through the heavens followed by clamorous thunder. The lovers heard nothing absorbed only with the exploration of each other. Cord lightly ran his fingers over the perfect breasts and down the flat belly to the area below. She was definitely ready. He eased upward and gently entered her; Peri clasped her arms about Cord's shoulders and wrapped her legs around him.

Cord had had sex many times, but this was his first experience at making love.

Can it be? Is this little veterinarian the woman for me—for the rest of my life? Forever? Is this little beauty the one? Is she my soul mate?

Outside, in the pounding rain, a ghastly form floated in deathly silence as it drifted effortlessly over the marsh. The tall eerie figure was angel-white and gave off a silver aura while it glided inches above the ground. The 18th century tribal dress clearly showed him a Seminole Chief. Blood was dripping from its headless throat, as it moved smoothly across the soggy surface. Never making contact with the earth, it made its way to the Cessna.

The creature was ubiquitous having the ability to appear and disappear at will. Time and distance made no matter. It paused at the Cessna as if confused and curiously examined it.

448

Through the howling rain, it faded into the darkness only to immediately reappear at the lodge. The wraithlike creature circled the cabin then suddenly materialized by the sliding glass door of the bungalow where it stood stone still for an hour.

Again, it evaporated into the dark night and re-emerged. Silently it eased up to the bedroom window.

Peri was enthralled with Cord's muscular body pressing against her. Her eyes glazed in this moment of splendid enchantment. She was in love. She was truly in love with this magnificent man.

They lay naked on their backs. A glow of light filtered through Peri's eyelids. "Cord!" she cried, digging her fingernails into him. "A light! There's a light at the window!"

CHAPTER SEVENTY-THREE

Barrett Hunting Lodge Deep in the
Florida Everglades
September 21

Peri was standing at the cabin stove. "How do you want your eggs, lover?"

"Let's try over easy this morning instead of scrambled for a change."

"Yeah, me too," laughing she added, "but they might wind up scrambled anyway."

Cord had set out some left over steak from the night before while Peri pared potatoes. Sitting down to breakfast, they enjoyed eggs, fried potatoes, steak and steaming hot coffee. "Steak and eggs, good idea," she said.

"Yep, we used to get it all the time in the Navy."

"They fed you pretty good, huh?"

"Sure did. Flight crews got anything they wanted around the clock. Doctor Pepper, are you sure…?"

Peri set her fork down heavily. "Cord, I know what I saw," she cried, almost in tears. "Do you think I would make it up or I was dreaming?"

"No, certainly not Doctor Pepper, but I looked all over outside and didn't find a thing, not a trace—Nothing."

"Cord, do you remember that thing we saw at the slough that night?"

"Sure. Is that what you saw?"

"No, I didn't see a figure; all I saw was a glow out there in the rain. You know a kind of a silver white-like radiance. By the time, you looked it was gone. Just like that thing in the slough. It was there and then it wasn't."

"Please, Doctor Pepper, don't start that ghost crap again, you've been listening to Goose too much."

"Maybe I have, Cord. He really believes it, and I'm beginning to wonder myself if…"

"Yeah, yeah, yeah, Goose believes a lot of things about all that supernatural nonsense in the Glades. But, I assure you there is a logical and scientific reason behind those Seminole myths."

"Really," she said. "Then tell me, why don't Seminoles cast a shadow?"

Cord shrugged, "Wish I could answer that one, Doctor Pepper. Nobody knows, but as usual, no Seminole will say a damn thing about it. Not one."

Peri carried the dishes to the sink and began clearing the table. Cord said, "I'll be right back. I'm going to check the airplane and the runway. It should be dry enough to take off by now."

They tidied up the lodge and checked to make sure everything was where it should be. Outside Peri stood on the bottom step, which brought her up to face-to-face height with Cord, who was standing on the ground.

She flung her arms about his neck. "Kiss me, kiss me, my brave and bold pilot," she cried grinning at him.

Cord obliged wrapping his arms about her narrow waist and giving her a long lingering kiss. "C'mon, Doctor Pepper, let's go. You're..."

"Don't tell me, I already know," she exclaimed. "I'm burning daylight."

Once strapped in the Skywagon, Cord taxied to the far end of the strip. He had walked the soggy runway earlier that morning and cleared a few of the limbs and debris that had blown off the trees during the storm.

"Why are we going to the other end?" she asked.

"We always take off into the wind."

"Do you think its dry enough?"

"We're about to find out, Doctor Pepper, this thing has a lot of power for just this kind of situation. Hang on."

Cord dropped 10 degrees of flaps and applied full power. He held the control yoke in the full back position executing a soft-field takeoff maneuver, which would allow the aircraft to leave the ground as quickly as possible at low airspeed.

The Cessna lifted off the wet grass and Cord held it level with the ground building speed. "What's that buzzing noise?" Peri shouted.

"Stall horn."

"Is the engine going to stall?"

"Not now, Doctor Pepper, it's got nothing to do with the engine. A stall is when the airspeed gets too low and the wings lose their lift. The horn warns us when the stall speed is getting critical. I'll tell you later. Right now, I'm busy."

Cord retracted the flaps reducing the drag on the aircraft as it climbed into the morning sky. The storm had passed during the night and it was another a beautiful clear Florida day.

Since they had taken off to the west, Cord banked the airplane sharply east toward the Pend Oreille. They were still in a steep bank and close to the ground when Peri and Cord saw a flash of light.

"What was that?" she said. "A flashbulb?"

"Can't be. It's too big and not way out here. It looked like some kind of reflection, like someone signals sunlight with a mirror."

"Maybe it was from a windshield."

"Impossible," said Cord. "Nobody could get anything like that in here. It's probably just a piece of glass or an old scrap of aluminum; something like that."

Cord made several tight turns around the area and both searched the ground. The reflection showed itself for an instant only when he banked the airplane at a certain angle and from a certain spot.

"Haven't you ever noticed it before, Cord?"

"No, and we would have missed it except the storm must have blown some of those oak limbs and the Spanish moss away."

"I don't see anything now, Cord."

"No, neither do I. The only thing I can think of is maybe there is something tucked way back in that hammock. We could have never spotted it from the air until now. Whatever it is, it's well-hidden."

"Oh, so what," she said. "It's probably nothing."

"Yeah, probably nothing," he climbed the airplane higher.

Doesn't make any sense. There's no way any glass or tin could be down there way out here. Maybe it's just the sun bouncing off the water.   No, I don't think so—

Back at the Tidewaters, Cord and Peri walked out on the veranda where Wildgoose sat chatting with Darcee. The two women glared at each other, with eyes like daggers.

"Don't you have a home?" Cord said looking at Wildgoose.

"Yeah, but I like this one better."

"Doesn't Maria feed you?" Cord asked.

"Sure, but the food is cheaper here," smiled Wildgoose, swiping a tortilla chip through some nearby avocado dip. Darcee jabbed a straw at the ice in her tea.

"So what's up, Goose?"

Wildgoose said, "Never mind me for now. But I think you might have a little bad news from her," he bobbed his head at Darcee.

Cord looked at her sharply. "Bad news? Bad news like what, Darcee?"

"I hate to tell you, Cord," she replied, staring astringently at Peri, "But we've taken a hit on our banks in Tallahassee and New Orleans."

"Damn it!" he exclaimed, slamming his fist on the glass table. "This bullshit has got to stop! A hit? A hit like what, Darcee?"

"One million in Tallahassee and three million in New Orleans."

"What's that now? Fifteen million dollars missing and unaccounted for?"

"More like sixteen, if you count the million missing from Tallahassee," she answered, "all in even figures."

Wildgoose broke the tension. "Well Barrett, if you have lost 16 million in the past few days the way I figure in another 75 years you're going to be broke."

Cord ignored Wildgoose's taunt and in a calmer tone he said, "Does my uncle know?"

"Yes, I met with him this morning while you two were so loudly absent," she snarled, giving Peri another icy scowl.

"And?"

"And—he is beside himself," said Darcee. "I think he is about to call in the federal people. He doesn't want to, but we may have no other choice."

"What about this gal mother hired up in Lakeland, Michelle Stewart, is it?"

"Funny you should mention her, Cord," said the tall redhead. "She called Ted while I was there."

"Well?"

"According to your uncle, Ms. Stewart said that she was closing the gap and had her best computer people working on it. The one thing her people have narrowed down and are sure of is the thievery has to be from our computers here in Florida."

"But how?"

"We don't know," she said. "The only thing her computer people know for sure is that our secured bank codes are being used and no one can figure out how they are getting them, especially the generated code— that is such a short window, every two minutes it changes. And now the additional biometric fingerprint scan of the person making the transaction, explained Darcee."

"It's just impossible," Cord exclaimed.

"I can only tell you what they tell me. If they are being sent from our computers here then I should be able to trace it. But I haven't and I've given Ms. Stewart that report. Someone somewhere is pretty clever."

Wildgoose spoke, "How could anyone, but Mrs. Richardson and Mr. Bradshaw get to the computers in the main Barrett Bank in West Palm, except maybe your uncle?" speaking of the bank's two senior vice presidents in the West Palm headquarters.

"Good point Goose, just a select few have access to our computers and they have been with us for years.

The other computers are downstairs here at the Tidewaters, my laptop and Uncle Ted's office or laptop and they are all accounted for. The only way anyone could gain access is if Uncle Ted, a West Palm V.P. or me let them in, and they would have to have both code and a biometric swipe of a finger."

Cord rose, "I'm going into West Palm Beach and see my uncle. We've got to put a stop to this somehow." Sensing the animosity between the two women, "Doctor Pepper, why don't you come ride with me?"

Peri stood, as did Wildgoose. "Here," he said, "I'll get these." He scooped up the chips and the dip and grabbed the empty tea glasses.

"Staff will get those, Goose," said Cord.

"Aw, that's all right. I'm going that way anyhow," he remarked. "Besides, I need to keep Miss Julia happy as possible, so she will keep on feeding me." Discretely he pocketed Darcee's glass.

Cord laughed, "Yeah, we all do. She's the one who feeds us." Turning to Darcee, he said, "Darcee, let me know when you are leaving again." She nodded complacently.

Cord, Peri and Wildgoose walked through the kitchen and were heading to the backstairs, when Miss Julia began her customary scoldings and admonishments.

Wildgoose wrapped his arms around her portly shoulders and gave her a big noisy kiss on her forehead. "Now Miss Julia, darling, you know how passionately I have been in love with you all these years."

"Don't you go a-huggin' and a-kissing on me, George Washington Wildgoose!" she cried waving a long handled wooden spoon at him. "I kin still tan yo fanny jest like I done yo…."

"Yes, we know," they all laughed, charging toward the back stairs.

"Lordy, Lordy…dem boys is gonna be the deff of me yet."

Downstairs in the rec room, Wildgoose said, "Cord, I need to see you for a minute."

"What's up, Goose? You can talk in front of her."

Wildgoose looked uneasy but said, "See this little vial?" He pulled a small eyedropper size bottle from his pocket.

"Yeah, what is it, Goose?"

"Just a hunch I have. I need to get into your computer room, Cord and access to the computer center at the main bank downtown."

"I can let you in here, Goose, but I don't know about downtown."

"I can get in if you are with me or if Uncle Ted says so."

"Okay, Goose. We can take a look here, but it takes two keys. I have one, but I will have to get the other out of my safe."

"Good Cord. We'll meet you at the computer room."

"Okay, I'll be right back. Better wait for me here or else Max will make enough noise to wake your namesake up at Mount Vernon."

Cord unlocked both the deadbolts securing the computer office and punched in the access code on the door.

"Cord, you and Doctor Pepper wait out here. I'll just be a minute," said Wildgoose shutting the door, leaving Cord and Peri by the always on the alert Max.

Emerging minutes later, Wildgoose said, "All right, let's head to West Palm."

At the driveway, they met Darcee. She looked at Cord and gave Peri anything but a congenial stare.

"Oh Cord, I'm glad you're still here. I'm off to Little Rock."

"Little Rock?"

Before Darcee could answer, the moment was shattered by a large macaw alighting on her shoulder. Flapping its wings vigorously trying to maintain balance, the bird squawked, "Pretty Max, Pretty Max," and ducked its head into Darcee's breast pocket. Emerging with a spray of sunflower seeds in her powerful jaws, she crushed them with ease spewing shells in every direction. "Pretty Max, Pretty Max," the bird cawed.

Forcing the parrot on her forearm, Darcee put her face against its beak. "Bad girl, bad Max," she scolded. "Go home." She arched her arm into the air and the bird reluctantly took flight back to her long perch at the Tidewaters.

Darcee returned her gaze to Cord. "Yes, we need an audit in all four of our Little Rock banks."

"Is Captain Sawber taking you in the Gulfstream?" he asked.

"No, I'm going to commercial out. I think the Gulfstream has been reserved by your mom."

"My mother? Where is she going?"

"Either your mother or maybe one of your sisters. I don't know. I didn't ask."

Cord said, "Darcee, you are welcome to take any of the other company jets." The luxurious Gulfstream was reserved only for family and guests and rarely used by employees.

"Thank you, but I have already made reservations. I'll see you in a few days." They all said a parting farewell this time with a more phlegmatic quid-pro-quo.

After explaining the situation to Ted Barrett, he reluctantly agreed to allow Wildgoose into the computer center two floors below. He called Georgette Richardson, the Barrett Senior Vice-President whose duties, among other things were overseeing the computer center.

"Georgette's not answering her phone," said Ted. "She's probably away from her desk. Maybe she's in the computer complex."

They passed the guard at his desk and used the access codes to the computer room. "The lights are off, that's strange. The lights are always left on," remarked Ted, flipping on the light switches. At that moment, a distinct odor struck them.

"Ugh!" groaned Wildgoose. "Did somebody barbecue a bear in here?"

Georgette was sitting in a swivel office chair at the main terminal, with her back to them. She didn't turn around. Cord walked over to the chair in front of the rows of blade servers. Turning it around, he was met by a gaping stare. One eye had been gouged from its socket; the other hung down on the sunken cheek.

The jowls sagged grossly. A small caliber bullet hole stared at them from between the absent eyes. Georgette's right hand third finger was missing.

Wildgoose noticed the top of her blond head was stained with a deep crimson color. Georgette gawked at him with an eyeless face.

"Oh, my Gosh!" screamed Peri throwing her hands over her face.

"Don't touch her, Cord," Wildgoose exclaimed. "She was killed here."

"How, how—do you know?" stammered Cord.

"Look, at the blood splatter. The body still has a little warmth and not stiffening much, so rigor hasn't set in yet. She has only been dead for an hour or so. And see those powder burns? She was shot up close maybe just an inch or two. Cord, I thought you said nobody could get in here."

Not waiting for an answer, Wildgoose said, "Do you know her?"

"Yes, of course," said Ted. "Georgette is one of our senior vice-presidents."

"Better call the police, Uncle Ted," said Wildgoose. "The killer may still be in the building. Have security lock down the entrances. And everyone needs to carefully step out of the computer center."

"We need to keep the media at bay as much as possible," said Ted.

"Cord, you and Doctor Pepper go back to the Pend Oreille. I'll stay here for the medical examiner and CSI."

"Okay Goose, we'll meet back there." He put his arm around the sobbing Peri and they made for the elevators.

At the Tidewaters Cord and Peri rested on the wrap around balcony. Cord was sipping a vodka and tonic while Peri opted for a frozen lime daiquiri. "Here comes Goose," said Cord, pointing to a truck coming around a steep turn on the four-mile driveway. The white fence rows were adorned with blooming colorful pink and purple bougainvilleas.

Wildgoose soon emerged on the veranda munching a handful of chips he had filched from the kitchen when Miss Julia wasn't looking.

Cord said, "Big Injun detective want-um drink of firewater?"

"Big Injun detective want-um double," he shot back. Cord signaled a passing white-coated staff member.

"What did you find out downtown, Goose?"

"Not much. It appears that no one knows anything. It looked like something from a horror movie with her eyes removed from their sockets. It appears they have found a way around the biometric scanners."

"How come nobody else was in the computer complex at the time of the killing and what about the guard?"

Wildgoose said, "Aha, Dick Tracy, now you have hit on the mystery. How indeed? We know the killer had to have a silencer or someone would have surely heard the gunshot. However, the two regular employees that work the computer center downtown, well one's on vacation and the other never showed up to work today, which is very unusual for him. The guard received a call to go down to receiving to bring up some new software. By the time he looked for the package it was not there, he was gone for about 30 minutes."

"Humm," sighed Cord "do we know who called him."

"No, not yet, Cord," said Wildgoose, "I hate to change the subject, but I need for you to let me back in the computer room downstairs."

"Goose, what's on that redskin mind of yours, what's going on?"

"Just a hunch, Cord, just a hunch, that's all."

"Bet you five bucks your hunch is a dead end," said Cord.

"How are you going to pay up if you lose, Mr. Trump? Mortgage the ranch? Anyway, I won't have any answers for a few days."

"Okay," said Cord. "That might work out well. I'm off until the 30th. Doctor Pepper and I are going to fly Uncle Ted up to Tallahassee in the Baron tomorrow."

"We are?" said a startled Peri.

"Yep," said Cord. "I'm pretty sure Uncle Ted is going to run for governor and he wants to go up to Tallahassee and test the water."

"Perfect," said Wildgoose. "You ready?"

"Yeah, let's go. Doctor Pepper, you coming?"

"You guys go ahead. I think I'll run down to the stables and check on the mare and the foal."

The men nodded and started for the stairs. "Hey Cord, what time is dinner?" asked Wildgoose.

"Same as always, doesn't Maria keep any food at your place?"

"Sure, but I have to drive home all the way around the cove. How can I do that on an empty stomach?"

"Okay, okay, Goose. I'll tell Miss Julia to set out another plate."

"No need."

"What?"

"No need, Barrett, I already told her."

Cord opened the dead bolts and punched in the security code for the computer room. "It's dark in here," said Cord, flipping on the lights.

They were greeted by an inimitable smell. Both men gasped and stood frozen in their tracks.

The shirtless man was hanging from one of the large ceiling beams.

CHAPTER SEVENTY-FOUR

Pend Oreille Ranch
September 21

The Pend Oreille's computer offices were tastefully constructed in a wooden theme. The walls were sheeted with an expensive tongue and groove white oak accented with an open ceiling supported by strong six by six cedar beams. Desks and smaller computer stations sat next to the blade servers. Swivel chairs rested behind the desks. A round conference table was at the center of the room.

The man's body hung limply from the main cedar beam suspended by a thin rope. As before, like Mrs. Richardson, the eyes had been pried from their sockets, one was missing and the other dangled on the sagging cheek staring vacuously into nothing. The tongue drooped forlornly from the corner of the mouth. No sign of blood or physical trauma could be seen even though the third finger from the man's right hand had been severed. Urine stained the front of the trousers. An unimpeachable odor told them the man had fouled himself. When the heart stopped beating, everything stopped. The man was clearly dead.

Cord started to bolt toward the sagging corpse when Wildgoose threw his arms out like a school crossing guard.

"Stop Cord, stop!" he shouted.

"Goose!"

"Wait Cord, this is a crime scene. Stay here."

Wildgoose edged over to the dangling body. He felt for a pulse knowing only too well, there wasn't one. "He's dead Cord, but not by much, the body is still warm."

"He's not supposed to be here, Goose. He works downtown."

"He wasn't killed here, Cord. See how the head has been snapped sideways. No bruising or contusions in the neck area."

Wildgoose interlocked his arms making a jerking motion. "This was a professional hit; the neck has been snapped sideways like this. Very neat, very clean. It severs the spinal column in a millisecond. The killer, whoever he might be is definitely a pro. Like I said Cord, this poor bastard is gone but not by much."

"That means whoever did this is still on the Pend Oreille," Cord exclaimed.

"Maybe; he's probably had time to get away, but I wouldn't bet on it."

"Or else he lives here," mumbled Cord.

"Could be, but right now we'd better call the sheriff's office."

"Yeah Goose, for sure."

"And Cord, tell them we're going to need someone to tell us who this guy is, or was, and to send a M.E. and their CSI unit too."

"No need to ID him Goose, I know who he is."

"Oh?"

"He was one of our senior vice presidents like Mrs. Richardson; he worked in the computer information services unit. Bradshaw is the name. Leonard Bradshaw."

"Cord, I think you should take your Tallahassee trip a day early and get out of town. I will wait for the sheriff's people. Round up your uncle and Doctor Pepper, and get the hell out of here."

Cord bolted for the door. "Oh, good grief! Doctor Pepper!" Cord shouted. "The killer could be after her too!"

He ran full speed towards the stables.

CHAPTER SEVENTY-FIVE

Pend Oreille Ranch
September 24

It had been an uneventful flight to Tallahassee and they spent an extra day in the small city. Three days passed and Cord was anxious to get back to the Pend Oreille, but Ted advised him to take an additional day to allow things to cool at the ranch. Ted had scored impossible to get tickets, a gift from the governor, the Florida State Seminoles hosting their rivals, the Fighting Irish of Norte Dame.

Both Ted and Cord had attended college at Florida State and they enjoyed showing Peri around Florida's capital city and the university. Since they were alumni and former Florida State athletes, they were awarded excellent seats.

Later Peri remarked, "That was the first time I have ever been to a college football game."

"What about all those years in college and vet school, you never went to a game?"

"Couldn't," she said. "I was too busy waitressing, slinging chili and studying. I never had the chance or the time to get into that college kid rah, rah stuff."

Although Peri intended to make a joke of having to struggle during her college and graduate years of study, neither man laughed. They had been born of privilege and great wealth. Neither had any comprehension what it was to battle daily to make ends meet.

The following day Wildgoose, Peri and Cord sat on the veranda sipping a tequila sunrise. They did not sit at the table, choosing instead the rocking chairs. The sun was beginning to sink over the cove and they were discussing the events of the past few days.

"What did you find out about the murders, Goose?"

"Things are still kind of foggy, Cord. One thing that raises eyebrows is that Richardson and Bradshaw are the only ones who have the computer codes and biometric entries except for you and Uncle Ted."

"Yeah, I figured that, Goose. But how could anyone get an authorized computer, the monthly code, the generated code and have the necessary a biometric access to siphon millions from our banks?"

"Exactly, Cord. That could mean only one thing. It has to be an inside job."

"I guess you mean Richardson and Bradshaw are connected? That's hard to believe. They are career employees and have been with BDI for years. What could they have gotten themselves involved in?"

"It sure looks that way. Nobody else has access to the codes. Another mystery is how somebody is getting into your offices here at the Tidewaters. And they would have to have the two keys, entry code just to get into the computer room here and then know the monthly code and have access to the code generator you keep here in your safe to make it work."

Peri spoke for the first time. "Does biometric mean what I think it does?"

"Depends on what you think it means, Doctor Pepper," answered Wildgoose. "The bank's biometric system identifies users by fingerprint and or by scanning the iris of the eye. It is very distinctive and provides an irrefrangible signature."

"It looks like we have no other choice. We're going to have to call in the feds," said Cord.

"Yep, that's what Ted and I figure too," said Wildgoose. "We do know this for sure. The bank codes are being leaked somewhere. Someone has found the monthly code and code generator, even though they all have been accounted for."

"Goose, anything else on the murders or who's doing it?"

Peri spoke her voice breaking. "Those eyes! What kind of sicko would do such a thing? How horrible."

"I can answer that, Doctor Pepper," said Cord. "Gouging eyes was a signature of the Seminoles. They believe if a person doesn't have eyes they can never get into the land of the blue light and must wander amid the eternal winds in darkness; not only that, it scared the crap out of the white settlers and soldiers."

"Ha! That might have been true in the 1800s, but a few things have changed since then," said Wildgoose. "The Seminoles have no involvement in this at all. Someone is sending you a message, Cord."

"Me? A message?"

Peri broke in and said, "I need something pleasant right now. If it is okay with you boys, I need to check on the foal and mare."

Cord said, "Okay but be careful, call up here if you are going to be more than 15-minutes."

Peri replied, "You got it." and left Goose and Cord discussing the horrors of the day.

"Yes, you! You could be next. Here in south Florida, the human body decays quite rapidly. The stolen fingers of our victims will become useless quite quickly, so will the eyeballs. Uncle Ted also added an iris scanner in addition to the fingerprint scanner. However, you only have a fingerprint on file for the biometrics scanner when I checked after Mrs. Richardson murder."

"Uncle Ted ordered the fingerprint biometric scanner installed earlier this week as an additional layer of security. But what is this about an iris scanner?" asked Cord.

"Yes, while the security installation personnel were installing the fingerprint scanner, they also suggested an iris scanner as even another layer of security. You left the office before they could add your iris scan into the security system. But does the thief know that? You or Uncle Ted could be next." Goose softly stated. "Cord, humor me again and tell me or show me how you personally do a transaction. I think I must be missing something."

"Okay, Goose, if it will really help. As for the Tidewaters' computer room, you need the two keys, one that is in my safe and the other on my keys, and punch in a code to gain access to the room. Once inside, I would have to be able to communicate with our headquarter servers through the company's intranet, a VPN via an Internet connection. I open up the transaction program and enter my user name and the monthly password. Next, it asks me for the biometric fingerprint. I place my middle right-hand finger on the scanner and it confirms who I am. Once confirmed, I set up the transaction with the necessary account data, to and from accounts, and other necessary data like the amount, type of currency, and the account owner's information. I press okay and a final window opens, it asks for the final verification, the code from the code generator." Cord removed a small pager-looking device from the safe in the Tidewaters and showed it to Goose."

Goose looks at the device and asks Cord, "This safe looks ancient, Cord. Someone with safe tumbler skills could break easily into it."

"Come on Goose, it's not the old type of safe, anyway no one here would ever try. You think Miss Julia or Mister Ironside would do break into the safe and kill Richardson and Bradshaw."

"Cord, I am just saying it is not the most modern type of safe and its style has been known as not the securest around. Never, mind the safe since you must take the code generator with you when you're working flights for TGI."

"Actually, Goose, I have a second code generator I take with me while flying, since this one always stays at the Tidewaters. The other code generator is in my flight bag locked in the pilots' room at MIA. The pilot room is locked and only flight crew can access it."

"Cord, if you had to make a transfer while flying, how do you go about making it then?"

"First, I have to be at my hotel or in the airport for the Internet connection to Barrett Banks headquarters servers."

"Cord, what do you access the server with? Interrupted Goose.

"My laptop, it has the transaction program installed. The security installers left a box in the Tidewater computer room, with a biometric fingerprint scanner. It just plugs into my laptop with a USB cable. Other than being elsewhere it is the same process as here at the Tidewaters." Cord concluded.

"Cord, let me see your laptop?"

"Oh, it is also in my flight bag. All my charts are on it. I have a tablet here with my charts when I fly the company's planes."

Goose's piercing Seminole eyes just stared through Cord.

"Goose, I do not like that look. How do you expect me to stay in touch with BDI or Barrett Banks, when I am out of town? I always keep password generator in my flight bag. No one in the pilot's room would know what it goes to or like in Denver last trip; I took the bag with me to my room. It is perfectly safe."

"Maybe or maybe not, as I'm starting to see it."

"Goose, you think I have caused the missing money."

"I'm not quite sure—we'll have to see. I will make sure we find out."

Cord reassuring Goose, "Whomever they are would still need the monthly code and scanner if they got my flight bag. And here Mr. Bradshaw would have had to give the murderer the access code to the computer room before he was killed."

"Cord, that's not too hard if Mr. Bradshaw was being threatened. Whoever is behind this had Bradshaw open the safe or did it themselves, got the second key, and code generator. He had his own primary key and they took his finger to swipe and his iris to scan."

Peri walked back in, squirmed and gulped, "Who could be so sick?"

"You'd be surprised what people will do for money, especially millions," Goose responded with his official voice.

"So Goose, what do you think the message is they're sending me?"

"I still not sure, but you need to be careful." Sounding now more like a friend than an agent, "I'm not sure just...yet, but don't go anywhere alone."

"I won't. I have always Dr. Pepper with me and you." Cord smiled down at Peri.

Wildgoose eased out of the rocking chair. "Well Barrett, if you're too damn pitiable to feed me then I'll just go home."

Cord reflected on the Seminole's epicurean appetite for a moment. "Goose, feeding you is like trying to fill up a running garbage disposal. But wait a second, there's one more thing."

"Yeah?"

"The other day when we took off from the hunting camp I spotted something shining in one of the hammocks."

"Like what?"

"I don't know, maybe it's an aircraft wreckage. It's got to be something. I want to check it out. Are you free tomorrow morning?"

"Not in the morning, Cord, I have to go to the Miami district office and check on a few things. I can meet you here about two."

"That'll work. Goose, see you tomorrow."

The next day shortly after two, Wildgoose found Peri and Cord at the stables. "You think we should try to go out in the Glades this late?"

"No, we will wait until tomorrow, Goose. It will be an all-day-er so we need to get an early start."

"Are we taking the airboat or a swamp buggy?" asked Wildgoose.

"The airboat, there's no other way in there."

"I think we should take the swamp buggy, Cord. If there is anything in those Glades, it's got to have a way to get in. If there's a way in, I'll find it."

"Okay, suits me. Doctor Pepper, do you want to go?"

"Are you going?"

"Yes, of course."

Peri jammed her hands on her hips. "Then I'm going too," she firmly stated.

"All right, see you in the morning," said Wildgoose. "You two get a good night sleep." Winking at Cord and shaking his finger at Peri, he said, "Separate rooms tonight, Doctor Pepper."

Peri wrinkled her nose at him. "Not in this lifetime, Agent George Washington Wildgoose," she flatly declared.

Wildgoose started to walk back to his truck. Stopping, he turned. "Oh, Cord, I almost forgot. Here's your killer." He handed Cord an envelope.

Cord tore open the envelope.

"El Diablo!" Cord almost shouted. "What— What? What would a major leaguer like him possibly want with us? Why?"

"Why do you think, Mr. Zillionaire," said Wildgoose. "I told you someone was trying to kill you, but you won't listen."

"He may be right, Sweetheart," Peri quietly said.

Wildgoose said, "That's not all."

"There's more?"

"A lot more, Cord. I have a balloon buster for you, a real shocker. I need to go to my truck and get a file. I'll meet you two upstairs on the porch."

Cord had drawn two beers from the bar tap and Peri had iced tea. They were sitting by the table on the veranda.

"Here," said Wildgoose, sliding a thick FBI file to Cord. "I made copies of everything, INTERPOL's too."

"And?"

Wildgoose paused for a moment. He took the band from his ponytail and shook his hair loose. "We were finally able to finger El Diablo. We know who El Diablo is."

Cord opened the bulky folder and read. He sat in stunned disbelief. There's…there's got to be a mistake," he stuttered.

"No mistake," said Wildgoose. He jabbed his finger on a name in the file.

"That's El Diablo."

CHAPTER SEVENTY-SIX

Pend Oreille Ranch
September 25

A clear morning blanketed the Pend Oreille. The Contractor settled on the dry ground under the walkway to the boathouse. Through the scope of his best friend, the contractor watched Peri, Cord and Wildgoose emerge from the backstairs and climb into a government pick-up. Secured on a trailer behind the truck was an amphibian four-wheeler with extremely wide balloon tires, built especially for grinding through swamps and marsh.

The Contractor had scouted the area thoroughly checking position, weather and vantage point. He had made his way from the county road on foot. To avoid the security cameras, he slipped inside the chain link fence and waded near the shore of the cove, along the four-mile driveway leading to the Tidewaters. Sometimes in waist deep water but most often-in water up to his knees.

Once on the dry area under the boathouse he was comfortable. The Contractor reached for his thermos, poured a cup of clam chowder, and opened a packet of crackers.   He would eat the sandwich later.   It was going to be a long wait, but his time in the jungles of Vietnam and the demands of his profession had taught him patience.

Ugh, he thought, *stale.*   He tossed the fusty crackers in the water.   Opportunity may be slow to come.

Cord Barrett will die today.

He waited.

CHAPTER SEVENTY-SEVEN

Deep in the Florida Everglades
September 25

They drove along the seldom-traveled County Road 9 cutting through the heart of the Everglades. Wildgoose said, "Look! See that?"

"See what?" said Cord and Peri.

"Take a look at those gumbo limbo trees?" The gumbo-limbo is a species of the many hardwoods, which grow on the numerous small islands throughout the Everglades. They produce a large yellowish-green fruit, which provides a food source for the animals.

"See how the limbs are bent just a smidgen and how the moss is leaning back a bit?"

Both Peri and Cord shrugged. "No, we don't see it Goose, but so what?" said Cord.

"Look at the other moss," he said. "It's all hanging straight down and shifting with the breeze a tad, but that moss is clinging to the limbs and tilting back just a hair. About cab high, I would guess. Someone has driven a rig through there."

Wildgoose drove the truck into the thicket of wild oaks and gumbo-limbos surrounded by a nest of palmettos. The dangling moss covered the windshield obscuring their visibility for a moment.

"There's your mystery road if you want to call it a road," he said, gesturing forward through the windshield with the flat of his hand.

"I don't see anything but swamp," said Cord. "But lead on, Rand McNally."

Wildgoose drove for a half-hour over the incredible rough terrain winding through the mire and brush until they came to what appeared to be a half circle clearing cut in a cluster of pines.

"We'd better unload the buggy here. This poor old truck can't go any further in four-wheel," said Cord.

"You're right," said Wildgoose, bobbing his head toward a thicket. "Somebody else had the same idea. Take a look."

"Take a look at what?" said Peri.

"My, my," sighed Wildgoose. "You pale face; yellow hairs couldn't find your asses with a wraparound mirror. Look!" He walked over to a coppice of hardwood trees and pulled back a bulk of palm fronds.

"A swamp buggy," Cord exclaimed. "What the hell?"

"Exactly. An amphibian just like ours," said Wildgoose. "Except this one has tractor tires and we have four-foot balloon tires. But the engine sits high same as the one we have."

"Makes the tracks easy to follow," said Cord. "Let's go."

Peri took a tissue from her pocket. "Just a minute," she said walking behind the clump of brush.

"Hey Doctor Pepper," called out Wildgoose. "Don't forget the paperwork and remember to flush it."

"And, Doctor Pepper" sang out Cord, "I remembered to put the lid down just for you."

Peri put her thumbs in her ears and waving her fingers stuck her tongue out at them. "I'll only be a second," she said.

Laughing, the two men unloaded the buggy from the trailer. "You drive the jets, Barrett, I'll drive the buggy," said Wildgoose. "Besides, you white-eyes would never find your way."

"Okay, Red Cloud, lead on."

Peri reemerged and climbed aboard the swamp buggy.

Wildgoose steered the buggy through an endless circuitous route over the rough floor of the Everglades, sometimes with water coming to the top of the wheels. Suddenly he stopped and pointed to a glimmer sporadically blinking through the undergrowth and scrub pines.

"There's your shiny whatever it is, Mr. Barrett."

Wildgoose pulled the swamp buggy into a wide clearing and neatly tucked under a hammock of tall oak trees. Almost completely hidden in the hanging moss they saw a long aluminum shed.

"What is going on here?" exclaimed Cord. "That's on Pend Oreille property. How could they get all this stuff out here?"

"Simple, Cord, they did it the same way we built the hunting lodge, a piece at a time."

"But Goose, how did they get it here?"

"Had to be by airboat, Cord, a regular boat would never make it. If they had gone by land, they would have worn much more identifiable path than we used getting in here. Obviously they didn't want to leave any trail, so they had to move everything through the swamp by airboat."

"Yeah, our hunting camp has to be somewhere over there," he pointed.

"It is," replied Wildgoose. "This place is well done. There's water on three sides. Whoever it is, they built a small dock for the airboats. Hey, Cord," he said, "Take a look at those." Wildgoose pointed to some white bits and pieces on the ground scattered about the clearing.

"Yeah, Goose, I saw them."

"What does that tell you?"

"Not much other than confirming what you already told me. I still can't believe it, Goose."

"Believe it, Barrett."

The three cautiously approached the single door to the barn-like structure, not knowing if anyone was about or not. Wildgoose stopped them. "Nobody's here," he said. "But look, there's a couple of padlocks and deadbolts too. Somebody does not want any visitors."

"Now what?" said Cord.

"I have some bolt cutters in the amphibian, Cord, your call."

"Get them, Goose. This barn or whatever is on my property and has no business being here."

Wildgoose returned with a pair of long handled bolt cutters and a flat crowbar. The padlocks snapped off easily. Cord and Wildgoose leaned together on the crowbar and after considerable effort, the door splintered open.

"Stay here, Doctor Pepper," ordered Cord.

There was plenty of adequate illumination inside from a skylight. Wildgoose and Cord's attention was instantly focused on the opposite side of the edifice. Neatly placed and leaning against the far wall, the eyes of two dead bodies stared at them. Mouths gaped open and a hole from a small caliber bullet was neatly centered in their foreheads.

CHAPTER SEVENTY-EIGHT

Deep in the Florida Everglades
September 25

Cord and Wildgoose had no way of knowing the corpses gawking at them with vacant eyes were the two who had delivered the white powder to Bucky Wooster. They stood and gawked back in stunned awe.

"Jeez," muttered Wildgoose. "We're getting more dead bodies around here than Custer had at the Little Big Horn."

"Something huge is going on." Cord said. "Take a look at this, Goose," he pointed to a large heap of brown packages stacked from floor to ceiling.

"Don't touch it Cord," said Wildgoose. He took the Bowie Knife from the sheath strapped to his waist. The razor sharp edge easily sliced through the side of one of the brown packages. A white powdery substance cascaded to the floor. Wildgoose licked his finger and touched the powder to the tip of his tongue.

"Cocaine."

"Cocaine!" Cord exclaimed. "Cocaine on the Pend Oreille?"

"Makes sense, Cord, if you think about it, what better place to hide it than in the Glades? Who would ever discover anything way out here on a ranch the size of Montana? Then it's just a simple matter to load up and distribute it in Miami, Lauderdale, West Palm and so on."

Peri's voice came from behind them. They had almost forgotten about her. "Hey Cord, what's this?" She reached for a dark blue suit in dry cleaners cellophane hanging by the door. "It looks like some kind of uniform."

Cord came closer. "It is a uniform. A TGI uniform, hat and all!" he exclaimed. "What the…?"

"Can't be yours, Cord, too small," she said.

"Not by much. But what would a company uniform being doing out here?"

"How tall is Captain Sellers?" asked Peri.

"About the same as this," said Cord, holding up the hanger. "But I can't imagine him—He's as straight as the Pope. What would his uniform be doing way out here in the Glades?"

"Are you sure, Cord?" asked Wildgoose.

Before Cord could answer, Wildgoose headed toward a small desk resting at the opposite corner from the splintered door. "What's this gizmo?" he said picking up a small box-like device, about the size of two decks of cards.

"I've seen those before," said Cord. "It's a projector. They use them in our training classes at TGI. It takes an image or video from a computer or laptop and projects it on a screen, greatly enlarging it and it's in high-definition."

"We had the same in our classes in vet school," spoke up Peri. "It's called a HD video projector."

"It couldn't work out here," said Cord. "No power."

"Sure it could," said Wildgoose. "It's solar powered. It takes in sunlight through the windows and stores the energy in a small battery."

Cord gave a solicitous look. He turned on the machine and aimed it at the darker wall towards the rear of the structure.

The three walked around and gazed in the direction of the projector image. Cord said, "Well, Goose, there's your ghost. And here's an amp with a bullhorn, no wonder the scream was so friggin' loud."

Wildgoose's jaw dropped when they all stood staring at the headless image of the blood dripping Chief Osceola.

"I—I don't understand," stuttered Wildgoose.

"Simple, Goose, whoever is running this operation is capitalizing on an old Seminole myth to scare people away from here."

"Apparently it was working," said Peri.

"No doubt Doctor Pepper," said Cord. "No wonder we never could find a trace of anything because whoever it is was in behind this thing was shining it toward us."

"But what about the screen?"

"You don't need one, GW," said Peri. "All that's needed is a light fog, mist or rain something like that; anything that will reflect light."

"We'd better get going," said Wildgoose. "It will be getting dark before long."

"Let's keep this quiet for now."

"No, can do, Cord," said Wildgoose. "We got two dead bodies and we have to notify the DEA and the FDLE. This is a big time operation, plain and simple. We don't have any choice."

"FDLE?" questioned Peri.

"That's the Florida Department of Law Enforcement; it's the state equivalent to the FBI," said Wildgoose.

"We'd better get going and get out of here before dark. We still have to load the swamp buggy back on the trailer," said Cord.

They were just exiting through the fractured door when a soft sound caught their attention.

"What was that?" snapped Peri.

"What was what?" said Cord.

"I heard it too," Wildgoose said, "something human."

"Someone is here," whispered Peri.

CHAPTER SEVENTY-NINE

Deep in the Florida Everglades
September 25

They cautiously made their way back into the aluminum building and eased to a narrow aisle behind the stacks of cocaine. Wildgoose put his fingers to his lips beckoning silence. He pointed to a low door barely high enough for a crawl space. From inside came a faint moaning and sobbing sound.

"Where's your pistol, Goose?" Cord whispered.

"In the truck."

"In the truck? That's ten miles away!"

"Shh Cord, you'll wake up the whole damn swamp," whispered Wildgoose. With the bolt cutters, he shattered the padlock on the small door. Wildgoose unsheathed the Bowie.

They were met by an array of foul odors. Huddled together were two pre-teen young girls and a boy of about nine. The rancid smell of feces and urine stung their nostrils. There was a gallon milk jug half-full of dirty water nearby and a couple bowls of cereal type foodstuff strewn on the floor.

The children clad only in ragged underclothes huddled together and shook in terror at the sight of Wildgoose banishing the large knife. They were frozen with fear of the Indian bending over them.

Cord grabbed Wildgoose by the belt and pulled him back. "Doctor Pepper, I think maybe you better handle this."

"Oh, how horrible," Peri exclaimed. She looked in the enclosure and spoke softly to the youngsters still cowering together.

"They don't understand a single word," she said. "GW let me have your badge." Wildgoose handed her the shield.

"They can't be more than eight or ten years old," said Peri, as she quietly and gently talked to them. "Okay, all is okay now, see police," she said. The kids seemed to understand the badge and after many long minutes of coaxing, they hesitantly emerged from the filthy dungeon.

"Cord, we have to find something for them to wear. They can't go around half naked," said Peri.

"I don't know what to do about that, Doctor Pepper—Wait a minute," he said grabbing the TGI uniform from the hanger. "Can we cut this up?"

"We'll have to make it do," she said. "These poor little things are scared out of their minds. I wonder how long they have been here."

"We need to get these kids to Miss Julia and get clothes and some hot food in them," said Cord.

Wildgoose said, "As if cocaine is not bad enough, now it is white slavery and human trafficking? No doubt they are selling these young kids to rich sugar daddies no telling where."

"Bastards like that should be hung up by their balls," exclaimed Peri.

"Now, now, Doctor Pepper," said Cord soothingly. "That's a bit uncharacteristic for the future Mrs. McCord Barrett to talk isn't it?"

Silence fell around them. After a moment she exclaimed, "The future what?"

"The future what?" repeated the stunned Wildgoose.

"You heard me," said Cord. "I said the future Mrs. McCord Barrett."

Cord gave her a stone stare. "I've made up my mind, Doctor Pepper; now you have to make up yours." Tears began to sting Peri's eyes.

Peri and Cord stared at each other. Wildgoose broke the trance abruptly changing the subject. "Let's get these kids to the Tidewaters; it's going to be dark by the time we get out of here. C'mon, now you're burning daylight."

They were back to the half circle clearing and about to climb aboard the amphibian, when Wildgoose stopped. "Wait," he said. "You hear that?"

Cord and Peri heard nothing. "You're hearing things, Goose."

"No, listen," he said.

Then they heard it. A steady hum reverberated through the dense jungle of the Everglades.

The children heard the sound and began to shake in terror.

"It's just an airplane," said Peri.

"No airplane," said Wildgoose. "It's an airboat and it's coming here."

CHAPTER EIGHTY

Deep in the Florida Everglades
September 25

The tall, stoic driver skillfully steered the airboat through the maze of small islands and the clumps of reeds and sawgrass. Keen eyes sought through the mist of the rooster-tail spray kicked up from the powerful blades of the propeller until they rested on exactly what they were seeking. From the seat high in the boat, the driver cut the power and allowed the flat-bottomed craft to glide under a clump of mangrove trees.

The mangrove's limbs extended out and draped down to the water line. Its roots were above the water reached as high as the boat gunnels in a bow-like fashion. They looked like a giant spider with its legs draping down into the water anchoring into the rich bottom of the swampy savannah below.

This was precisely what the figure wanted. Once the boat was completely hidden under the dense camouflage of mangrove limbs, a line was securely fastened to an arched root.

The driver got down from the high seat and approached the two dead bodies, a man and a woman, on the front of the boat. With a long bamboo stalk, the depth of the water was probed.

Eight feet, that should be plenty.

The figure meticulously checked the heavy chains wrapped around the bodies and running through a 30-pound concrete cinder block. The staring eyes and the small caliber bullet holes in the center of the foreheads were callously ignored.

With some difficulty, the figure hoisted the man's body over the side and watched it disappear. The expressionless face stared back from under the tea colored water as it sank out of sight.

The woman, smaller and lighter was easier to winch over the side. Her blond hair drifted for a moment in the soft motion of the water. She too stared back while she descended into her dark watery Everglades tomb.

The driver brushed his hands together.

That's that—No coup de grace for you folks. Bad day for you—good day for the gators.

The figure tossed sunglasses and a pair of wide brimmed Panama hats after the sinking corpses. A phony Van Dyke goatee followed into the mire. Releasing the ropes, the figure restarted the powerful 180-horse Lycoming engine. Bringing the boat about abruptly, the driver navigated the tangle of small channels and sawgrass.

I have to get rid of those kids and I still have to dispose of two more bodies. There's no chance of finding my way out of here at night. I've got to get back before dark.

The driver steered the airboat toward the aluminum shed.

CHAPTER EIGHTY-ONE

Deep in the Florida Everglades
September 25

"Quick," exclaimed Wildgoose. "Doctor Pepper, hide the kids over in those palmettos. Cord, you come with me."

Peri quickly gathered the youngsters and made a run for a thicket of palmettos bordering the half-circle clearing. Hunkering them down under the cover of the palmetto fans, she touched a finger to her lips making the international gesture to be quiet. Recognizing the sound of the airboat, the children shivered with fear but nodded that they understood.

Peri held out the flat of her hands indicating stay here. Again, they nodded understanding. Peri made a dash across the cleared compound and crowded behind Cord and Wildgoose.

"Doctor Pepper, what are you doing here?" exclaimed Cord. "I told you to wait with the kids."

"No, you didn't," she said. Peri started to say something else when Wildgoose shushed her.

"Keep quiet," he ordered. At that moment, an airboat banked sharply around a steep corner at a high speed. The driver cut the engine and the boat glided smoothly to the small dock.

From their hidden vantage point, the three glanced at each other. "Just who we thought," whispered Cord.

The figure alit from the boat and was tying a line to a dock cleat, when Wildgoose and Cord crept up from behind. Following the men, Peri stepped on a small twig. At the snapping sound, the figure jerked around.

"What? What are you doing here?"

"I might ask you the same question," replied Cord.

"Good afternoon, Mr. Barrett."

"Good afternoon, El Diablo."

CHAPTER EIGHTY-TWO

Deep in the Florida Everglades
September 25

"So, you think you finally figured out who I am."

"It wasn't all that difficult when you apply a little science," said Wildgoose.

"What are you talking about?"

Cord spoke. "Easy enough Darcee, or do you prefer El Diablo?"

"Screw you," she barked.

"Aw, that won't be necessary," said Cord. "Goose here, borrowed a little Agar…Agar…"

"Agarose Gel," said Peri. "It's an electrophoresis process which isolates RFLP."

Darcee reached under her shirt and produced a small caliber pistol. Leveling it at them, she said, "What the hell are you talking about, shorty?"

"RFLP, Restriction Fragment Length Polymorphism," said Peri.

"I don't need any chemistry lesson," snarled Darcee.

Peri continued, "In other words Deoxyribonucleic Acid. Simply put: DNA."

"For someone who is supposed to have a genius IQ you were pretty careless, Darcee," said Wildgoose.

"That doesn't prove a thing."

"I'm afraid it does, Miss El Diablo," said Cord. "Goose spread some of this Ag…"

"Agarose Gel," Peri repeated.

"Yeah, Agarose Gel," said Cord. "Goose coated the computer keys at the bank's main servers with it and he did the same on the computers at the Tidewaters. Once we were sure that you had touched the keys, he took a trace tissue sample to the crime lab at the FBI. Their lab did the rest. Also, Goose matched your fingerprints."

"I was in Tallahassee and other places. How could it have been me?"

"That's easy, Darcee," said Cord. "Haven't you ever heard of an FAA flight plan? You chartered a jet from Sky Ventures Aviation, simple enough to check. But the real clincher, haven't you ever read anything by Dr. Arthur Canon Doyle?"

"What the hell are you talking about, Barrett?"

"He wrote the Sherlock Holmes novels. But what I'm referring to is in, *Silver Blaze*, the dog that didn't bark. That's the way Holmes figured out who was the perpetrator. The guard dog didn't bark, so it had to have known the bad guy."

"So?"

"So—you are the only person who could have gotten past Max. Besides, see those white things on the ground over there? Sunflower shells; tells me Max has been here."

Darcee laughed. "Yes, my dear friend Max drops by for a visit and treat occasionally."

Cord spoke piercingly, "I see that not only have you been bilking our banks out of millions, but you are trafficking kids and cocaine as well."

"How perceptive of you, Mr. Barrett, but how wrong you are, the cocaine is only a sideline. You know pocket change. The kids are merely bargaining chips."

"Bargaining chips?"

"Yes, bargaining chips. You would be amazed how easy it was to negotiate with Mrs. Richardson and Mr. Bradshaw. Once I snatched their kids, they became very cooperative indeed and extremely easy to deal with."

I knew there was something," exclaimed Cord. "Brad and Georgette were with us for years and ...."

"Now Cord, you aren't that naïve are you? You would be surprised how cooperative people can get when you have good bargaining chips like their kids. Too bad, they have to die today. Just like you."

"No, you can't!" cried Peri, taking a step forward. "The kids—the children—they're gone. They're not here! They…."

Darcee jabbed the pistol in her direction. "Get back shorty, and don't insult my intelligence like that again."

Cord gave a look of capitulation as if surrendering to defeat. "Okay then, if we are about to die how about clearing up a few things?"

"Sure, Mr. Owner of the whole planet, I've got plenty of time. Unfortunately, you don't."

"We could rush her," whispered Wildgoose.

"Don't even think about it, Tonto." Waving the pistol she said, "This is an automatic I could drop all three of you in a second."

She's right, thought Wildgoose. *There's got to be another way out of this—*

"What about you and me? What about us?" said Cord. "Didn't we start off…?"

"Us?" exclaimed Darcee. "Us? Ha, ha. Don't make me laugh. There never was an 'us.' You like big tits and I have two of them. Getting to you was a snap. But now, your uncle, well, that was another can of worms. Besides, Barrett," she said, jabbing the pistol toward Cord's midsection, "You were very predictable. You have a dick and a couple of balls in there, so I knew what you were after; not exactly my cup of tea, if you know what I mean."

"Are you saying…?"

"Exactly," said Darcee. "But take Doctor Pixy there—She's more to my liking, if you follow my drift."

"Why is one of my uniforms out here?" interrupted Cord.

"It's not your uniform, it's my uniform."

"Yours?"

"Yes mine. It was so sweet of you to leave your bag in the crew room."

"And the uniform…."

"I knew you were flying out of Miami, and if you don't bring your flight bag home, you leave it in MIA's crew room. Other times you would leave it in crew rooms of other cities where you overnighted or like Denver in your hotel room. Easy access with my TGI uniform, I would simply don the uniform; tuck my hair under the hat. Moving on, so, since Mr. Bradshaw and Mrs. Richardson were kind enough to supply me their codes and biometrics accesses and since your Uncle Ted keeps his monthly pass code taped under a drawer in his desk, it was easy. All I had to do then was get into the Tidewaters' computer room to make the transaction. Once I even made a withdrawal from your laptop in the crew room."

"I thought so," said Goose, "Cord, I had a feeling your flight bag contents were used."

Cord snapped, "Stop the blame game." Then speaking to Darcee, "That's why you were able to get by Max. "What good is it for you to kill us, anyway? The FBI already knows that you're El Diablo."

"Cordie, my boy, you are getting smarter by the minute and I like tidy endings," said Darcee.

"But that's not the whole story is it, Miss El Diablo?" said Wildgoose mordantly.

"No, it's not, Cochise," said Darcee. She aimed the pistol at him. Her finger closed tightly on the trigger housing.

CHAPTER EIGHTY-THREE

Deep in the Florida Everglades
September 25

They waited for the loud bang. Wildgoose said,
"Why did you have to murder all those people?"

"Now, now, GW, murder? That's not a very nice
word," said Darcee. "Elimination, now that's a more
gracious term. The best way to keep a secret is not to
share it. So, I eliminate them." She smiled making a
rhyme. "Those in the know, just have to go."

"It looks like your little scheme is working," said
Cord.

"No, not at all like I initially planned, Cordie my
boy. My thoughts were to marry you. Then you would
meet with a most unfortunate accident."

"Sounds like a plan," said Wildgoose disgustedly.

"It was until this petite little harlot showed up,"
she juggled the gun in Peri's direction. "Everything
was going perfectly until Cord's hard-on got to thinking
for him and this little whore with half my brains and

none of my tits wriggled her ass. Tell me, Cordie boy; is she pretty good in the sack?"

Cord said nothing and glared at her. Peri lurched forward. Cord grabbed her. "Ah, ah, sugar britches…. Temper, temper," said El Diablo.

Still training the pistol at them, El Diablo hopped down from the dock facing them with her back to the swamp. She was careful to keep an adequate distance away. Nodding at Peri, "I wouldn't mind taking her for a test drive myself, but as you can see, I'm pretty busy right now."

"If you did get BDI and the Pend Oreille you couldn't run it," said Cord.

"I wouldn't have to. You have thousands of people who run things for you. Get real, Barrett. I would simply sell out and continue on with my other business interests."

"Yeah, like crime and killing people," snarled Peri.

"Exactly, little person," said Darcee. "Where I really missed the boat was not getting my hands on Phoebe and that triggering mechanism. I could have held the whole world hostage with that thing. But now, I guess that's a moot point and another story."

"So that was you," said Cord.

"Yes, of course it was me. I sent a couple of my business associates up to North Carolina to have a chat with that old bastard commander." Darcee snickered.

"I tell you, he was one tough old codger and stubborn as the day is long. But he came around when we offered the ultimatum."

"Ultimatum?" said Wildgoose.

"Yes, an ultimatum, GW. The deal was to tell us what we wanted to know or watch his granddaughter's brains splattered all over his quaint little mountain home. To coin a phrase you might say I made him an offer he couldn't refuse."

"Yeah," said Peri, "Like killing his family."

"Right again, sweet panties."

"How did you know?" said Peri.

"Oh shorty, you're getting as dumb as these two. I got a call from the Pend Oreille telling me what Cordie boy and his faithful Indian companion here were up to."

From the Pend Oreille? thought Cord. *Impossible! Or is it?*

"Well—if there's nothing else," said Darcee, "I hope you believe in Jesus. It's time for you to meet him."

Cord said. "You may get away with what you have already stolen, but there won't be any more. Our computer people have…"

"You mean Michelle Stewart and her crew? Sorry to disappoint you, but she's a little behind. I anticipated her finding out too much too soon, so I programmed the computers at the main bank to download all the money to my accounts in Switzerland and the Caymans."

"That's impossible," exclaimed Cord.

"Sorry, but it's not impossible if you know how," she smiled. "And, by the way, I should be able to live quite comfortably on 75 or 80 billion bucks."

"Not to rain on your parade, El Diablo," said Cord, "All the BDI computers have been shut down until Monday, so you are lying."

"Of course they have, Cordie my boy. But I added a little program on the server that allows transactions to be sent on a certain time and date. It no longer needs to be when you're sitting at the computer. The program is so stealth that even the best hackers in the world haven't learned to hide a file like I can. The transaction will start first thing Monday morning at nine. I've got everything I need to access and control all of the Barrett Bank's servers and computers; I have pre-programmed transactions set all day Monday. By close of business day, I'll be 80 billion dollars richer and no one will be able to locate me. Now that both Bradshaw and Richardson are unable to get to the servers and try stop the transactions if they knew about them they would not have been able to stop the transactions."

"So there is no one to cancel the transactions," sighed Cord.

"Exactly, no one even knows about the preset transaction except the four of us. Soon it will only be me. Now as a last gesture, how about you folks walking over this way so I don't have to drag your heavy dead asses." She waved the pistol toward the airboat.

Not exactly the obsequious type, Wildgoose said acerbically, "Fuck you."

"Tsk, tsk," she scolded. "That would be nice but sorry, I just don't have the time; besides, is that any way to talk when you about to see if Saint Peter will open the Pearly Gates for you?"

"We are not budging," said Wildgoose, looking around at the darkness beginning to settle over the Everglades.

"Fine by me, GW, I'm sure Cord and Dr. Sweet Cheeks here will be happy to lug your dead butt for me. And since you like being such a smart ass, you're first."

High in a nearby mango tree, a pair of yellow eyes stared fixedly below. Its jaw muscles flexed and tightened in anticipation of a succulent feast.

Darcee leveled the gun directly at Wildgoose's head and squeezed the trigger.

CHAPTER EIGHTY-FOUR

Deep in the Florida Everglades
September 25

At the exact instant Darcee pulled the trigger, a blur came streaking from the top of a tall mango tree in a nearby hammock colliding with her shoulder with incredible force. Darcee awkwardly tumbled backwards toward the marsh heaving the gun spinning in the air just as it exploded sending its missile millimeters over Wildgoose's head. He felt the heat of the projectile scorching his scalp.

"Hi 'ya, Max. Pretty Max, pretty Max," squawked the bird. Darcee had been holding the pistol in the same manner in which she fed the large parrot its favorite delicacy of sunflower seeds. Max, assuming she was in for scrumptious treats, lit on her shoulder flapping her wings in Darcee's face, making quite a ruckus and squawking with delight. The collision knocked gun into the air forcing Darcee to lose her balance and stumble backward into the mire.

"Darcee, no!" shouted Cord, bolting toward her.

"Cord, stop!" bellowed Wildgoose grabbing Cord's shirt. "Quicksand!"

"Quicksand? Oh, my god!" screamed Peri. "Cord, do something!"

Panic stricken, Darcee began to thrash and writhe fighting against the suction of the slime tugging her down into the bog. Her arms beat the air fiercely.

"Darcee!" shouted Wildgoose, "Don't fight it. Relax and lie back. The mud will support you."

Darcee never heard him. Terror ripped through her body as survival instincts demanded she resist the dreadful fate lurking below. Because of her resistance against the pull of the bog, Darcee was sinking quickly. The sucking quicksand was covering her breasts. Her eyes bulged in horror as she discerned her inevitable doom. It was only a matter of moments.

"Quick, Cord!" yelled Wildgoose. "Get the rope out of the buggy. I'll try to find a pole or stick. Hurry, we don't have much time!"

Cord dashed to the amphibian and Wildgoose rushed into the woods. Peri stood frozen and couldn't move. She watched in shocked horror at the doomed El Diablo slowly sinking to her chin in the unrelenting quagmire.

CHAPTER EIGHTY-FIVE

Deep in the Florida Everglades
September 25

Cord sprinted back with sturdy rope and found Wildgoose with his characteristic adroitness already back to the edge of the quicksand. Wildgoose was desperately trying to reach the doomed woman with a bamboo pole. Only her hair floated above the mire.

"Too short, quick, let me have that rope!" he cried. The scarlet hair had slowly disappeared. A desperate arm was waving frantically above the surface.

Wildgoose heaved the rope toward the thrashing wrist. He cursed. "Missed!" he cried. Wildgoose recoiled the rope and threw it again. This time hitting the disappearing hand, which was now hanging limp.

"Too late, there's nothing we can do," muttered Cord.

Nothing but a few bubbles and the silent gurgling belching from the quicksand as Darcee, El Diablo, was swallowed into the eternity of her endless, bottomless and lightless sepulcher.

"Too late, she's gone," said Wildgoose despairingly. Cord put his arms around Peri. The three stood in stunned silence as the darkness and stillness of the mysterious and infinite Everglades shrouded them.

Peri looked up at Cord, her beautiful eyes fixed on him. "I love you," she whispered.

"I love you back, Doctor Pepper," he murmured softly. They held each other's gaze for a long moment.

"Okay, saddle up. Let's round up those kids and get back to the Tidewaters. C'mon, Doctor Pepper, you're...."

"You don't have to tell me. I know, I'm burning daylight."

CHAPTER EIGHTY-SIX

Pend Oreille Ranch
September 26

Cord and Peri sat down for breakfast on the veranda. Peri poured a glass of grapefruit juice and swatted at a visiting fly hovering over her plate.

"Cord, have you called GW to come over so we can hash all this out?"

"I don't have to call him, Doctor Pepper. Goose is like a bloodhound. He'll smell these ham and eggs all the way across the lake. He will be here shortly, trust me."

"Cord, don't you think it's time to start calling me Peri instead of Doctor Pepper?"

"Sure do, Doctor Pepper."

As Cord was speaking, Wildgoose poked his head from the open sliding glass door. "Ahh, ham and eggs this morning—"

Cord looked at Peri. "See? What did I tell you? Sit down, Goose, there's your plate." Wildgoose was already chewing on something he had obviously ripped off in the kitchen behind Miss Julia's vigilant eyes.

"Goose, did you get the children taken care of?"

"Sure did. I turned them over to juvenile at the sheriff's office last night and relatives picked them up right away. While I'm thinking about it, Cord, the sheriff and the feds want to talk to us."

"Yeah Goose, I figured as much. Has Timmy had any luck?"

Wildgoose had summoned Timmy late that night to try to crack Darcee's codes and stop the downloads in the offshore banks.

"Not yet, Cord. But we can check with him after breakfast."

Cord and Wildgoose stood to leave. "Doctor Pepper, you going with us?"

"No. You two go ahead. I have to inoculate the foal and look in on the mare. I'll catch you later."

They found Timmy still tirelessly working at the FBI computer. "Whatcha got Timmy, anything?"

"No sir, Mr. Wildgoose. Any code is breakable, but it takes time. Even with the information and codes you gave me, I cannot get in yet, since it take two different persons to enter their information simultaneously."

"How much time do you need, Timmy?" asked Cord.

Timmy had set up three computers; the three monitors each showing a blur of numbers and codes attempting to gain access. He interlocked his fingers and stretched his arms. Yawning he said, "Hard to say, Mr. Barrett. Could be any second or it could take days."

"What?"

"Yes sir. See," he said, dragging a thumbnail across a nearby screen as it flashed a series of letters and numbers as the different hacking codes ran. "I am trying everything I know. I have also reached out to the hacking community for other ideas; the BDI Industries have set up the newest and best security of our times. It's at a security level that even the best of the best hackers haven't broken yet."

"Richardson and Bradshaw were the best security specialists we could find on the planet, without them, I don't know how we are going to be able to stop the preset transactions. Timmy, you have to keep trying or tell me who we can get to stop that download and transaction before Monday."

"Mr. Barrett, you may have to keep the system shut down until we can figure out a way."

"We can't do that, we have customers who want their money," exclaimed Cord heading for the door.

Holding up a notepad, Timmy said, "Hold on Mr. Barrett, I have found a way and it can stop the download, but you have to be there in person to do it. I can't stop them from here electronically, at least not yet, sir."

"Well tell me, Timmy."

"What are you going to do, Barrett?" asked Wildgoose.

Cord was already on his cell phone. "I don't care if he is on the golf course. Get Captain Sawber and his number one crew to the airport now and have the Gulfstream and the Sabreliner fueled and catered for a long flight."

"What—what's going on, Cord."

"C'mon, Goose. I'll explain later, right now we have to go. Today is Sunday. One of us has to be in Switzerland and one of us has to be in the Caymans tomorrow morning by nine o'clock their time, or every cent we have in the BDI banks will be gone."

Cord called Peri on his cell phone. "Get back to the Tidewaters right away and wait for me," he ordered.

Back at the ranch, they encountered an anxious Peri waiting on the veranda. "Doctor Pepper do you have a passport?"

"Ah yes, sure Cord," she stammered, "But I've never used it."

"Good. Get it. Goose will drive us to the airport."

"Sure Cord, okay. You mind telling me where we are going?"

"We are not going anywhere, Doctor Pepper. You are going to Switzerland and I am going to the Caymans."

"What?"

"I'll explain on the way to the airport. I have to have someone I can depend on and totally trust 100 percent. That's narrows it down to my uncle, Goose and you."

"I need to pack a few things," said Peri, still shocked.

"No time, Doctor Pepper. Just use your BDI card and buy whatever you need when you get there."

"Let's go."

CHAPTER EIGHTY-SEVEN

Pend Oreille Ranch
September 26

Under the boathouse, the Contractor's endless patience had paid off once again. His target was standing by the wooden railings along the long veranda and appeared to be in an intense conversation with an attractive young woman.

The Contractor squinted through his scope.

No clear shot from here—the woman—too close—

He edged into knee-deep water and moved a few steps sideways. Much better—He rested his best friend against one of the piling cross braces. Now he was ready. Everything was perfect.

Let's see. About seventy-five yards—no wind to speak of—no worries about atmosphere or elevation. Better add one click—

The Contractor twisted a small knob on the riflescope making the adjustment for 75 - 100 yard range. He heard the familiar click. He narrowed his eyes and peered through the scope. He waited until Cord turned.

No head shot—too messy. I have to be careful and make sure the girl is clear. I need a chest shot. Ah, there it is—I've earned my fee on this operation. Hold it right there, Mr. Barrett—

The Contractor focused the scope on the center of Cord's chest. His finger eased onto the trigger of his best friend. He gently applied a slight pressure.

Suddenly the contractor felt an abrupt gush of excruciating pain shoot upward through his body like a surge of lightning.

Oh, my god! A bear trap? Who would set a bear trap in water? My leg—Oh, my god! My leg!

The Contractor felt his leg being shattered as he heard the gruesome sounds of bone being crushed into pieces. Something with the strength of a bulldozer was wrenching him into the brackish water. He was flung on his belly and being dragged backwards. The Contractor thrust out his arms and dug his fingers in the beach sand up to their knuckles. Something was effortlessly pulling him into the water.

The Contractor realized that he was under the briny water traveling at high speed. He vainly kicked with his free leg and desperately fought for breath. Everything was passing through his mind very slowly. He thought of his boys and his spacious five-acre home in nearby Jupiter. He could clearly see the face of his beautiful wife smiling at him from the door as if he had just returned from a business trip.

I am in a dream—none of this is real. Everything is passing so slowly. It is all so surreal. All around me is turning dark. I can no longer feel the pain. I can't feel anything—Darkness—

The Contractor's drowned and his mangled body was tucked into a fissure under the calm waters of the cove bordering the Pend Oreille Ranch. Eternity was waiting and his penitence yet to be determined.

Goliath and company would dine well tonight.

CHAPTER EIGHT-EIGHT

Pend Oreille Ranch
September 26

By the time they arrived at the airport, Cord had given Peri the instructions and explained where she had to be the next morning. Captain Sawber and his crew, a co-pilot and a flight attendant were already at the airport standing by the silver Gulfstream with the longhorn steer horns painted on the tail above *Pend Oreille Cattle Company, BDI, Inc.*

"You are taking the G-5," Cord said to Peri. "It is fully catered with anything you want and sleeping quarters if you get tired."

"But—but, Cord," she stammered. "Isn't this your family's personal plane?"

"No buts, Doctor Pepper, the Gulfstream has the range to take you north and over."

"North?" she exclaimed. "To Switzerland?"

Captain Sawber lit the engines and they were spooling up. The RPMs began a deafening whine.

"Yes, Doctor Pepper, it's called the polar route. You won't turn east until a little past New York."

"Polar what?" She shouted over the engines.

"Never mind, Doctor Pepper, it's shorter and quicker that way, trust me. Just go!" He exclaimed. "Krissy is the flight attendant. Just ask her for anything you want." Cord smiled, "There should be plenty of Dr. Pepper on board."

Peri scrunched her face. "Ugh, very funny. First time today," she muttered and raced up the stairs of the screaming jet.

They watched the Gulfstream taxi out. Cord turned to Wildgoose. "Goose you stay here and keep an eye on things at the Pend Oreille. I'm taking the Sabre down to the Caymans."

"Have you called the State Department?" asked Wildgoose.

"Oh yeah, I forgot. We can't fly over Cuba without a clearance," said Cord. "Well, screw it. We're going anyway."

"Mr. Barrett," said the co-pilot standing nearby, "You are a pilot; you know we can't do that. You can't overfly Cuba without State Department approval."

"You are right. We'll have to go around Cuba."

"Do you have that kind of range in this thing?"

"I think so, Goose. It will be cutting it awful close. I'll be back tomorrow night. Catch you later."

"Yeah, Big Chief, catch you later."

CHAPTER EIGHTY-NINE

Geneva Switzerland
September 27

Shortly after dawn, Peri was enjoying a splendid view of Lake Geneva enveloped by the breathtaking snow-capped mountains and the city of Geneva off to her right as Captain Sawber made his final approach and gently touched the jet down on Runway Two-Three at the Cointrin International Aéroport. Geneva is located in the French speaking Republique et Canton de Genéve in southwestern Switzerland.

A uniformed driver and a female English-speaking attendant were standing smartly beside the open door of a dark Mercedes Limousine. Captain Sawber set the parking brake and spooled down the engines.

"What is your pleasure, mum?" asked the woman.

Peri replied, "I'm—I'm not sure."

"We are instructed to deliver you to the Banque de Candolle Mallet et and Cie, mum."

"The what, please?"

"The bank, mum." She gestured to the limo door. "There is a breakfast bar for you, hot coffee, pastries and juices. If you please, mum." She waved her hand for Peri to enter the limo.

A short time later the limo pulled up into the reserved parking at 60 Route des Acacias and the attendant was out and opened Peri's door the instant it stopped. She bowed slightly and extended an open palm toward the bank door.

"If you please, mum."

Peri glanced at her watch set seven hours ahead of Florida time. *Perfect—*

Peri did not appear to be in a hurry and admired the expensive paintings adorning the bank walls and thought how different the Swiss banks were as to what she was accustomed to. A red-faced and very anxious bank manager stood immaculately attired in a dark blue business suit nervously wringing his hands.

"Doctor Pepper, I presume?" he inquired. Peri nodded. "I am Günter Steinberg, the bank CEO, this way, if you please."

Far away in the Grand Cayman Islands, Cord strode anxiously into the Banko Caribbean, Georgetown.

"Mr. Birmingham, please," he said to a tall attractive black woman neatly dressed in a dark yellow suit.

"Mr. Barrett?" Cord nodded. "Mr. Birmingham is expecting you." She ushered him into a wide opulent office. A portly dark skinned man stood from behind a cluttered desk.

"Sit down, Mr. Barrett, please," he said with a thick British accent offering his hand. Cord shook it. They exchanged brief pleasantries. "Mr. Barrett," Birmingham continued, "Before we begin any business I have a most urgent message for you."

"Urgent?"

"Yes, it is noted extremely urgent. You are to call a Mr. Wildgoose at this number immediately." Cord recognized the number and reached for his cell phone.

It was answered right away. "Goose, what's up?"

"Cord, I been trying to reach you," said Wildgoose's familiar voice. "I have some good news and some bad news."

"Better give me the good news, Goose; I'm not in the mood for any more bad news."

"Okay. You will be happy to know that Timmy stopped the download this morning about two and he was able to stop the transactions so they don't have to be done from both there and in Switzerland. So looks like the BDI bank money is safe except for the 15 or 16 million she's already bilked out of you."

"Whew, that really is good news, Goose." Cord exhaled a lungful of air. "So, shoot, what's the bad news?"

"Are you sitting, Barrett?"

"No."

"Well sit down; because you ain't gonna believe this one."

CHAPTER NINETY

Geneva, Switzerland
September 27

Exiting the bank, Peri asked the driver to take her to a shopping mall, the finest in Geneva. She was tired of dressing like a ranch veterinarian and she needed a new wardrobe. After all, Cord had told her to buy whatever she needed, didn't he?

Fifteen thousand dollars later, she asked the new purchases be delivered to the hotel. A half hour had passed, when she strode up to the desk at the Hotel des Bergius Geneva where room prices start at $1,300 per night.

Since arriving in Switzerland, Peri had attained a much more authoritative attitude. Her walk was bolder and her posture more erect.

"Puis-je vous aider?" said the clerk.

"I am Peri Pepper. I have a reservation."

"Yes of course, Doctor Pepper," he said in English. "You are in suite 501. Luggage?"

Peri shook her head no. "It will be delivered later."

The clerk handed her a plastic key and nodded toward an open elevator. "Enjoy your stay with us," he said. "Your party is waiting."

My party? What party? Am I having a party?

Peri inserted the key into the door slot by a red dot. It was quickly replaced by green. She waited for the click. Peri opened the door.

"It's you. Oh, thank God!" Peri exclaimed. She felt two strong arms embrace her and her skin tingled as kisses ran up and down her cheeks and neck. "I was so upset," she breathed. She began to say something else, but her words were cut short by a tongue slipping past her lips.

Four hands were caressing, groping, touching everywhere. Breaths came in small gasps as excitement was exchanged. Clothes were ripped off and strewn on the furniture and floor. The kisses grew deeper and deeper. Searching hands explored the other's body. Fingertips felt as they were wired with electricity. They fell back on the king size bed in full embrace.

Soon they were nude. Peri's kisses made their way down to her lover's abdomen and lower. She looked up abruptly. "You shaved!" she exclaimed.

"And you didn't," a voice laughed back at her. "Oh, Doctor Pepper, love of my life. I have missed you so."

"And, life of my love," uttered Peri, "I missed you too."

CHAPTER NINETY-ONE

Geneva Switzerland
September 27

Two hours and several orgasms later, Peri and Darcee lay nude on the bed howling with laughter as they talked of the recent past events. Darcee poured Peri another flute of the Krug Clos de' Ambonnay chilled in a bucket of ice resting on the nightstand.

"Here," Darcee said. "Good stuff. I had it flown in from France."

Peri reached for the black bottle. "I've read about this. It's from Northern France and the Vineyard is only about an acre of land. It's supposed to be the best in the world."

"If it's not it's damn sure one of the most expensive. This little baby was 8,000 bucks," smiled Darcee.

"I guess we can afford it giggled Peri," stroking Darcee's bare belly.

Darcee grinned, "I charged it to Barrett Diversified Industries. They can afford it better than us."

Both were laughing. Peri said, "Can you imagine the look on Cord's face when he finds out all this? His true love, Doctor Peri Pepper, or should I say his Dr. Strangelove is wrapped in the arms of a BDI auditor on the other side of the world!"

"He will be cross-eyed! Funnier still," exclaimed Darcee through her tears. "What do you think our dear daddy, the good Reverend Joshua Pepper, would do it he could see us now?"

"Oh, my gosh," said Peri. "He would be flipping cartwheels in his grave."

They were still chortling when Peri took a more serious note. "I was so worried about you getting out of that quicksand."

"Not to worry, little sister. I tied a rope on one of the dock pilings and hid it barely under the surface of the quicksand, just like I told you. I knew it wouldn't sink in that thick mush so once I went under, I simply grabbed the rope and pulled myself under the dock behind the hyacinths and lily pads. From where you all were standing they could never have seen me."

"I know," said Peri quietly. "But still I was worried about you."

"No problems, love. Everything went exactly like we planned from meeting Cord in Denver to now."

"But I have to say I really did like Cord. Another time and another place, it could have been the real thing," Peri said softly.

"Not to fret, little dear. I could hear every word you all were saying and it was getting dark. Besides, they had those pesky kids to worry about. So, I waited until I knew you all were out of earshot and I jumped back in the airboat."

"Maybe Cord and I couldn't hear it; that's for sure. But GW, you never know about him. It's like he has some kind of radar out there in those Glades."

"I know. He's a peculiar dude. One thing's for sure; I watched and he never did throw a shadow anywhere."

"I can't explain it either," said Peri. "It's got to be an Indian thing."

Darcee edged closer and rubbed her erect nipples against Peri. "Wait a sec, big sister," said Peri. "You said everything went exactly as we planned. I don't think so."

"What do you mean?"

"There are a lot of things, Darcee. Our first plan was for one of us to marry Cord and then do him in, remember?"

"Oh, I remember all right," said Darcee. "He wasn't taking the bait with me so that's why we came up with the Denver plan with you."

Said Peri, "Yeah, that worked out pretty well, but I found out at the bank this morning that pimple-faced, skinny little snot Timmy blocked our transactions."

"I know," said Darcee. "But the good news is we still scored a cool 16 mil. That's eight million apiece."

Peri smiled, "No, not quite 16 million. The banks charge a $15 dollar transfer fee."

They exploded in laughter. "Well then, little sister, you can take the 15 bucks out of my share."

"Okay, I will," scrawled Peri. "But we could have done a lot better if we had gotten our hands on that Phoebe thing. We could have held the whole world by the balls."

"Maybe we still can," sighed Darcee.

"No, not a chance, not anytime soon. We will have to wait quite a while before things cool off in Florida. Let's just hope that old woman and Major Douglas are still kicking. They are the only ones who know where the triggering mechanism is."

Darcee rubbed her breasts against Peri again. "Poor Cord," she whispered in Peri's ear. "He was such a dufus, always thinking with his play toy; never with his head or the head on his shoulders anyway."

"Cord wasn't a bad guy."

"No, he wasn't," agreed Darcee. "Too bad, I think he was really in love with you. And as a matter of fact, I thought he was a pretty good lay."

Peri smiled. "Yes, he was. I was falling in love with him too. I think I already am. In a way, I wish things could have been different."

Peri smiled and rolled on top. Darcee spread her legs. They kissed deeply. "Poor Cord," said Peri softly. "A good lay maybe, but the dear boy always had an identity problem."

"A what?"

"An identity problem, he never could figure out who was who."

CHAPTER NINETY-TWO

Pend Oreille Ranch
September 27

On the Tidewaters veranda, Cord sat solemn faced staring at the calm waters of the cove. A house staff member appeared.

"Big white chief want-um firewater?" said Wildgoose. Cord answered by waving his arm- indicating no, but said nothing.

"Cord, I know all this is a kick in the nuts, but you have got to get over this mess. You have to go back to work in a couple days and you can't do that looking like you just left a funeral. Besides, the insurance companies will stand good for most of your bank losses."

"I know, Goose, I know. It's not the money; I could take the hit on that. But all this is hard to swallow in one gulp. I really loved her."

"I know you did, Cord. But you have got to move on. There is too much to attend to, and the insurance investigators will be here this afternoon. They will find her."

Cord looked up at an approaching white coat. "Hello Mr. Ironside, what's up?"

"Mista Cordie, suh, this here letter jest came for you, suh. It say special delivery and it say personal, suh."

"Thank you, Mr. Ironside."

"Sumthin' else, Mr. Cordie, suh."

"Yes?"

"Me and Paco, suh. We go down to the boathouse to make sure the bar and frigerator be stocked. Paco, he finds a rifle right on de shore, suh. It be a real beauty it is."

"Thank you again, Mr. Ironside. Please ask Paco to bring it to Mr. Wildgoose. I have a feeling the FBI will be very interested in that rifle."

Cord turned to Wildgoose. "It's hard to fathom that this whole charade was perfectly orchestrated and choreographed from the first time I saw her in Denver."

"It may be hard to accept, Cord. But sadly enough it's true."

"But—but, Doctor Pepper was…"

"Hold it right there, Cord. That old Indian woman was right. She had her pegged from the start."

"I know, Goose. But it stretches my imagination to even dream that Doctor Pepper would or could ever be involved with someone like El Diablo. It just doesn't fit."

"It does if you think about it and add up all the facts, Cord. In fact, Peri and Darcee…"

Cord interrupted. "Yeah, Darcee was El Diablo, who would have ever thought that?"

"Ah Cord, you have a few nouns mixed up. Darcee is not El Diablo."

"If she's not El Diablo who the hell are they working for?" Cord exclaimed.

Before Wildgoose could answer, Cord tore open the special delivery envelope. "No return address," he mumbled. "Goose, what's this?"

Wildgoose read: "You've been DEWERCS."

"Goose, what the hell is D-E-W-E-R-C-S?"

Wildgoose gazed at the writing for some time. He smiled and looked at Cord. "Read it backwards, Cord."

"That's S-C-R-E-W-E-D. Screwed? You've been screwed, and it's signed E.D. It can't be, Goose, El Diablo is dead. We saw it ourselves."

Wildgoose let out a chest full of air. "Cord, my dear brother, you have missed the whole picture." He reached for a thick FBI file. Running his finger down the page, he stopped. "Look, Cord, here's the brains and the sadistic force behind it all."

Cord stared at the print in disbelief. "No!" he gasped, "Never in a million years. It can't be!"

"No question about it, Cord. It's always who you think are the quiet, shy ones."

"Impossible, Goose! It had to be Darcee."

"Sorry, Cord. That's exactly what they wanted you to think. It's true. Here's the proof," grabbing the printout and jabbing his finger on the name.

"El Diablo is none other than Doctor Peri Pepper."

CHAPTER NINETY-THREE

Miami Intl Airport
October 2

Cord shucked his coat and hat and hung them on the crew rack in the cockpit. "Hey, Capt-em Luke, San Francisco this morning?" he asked getting into the right seat and reaching for the shoulder harness.

"Pre-start checklist."

"Yep, San Fran again," sighed the captain. "Weather looks pretty good most of the way. We're ready for push back."

The apron tug pushed the big Boeing out to the startup area. Luke reached above and squeezed a small switch kicking in the fuel to light the whining turbine. "One to ground. We have ignition on number one."

"Fire in the hole," grinned Cord. "Lighting number one."

Soon they had reached their cruising altitude of 33,000 feet. "Is Andi our lead this month?" said Cord.

"Sure is. You want some coffee?"

"Yes, please. I could do with a cup. Anything exciting going on at your place, Luke?"

"Oh yeah, big time excitement," said the captain. "Let's see, I reupholstered the back of a rocking chair. And Carolyn is all fired up about some avocado seeds she planted."

"Avocados?"

"Yep, avocados, damnedest thing you ever saw. Everyone told her they would never grow in Texas, but the dern things are almost knee high."

"And that's excitement?"

"Around my place it is. Anything happen with you?"

"Nah," replied Cord. "Same-old, same-old."

"Not from what I've read in the papers and heard on the news. They say they got El Diablo somewhere around your ranch. The news says he's dead."

"Yeah, that's what they say, Captain."

"How did they catch him?"

"Almost too simple, Cap. We have a plant down there in the Everglades, it is so rare the government, and the state set up security cameras to protect it from poachers. They had a couple cameras hidden on the Pend Oreille down by the boathouse. Anyway, El Diablo's partner came sneaking around in the dark of night and got caught on the cameras."

"What kind of plant could be so important?"

"It's very rare, Cap, and the only place in the world it grows is in the Everglades."

"What's it called, Spark Plug?"

"Phantom Orchid."

EPILOGUE

DAVE and RITA - Are happily married living in Clewiston, Florida

CAPTAIN CLAYTON CARSON - Landed that night at McCarran Airport, Las Vegas, into a sea of flashing blue lights. He is no longer a pilot for anyone, anywhere.

KYLE MacFARLAND - With the help of Chief Pilot Spencer was hired as a flight officer with TGI.

PETE OGLIVIE - Was sent to rehab and transferred as a tower operator in Livingston, Montana, never again to work the radarscopes.

BETTY LOU GOMEZ - (Bouncing Betsy) is still the center supervisor in Denver.

ANDREA MAROKRIS - Remains a lead flight attendant with TGI.

CAPTAIN LUKE SELLERS - Retired from TGI and spends his time in his home in Texas and touring the world with his lovely wife Carolyn.

COMMANDER JAKE GALVAN, HIS WIFE LISA and GRANDDAUGHTER KAITLYN - Quietly enjoy the peacefulness of their North Carolina mountain home.

MAJOR LYNN DOUGLAS - Remains in the Indian village with his medicine woman, Christine, as far as anyone knows.

MISS JULIA - The undisputed matriarch of the Tidewaters is still barking orders and keeps the staff jumping.

TED BARRETT - Was elected Governor of Florida the following November leaving Gary Wildgoose to run the law firm and BDI Inc.

THE SEMINOLE VILLAGE and THE LAND OF THE BLUE LIGHT - No one has ever spoken of it since.

GEORGE WASHINGTON WILDGOOSE - Attends to his duties as an FBI Special Agent for the Native American tribes in South Florida and waits for Cord to stumble over their next adventure.

MCCORD BARRETT - Is still flying the line for TGI completely nescient of the adventure lying in wait just ahead.

DARCEE CORBIN PEPPER - Unknown.

DOCTOR PERI PEPPER - Also unknown.

ACKNOWLEDGEMENTS

Many people have contributed to this writing one way or another. I am in your debt and offer my sincere thanks to Michael and Maria Mahoney, Nella Goff, Jack Galvan, Joe Termina and Stephen Steinberg.

A special thank you and sincere appreciation to my editor and dear friend, Laurel Galvan, whose infinite patience with me, superb graphic and editorial skills made this possible.

AUTHOR'S NOTE

I am always pleased and flattered, to hear from my readers. Thank you.

However, if you visit my website at www.josstallman.com, I will receive your correspondence much faster than writing my publisher, Author's Bridge or via snail mail. So far, I have been able to keep up with all the mail and answer you accordingly, and I will try to continue to do so.

Please do not forward me attachments. I will not download them for obvious reasons. Please do not place me on your mailing lists for jokes, prayers, political causes, charities, etc. I simply do not have the time to download and peruse them, but thanks anyway.

I appreciate your kind offers and suggestions for upcoming novels, but it is my policy to write only what is generated in my own mind, from my own experiences and from my own imagination, but thanks. If you have a good idea for a book, write it yourself.

I am grateful for those of you who catch typos and other errors, but please take heart: I am well aware of them by now and must assume 100% fault for each and every one.

For those of you, who wish to schedule book-signings, events, guest speaker or appearances, etc., please contact my publishing coordinator and webmaster at CyberDiamond, LLC., LAUREL GALVAN at laurel@cyberdiamond.net or 320 Mamie Cook Road, Boone, NC 28607-7844.

For those of you who may be interested in buying literary rights such as films, television, copyrights, or any other related legal matters, please contact my attorney: STEPHEN STEINBERG, Esq. at stesteinberg@comcast.net or Steinberg Law Offices, 48 Brant Avenue, Clark, NJ 07066-1534.

I appreciate your patronage and wish you well. *KEEP READING!*

Blue Skies,

Joss Tallman

ABOUT THE AUTHOR

Joss Tallman is the busiest retired person I've ever met. Joss is a fifth generation native born Floridian and graduated from Florida State University and from law school in Washington State.

Tallman began his career as a law enforcement pilot with a Florida State Police Agency. After serving as a prosecutor with the State Attorney's Office, he returned to his first love of flying both commercially and as an FAA Designated Pilot Examiner.

Although retired, Joss remains active as a legal aviation consultant and is often a guest speaker at various events. He still holds an FAA Airline Transport Rating and flight instructor certificates. He has been an adjunct professor at Palm Beach State College since 1994.

Tallman's first published book *Amarillo Rose* received great reviews. Now, he definitely has the writing bug, along with his great skills of bringing his fans to the edge of their seats with his great stories. Find out more by visiting his website www.josstallman.com.

Tallman makes his home in south Florida with his little dog Toby. He enjoys fishing, flying his airplane, and, of course, writing.

~Laurel L. Galvan